OLLIE SLEIGHT

MITHRAS MURDERS

I would like to dedicate this book to my family who have all, at one time or another, encouraged me to continue this through to the end.

In particular I would like to thank Sarah Furneaux who convinced me that it was worth publishing, also Dr Hayley Allen for her invaluable advice concerning medical matters used within the novel.

Lastly, I would like to thank Neal Pulla without whom this story would never have been written.

First edition

Published 2006 by
The Square Design & Print Co. Ltd.
43 Garamonde Drive
Wymbush Industrial Estate
Milton Keynes
Buckinghamshire
MK8 8DD

Telephone 01908 305018
Fax 01908 260901
Email: info@thesquareguide.co.uk
www.thesquareguide.co.uk

All rights reserved.
No reproduction, copy or transmission of this publication may be made without consent of
The Square Design & Print Co. Ltd.

ISBN Nos. 0-9544810-8-9
978-0-9544810-8-7

Cover design by
Jan Allen

Printed by
The Square Design & Print Co. Ltd.

Ollie Sleight has asserted his right under the Copyright, Designs and Patents Act 1988 to
be identified as the author of this work.

All the characters used within the book are fictional and are from the author's imagination.
Any similarity to persons past or present is entirely coincidental. All dates and locations
mentioned have been adjusted by the author to fit within the story.

CHAPTER ONE

"So there you have it! Unfortunately we've run out of time yet again. I would just like to thank tonight's guest for joining us – the current world light heavyweight champion, Mr John Conteh. To play us out this evening we have Elton John's latest hit 'Lucy In The Sky With Diamonds'. Until tomorrow then..."

William James flicked the 'off' button on the Blaupunkt radio then listened as the rain drummed noisily on the fabric roof of his speeding car.

Geta – his real name, and then only to his closest of friends, thirty five and happily unmarried – aimed the large dark convertible with little skill or regard and sped between the evening's traffic on the busy A5, oblivious to the angrily flashed headlights coming towards him.

He took a moment to glance down at the illuminated clock display on the dashboard. It read 6.30pm. He smiled to himself, pleased that once again he had been able to get away early.

He worked in the City of London just a short walk from Fenchurch Street and had done for almost two years now and despite the travelling loved it. Being self-employed it often meant long days and late nights. Today though was Thursday and, just like most Thursdays by working through his lunch he had finished early and now contented himself in the knowledge that, with any luck, he should be in bed by 10.00pm.

Thursday was Lucy's night.

He had met her by chance almost seven months ago. The Lord Nelson, as he remembered, a pub close to his office. Since then they had seen each other almost every lunch time and nearly every Thursday evening.

She would travel up by train to Wolverton where he would meet her. They would usually find a quiet pub or have a meal somewhere and return to his home where she would stay the night, catching the early train together the following morning.

As William reached the familiar outskirts of home, the headlights from his car singled out the large white reflective road sign for Towcester.

Reading aloud the Latin name printed below in italics "LACTODORUM" he smiled and slowed the car. Turning his dark blue Mercedes left, he pressed the accelerator down and sped along the winding driveway, the rear wheels kicking up small stones.

The wheels locked momentarily before the car came to rest in front of the large double door of his garage. Pulling the grey leather covered visor above his head down, he pressed the 'up' button on the remote and peered ahead into the dark and beyond the driving rain. The two chrome wiper blades skimmed in a great majestic arc across the windscreen allowing him only brief glimpses of the rising door.

From somewhere deep within the garage a small green light flickered then glowed brightly, indicating that the door was up. He engaged 'drive' and moved forward slowly on tick over.

Replacing the remote back onto the visor he watched in the rear view mirror as the door slid silently down behind him and gave an audible click as it locked firmly in place. Pleased to be home and in the dry he switched off the ignition and stepped out from the car. He made his way carefully in the dark to the internal entrance which lay at the far corner of the garage.

His finger stabbed out the sequence of numbers on a dimly lit panel that would disarm the alarm system and release the door.

Once inside, he switched on the light in the hallway, stepped out of his new Loake shoes and went through to the lounge. Tossing his jacket onto the arm of the white leather settee he made his way into the kitchen, reached out for the light switch, pressed it then cursed technology. With the kitchen only partially lit from the light of the hall he filled the kettle. He stood in the dark; the house was quiet, almost as if it was holding its breath, his fingers tapped to an imaginary rhythm on the white melamine worktop.

William James was blissfully unaware of the small powerful figure that moved silently along his hallway. Had he realised he would have almost certainly wished himself far, far away.

That single moment in time when William became aware was just as the heavy club hammer struck him full in the face, destroying his nose and mouth.

When he awoke, somewhere far off he could just make out the ringing of a telephone. He held his breath as he heard a familiar voice. It was his own, then Lucy spoke. He recognised her soft tone immediately but couldn't hear what she was saying. Then silence. He was unable to move and tried desperately to look beyond the confusion that overwhelmed him, he was aware of someone pulling on his arm then suddenly a loud crack filled the room as steel met steel.

With consciousness came the awful reality of intense pain, at first from his face and now up from his hands, travelling along his arms to meet in the middle of his chest. To add to his distress he could no longer feel his feet. He tried to lift his head but the effort was too great. With a painful sigh he let his head drop back heavily onto the hard floor.

Panic struck him through a swirling mist that hung like a whitish veil over watery eyes. He tried to scream out but could only manage a muted gargle. He spat blood and pieces of teeth and gasped for air.

William felt a wave of shock forge through him. He tried feebly to raise his aching body up from the hard wooden floor but failed. It was as if an invisible force held him down.

His last moments began slowly in that darkened room; a feint glint from a blade as the complicated network of vital veins and arteries were severed. Eye's wide and snorting through his nose like a dying pig he could only watch in horror as his life spilled out onto the floor from the deep and vicious wounds that were now being savagely inflicted upon him.

The final act of humiliation came from a swift single stab that caused his body to arc violently upwards. A pool of yellow green water grew on the floor and trickled in various directions.

The small figure stepped back for a moment and sighed impatiently as he watched his victim convulsing uncontrollably before him. There were still a few things to be done, traces to remove before the ordeal was over.

Moving forward again, he stood over his victim,

dressed only in a simple purple robe, and watched with little remorse as William James gasped, hissed air then slipped from this world. Taking care not to tread in the growing pool of blood and urine, he stepped over the mutilated figure and pulled at a towel that hung from the handle of the cooker door. He cleaned the blood from the hammer and let it drop into a small velvet drawstring bag. He glanced down and smiled, his thin lips drawn tightly over yellowed teeth set in a ghoulish white background.

Cautiously he ran the razor-edged blade across the reddening towel then slid it noiselessly into the highly ornate scabbard that hung heavily from his waist.

Letting the towel drop he reached down and pulled violently at the thin silver chain that hung discreetly around the victim's neck. It snapped easily, leaving an almost undetectable thin red line, the only evidence of its existence.

He slid the small silver object from the chain and placed it carefully between his narrow lips, allowing the chain to drop to the floor. Crouching down low over his victim he produced a tiny pearl-handled knife from around his neck.

His skilful use with this small fine edged blade excited him. His breathing became heavy and erratic. A thin trickle of yellow white saliva oozed from the corner of his mouth and ran slowly down to his chin. He wiped it quickly away on the back of his hairless hand.

Finishing his gruesome task, he allowed himself a feint almost unnoticeable smile as he savoured this special and very private moment, his breathing now quieter, more controlled. He produced a second, much smaller bag and unfastened the thin leather thong that held it closed and removed a small clay cylindrical container. He leant his weight for a moment against the kitchen wall, his head tilted back slightly as he listened to the silence around him. Then taking a long but measured breath he glanced down at his lightly clenched fist. Slowly, very slowly he opened his hand, smiled broadly and raised it to his nose. With eyes tightly shut he sniffed at the small red object that lay wet in his palm. This was a secret place only he could visit and he adored it.

Reluctantly he opened his eyes then, removing the lid, tilted his cupped hand slightly allowing the object to roll from his palm into the container. Once the lid was in place he replaced it back into the bag and tied the thong tightly.

He stepped into the hall and paused for a moment, framed by the doorway. He shielded his eyes from the bright light and turned, permitting himself one last look before proceeding along the hallway to a small door set under the stairs. He pulled at the brass handle, then stooped down and recovered a long grey trench coat from its hiding place. Slipping the coat over his shoulders and making sure that he had fastened the belt tightly, he switched off the hall light and stepped out into the cold, wet January night.

Not more than eight miles away, a slim, well-dressed figure replaced the telephone back onto its rest and stepped out from the booth. The cold night air cut savagely through her light jacket. She rubbed her arms briskly with numbed hands and headed for the waiting room, its brightly lit sign above the door a seemingly welcoming haven. She gave the heavy plate glass door a shove with her shoulder and entered.

A lone figure sat huddled at the far end of the room clutching a crushed beer can. The stale smoke filled air was in stark contrast to her fresh, youthful beauty.

She felt nervous and confused and was immediately aware of the seated figure staring at her which only served to heighten her feeling of vulnerability. She went over to the window arms folded tightly across her chest, her face pressed up close to the glass squinting into the gloom outside. Shortly a distant metallic voice announced the imminent arrival of the 21.30 to Euston, London. She straightened, glanced over at the seated figure then pulled open the door and stepped out into the fresh air.

Ten minutes later she was settled into the comfortable first class seat of the Inter-City train.

As it made its rhythmic clatter along the track, her mind pleasantly recounted their relationship. It had been good, in fact excellent, especially in bed. She had been honest with him from the start: he had not been the first but, as she recalled, this hadn't bothered him. She peered into the darkness, her reflection on the train's grubby window stared blankly back at her like some ghostly visitation.

At 22.10 the train slowed on its approach into Euston and with practised skill the driver brought around one hundred tons gently to a halt. Suddenly the door at the far end of the carriage swung open. "End of the line folks. Euston," the guard shouted as he made his way down the train. "End of the…"

His booming voice tailed off abruptly as the door slammed shut behind him. She quickly gathered together the few possessions she had placed on the seat beside her and made her way to the door.

To her surprise it had been held open for her by a lean, athletic-looking young man with dark eyes and hair to match. He had cheekily winked an eye at her; she smiled but looked away quickly as she felt her face flush and quickened her pace along the platform and up the gentle slope towards the exit. Approaching the ticket collector who sat with sagging shoulders in his dark wooden kiosk, she slowed up and was jostled from side to side as other passengers pushed past impatiently. After a lengthy search of her bag she eventually found her ticket and presented it to the now frowning collector who snatched it rudely from her hand.

Moving out onto the station's brightly lit concourse she was shocked to see the amount of young and homeless that wandered around aimlessly so late at night. Many rummaged expectantly amongst the decaying rubbish stacked up in dark corners while others sat with their backs to the cold glass-fronted windows of shops now closed.

One young girl who was sat cross-legged on the cold floor, a bedraggled dog at her side, had begged for money from Lucy as she passed. Lucy deliberately ignored the girl's pleas for fear of encouraging others, and quickened her step. This action prompted a torrent of verbal abuse from the girl. Now almost running she spotted a row of empty telephone booths to her right. She would ring William again and leave a message.

The first was out of order, the same with the second. The third, thankfully, was working. Picking up the handset and taking care not to hold it against her ear or touch it to her mouth she pushed at the worn numbers on the cold metal key pad and waited quietly for the connection to be made. She stared blankly at the list of area codes that were screwed tightly to the wall of the telephone booth then gagged as she watched in horror a thick strand of green white mucus slide slowly down its smooth glass surface, a calling card from the previous occupant. She put her hand up to her mouth and swallowed bile. She was cold, hungry and tired and so desperately wanted to be home and tucked up safely in her bed.

Tapping her foot impatiently on the cold floor she listened, one ring... two rings... three rings then the answerphone cut in.

"William, its Lucy, can you hear me?" She paused. "I waited for almost an hour, please ring me." Then hung up.

William could hear Lucy, only just, but not for long.

CHAPTER TWO

Emit Hart was dining alone at the Hatton; a comfortable hotel situated within the picturesque Buckinghamshire countryside, and hidden discreetly from the road by tall poplars and proud oaks. Its location was only evident to the very observant by the two large stone pillars that flanked its impressive block-paved driveway.

Almost two years had passed now since the sudden and inexplicable disappearance of his young wife Jill. He had spent much of this time alone, not out of necessity, as they had many good and loyal friends, but from choice.

Jill had become the most important thing in his life. Not just a wife and lover but more importantly over the years she had become his closest friend and confidant. He knew that she would always be a very hard act to follow.

Born in the Republic of Ireland in a small hamlet just south of Dublin, he had enjoyed an adventurous childhood in an untroubled and beautiful part of the country. Although no longer young, he was still attractive to women. At six foot two with steel blue eyes and dark hair he had often won the hearts of many, his soft melodic accent proving just too hard to resist for some.

With an appetite in keeping with his large frame he had made short work of his meal, which this evening had consisted of prawn cocktail to start with, followed by Chateau-Briande which was normally for two, mange tout, a favourite of Hart's, sauté potatoes and French beans. All washed down with a fine bottle of white Chateau Neuf du Pape, his favourite Burgundy. Although tempted he declined the sweet trolley and settled for coffee and an Irish whisky in the comfortable lounge.

The maitre-de, dressed in an expensive dark wool suit straightened his silk tie as Hart approached.

"Have a nice evening, Mr Hart," he said pleasantly opening the heavy door.

"Thank you, I shall."

Turning right Hart strode purposefully along the hallway towards the lounge, stopping briefly to select something to read from the highly polished brass rack that displayed a selection of papers and magazines. Deciding on a current edition of the Tatler he pushed on the large oak door that led into the lounge. Although heavy it swung open easily on its well-oiled brass hinges. This was Hart's favourite room with its wood-panelled walls, large open fire and blood red carpet. He stood for a moment listening to the spitting and cracking of the wood which burnt fiercely in the wrought iron grate, feeling even at this distance the heat on his face. Then turning slowly to his left he soon found what he was looking for and made his way towards the corner of the opulent room.

He settled back in the large red leather winged chair and made himself comfortable. Looking around the room it at first appeared deceptively empty. Here and there the odd cloud of cigar smoke curling lazily upwards was the only evidence that not everyone was still dining.

Hart pushed his back into the chair deciding to take full advantage of the relaxed atmosphere that this wonderful room offered, occasionally tuning in to conversations going on around him.

One in particular now held his attention. A young couple sat a short distance away to his left. The girl was slim and well dressed in a short red skirt and a figure hugging black top. Her perfume was strong and expensive, but not overpowering.

Her partner was heavily set, square jawed with dark curly hair and wore a large gold bracelet on his right wrist.

Hart became fascinated by their conversation and soon came to realise that they were both married but not to each other. Their liaison at the hotel had been carefully planned, and the pair now discussed in detail how viable each of their stories had been to their respective partners.

The tall blonde with the straining top was obviously beginning to doubt her alibi. Her companion, although looking a little disappointed, was doing his level best to reassure her.

"Would you like a coffee, sir?" a polite voice asked.

Hart looked up then nodded as the waiter placed the silver tray down onto the small round table.

"Black or white, sir?" he asked sliding the table forward.

"White, please," He muttered impatiently, keen to hear the outcome of the conversation. Shortly his whisky arrived complete with paper coaster.

Disappointingly the young couple had now moved over to the bar and were sat on tall stools, faces almost touching.

Hart sighed, picked up the heavy lead crystal glass and slowly swilled its amber contents around before putting it to his lips. He tipped his head back and held the whisky in his mouth for a moment feeling the liquid burn, then swallowed.

Sitting back he casually thumbed the pages of the magazine, deliberately skipping the first few which appeared to be mainly about Prime Minister Wilson's latest response to the recent IRA bombings. As an Irishman this sort of news was never well received by Hart. His attention was drawn instantly to an article on the forthcoming fight between Muhammad Ali and England's hopeful, Joe Bugner. Once a keen amateur heavyweight himself and talented enough in his day that many of his friends thought he could have turned professional, this so called gentleman's sport rated very highly on Hart's list of interests.

He had almost finished the page when a voice whispered discreetly.

"Excuse me, sir."

Hart was startled for a moment by the polite but firm voice.

"Mr Hart, I am sorry to disturb you, sir, but there's a policeman asking for you in reception."

For a split second Hart was unsure that he had heard him right.

"Should I show him through?" The waiter asked with a slight frown.

"I suppose you had better." A bewildered Hart sat forward, flung his head back and finished off the last of the whisky.

Removing a cigarette from its packet, he struck a match on the side of the box and waited for the bright flare to calm. He drew long on the cigarette inhaling the dark blue smoke deeply then let it out in a series of small but deliberate bursts.

Keeping one eye on the door he continued flicking lazily through the pages of the magazine though it was now obvious that it held little interest for him. Soon the waiter appeared in the doorway. Hart stood as they approached, quickly stubbing the newly lit Raffle into the heavy cut-glass ashtray.

"Inspector Hart, it's nice to meet you at last, I've heard so much about you. I'm DI Stacey."

Hart clasped his outstretched hand, felt his grip, and made a mental note never to upset this young man.

"All good I hope?" Hart responded with typical wit.

"But of course."

"Please take a seat. Can I get you a drink?"

"Coffee would be good, thanks." Stacey pulled up a chair and sat.

"And I'll have another whisky, I think," Hart smiled passing his glass to the waiter.

DI Stacey was a large fit-looking man who obviously worked out, aged about thirty with short-cut hair and cool grey eyes. He had, Hart decided, the sort of looks and confidence that would make meeting members of the opposite sex for the first time a doddle.

"So, what do you think of Buckinghamshire, sir? A bit quieter than London, eh!" Stacey asked looking around the room in a way that only policeman seem able to do. Then, as though satisfied it contained no-one on the local wanted list back at the station he made himself comfortable in the soft leather chair.

"Yes, a bit," Hart replied with a slight slur. The wine that he had drunk earlier together with the strong Irish whisky was now taking affect.

"Although I'm not exactly a stranger to these parts," he continued. "My wife was brought up around here so we often came back here to visit her family and friends."

Hart figured Stacey already knew all about his wife. She had been the daughter of a local well-respected businessman who, after her baffling disappearance, had attempted suicide on two occasions. Only his wife's love and determination had got him through it. Her disappearance had been one of the main reasons for Hart's decision to leave 'The Force' and move back to Buckinghamshire. It held many memories for him. He had spent several months looking for a house. He particularly wanted to live in or around the town of Buckingham as this had been where Jill had lived as a child and had spent most of her teenage years. Although she had moved to Nottingham while studying at the university, once graduated she had soon returned to Buckingham, but not back with her parents. Instead she had rented a small flat above the newsagents in the centre of the town; in fact this had been where they had first met.

Hart had called into the busy shop on his way to Oxford. They had spoken briefly. He couldn't remember now what about, but he remembered that he had liked her. They had said goodbye and went their separate ways.

Luckily he had met her again by chance several days later in a small country pub close to the village of Greens Norton.

That day Hart would remember forever. They had lunch together then spent the rest of the day strolling down by the canal in the warm sunshine, pausing occasionally to help tie up brightly painted narrow boats to badly worn cleats.

He had been surprised to learn that unlike many that graduated she had decided not to follow medicine or law. Instead she joined social services. After a couple of years she was running her own department responsible for the re-education and support for young women that had run away from home.

In particular, Hart recalled that she'd had a special interest in those that had become alcoholics or drug addicts. Regrettably many turned to prostitution in an effort to pay for their addictions. It had become obvious to them both that day that they had much in common and should see more of each other, which they did.

Happily they were married twelve months later in the large and picturesque church that stood in the very centre of Buckingham town. It had been kept deliberately low key with only close friends and family invited.

"I'm really sorry about your wife. Is there no chance of finding her?" Stacey shifted in the chair looking closely at Hart for an expression of hope. Seeing none he now looked decisively uncomfortable and wished he had not asked.

Hart shook his head pausing for a moment as the waiter arrived with the whisky and a small silver tray complete with coffee pot, matching cup and saucer. He set them down on the small glass table and left.

"I suppose like anything there's always hope Stacey," he said raising the glass to his lips. After all this time Hart had been forced to admit publicly that he had now more or less given up hope and accepted the theory put forward by the investigation team. It had been hard at first, but deep down he knew that they had probably got it right. Because of her line of work it often involved confrontation. Confrontation with people that lived in a world far removed from normal rational every day life. A world where violence and intimidation went hand in hand. These people were capable of anything and would stop at nothing to get their own way. Hart had often warned.

Whether it had been as the police thought, a drug dealer or pimp that had abducted her, it was unlikely now that anyone would ever know.

Both men sat quietly for a few moments then, Stacey broke the silence, keen to change the subject.

"So, how long are you staying here then?" he asked taking the opportunity to check out the room again.

Hart sat forward running his hand slowly over his head. "Only until Wednesday, that's when the builder is scheduled to finish up."

"Well, not long to wait. Have you been back to see it?"

"Oh God, yes, I wouldn't leave it all up to my builder. John is actually very good but he can get a bit carried away so occasionally it's been necessary to put the brakes on," Hart said with a tight grin then tilted his head back and drained the contents of his glass.

A sense of relief settled over Stacey as their conversation became more relaxed. Picking up the silver pot he poured the strong-smelling coffee into the cup, then dropped two roughly hewn brown sugar lumps into the liquid and stirred briskly.

"You're not from around here, are you, Stacey?" Hart rolled the glass slowly between his palms. "You have a slight accent but its not Northamptonshire, is it?" he added confidently.

"No, sir, Norfolk."

"I thought so. What part?"

"Kings Lyn, though I've lived here now for some twelve years or more."

Hart placed the empty glass down onto the table.

"Have you been in the job long?" Hart asked curiously.

"Only about fourteen months, sir, well, with CID that is. I joined the force straight from school, did my training at Aylesbury and was then stationed at Bletchley. From there I was moved to Wolverton where I am now. Actually it was while I was stationed at Aylesbury that I met your old assistant."

"Mike," Hart cut in enthusiastically.

"Yes, Mike Sharp." Stacey sat forward and placed the cup on its saucer. "We still keep in touch. Occasionally we meet up for the odd pint or three," he joked.

"Is he still with Scotland Yard?"

"Yes, in fact it was Mike that suggested that I should come and find you."

Although Hart was desperate to learn more he was more than a little keen to find out what his close friend was up to now.

"How is the old bugger? I bet he's still telling that lovely wife of his how overworked he is."

It had always been a standing joke amongst their team how he was forever complaining to his wife how busy he was and how they overworked him. The reality, though, was quite different. Mike had always been a keen carp fisherman and any opportunity that presented itself and he was off. It baffled everyone how he got away with it but, amazingly, he always did.

"Yes! He's doing fine, sir, and still fishing, I believe,"

Stacey beamed.

"Good," replied Hart sincerely. "I like Mike. You could always count on him if you were ever in a tight spot." He glanced down at his Timex and was surprised to see that it was almost 10.30. Then, looking back at Stacey, he added, "Anyway, Stacey, I'm intrigued, why, would Mike suggest that you come and find me, and more to the point how the bloody hell did you know I was staying here?"

"It was Mike. He told me that you had taken early retirement and that you had moved to Buckingham. It was him that gave me your new address," Stacey answered proudly. "I went their yesterday and spoke with your builder. He said to try here." Stacey sat forward on the edge of the seat and removing his jacket swung it over the back of the chair. "So here I am."

Hart's baffled expression prompted Stacey to supply some quick answers.

"I guess you must be a bit curious why Mike would want me to find you?" he said, lounging back into the chair.

"Well, I would be lying if I said no," Hart replied calmly. Stacey's admiration for this softly spoken Irishman was obvious, he'd heard so much about him over the years and knew that the respect that Mike had for him was immeasurable.

"As you will appreciate this is all highly confidential. In fact I suppose now that you are retired I probably shouldn't even be discussing this with you, but to be absolutely honest with you I just don't know what to do next." Stacey poured himself more coffee.

"At the moment I'm involved in a local murder investigation. It's actually my first serious case and to be perfectly blunt about it I'm in danger of fucking up big time. I'm now totally out of my depth and I really don't know what to do next." Stacey leant forwards in the chair and lowered his voice slightly. "I rang Mike yesterday morning in the hope that he might be able to give me some advice. Anyhow, I explained to him briefly what had happened and, well, he got pretty excited. He started blabbering on about how similar it was to something you and he had been involved with in the past and said that it was imperative that I found you, hence this visit."

Hart frowned as his interest mounted, "And?"

"Well, on Friday, that's Friday just gone, we were called out to an address in Towcester. Towcester is about eight miles north of here."

"Yes, I know it,"

"Anyway, when we arrived the uniformed lot were already there and had cordoned off the area. It was a large house, which stood in its own grounds just on the outskirts of the town overlooking the racecourse."

Stacey paused momentarily as Hart ordered two coffees and a couple of large Irish whiskies from a passing waiter.

"Make them mugs, would you? I can't take those daft little cups seriously," Hart added with a grin.

"Anyway, Mrs White who was employed at the house as housekeeper had raised the alarm. She had arrived as usual at 9.30am; entry to the house was via an electronic keypad, which shut off the alarm system at the same time unlocking the door. All very high tech … anyway, Mrs White, believing her employer to have left for work as usual, had set about her normal daily routine, which consisted of a small glass of sherry followed by a relaxing hour or so reading the local paper. She had admitted that it was very unlike her but she had nodded off. When she woke it was almost midday and the telephone was ringing. She had got up to answer it but it had stopped before she had the chance to pick it up. She had added that it couldn't have been ringing for very long as the answerphone had cut in. Anyhow, having now been woken she decided that she would go and put the kettle on before starting work, have a 'cuppa' as she put it and wake herself up. It was then that she found her employer, Mr James."

Stacey hesitated as the waiter arrived carrying a large tray, both men watched as the whiskies together with the coffee a dish of nuts and a small plate of biscuits were placed onto the table.

"The first people to arrive at the scene were the ambulance crew. Unfortunately there was nothing that could be done for Mr James so they did their best to comfort Mrs White who by now had been reduced to a babbling wreck."

Stacey leant forwards, dropped a couple of lumps of sugar into his coffee and stirred briskly, spilling most of the contents onto the table.

"What time was it when you arrived?" Hart enquired pleased at how easy it was to adopt the role as amateur detective now.

"About 13.20 hours. We couldn't get there any earlier. We were out on another shout unfortunately. It turned out to be a waste of time anyway." Stacey offered the plate of biscuits to Hart. "By the time we'd arrived so had Forensics, the doctor and most of the local bloody press."

"How the hell did the press get wind of it so quickly?"

"The thing is, sir, that very little goes on around here and apart from a few women that appear to have gone missing recently it's relatively quiet," as soon as Stacey had said it, he regretted it.

"Yes, of course. Stacey, you mentioned missing women. Exactly how many have gone missing?" Hart didn't intend to let this go.

"Six now, I believe."

"Over what sort of period?"

"About ten months. Most, if not all, appear to have been working girls if you get my drift," Stacey said snapping a biscuit in half in the hope that this action might put an end to the subject.

"And any ideas on where they may have gone?" This was getting better by the minute Hart thought.

"Not personally, sir. However, the team working on the case apparently believe that some, if not all, may have moved to London ... better money there I suppose."

Stacey shifted uncomfortably in the chair quietly cursing to himself that he had been foolish enough to even mentioned missing women.

"And suppose there's more to it than that?" Hart argued.

"Like what, sir?"

"I don't really know but kidnapping seems to spring to mind."

The expression on Stacey's face showed that he didn't like the way this conversation was going. He knew that Hart would obviously be very keen to explore any possible connection with his wife's disappearance and these more recent ones.

"We don't think so," Stacey deliberately put more emphasis on the word "we" in an attempt to assert some authority on this debate, "in fact," he added, "the team are convinced that there is no reason for concern. I know for instance that all the addresses were checked out and in each case everything was gone, no evidence of anyone still living there. All six had owned cars. Traffic were alerted and together with the investigation team they checked out all the obvious things like second-hand car dealers in the area just to make sure that none of the cars had been sold on – nothing."

"What about breaker's yards, were they checked out?"

"I don't know for certain but I'm sure that they would have thought of that," Stacey replied rather coldly, "Anyway, it's not uncommon in that line of work to just up sticks and go – trouble with a pimp or something."

"I guess so," Hart could tell that this wasn't going to go anywhere and decided to back off then added as an afterthought, "What about the electoral register – was that checked out?"

"I really don't know, but personally, I wouldn't have thought so. They're simply not bothered. Here one day, gone the next, they don't normally stick around in one place long enough to be concerned with things like that. I do know that all the addresses were rented properties, which again is quite commonplace," Stacey recalled.

"Do you have any information on the victim yet?" Hart asked, keen not to lock swords with Stacey.

Stacey shook his head and sighed. "Not a great deal, sir, only that he was in his mid-thirties, he'd bought the house almost nine months ago. We're still waiting for confirmation on the actual date though. As far as we can make out at the moment it appears that he paid cash for it, which we obviously find a bit suspect as does Inland

Revenue who as you would expect are very keen to look into it. Anyway, before that we think he may have lived in Essex. We've asked the Essex police for any information they might have on him; but we're still waiting for them to come back to us. Apparently he worked in London – well, that's what his housekeeper has confirmed."

"Doing what?" Hart asked cupping his hands around a cigarette as he lit it then blew the smoke out the corner of his mouth.

"Evidently very little. I have two of my lads going through his paperwork at the moment to see what they can dig up."

Hart inhaled the smoke deeply and held it in his chest for a moment waiting for Stacey to continue.

"Most of what we know about him to date we've learnt from the housekeeper,

Mrs White," Stacey offered.

"I know it's probably a bit early but have you had the results back from the post mortem?" The smoke erupted from Hart's mouth in a series of dense clouds.

"Not as yet, we're still waiting to hear from the pathologist. Any day now, so we're told. Bit of a backlog evidently." He said raising his glass then promptly emptied the entire contents in one go.

"How was he killed, Stacey?" It hadn't even occurred to Hart until now to ask this most obvious question.

"Well, sir, when we arrived I asked a female colleague on my team to go and sit with Mrs White in the ambulance while we went into the house. Anyway we – that is DS Jones and myself went straight through to the kitchen which is where Mrs White had found him. Fuck me! Honest. We were just not prepared for that, I can tell you! It was a scene straight from a horror film."

Stacey was visibly agitated and looked at Hart for some reaction. Hart signalled to the waiter again who hurried over and two more whiskies were ordered.

"It was little wonder that Mrs White was in such a state, it was difficult enough for us to take in. There was blood everywhere, and I mean everywhere. Whoever murdered him was one sick individual. They had literally nailed him to the floor, bloody crucified him Hart."

Stacey was now standing; his last few words hung in the air like stale smoke, and far from keeping things quiet he now had the undivided attention of most of the guests seated in the lounge. He ran his hands through his hair and glanced around him mumbled something incoherent then walked over and stood by the window, gazing through a gap in the curtains at the night sky.

Hart knew from bitter experience that in Stacey's sort of job you were expected to put aside any feelings that you might have and simply get on with it, after all, it was what you were paid to do. If you couldn't do that then you didn't last long. It was almost like riding a bike. If you stopped pedalling, you would fall off.

The waiter arrived with the whiskies and placed both on the table.

"Stacey, come and sit down." Hart tried to put some authority into his voice although somehow it didn't come over, but happily Stacey did.

He sat himself down heavily. He looked tired his face now ashen and drawn. Hart slid the whisky across the table towards him. Picking up the glass Stacey gulped down the contents.

"I bloody needed that," he said just managing a

smile, the fiery liquid bringing colour to his cheeks almost immediately.

"Would you like a refill, Stacey?"

"I had better not, sir, I'm driving," he chuckled.

"Look, Stacey, Mike's right. Listening to you this evening I know exactly why he was so keen for you to find me. I can help you with this, but not tonight. It's Sunday, it's late and, to be honest with you, you look like shit. You need to get yourself off home, get your head down for a few hours."

Hart didn't feel particularly tired himself, although as he stood his legs informed him otherwise.

"Perhaps if you agree I could meet with you at your office tomorrow," Hart suggested helpfully.

Stacey got up from the comfortable chair and looked a bit unsteady on his feet. At first Hart wondered if it had been the whisky but Stacey assured him that it was just tiredness.

"I think that's an excellent idea, sir." Stacey's expression had mellowed.

Hart stubbed the cigarette out in the glass ashtray and pushed it to one side.

"I'll walk with you to your car, Stacey. I could do with the fresh air."

As they made there way out of the lounge Hart realised that many of the other guests had already gone to bed. They walked through to reception, which Hart was surprised to note was now unmanned, passing through the heavy oak doorway and down the worn stone steps, both shivering as the cold night air hit them. Standing quietly for a few moments they gazed up at the clear night sky. Stacey rubbed the tiredness from his reddening eyes.

"Sir, about tomorrow. If you speak with reception in the morning I'm sure they'll give you directions to the police station, it's easy to find anyway. It's at the far end of Wolverton high street on the left between the fire station and the school, you can't miss it!"

Hart lit another cigarette inhaled deeply and blew the smoke high into the air, watching it spiral upwards.

"Don't worry, Stacey, I'll find it okay. You get yourself off home," Hart said giving Stacey a firm but friendly slap on the back.

"Take it steady, and I'll see you in the morning nice and early."

"Yes, sir, I shall. Good night, and thanks."

Hart watched as Stacey made his way still rather unsteadily across the gravel car park towards his car.

He stood just long enough to watch him pull out from his space and disappear down the dark tree-lined driveway, then walked back to the warmth and comfort of the hotel.

CHAPTER THREE

Ten miles to the north of Wolverton stood the old market town of Olney, pronounced "Ony" by the locals. For over three hundred years it was the heart of lace making and employed most of the townspeople and was famous locally for its pancake race which ancient documents show had been run almost every year since 1445.

With its limestone buildings and wider than normal high street it had become a popular attraction to visitors who came to wander around the many antique shops that fronted its market square, or to simply sit in one of the town's many tea shops.

Monday wasn't normally market day, as it stated on the public notice board, it had been changed for one week only to allow for drainage repairs in market square. The weather although cold was still dry, the air filled with the pleasant smell of bacon frying. A large queue had formed alongside the hot dog van.

People chatted and laughed. Many were busy bartering with grinning market traders. All were unaware of the small figure that stared down on them from slightly parted curtains above.

The observer, pale and drawn with closely shaven head and eye's like a flame of fire, snorted through his nose sending a fine but unpleasant mist onto the window.

He was simply dressed; his robe was of fine purple silk with gold edging, a lanyard of plaited gold around his waist and leather sandals on his feet.

He stood alone in a poorly lit room darkened by heavy gold curtains, the air thick with an acrid, sickly sweet smell that went unnoticed.

The silence was broken only by the rhythmic ticking of a clock somewhere distant.

The room was richly furnished. Although there were no carpets; highly ornate rugs covered the superb and carefully polished wooden floor.

Against one wall was a simple but low sofa with no back, to the left of this a narrow wooden table with ornately carved legs displayed a short sword complete with ruby encrusted scabbard supported on an ivory cradle. Ahead of this a small bag fastened tightly at the top looked oddly out of place. Against the opposite wall stood a similar sofa with a large square table positioned to the front. Placed carefully on top were three small plain, brick-red clay containers.

The walls were adorned with figures painted in rich vivid colours framed in gold. Many were of young women; most were dressed in white, some were nude.

The few men shown were dressed in deep crimson; all appeared to be enjoying each other as they played out their orgy scene.

Lit only by a few small oil lamps positioned strategically around the room the walls appeared to tremble in the soft golden glow magically bringing life to the still room.

Bored with the scenes below, he took great care to close the gap in the curtain, running his hand slowly over the join and, once satisfied, turned and quietly made his way over to the table.

Once seated, he moved the clay containers with care

around the table, spending much time arranging, then re-arranging – they had to be just so!

Satisfied at last with their positions he slowly lifted the lid from the closest and placed it carefully to one side. Using slender, well-manicured fingers he played carefully with its content, moving it from one side of the container to the other. He omitted a low gargling sound from somewhere deep within his throat. Saliva building up in his mouth caused him to swallow hard.

A smile formed but was soon checked as he picked up the cold soft object. Holding it delicately between finger and thumb he squeezed it gently. Clear fluid appeared on its surface. He held it close to his nose, sniffing gently at its sickly sweet aroma. He pushed his pointed tongue out between thin cruel lips and licked the small orb, tasting its unusual but distinctive flavour.

With a broadening grin he placed it onto his tongue then allowed it into his mouth, sucking gently at its juices, then rolling it around his mouth with his tongue, feeling its texture, cold like a grape – perhaps softer, he thought – all the time resisting the incredible urge to crush it between yellowing teeth.

Eventually and almost reluctantly he put the object back into its container and replaced the lid. Slowly he lay back on the sofa, with eyes closed and in a personal mood of near delirium he relived with excitement those wonderful moments.

Almost twelve miles south of Olney the pale blue Escort Mexico turned from the main road onto the industrial estate, its young driver keeping a finger on the button to bring the volume of the Sony 8-track down to an almost normal level.

Taking a left and then a quick right the car came to an abrupt halt outside a tidy new unit on what is known locally as Kiln Farm.

The Kiln Farm industrial estate was built two years ago by the newly formed Development Corporation and was provided especially for the smaller businesses. It contained around thirty factory units of varying sizes.

All but one unit proudly displayed company names and description of work done.

Before the driver of the Escort could get out of the car a second vehicle pulled alongside, only inches from its door.

The young escort driver scowled and threw the driver an angry look as he made eye contact, then burst into a fit of laughter. Then, thrusting his middle finger into the air he laughed louder.

The driver of the second car revved the engine aggressively then suddenly without warning, and with rear wheels screeching as rubber tried to grip tarmac, reversed at speed bringing the car abruptly to a halt with all four wheels locked only inches from the kerb.

Stepping from their cars they both exchanged well-practised verbal abuse before ascending the stone steps that led to the factory's main entrance.

"Get a move on, Neil, its cold enough to freeze the balls off a brass monkey!"

Neil struggled for several seconds before locating the correct key then, pushing the door open, switched on the lights and watched closely as his friend punched in the four-digit code to disarm the alarm system before locking the door.

The small but well furnished reception area looked good, it had to. As both men made their way along the narrow hallway they systematically switched on the lights to the three small offices to their left. Each office equipped with desk, chair and cupboard.

"I'll go and stick the kettle on, Steve, you get that bloody heating going. It's freezing in here." Neil spat the words through chattering teeth and headed for the kitchen tucked away in the far corner.

Steve turned the thermostat up, switched on the radio and then waited as the two rows of double fluorescence burst into life, illuminating below them two very large grey printing presses, both German, the engraved plate bolted firmly to the side of each displaying proudly that both were assembled in the small town of Heidelberg. In a matter of moments Steve had thrown the main isolator switch to both machines to the green on position activating their delivery lights. Then, checking that all the trip switches were closed, he went to the front of each press in turn and stabbed his finger on the small square black button marked RUN.

Simultaneously a loud bell sounded from the rear of each press as it came to life, the large impression cylinders rotating slowly as the feint hum from the powerful electric motors grew louder.

"Here we go mate," Neil said handing a mug to his colleague.

Half an hour later, with plates fitted and ink ducts full, both presses were up and running, producing around six thousand impressions per hour.

Each SRA2 sheet carried twelve images, each image printed four colours both sides and all perfect reproductions of a United Kingdom ten-pound note.

Each press would produce £72,000 per hour; they would run for a minimum of six hours per day.

They had started printing two days ago and if all went to plan would finish in five days' time. Allowing for waste they were aiming to produce around six million pounds sterling.

This print shop was unlike any other. It employed no staff. It had no customers and no telephone, it never invoiced anybody and never would and in approximately five days' time would be out of business.

CHAPTER FOUR

Hart was woken up at 7.30am by the intermittent buzzing from his room's telephone, the pleasant voice on the other end reminding him that he had asked reception for an alarm call before going to bed. He thanked her and replaced the receiver. Hart never woke well and surprised himself at how polite he had been, especially since suffering a slight hangover.

Swinging his legs out of the bed he went over to the window, pulled back the heavy curtains and was greeted with blue skies and warm sunshine. The room was stuffy with little air and he now wished that he'd asked for a non-smoking room.

Once showered, he dressed in a comfortable blue suit – his only suit – gave his shoes a quick polish with one of yesterday's socks, slipped on his shoes and hung the notice on the outside of the door announcing that the room could now be cleaned, then headed for the tiny lift at the end of the corridor.

The restaurant was situated to the back of the hotel overlooking the open countryside. It was south facing and in the mornings if the weather was kind the room would be awash with sunlight.

He picked his way past other diners and went and sat at a small table over by the window. A young waitress in a short black skirt came over carrying a silver pot in each hand. He declined her offer of tea or coffee and asked for orange. Shortly a second waitress came to his table and he placed an order for breakfast.

Hart exchanged pleasantries with the couple to his left. To the right and three tables down he noticed the girl with the straining top and her companion. They looked pleased enough with each other so Hart guessed that they must have managed to come to terms with their alibis.

He enjoyed a full English followed by two cups of strong black coffee and a browse through the local paper. Happily he noted there was no mention of the murder.

Thanking the staff on the way out of the restaurant he wandered into reception and waited until the person in front of him had finished talking with the receptionist before asking for directions to the nearest petrol station, "and preferably one that's close to Wolverton police station." He added quickly. Then scribbling down a few notes on a sheet of hotel letterhead he thanked the girl and headed for the oak door. As he passed the old grandfather clock that stood guard by the doorway it chimed, out of habit Hart checked his watch before stepping outside.

The January air although brisk was pleasingly refreshing and did much to clear his aching head. He considered a walk around the impressive grounds, but thought better of it and lit the first cigarette of the day, carefully protecting the flame of his lighter with cupped hands from the gusting wind. He let the lid of his chrome Zippo snap shut and slid it back into the half empty pack of Raffles and dropped the pack back into his jacket pocket. He took in a lung full of smoke then wandered across the car park, his mind recounting the conversation with Stacey from the previous evening.

He had, as he remembered, been very upset with

events. Obviously the discovery of the body and what had taken place in that house had been a traumatic experience for him, a far cry from petty theft and marital disputes.

Hart was confident that given the information that he had to hand, it would prove of great assistance to Stacey, and should go a long way to answering some of the questions that he undoubtedly had.

He had at one point been tempted to tell Stacey all he knew but had sensibly decided against it, which on reflection now was probably a good thing particularly in view of how much he'd drunk. He might have said too much.

At first Hart had difficulty locating his car. When he'd arrived the car park had been relatively empty. Now it was full of expensive toys. He allowed himself a feint, almost cynical smile as he mused how out of place his battered old Cortina looked amongst its company now.

It started as always with reluctance, the engine coughing into life. He waited the usual five minutes until the engine settled, then engaged first and moved out of the car park and along the drive, stopping at the entrance briefly before pulling out into the lane.

Hart found the petrol station exactly where the receptionist had said and directly opposite his next port of call. The Police Station, it was typical of a small town, built in the late fifties early sixties and now in need of several coats of fresh paint. Hart waited for the petrol attendant to bring back his change, thanked him then turned the ignition key. This time the car started straight away. Pulling away from the pumps he crossed the Wolverton road and drove into the station's car park.

Locking the car he sprinted across the car park and up the concrete steps deliberately missing out every other step then paused at the top for a moment feeling distinctly unfit before pushing open the twin wire-enforced glass doors.

He was immediately hit by the pungent and unmistakable smell of disinfectant, common practice in most police stations and a popular method for disguising the drunks of the previous evening.

Like most police stations the small reception area was sparsely furnished. Two vinyl covered benches stood against the wall, both bolted securely to the tiled floor. Smooth surfaces made cleaning much easier. On the wall above each, large posters warned of crime increases in the Buckinghamshire area. Ahead of him and directly opposite the door was the reception desk complete with toughened glass and speaker grill.

Placing his face close to the grill but making sure not to make contact with it he asked for DI Stacey. His unmistakable Irish accent brought an immediate response from the officious WPC.

"Who shall I say is asking for him?" She asked peering over the top of her silver-framed glasses.

"My name is Hart, Emit Hart."

"Ah! Mr Hart please take a seat, sir. I'll let him know that you're here," she said sliding off her chair, "I believe he's been expecting you," she gave Hart a pleasant smile before disappearing through the door directly behind her.

Hart did as she had suggested and sat down, the numbing ache now developing in his upper leg a sobering reminder to his obvious lack of fitness.

Shortly she returned with Stacey hot on her heals and smiling broadly.

"Come on through, sir," he said pointing towards a door to the left of the reception desk. There was a faint almost inaudible buzz followed by a distinct clunk as the WPC activated the electronic switch down by her side that allowed the re-enforced door to be opened.

Hart entered the inner hallway as Stacey came out of the front office, his arm extended. They shook hands warmly as Stacey ushered Hart towards his office.

"How's the head, Stacey?" Hart enquired with a wry smile.

"Fine, sir, though I probably shouldn't have driven. The wife was a bit pissed off when I got home. Apparently we were supposed to be out with the neighbours," he said raising his eyebrows.

Stacey's office was smaller than Hart had imagined but appeared well organised. Against the far wall a large white marker board stood balanced on a wooden easel, on it and drawn in red marker pen was what at this distance appeared to be someone's family tree, complete with photographs.

To the left of it a large map was pinned to the wall. To the right of the map stood a line of grey painted filing cabinets that had obviously seen better days.

The wall to Hart's right was relatively clear apart for a small battered desk pushed up under the only window in the office. In the centre of the room two desks were arranged in an "L" shape.

Stacey slid a chair forward. "Here you are Sir, take a seat," he invited, "how about a cuppa?" Stacey asked looking just beyond Hart.

Hart turned around as he realised that they had been

followed into the office. The young woman framed in the doorway was tall very slim and had the sort of looks that woke you at night. Hart made a conscious effort not to get caught looking at her bust, but was. Although she didn't seem to mind Hart did note a slight colouring of her cheeks.

"This is WPC Michele Glinn Sir, she's one of my team, everyone around here calls her Mitch though, isn't that right?" he said with a friendly smile.

"Sir," she acknowledged giving an almost undetectable nod of her head.

Hart stood, smiled and shook hands, probably for a little longer than he should have.

"It's good to meet you Mitch, and before you ask, yes I'd love some tea." Hart could sense her shyness as he let her hand slide from his, her perfume lingering for a moment in the still air and then, like her, disappeared.

When Hart turned back Stacey was grinning.

"Bloody gorgeous, isn't she?" Stacey lifted his eyebrows and broadened his grin.

Hart nodded, feeling for some inexplicable reason slightly embarrassed.

"I'll tell you something, sir, not only good looking but nice with it if you know what I mean, and very conscientious."

"Has the wife met her yet?" Hart asked with typical Irish humour.

"Unfortunately yes, and I have to say not too happy about it."

Hart could smell perfume again, which signalled the arrival of the tea. WPC Glinn came in and set the tray down on the desk.

"Mitch, don't disappear. I would like you to stay if

you would?"

During the next forty five minutes that followed Hart learned from Stacey that he'd been able with a few white lies to second Mitch from uniformed duties to assist him and his small team. Towcester police were also involved in the investigation with both forces reporting to Bletchley.

"I know its early days Sir, but we just don't seem to be getting much help, especially from the top. It's as though they're just going through the motions." Stacey said fiercely.

Hart sat motionless, his legs crossed and arms folded as he listened, all the time weighing up what he should say, or indeed what he could say. Too much information could sometimes be as harmful as too little.

"We really could do with your help, sir. However, I must warn you that we will have to keep things very close to our chest. Can you imagine the fuss they'd make if they were to find out at Bletchley that I had involved a retired Detective from Scotland Yard? I'd be back in uniform for the rest of my bloody natural." Stacey's look of concern was not unjustified.

"I'll tell you what I can, Stacey, but this is definitely off the record. If you want it official then you'll have to speak with Mike."

Hart sat forward in his chair. "Almost a year and a half ago now a body was discovered in an apartment in London – Kensington to be exact. I was put in charge of the team that was to investigate the murder. My assistant was, as you now know, DC Mike Sharp." Sharp was well liked and had gained an amiable reputation among other detectives at the Yard as someone who could be relied on to be dogmatic and very thorough. Qualities of which became evident during the investigation.

"We had very little to go on at the time. The victim had been struck by something heavy. The blow had been to the face and by all accounts had been devastating." Hart paused. "Most of the front teeth had been snapped off at the gum and the nose was badly broken. The GP at the scene was Dr Peter Warren, a good friend of mine."

Hart turned to Mitch. "He stated at the time that although the blow had been hard it was unlikely that it would have caused the victim to lose consciousness. It would have left him in a great deal of pain and definitely unable to prevent what was to happen next."

Hart rubbed his hand briskly on the top of his right leg then stood and walked across the room with a slight but noticeable limp.

"The killer had then laid the victim out on the floor. A large square nail, almost eight inches in length, had been driven through the palm of each hand with a third through both feet effectively nailing the body to the floor. Put more simply, he had been crucified.

"Almost two months later we had a second killing." Hart went to his chair and sat back down. "Although it wasn't on our patch so to speak due to the similarities both Sharp and I were asked to take charge of the investigation." Hart lifted his mug and drained it before continuing.

"The body had been found in a small flat above an Italian restaurant not far from here – Dunstable to be exact. Again, as with the first, he had been hit in the face, though this time he had been nailed firmly to the dinning room table. The wrists and throat of both victims had received deep wounds, and each had received a single stab wound to the crutch area."

Hart then went on to explain how during the investigations it had come to light that although both victims had been found in completely different locations they had, apparently, been loosely connected.

John Marshal, the first victim, worked for a large and well-known group of property agents who had offices throughout the United Kingdom, France and Italy.

The second was Raymond Thornton-Allen, a commodities trader employed on the Stock Exchange.

Both were believed to be of Mediterranean origin and both had belonged to the same exclusive London club known as "The Cleaners". The membership of this club appeared to be made up of traders from the Stock Exchange, barristers, medical consultants and the odd policeman.

Hart could tell from their blank expressions that both Stacey and Mitch appeared confused by this latest news.

"It was a stroke of luck really!" Hart added quickly. "One of our team had been going through the victims' mail. Luckily for us the club had sent out renewal notices to all of its members. These renewal notices had been found at both addresses." Hart took a breath before continuing. "When eventually we were able to get hold of the membership list from the club both were confirmed as members." He hesitated for a second. "The membership list is, I believe, still with Mike Sharp despite, I might say, attempts by the club to stop it from leaving their premises."

"Why were they being difficult about it?" Mitch threw

Hart an odd look.

"Because, Mitch, many of those names listed were of people that should have known better." Hart smiled, he had detected something in her, in a look, just for a split second before she checked it. There was so obviously something between them, some attraction. His stomach did a flip as he realised that there was something about this woman that he liked.

Since Jill's disappearance Hart had always felt a twinge of guilt if he had occasion to meet a member of the opposite sex that he liked. It was silly really. He knew deep down that Jill would have wanted him to meet someone and perhaps even remarry. They had often spoken on the subject, particularly in view of his line of work.

He had joined the force straight from school, which had been against his parents' wishes and at the time had caused much friction. It had always been taken for granted by his family that once he'd finished school he would follow his brother's example and join the family-run heating business and work alongside his father in Ireland.

Hart, though, had other ideas. The very thought of spending hours in cramped and dark boiler rooms appalled him.

Although being a policeman had its own risks looking back on it now he had made the right choice. It had taken almost ten years and many early deaths before the civilized world realised the dangers of Asbestos. This fine powdery substance had proved fatal to most that had worked with it and over a few years had claimed the lives of his father and two uncles.

His mother, he recalled, worked for hours on end,

sewing at home making ladies clothing for someone he only remembered as Mo.

At the age of twenty-six and after many miles walking the beat Hart had made it into CID, and eventually after much success locally was drafted to Snow Hill in London where he joined an armed response unit. After three years with them he was moved back into CID, this time though based at Scotland Yard where he remained until he decided to take early retirement.

Despite all his efforts and many contacts Hart had been unable to unearth anything on his wife's disappearance. This eventually had driven him out. He had simply lost interest in the job. In fact, up until quite recently he had lost interest in more or less everything.

He knew the moment that Stacey had asked him that this opportunity to help investigate was what he needed to get his life back on track, what he hadn't figured on was Mitch, she had come right out of the blue.

"How far did the investigation get before you retired, sir?" Mitch asked as she turned around. "Were there any suspects or arrests?"

Hart's eyes narrowed as he shook his head. "None I'm afraid. Needless to say we drew a blank on just about everything. It was bloody frustrating. Both victims appeared to have very little past and almost certainly false identities and we had absolutely no motives to go on. We – I mean DC Sharp and I – were eventually told by those above to call it a day, it was a surprise to all of us I can tell you. Evidently it was felt that too many man-hours were being spent investigating without any results. You know what its like, even the force is money driven."

"Who did you report to, sir?" Mitch asked curiously.

"Superintendent bloody Cave, a right bastard if you excuse the French. He'd only been with the Yard for about a year. We never got on. He was always there ready to stick his nose in. The bloody times I crossed swords with him. He alone probably wasted more police time than any other on the force." Hart's normally calm Irish accent had moved up a gear. "Anyway why do you ask?"

"No reason really, sir, I just think it's odd that you have two identical murders. Neither of them by any stretch of the imagination could be considered commonplace or even unconnected, and yet your boss decides to pull the plug on it?" She deliberately exaggerated her baffled expression to add weight to this observation.

"Actually the case has never been closed officially," Hart interrupted. "It's just become yet another series of unsolved murders, and God knows we have a few of them. As you might expect both Mike and I were devastated when we were first told. The only good to come out of it was that they moved Cave on. Where, though, nobody ever found out."

"Was there anyone responsible for monitoring the case once they'd pulled the plug on it?" Stacey cut in.

"Oh! I think that they probably did initially, but not for long, I wouldn't have thought. Too many other things going on," Hart replied with a tight smile, his tone almost back to normal.

"Did either you or Mike have any ideas why they may have been killed?" Mitch enquired curiously.

"Perhaps not an idea exactly, but we did have an opinion. Unfortunately for us it was an opinion that nobody else seemed interested in."

"Which was what?" Stacey asked sitting down.

"Well, both victims, as I said earlier, were believed to be of Mediterranean origin, or at least that's what was thought at the time by Peter, or I should say Dr Warren. Anyway, over the weeks that followed we interviewed several of their work colleagues and associates and this idea appeared to hold up. We were told that both were well educated and spoke very good English, albeit with a slight accent. Both were very private people, kept themselves to themselves, if you know what I mean. Once work was finished they were gone, neither getting involved in after-work drinks or parties. And interestingly in both cases, despite exhaustive searching by our investigation teams, we were unable to find any passports amongst their possessions. In fact, neither had anything that dated them beyond two years or so, it's as if they just appeared from nowhere."

He made eye contact with Mitch and smiled. "At one point we even had Interpol looking into it, still bugger all." Hart was hoping for that look again but it didn't show.

"What was your gut feeling though, sir? You must have had one," Stacey asked curiously.

"Of course. Personally – and I might add that this opinion was shared by Mike – I think that it was highly likely that both these men were involved together in some kind of gang work, perhaps in Spain or Italy, and for whatever reason came to England, maybe to broaden that work or simply to escape it. Who knows?" Hart replied shrugging his broad shoulders.

"Do you think then, that they may have been followed over here and murdered by their own people?"

"It's possible."

"So our killer or indeed killers might also be foreign?" Stacey offered.

"Pretty likely I would say, wouldn't you? But with little or nothing to go on it's not going to be easy."

"Then let's hope we have more luck with William James. Perhaps this time the killer has given us a bit more to go on," Stacey observed.

Hart stood, stretching his large frame pleased that his leg had now recovered and stared up at the white marker board. After a few moments of thought he tapped his index finger several times on the less than perfect photograph of William James's house. Then turning he gave an encouraging smile.

"I think it might be a good idea for us to pay a visit to William James's home, have a quick look around, what do you reckon?"

Hart's melodic tone received no immediate response. He clapped his hands together loudly.

"Well, come on then, what are you both waiting for? By the way, Stacey, where are you keeping Mr James?"

"He's on ice, you might say, down at the mortuary," Stacey answered lifting his weight out of the chair.

"I'd like to pay him a visit too if you have no objection," said Hart opening the door. "There is something I want to check out. By the way, have you had those results back on the post mortem yet?"

Hart didn't want to go into too much detail with Stacey at this stage. It was a long shot anyway but one he felt well worth looking in to.

"Not yet, sir, although I do know it's ready. Evidently we had a call from the pathologist this morning to say that it could be picked up at our convenience."

"Well, I think we'll start with the house, don't you?" Hart smiled and clapped his large hand on Stacey's shoulder as he passed into the corridor.

"Mitch, would you bring the car around to the front please?" Stacey called back.

Still holding the door open Hart watched with interest as Mitch gathered a few items from Stacey's desk.

"Thank you, sir," she said clasping a file to her chest as she hurried after Stacey.

Closing the door Hart quickened his step to catch her up. She was, he decided, about five, eleven, maybe six foot, very slim. The light blue suit that she wore was cut well and hugged her body closely. She had a smallish bust, he remembered, but Hart didn't mind that; he could never understand the male fascination with large busts anyway. Her skirt although knee length, revealed shapely legs. Her hair was cut short – very practical when you spend most of your time out in the elements. Hart was pleased to note that she wore no wedding or engagement rings.

Stepping into the outer office Mitch activated the door release then, with her head tilted slightly to one side, smiled and added, "If you go through there, sir, I'll meet you around the front in a moment."

"I'll look forward to that," Hart replied cheekily, confident that he had seen that look in her eye again.

Outside Stacey was stood at the foot of the steps talking to a young uniformed officer who appeared agitated. Hearing Stacey raise his voice slightly Hart decided to keep away as the lad was obviously getting a ticking off. Lighting his second cigarette of the day he reflected on what he hoped hadn't been his imagination.

"It looks as though it could rain!" Stacey said as he approached Hart.

Hart pulled his collar up around his ears and thrust his hands deep into the pockets of his coat. "I don't understand how the weather can change so quickly," he said, smoke spilling from his mouth.

"It's that time of year," Stacey offered, then turning to Hart added soberly, "Be honest with me, sir, do you think we stand much chance of finding this bastard?"

Hart noted Stacey's tone then, letting the cigarette drop to the ground, twisted his foot over it. "I think you need more luck than we had," he said rather bluntly.

"Then let's hope we get some, sir," Stacey said turning as he heard an engine start, the distinctive sound reverberating along the narrow alleyway. "I will get him, you know." Stacey hissed confidently.

"I hope you do, Stacey, I really do."

In the car, the sun now replaced by light rain and with Mitch struggling to keep the windscreen from misting up, they made their way from the car park.

Once they were out of the town the traffic became much lighter and with the heater turned full on Mitch sat back happy now that she could see better.

Stacey leant forward and rummaged around in the glove box for a few moments, spilling most of its contents out onto the floor until he found what he was looking for.

"Mint anyone?"

"You can't eat those!" Mitch said in horror. "They've been in there months, Stacey."

"Watch me!" He held the pack over his right shoulder.

"Sir, can I tempt you?"

"No thanks," Hart replied, his face pressed up close to the side window.

"You know, there is something, sir," Mitch said turning the fan down on the car's heater for a moment. "It's probably nothing but I have just realised something." She hesitated as she changed down before accelerating past the car in front. "The first killing was in Kensington. That's London, right?"

"Yes," Hart answered, his face still pressed against the window.

"The second was Dunstable, and now we have this one in Towcester."

"You've lost me," Stacey said shrugging his shoulders.

As they sped along the road Mitch pointed to a small green road sign ahead.

"The A5, sir, they're all connected by this old Roman road," she offered as they shot past the sign. "Don't you see? The killer is moving north up the A5 – First London, then Dunstable and now Towcester." She risked a glance at Stacey in an attempt to gauge his reaction to this idea.

"Bloody hell, Mitch, you could have a point." Hart swung round.

"A truck driver perhaps or company rep. Someone who, uses this road regularly."

Stacey's heart took a sudden leap at this latest revelation.

"Unfortunately that's not going to be easy to follow up. Have you any idea how long the A5 is? He could be travelling from anywhere," Hart said disappointedly.

"Yes, but as yet he's only killed between London and Towcester, remember," Mitch said confidently.

"That's still about seventy miles though," Stacey added quickly.

"Mitch, pull over for a minute would you?" Hart asked.

Mitch slowed up then, indicating left, turned the car into the entrance of a farm.

"Leave the engine running, we may have to move. Mitch's idea could be right on the button." Hart laughed, hardly able to believe something that now appeared so blindingly obvious.

"What?" Mitch quizzed.

Hart slid across to the middle of the seat and rested his arms across both front seats. "It's so bloody obvious it almost hurts."

"It's only an idea," she added.

"I know, and a bloody good one at that!" Hart beamed.

"So where do we go from here?" asked Stacey.

"Obviously the discovery of this third body adds considerable weight to Mitch's idea but, we're still missing something. There has to be something else that they all have in common."

"Maybe it's the club," Mitch responded.

"The club?" Stacey repeated blankly.

Mitch rolled her eyes, "Yes, the club. Call it women's intuition if you like but, I'll bet you anything you like that William James is, or rather was, a member of The Cleaners."

"We need to get the membership list from Mike Sharp and check it out. If he was a member then he'll be on that for sure." Hart said confidently.

"I'll get Mike to stick a copy of it in the post as soon as we get back," Stacey added.

"If Mitch is right and it turns out that he is on the list, what next?"

"Then our next port of call will be to find Cave." Hart's Irish temper was now evident.

"Why do we have to find your old boss, sir?" Mitch watched as Hart's face reddened further.

"Because, Mitch, Cave was one of the names on that membership list, and I believe that's why he was moved. He was instrumental in calling off the investigation in the first place and those above agreed with him. They were forced to, you see. They couldn't risk the bad press that they would inevitably get once it became public that a high ranking police officer was involved in syndicate like The Cleaners. It was easier to close it down and move that bastard Cave out of harm's way." Hart's accent thickened as his temper rose.

"Does anybody know where he ended up?" Stacey asked.

"No! But he won't be that hard to find. I'll get Mike on it when we get back, I'm sure he'll be only too pleased to help." Hart said with just a hint of cynicism.

"For now, though, I'll settle for a quick look around Mr James's home, shall we?"

Engaging reverse Mitch swung the car around and was soon back on the A5 and heading for Towcester.

"That's it, sir, ahead over on the left."

Set far back from the road the large house was just visible through the trees. It was just as Mitch turned into William James's drive that Hart spotted it. A small wooden plaque screwed to the gate post read MITHRAS. His mind engaged overdrive as he tried to think back, suddenly, without warning a large uniformed figure stepped out from nowhere effectively blocking their path. Mitch braked hard bringing the car to a skidding halt on the gravel drive. Recognising Mitch as the driver he broke into a smile that showed off a near perfect set of white teeth.

Mitch wound her window down as he slapped his large hand onto the roof of the car.

"Well, well, well. If it isn't me old mate Mitch," he bellowed in a broad Northamptonshire accent. "Come to see how us poor old buggers put up with the elements have we, me duck?"

Mitch smiled warmly at her large friend and gave his hand a reassuring squeeze, and replied cheekily, "You big softy, if I had known that it would be you standing guard I would have brought along a nice thick blanket."

"Now, now, let's keep it clean, missy, or you'll have some explaining to do to that nice Mr Stacey sat by your side."

"Hello, Rob, how's life treating you?" Stacey smiled.

"Not bad thanks. I'm off duty in another hour or so, then it'll be down to some other poor sod to stand out here." He looked up at the darkening sky.

"Rob, has anyone from the press been down here today?" Stacey leant forwards.

The large policeman crouched down and rested his chin on the top of the door.

"No, lad, it's been as quiet as you like. I think the novelty of a murder has worn off now. They've probably got a fete to cover or something." He chuckled.

"Okay, Rob, thanks." Stacey gave Mitch a gentle nudge on the arm.

"See you later, Rob!"

"Now you take care, me duck," he said stepping back.

"And you, handsome," she said winking an eye

cheekily.

Mitch parked the car in front of the garage and got out. The rain and wind had picked up making it feel much colder.

All three pulled collars up around reddening ears and hurried towards the front door. Above the brass doorknocker hung a small clay sign. Hart ran his finger over the lettering.

"It's the name of the house, sir, MITHRAS."

The cold gradually seeped through their clothing numbing hands and feet.

Stacey pulled away the black and white striped tape that had been strung across the door and punched the entry number into the small keypad to the side of the door. There followed a few distant bleeps and a metallic clunk. Stacey gave the door a firm shove with his shoulder sending it swinging inwards.

All three seemed to take a deep breath simultaneously as they stepped into the darkened hallway. Mitch visibly shivered and folded her arms across her chest.

"Jesus. It's colder in here than it is outside," She stammered hunching her shoulders.

They made their way along the hallway and into the living room. Someone switched a light on. It was obvious that money had not been an issue when it came to furnishing this large room. Silk rugs covered the highly polished wood flooring, in the very centre of the room a coffee table complete with ivory inlay was flanked by two enormous white leather sofas. The walls were painted in a light orange colour and were covered in framed prints of various sizes.

"These must be worth a bloody fortune!" Hart

whistled. "Look, they're all limited editions. This one here is one of ten," he said looking up at the large abstract. "He certainly didn't seem to have a problem when it came to spending money, that's for sure."

"This is interesting," Stacey had closed the door that separated the living room from the hallway. Hung on the wall behind the door was a small wooden sword held in place by two brass hooks. Lifting it from its rests he turned it over slowly in his hand.

"It's more than a little interesting," Hart said almost snatching the sword from Stacey. "I've seen one of these before."

It wasn't particularly well made, and certainly not made well enough to display on a wall. Hart turned to Stacey.

"We found an identical one to this at the Kensington address," he said passing it back.

"Oh! Yes, and while I remember that was named MITHRAS HOUSE too. I knew the moment we'd turned off the road and I saw the house name on the gate post that it seemed familiar. It wasn't until I see it again above the door that it all fell into place."

"What about the Dunstable address?" Mitch cut in.

"Don't know, but that will be something else for Mike to check out."

Leaving Hart to ponder Stacey went through to the kitchen, the light cast from the living room was just sufficient to allow him to make out the silhouette of the kitchen table that stood in the centre of the room whilst disguising for the moment at least the horror that the room held.

He fumbled in the half light for the light switch then, held his hand up to shield his eyes from the sudden glare.

"Oh shit!"

The voice from behind startled him. Mitch, who had followed him into the room, now stood motionless with her hand clamped firmly over her mouth.

Stacey put his hand on her arm and tried to push her back.

"Christ, Mitch, I'm sorry, I should have known better or at least warned you," he stammered looking at her shocked statue-like figure.

"Go and sit in there for a while. Hart and I can take care of this." He pushed her gently again hoping that she would relent.

"No," she said looking up at the ceiling. "I have to face this," and side-stepped him.

Hart, who now stood in the doorway, fought with memories that flooded into his numbed brain. Just beyond Mitch he could see the brownish red stains. They ran the length of the wall, across the kitchen table and ended in large drying pools on the wooden floor.

"Jesus, Stacey."

"That's where he was found." Stacey pointed to a white chalk outline that had been scrawled across the floor to mark the body's position. "Bit of a mess, sir, wouldn't you say?"

"That, Stacey, is a bloody understatement."

"We have to get this bastard," Stacey said turning to Hart. "We believe he'd removed the fuse from the fuse box to give him the element of surprise."

Hart picked his way carefully between bloodstains and drying puddles over to where the body had lay. Crouching low he instantly found what he'd hoped for.

Positioned roughly where the victim's hands and feet

would have been were three square holes punched into the wood flooring. He ran his hand gently over one of the holes then looked up at Stacey.

"These are identical to the nail holes found at the other addresses. I'll bet you a pound to a penny that the nails are the same too."

Standing up he moved around to where the victim's head would have been and sat on his heels. "Can you see this?" He pointed.

Almost two inches in height and scratched heavily into the wooden floor boards: XXIV/XLI.

"This too," Hart said triumphantly.

Mitch shot a glance over at Stacey but neither spoke. Standing, Hart began to make his way back towards them both. He had taken only two steps when he suddenly became aware that he had trodden on something. He couldn't say that he actually heard it but rather felt it – a crunch.

"What's that?" Mitch said excitedly, dropping to one knee. "Hold up, sir, don't put your foot down, there's something hanging from your shoe." She pointed her slim finger at Hart's sole.

"Hang on a minute!" Stacey moved away from the table over to where Hart was balanced, then bending down pulled firmly at the shiny object.

"It's a chain," Stacey exclaimed as it came away.

Hart held out a hand and Stacey let it fall into his palm. He held it up to the light between finger and thumb. It was slightly sticky and he could see small traces of drying blood clogging several of the links.

"A silver necklace, to be exact, Have you got anything on you that we can put it in?"

Stacey handed Hart a small clear plastic bag; he let

the chain drop then sealed the flap down and passed it back to Stacey for safekeeping.

"What do you make of the marks in the floor then, sir? You say you've seen them before?"

Hart fumbled for a moment in his inside pocket then produced a pen together with a small sheet of paper. Dropping to one knee he carefully copied the image onto the paper and passed it to Stacey.

"They look like Roman numerals to me, you know, Latin," Mitch suggested peering over Stacey's left shoulder.

"It is indeed Latin, Mitch, you are quite correct. It's a number, 2441 to be exact," he said taking the paper from Stacey's grasp and writing the number 2441 just below. "Any ideas?" he asked handing the paper back.

"None, I'm afraid," Mitch replied shaking her head.

Stacey stared blankly at the figures written on the paper.

"I'm sorry, Hart, nothing that springs immediately to mind, but I'll keep hold of this if you've no objection," he said folding the paper in half then slipping it into an inside jacket pocket.

Hart smiled, this was the first time since leaving Scotland Yard that someone had called him by his surname, something everyone had done when he had been in the force. It was oddly comforting. "Shall we?" He said gesturing towards the living room.

"Good idea. I think we've all had enough of this room, don't you?" Stacey made sure that his slight head movement at Mitch went unnoticed by her.

Leaving the horrors of the kitchen to the dark Stacey switched off the light and followed Hart into the living room. Hart sat with Mitch on one sofa while Stacey chose the arm of the other. He removed the slip of paper from his pocket again and unfolded it.

"Perhaps it's a date or something."

"If it is then why scratch the number in Latin? Surely it would have taken him longer to do? Anybody in their right mind would have wanted to be away from here as quickly as possible." said Mitch.

"Yes, but we're not dealing with someone in their right mind are we? We're dealing with someone who is far from being right." For that brief moment pictures flashed in front of Hart as clear as day, visions of those other victims. The characters scrawled across the floor, the mess. He turned to Mitch as the visions faded. "I think." He paused, "I'm sure that it's written in Latin because it means something to him, it's important to him."

"Perhaps that's it." Mitch sat forward placing her hand on Hart's leg. "We know from your doctor friend that they were foreign and you know yourself that their work colleagues all stated that neither were English. Italy must be the connection." She paused for a moment then as it hit her she jumped up. "Mafia!" she shrieked. "That would make sense wouldn't it? Perhaps they were members of the Mafia." She turned to both men waiting for some reaction.

"She may have a point," Stacey said turning to Hart. "We've known for some time that the Mafia are heavily involved in protection rackets, particularly around the Hatton Garden and Leather Lane area of London."

Hart sat back in the comfortable sofa and crossed his legs. For a few brief moments the room was silent. Somewhere in another room a clock chimed. Stacey gave Mitch a puzzled look and shrugged his shoulders.

"I take it that you're not sold on the Mafia idea," Stacey asked.

Hart sat forward and looked at his watch but appeared oddly agitated. He ran a hand over his head. "To be honest, no, not especially, but don't get me wrong, I think it's possible. Its things like the wooden swords and the fact that both addresses share the same house name. Before we jump to any conclusions I think we need to find out from Mike if anybody remembers seeing a wooden sword at the Dunstable address, or if the flat had a name rather than number."

"Perhaps the sword is a type of symbol or something, you know to the club I mean," Mitch suggested.

"Its possible I guess," Hart said stroking his chin, the vague expression shown on his face evidence enough that for the moment at least his mind was elsewhere.

"Do we know if William James had any visitors?" He said with a frown.

"According to the housekeeper there had only ever been the girlfriend at the house." Mitch produced a small black notebook from her pocket and flipped it open. "A Miss Lucy Reed. Mrs White confirmed to me that she had only met her once – appeared friendly but a bit shy." She closed the book and placed it on her lap.

"We need to track down the girlfriend, this Lucy Reed," Hart said simply. "See if she knows anything."

"I'll get on it as soon as we get back," Mitch offered.

All three agreed that although the house had already been searched thoroughly it was worth doing again even though they didn't really expect to find anything.

Just off the hallway Stacey had discovered a small cupboard that interested him as it contained the main fuse box for the house. Only six feet by four, its cramped conditions were not ideal for someone of his size.

He soon found what he was looking for and switched the light on, shielding his eyes from the bare bulb briefly.

He could now make out the fuse box up in the corner. It was covered in white powder – evidence at least that someone on his team had the sense to check it for prints.

He pulled at the plastic cover, which swung open easily, below each fuse a small label indicated clearly which fuse powered what circuit. All were firmly in place and each had a thin layer of dust except that is for the one labelled 'kitchen'. Satisfied with what he'd found he clipped the cover back in place. He was about to switch off the overhead light when something on the floor caught his attention. Squatting low he wiped his finger through a light film of mud that had dried on the stone floor close to the wall. The discovery of this confirmed to Stacey what he'd already suspected. Switching off the light he stepped into the hallway and closed the cupboard door.

"Hart!" he called. "Mitch, come and take a look at this."

"What is it?" Mitch asked as she appeared in the doorway of the living room.

"This is the cupboard that contains the fuse box. I think the killer may have hid inside it. He obviously removed the fuse to the kitchen. He knew that William James would have to come back to the cupboard to fix the problem. He would have opened the door completely unaware of who was waiting for him inside and then, Wham!" Stacey clapped both hands together loudly.

"If he had come in through the connecting door to the garage he must have either known the entrance code, or was able to get around it somehow. Inside the garage he would have been out of sight and free to work on the lock anyway," Mitch said confidently.

"The entry code for both the front door and garage are the same anyway," Stacey added.

"The cupboard is closer to the garage than it is to the front door. If he did come in that way that might explain the broken window in the garage," Mitch said. "When I interviewed Mrs White she had said that Mr James had left for work as usual that Thursday morning. She also mentioned that it had been raining heavily that day."

"That's why there's mud on the floor of the cupboard," Stacey tapped his knuckle a couple of times on the cupboard door. "The killer would've had more than enough time to get rid of any footprints between here and the garage that might have given him away."

"Can you imagine it?" Mitch whispered, folding her arms and hunching her shoulders. "Coming home from work or wherever, walking along your hallway past that cupboard, and unknown to you just inches away is your future just waiting to pounce."

"Or lack of it," Stacey added coldly.

"Obviously William James hadn't been too bothered about the dark or there was enough light coming in from the living room for him to see. Either way he hadn't done what had been expected of him. This change of plan would naturally have forced the attacker from his hiding place and into the open," Hart pointed out.

"And the rest we know."

"The assailant had then left the house, probably using the same route as he had entered it," Hart added.

"Exactly!"

"Well, I think you'll agree that we have a pretty

accurate idea of what happened leading up to that moment when William James' was attacked, we know the outcome of the attack, all we need to know now is who and why?" Hart's tone was less than encouraging.

"I know you don't hold out much hope of us catching this killer Hart but, as I said to you before, we will have him." Stacey's tone was firm, almost believable. He turned to Mitch expecting some support instead, she lowered her gaze.

"We have to get this bastard." He urged.

"It won't be for the want of trying Stacey that's for sure," Hart said conscious that morale needed a boost, "Anyway," he sighed, "I think I've seen enough in here for now, how about you two?"

"I agree," Stacey said quickly, "the sooner I'm out of here the better as far as I'm concerned."

Closing the door behind them Hart watched as Stacey rearmed the alarm system while Mitch replaced the chequered tape. Back in the car and with the heater up full again they headed down the drive the small hunched figure standing by the gate was obviously big Rob's replacement. Keeping his back to the wind with collar pulled up high in a futile effort to protect reddening ears he stepped to one side and waved them through.

"Where did you say you were keeping our Mr James?" Hart asked leaning on the back of Stacey's seat.

"He's at the Morgue in Stony Stratford. Do you want to call in on the way back?"

"Splendid idea, and if you know of somewhere we can grab something to eat even better."

CHAPTER FIVE

Almost one hour after parking alongside vans and trucks at the Sizzling Sausage café and now fully fed and watered, the trio, with renewed enthusiasm, were back in the powder blue Viva and heading towards Stony Stratford and their first meeting with William James – deceased.

Stony Stratford, or Stony as most locals referred to it, was a small market town which straddled the old Roman road Watling street, and almost exactly halfway between what was then two busy Roman settlements Magiovinium and Lactodorum better known today as, Fenny Stratford and Towcester. Stony was then a safe crossing point over the river Ouse and was in Roman times known as "the Ford on the Stone Street."

Several new estates had sprung up over recent years and, located only a mile or so from Wolverton, it shared popular rail links with commuters to London. It was also the only town for some miles that had its own crematorium, the position of which was easily identified by its fifty-foot high brick chimney.

Just beyond this, some seventy yards or so was the mortuary.

Happily for the Stony residents both buildings were situated on the very edge of the town, with the mortuary hidden discreetly behind two large grey-painted wrought iron gates. Beyond these and between neatly trimmed box hedging a block-paved drive led visitors up to its two large oak panelled doors complete with ornate brass furniture.

Mitch passed through the gates taking care to obey the five mile per hour sign and along the driveway, shortly coming to rest opposite the large doors.

A varnished sign positioned prominently on the marble steps read: NO PARKING in gold copperplate.

"There's a space over their, Mitch, next to the white Transit."

Mitch engaged reverse and moved back slowly. "It's a bit tight!" she said looking over her shoulder.

"There's plenty of room. Left hand down a bit, that's it, you're in." Hart applauded humorously.

"Thanks for the vote of approval, sir."

Mitch shot Hart a look that made him blush. The kind of look that women used to shut men up in a heartbeat.

She had been right, it was tight, very tight, and this had made it difficult for them to get out of the car. Stacey extracted himself with relative ease. Hart struggled but kept quiet, not wishing to reveal to the others the obvious effort involved in getting his large frame out.

They made their way across the drive deciding to take the shortest route, stepping over a low wall then making their way along the winding path towards the main building. To each side of the path was lawn bordered with flowerbeds still waiting to be planted.

Climbing the marble steps Hart grasped the large brass door knob and pulled open the door, the self closing mechanism requiring a surprising amount of effort to keep it from shutting.

Once inside the three made their way towards the reception desk, which was flanked on either side by large metal planters each containing an abundance of freshly cut flowers. Although the place was surprisingly pleasant and certainly not what they'd expected, the large wooden crucifix hung on the wall behind the desk was a sobering reminder to them why they were there.

"Good afternoon," Stacey said producing his identity badge from deep within an inside pocket.

The receptionist looked up, but only just.

"I'm DI Stacey. Is there anybody here that I could speak with regarding one of your guests?"

"And what guest would that be?" she replied coldly looking over the top of gold-framed glasses.

"William James," he replied leaning on the desk.

"Ah yes! We've been wondering when we would get a visit from you lot!" She slid her chair back and stood. "Please take a seat. I'll go and fetch someone."

"We'll stand if it's all the same to you," Stacey replied turning to his colleagues.

Moments later she reappeared, followed closely by a tall elderly man who looked, as Stacey said later, as though he could have done with a good meal and a comb. The knee length white smock that he wore exaggerated his skinny frame making him appear taller than he actually was. As they got closer the figure removed one of the white rubber gloves that he wore and ran his hand over his head in an effort to bring some control to his greying hair. He peered suspiciously at his visitors through large bifocals then, as they came into focus he pushed past the receptionist with both arms extended and grinned broadly.

"My God, Hart, I don't believe it. What the bloody hell are you doing here?" The two men hugged each other as brothers do.

"It's good to see you, Peter." Hart stepped back, "Stacey, Mitch, I'd like you to meet a dear old friend of mine. This is Dr Peter Warren. Peter, this is Stacey, or rather DI Stacey."

Stacey stepped forward and grasped Peter's hand firmly. "Pleased to meet you, Doctor."

"And this, Peter, is DC Glinn."

Taking hold Peter gently kissed the back of her hand. "A pleasure, DC Glinn."

"Please, call me Mitch, everyone else does," she said delicately sliding her hand from Peter's grasp.

"Still the same old Peter I see. Don't mind him, Mitch, he's one of a dying breed, what used to be known years ago as gentlemen ... few of them around nowadays," Hart reassured.

Peter gave Mitch a cheeky wink, which only added to her embarrassment before turning to his friend.

"Well, Mr Hart, I would hazard a guess that you have come to see our Mr James, have you not?"

Peter's face had now taken on a smug "I know something that you don't" look.

"I have, Peter, although only as an observer I might add."

"I understand. Perhaps you would all like to follow me then."

With all three following close behind, Peter led them down the neon-lit corridor to the left of the reception area. Stacey commented to Hart how the place reminded him of a good hotel. The walls were hung with Turner copies, the floor covered in thick pile carpet. It was only now that the reality of where they actually were hit home; the feint but unmistakable smell of surgical spirit, and the occasional clatter of metal in a room somewhere far off.

Not a hotel Hart thought, more like a hospital. Only this was no hospital. This was where you came when the hospital could no longer help you.

At the end of the long corridor Peter turned left, occasionally glancing over his shoulder to satisfy himself that everyone was still behind him. Turning right then left he stopped and pushed open the door marked Dr Peter Warren – Forensic Pathologist.

"Well, this is it!" he said holding the door open. "Grab yourselves a seat."

He waited until everyone had sat down then closing the door went over to his desk.

"Okay, first thing before we go through, I must warn you, our Mr James is not a very pretty sight. I make no excuses that in this line of work we don't exactly improve matters, but we do what we have to do I'm afraid." He said morosely.

Mitch shifted in her chair as she built up her own picture of what was likely to follow as Peter explained to them the role of the criminal pathologist and his considerable experience in an area which had always been very close to his heart, criminal profiling. This particular area of criminology required much skill which thankfully Peter had gained over many years of study and hands-on experience. He explained carefully to his captive audience his opinion of the killer, stopping occasionally to gauge their reactions. "This individual is compulsively motivated and what is most frightening is that I sincerely believe that he derives great pleasure from the act, he is pure evil," Peter left nothing to imagination, explaining the severity of the injuries and that in his humble opinion they were inflicted on the victim slowly to heighten the suffering. "He is without question a very sick individual and someone that you need to find very soon as I believe he will strike again."

All three sat in absolute silence listening to Peter who was a past master at holding attention once won. Hart knew from previous experience that he was preparing his two colleagues to face something unimaginable, something that was likely to stay with them for many years to come.

"Peter," Hart interrupted. "I assume from what you're saying that you believe we now have our third victim."

"Spot on, Hart. As I had said to you in the past, I felt sure that this killer would strike again. At the time I just didn't know where or when."

Peter, who had now become visibly excited at the thought of the chase, stood. "Okay then, if you're ready I suggest that we go in." He moved over to the door and held it open. "If any of you have any reservations about seeing him then now is the time to say," Peter said deliberately singling Mitch out.

"Thank you for your concern but I'll be okay," she said quickly.

Once outside Peter led them through a pair of swing doors and along a narrow passageway. The most obvious thing here was the lack of carpet. Even the splendid prints in the corridor hadn't made it this far. The light, too, was much whiter, more clinical.

"Okay, this is what I like to call my action room."

Without waiting Peter passed through the doorway, Hart only just managing to catch the wider than normal door before it swung shut.

The room was brightly lit, so bright that for a few

moments it hurt the eyes. There were several very large lamps that hung down from the white painted ceiling and somewhere above them an extractor fan hummed. There was a noticeable lack of windows, which together with the almost overwhelming heady smell of ether certainly did nothing to improve the atmosphere. The floor was tiled in plain white, which made it awkward to walk on. All four of the walls were tiled in a similar fashion. Along one wall stood three stainless steel benches, each with a variety of implements arranged in neat orderly rows that left the mind racing. A large set of polished scales stood to one side. Above the benches at eye level ran two rows of shelving which held a selection of different-sized jars. Hart observed that some appeared to contain body parts and hoped that this had gone unnoticed by Mitch.

Running through the centre of the room, which effectively cut the floor in two, was a channel, some six inches deep and almost twelve wide. At one end was a polished drain cover, at the other a large stainless steel table which sat astride the channel.

Hart's stomach did a flip as he spotted William James's body, which was laid out feet towards them on the mirror-like surface of the table.

As they approached, Hart checked Mitch's body language, looking for any sign of weakness.

"You okay, Mitch," he whispered.

Turning she smiled but Hart couldn't help notice a hint of that same chastisement in her look that he had received in the car. He made a mental note to himself to back off. Although he couldn't help his overprotective nature he had to admit that she was obviously made of sterner stuff than he first thought and certainly more than should be allowed for someone so young. The 'force' had definitely changed since Hart had been a regular cog in the machine.

"Okay, if you would like to gather around this." Peter tapped the surface of the table with his pen. "This is what in the trade is affectionately known as the slab."

All three stepped forward and positioned themselves around the table as though they were back at school and about to get their first cookery lesson.

"They were once made of marble," Peter rambled.

"Sorry?" Hart said turning to Peter.

"The tables, Hart, they were once made of marble, you know, that's why we call them the slab."

"Oh! Yes, I see."

Hart couldn't help but look again for signs of weakness in Mitch's stance. It was almost as if he longed to find her vulnerability. Perhaps it was his own weakness he was focused on. The need to protect; to be needed himself. Or perhaps it was just his attraction to her that scared him. Maybe it was he who needed protection.

Mitch glanced up and caught Hart's stare, which he quickly retracted, turning once more to William James's grey and lifeless form. A thin white cotton sheet folded over several times covered his genital region, offering him some dignity in death.

"As you can see, Mr James was probably aged between thirty and forty years. I would have said looking at his calf muscles and upper body that he had been reasonably fit."

All three of them stared blankly at the cold figure whilst Peter described in detail what was blatantly obvious, although it was debatable whether or not any of them was actually taking much of what he was saying in.

"I have established the time of death to be around eight."

"How can you be so certain?" Stacey asked.

Peter sighed irritably before answering what he felt should have been common knowledge.

"During an autopsy we inspect and weigh everything, all organs, body fluids and in particular stomach contents. I know, for example, that this chap ate a burger with fries and drank almost half a pint of fresh milk around five-thirty. You see, within two to three hours after eating just over ninety-five per cent of the food consumed will have moved from the stomach and into the small intestine. This process stops at the time of death, which enables a pathologist to estimate that time pretty accurately."

Peter hesitated for a moment before continuing.

"You will also note that, given that he has been dead for some time now, his skin tone is still quite olive in colour. It would be my considered opinion that like the others William here was not of British origin."

"Can you be more specific?" Stacey said turning to Peter.

"Not really other than to say possibly Spain, Italy, or perhaps Portugal."

"Hart, perhaps you would be kind enough to turn Mr James's hand over."

Hart reluctantly obeyed. He took hold of the arm and lifted it from the table. At first it seemed to resist his efforts. The flesh, which had now become cold and waxy, appeared tight. Carefully he turned the stiffening hand palm upwards.

"Please note the severe bruising to the palm and the wound in the centre. The left hand has suffered exactly the same injury as has his feet, if you care to look."

None of them appeared to want to but all did.

Stacey, whose complexion had now become slightly ashen and drawn, had taken hold of the other hand and was now inspecting the injury closely.

Peter turned to a small table to his left and took three large nails from a chrome dish. All were square formed and approximately eight inches or so in length. "These were found driven into the palms and feet of Mr Williams," he said, holding them out for inspection.

Replacing two of the nails back into the dish Peter moved around and stood next to Hart. He gently but firmly lifted William James's cold, lifeless hand and, to everyone's absolute horror, pushed the third rust-coated nail through the hole in the palm then slowly withdrew it, pulling up with it silky fine strands of raw flesh that clung to the roughened steel.

Hart finally noticed, out the corner of one eye, the reaction from Mitch that he had been waiting for. Her complexion had taken on a similar pallor to Stacey's and she reeled slightly.

"You will notice that the palm still bears quite heavy bruising in and around the actual wound. This would have been the result of the victim trying to pull his hand off the nail. Incidentally, the thumb and first finger on this hand have also been broken, or I should say crushed." Peter looked up for a moment before continuing. "This, I believe, was probably the result of an inaccurate swing with the hammer when striking at the nail."

Peter paused then looking over the top of his glasses

added, "Clear so far?"

"Crystal," Hart replied coldly.

"Moving on, or rather up should I say, you can see by the injuries to his face that the blow has broken off the front four upper and three lower teeth."

Peter pulled the swollen and blackened top lip upwards with two fingers.

"If you look closely you will note that the tip of the tongue has been bitten off, which as yet I have been unable to find. It's possible of course that he may have swallowed it. His nose is also badly broken."

All three stared at William James's wretched face, mouth open, lips drawn tightly across smashed teeth, the nose split exposing broken whitish bone and eyes wide and dry.

"Now we come to the interesting bit ... our man here, despite these awful injuries, actually died through massive blood loss. You can see that both his wrists and throat have been cut through and if you look here..." Peter stepped forward and suddenly without warning pulled back the white sheet. "You can see that he's also had an extremely deep stab wound to the genitals."

The reaction from both Hart and Stacey to this observation was almost simultaneous and instant and only shared by men.

Replacing the sheet Peter moved around to the victims head again. "I'm particularly curious about his throat though, which as you can see has suffered an extremely vicious and deep wound."

All three watched in silent horror as Peter pushed his first three fingers deep into the gash, then with some considerable force pulled the head violently backwards. There came a feint hiss as trapped air escaped from the chest cavity and the wound was laid open.

This final action was enough to break Mitch's cool. She excused herself and, looking very unsteady, made her way out of the room. Hart allowed himself a private moment of indulgence at this but was careful not to make the same mistake as before and ignored her departure as best he could.

Stacey, who had at this point gained some colour back, was now watching with renewed interest.

"Please, Hart, would you be good enough to pass me those clamps? I'm afraid that we'll have to get a move on otherwise he'll have to go back in the fridge for a while."

"These?" Hart asked holding up two stainless steel tools that he thought looked like clamps.

"No, to your right." Peter gestured irritably, taking care to keep the head pulled back. "That's it! Great."

He then with skilled dexterity, held open the wound with his left hand while with the right positioned the steel device into the opening. Once in position and using a scissors action, he jacked open the wound, which to both Hart and Stacey's horror made sickeningly loud crunching sounds as flesh parted bone.

Peter was now free to let go and stood back.

"What's happened to Mitch?" he asked curiously.

"I don't think she could take any more," Stacey said sympathetically.

"I think, Peter, that you sometimes forget, this is bloody hard on your constitution if you're not used to it, not to mention your stomach," Hart added.

"Hmm ... losing your appetite, old boy? Never thought I'd see the day." He shot Hart a comical look that was tactfully ignored. "Anyway, want to wait for your girl to come back?"

"No, Peter, I don't think she's planning to come back. Please continue, the sooner this is over the better."

Reaching up, Peter pulled a large multi-hinged lamp down. Then taking great care to position it just so, switched it on.

"Right, I'm afraid I will need you both to get rather close now," he said looking at both men in turn. "When I inspected his throat this morning, I have to admit that I did rather hope that I would find what I did find," Peter said looking directly at a now expressionless Hart. "Hart, I think, will not be surprised. You, Stacey, I hope will be," he added confidently.

Stacey moved closer, so close that Peter asked him to move back slightly as he was blocking the light.

Picking up a pair of long tweezers Peter leant forward and pointed deep inside the wound.

"Can you see that, just at the back, lodged between the two large muscles?"

Stacey nodded then swallowed.

In the bright light, deep in the wound and only just visible, something glinted.

Peter closed the fine tip of the tweezers over the object and, with practised skill, pulled gently. Initially there was some resistance, but then it let go.

With a long thick string of whitish mucus swinging from below the object he held it up to the light.

"Jesus!" Stacey exclaimed with obvious surprise. "It's a bloody coin."

With a plop, Peter allowed the coin to drop from his tweezers into the stainless steel tray filled with spirit that stood at his side, instantly turning the clear liquid red.

"Hart," Peter said turning to him. "I can guarantee

that this chap was killed by the same hand that killed the others. Everything to do with their deaths is identical." Peter waited for a response.

Something deep within came to life and rolled around in Hart's stomach. He quickly checked the faint smile that his face was now showing.

"Perhaps a second bite at the cherry?" Peter had spotted his reaction.

"Let's hope so," Hart replied, concealing his obvious delight.

"There is something else that you should know, Hart," Peter said replacing the tweezers carefully back onto the tray. "During the post mortem which we performed on the other victims we discovered something else, something really odd."

Turning to his right he picked up what at first glance appeared to be a stainless steel shoe horn. It was almost ten inches long with a flat at one end. Peter inserted it deep into the gaping wound, then with his free hand picked up the tweezers again and swished them around in the reddened liquid.

"We were under strict instructions that at no time were we to reveal what we had discovered," he said wiping the tips dry on a white towel that lay by the tray. "The reason for the secrecy, we were told, was that if and when a suspect was found this one exclusion from the evidence sheet would only be known by a select few and obviously the killer."

As Peter pulled open the wound, air escaped again.

"That evidence," he continued, "would rule out any cranks that might be tempted to volunteer themselves as the killer." He glanced up at Hart quickly. "Okay, let's get on, shall we? Can you see this severed muscle here?" Gripping the muscle with the tip of his tweezers he pulled at it until it was almost straight. "This is the trachea. It would normally be joined to this part below."

Hart watched with renewed interest knowing that he was about to learn something that had been kept from him during the original investigations.

"Wrapped around this muscle should be the cricoid cartilage."

Peter let his grip with the tweezers go and the thin strand of muscle coiled back up out of sight under the chin.

Hart felt fluid spray lightly onto his cheek; suppressing the revulsion that coursed through him he quickly wiped it away using the back of his hand.

"Speak English, Peter, we're not bloody surgeons," Hart hissed, throwing him a dirty look.

Then, pointing with the tweezers into the gaping hole that was once William James's throat, Peter explained. "Adam's Apple, Hart, all three victims have had their Adam's Apple removed by the killer."

Both men stood in complete silence as Peter's last statement sunk in.

"You see the cricoid cartilage is attached to the front of the trachea or, as you would call it, windpipe." Peter waited for a moment before continuing, then added, "I also believe that I now know what our killer used to disable his victims and then kill them ... the knife, I mean."

He let the wound close and removed the shoe horn.

"Let me finish up here then we can go back into the office and I'll explain all. Have you something that I can put this into?"

Using the tweezers again, Peter delicately picked up

the coin from the steel tray and swished it vigorously in the reddening liquid. Once he was satisfied that it was as clean as he was going to get it he let the coin drop into the plastic bag that Stacey had produced.

"Thank you," Peter said taking the bag from Stacey. He let the tweezers drop with a clatter into the tray then sealed the bag shut.

"Take care of this would you, Hart?"

Hart slipped the bag into his breast pocket and gave it a reassuring pat with his hand.

"I should step back a little," Peter instructed, reaching up for a showerhead that was hung above the table. Depressing the trigger he sprayed water over the torso and carefully directed the resulting flow of blood and body fluids towards the drain in the table. As they watched the reddening torrent run along and down into the drain cover it became obvious to them both why there had been a channel carved into the tiled floor.

"Right then, who fancies some tea?" Peter said with raised eyebrows. He replaced the large shower head back onto its mount, ignoring the silence that greeted him. Walking towards the exit Peter clapped his hand on Hart's back then turned to Stacey.

"Here's something for the record: did you know that it was your lot, Scotland Yard I mean, that were responsible for all this? They became so frustrated at the lack of evidence during their investigations of Jack the Ripper in 1888 that it led to the creation of the position of forensic pathologists." He waited for some reaction before adding, "And the word 'autopsy', well, it means to look for oneself. Very odd wouldn't you say?"

Hart was unimpressed by this revelation, which only managed to elicit a slight lifting of eyebrows from

Stacey.

They found Mitch sitting on a small wall in the sun. As they approached she turned and gave a smile. She looked a little better and stood as they got up to her. Hart put a hand on her shoulder.

"You okay?" he said sitting down beside her.

"Come on, girl," said Peter, waving a hand impatiently. "There's nothing like a nice cuppa to soothe the nerves."

Mitch tried hard to ignore Peter's offhand manner, and tried harder still to hide her blushing cheeks.

She turned sheepishly to Hart but said nothing.

Hart played stupid but wondered if he was about to be a part of a battle of wills. It was the last thing he wanted, to be at odds with Mitch. Totally the opposite, in fact. He stared at her smooth complexion, taking in the steely eyes that tried hard to shield her emotions.

"It's okay, you know, Mitch."

"What is?" she replied, taking care to hold her stare.

"In there," he said, motioning back to the mortuary building. "It's okay to—"

"Sir, I know you think I need protecting but I can assure you I can look after myself!"

Hart was taken aback for the third time that day. He felt his cheeks burn and tried as hard to hide it as Mitch did her emotions.

"Mitch, I'm sorry, I didn't mean—"

"Look, sir, I'm sure that when you joined the force things were different, but this is the age of equality and not everyone with a pair of tits needs a father figure."

Hart jumped back and furrowed his brow. He felt like he had been hit in the stomach. A father figure – was that how she saw him? That hurt. She had certainly had more luck in finding his weakness. Touche!

They sat in silence for a few moments, Hart nursing his bruised ego and Mitch looking decidedly uncomfortable all of a sudden.

"Sir," she said, her voice cutting through the awkwardness. "I'm sorry, that was really out of line."

"It's okay."

"No, it's not, you didn't deserve that. It's just that..." Mitch's expression softened along with her tone of voice. "Being a woman in the police isn't always easy."

"Mitch, it should be me apologising. I've obviously been out of the game too long."

Mitch managed a smile at that. "No, it's just me venting. I just get fed up with people trying to wrap me in cotton wool sometimes. I've got just as much ambition as the next guy but people just see a sheep in wolf's clothing."

"A wolf in sheep's ... oh, I get you."

"I'm good at my job, sir. I just want a chance to prove that."

Hart thought about offering some more words of wisdom but settled on a pat on her slender shoulder.

"You are good at your job, Mitch. Maybe an old guy like me's just not used to the competition, eh?"

Mitch allowed herself another smile. "You not so old," she said and shot Hart a look that made his heart skip a beat. "You ready for that tea, sir?"

Hart followed her into the building, trying to ignore the new feeling that swept over him as the self-assured figure stepped back and held the door open for him with a conspirital smile.

Inside Stacey offered them both a mug, which they gladly accepted, the piping hot liquid a refreshing welcome. The group sat for a while mostly without speaking as though trying to regain some inner strength when suddenly Peter's secretary appeared in the doorway clutching a manila folder. Jackie had been Peter's secretary for many years now and although he would have been the last to admit it, he could not do without her. She kept him organised, at times almost bullied him, but cleverly. She was also excellent when dealing with the press on his behalf, never letting them know too much. Both lived alone and many of their colleagues thought that one day they might make a go of it.

"Thanks Jackie." Peter slipped the elastic band off and opened the folder.

"You know, that was one hell of an experience back there Peter," Stacey said, "I don't think I could leave home in the morning, kiss the wife goodbye then be faced with that every day?"

Mitch avoided Stacey's stare, which she felt sure would be directed towards her.

"I'm not married." Peter replied flatly.

Hart glanced over at Mitch and gave her a reassuring smile, which she ignored. The shield was back up, thought Hart. He cleared his throat. "So, Peter, now that you've put us all through that ordeal, any ideas?"

Peter sat ram rod straight in his chair and took a deep breath as though he was about to do a length underwater.

"I can't, I'm afraid to say, give you a motive. What I can give you, though, is how and possibly when. Taking into account the amount of damage inflicted on the lower jaw it is my considered opinion that just as the other two unfortunate victims the blow to the face was done with a hammer, and judging by the size and shape of the bruising, it was almost certainly the same type of club hammer."

Peter had now removed from the folder several pages of neatly typed notes and ran his finger slowly down the index printed on page one.

"Ah! Here it is!" he said triumphantly and promptly removed a page. "I reported here that the blow would have severely stunned the victim; he may or may not have lost consciousness at this point. The killer had then positioned the victim on the floor, at this stage, Mr James was probably aware of what was going on but almost certainly unable to do much about it." Peter paused for a moment as he referred to his notes again. "I'm sorry to say that the rest is history, our unfortunate Mr James had then been literally nailed to the floor." Peter hesitated. "I also believe that some time elapsed between the actual crucifixion and the point when he was cut open. Oh! And before you ask, no there was no sign of any sexual motive other than the stab wound."

"Could our killer do all this and still remain relatively clean?" Stacey quizzed.

"It would be extremely difficult but not impossible if you were determined enough." Again Peter thumbed through his notes, "There's something else … I'm reasonably confident now that I know what type of weapon was used, and a strange choice in my opinion," Peter added with a satisfied air.

All three waited patiently as he rummaged amongst the confusion of paper that lay on his desk. If Peter did have an idea of the weapon used, then, this information would be invaluable to them. They at least could arrange a more thorough search of the area knowing what they were looking for.

"With all three victims we are confident that the throat injuries were sustained by one single violent slash of a blade. The depth of cut was so deep that in all cases it had almost severed the head from the body. To achieve this, the blade would need to be reasonably heavy and longer than a knife. We know from the stab wound that it was at least three inches wide." Peter replaced the notes and closed the folder. "In my humble opinion you should be looking for a sword – an odd choice, wouldn't you say?"

"Difficult to conceal, you mean!" Mitch cut in.

"Exactly." Peter slid his chair back and opened the centre drawer of his desk and produced a small brown envelope then stood up.

"Lastly we come to what I consider to be the most confusing items of evidence in these killing."

Tearing off the security seal he allowed the contents of the envelope to tumble out and clatter together on the melamine surface of the desk. All three watched as both items spun and danced together, glinting under the artificial light of Peter's clinical room.

"Hart, if you would be so kind." Peter held out his hand.

Hart removed the small plastic bag from his pocket and handed it over. Pulling the seal away Peter let the coin drop into his hand, then, placed it next to the others on the table.

"Why the use of coins?" Stacey exclaimed. "It just doesn't add up."

"Exactly right, but you see, Stacey, these are not just ordinary coins, these are quite rare ... Roman, you see." Peter celebrated his power again for a moment. "They are each over fifteen hundred years old."

"Silver Denari, or rather Danarius," Hart interrupted reacting to Mitch's confused expression.

Stacey scooped all three of the coins into his large hand and examined them closely one by one.

"Stacey, how the hell can you hold them?" a horrified Mitch exclaimed.

In a knee jerk reaction Stacey immediately let the coins drop back onto the table and rubbed his palms vigorously together.

"Its quite all right, they have been cleaned." Peter allowed his smile to grow wider while arranging them so that each coin was face up and in order. "For the record, this one here, you will remember, Hart, we retrieved from the throat of our first victim, Mr Marshal." Peter picked the coin up and turned it over. "As you can see, it's in remarkable condition considering its age."

Sliding forward the second coin, he continued. "This one came from the throat of Mr Thornton-Allen, our second unfortunate soul."

Lastly he picked up the third. "And finally we come to the most recent addition to our little collection here and that found inside William James. Again, this appears in excellent condition." He flipped it over in the palm of his hand.

"You will be pleased to know that earlier today I rang a very good friend of mine, a James King who is the curator at the British Museum in London. I explained very briefly about this murder and in particular my discovery of a third coin. He kindly put me in touch with their resident expert in Roman history, Mr Anton King, no relation I might add, and a strange chap as I remember."

Peter held the coin up to the light.

"Anyway, he was extremely interested when I told him of the coins, so much so in fact that he suggested that I send them to him. He said that coins were one of his specialities.

"I think that rather than send them to him we should take them to him, what do you say, Hart?" Stacey suggested.

"Yes, I agree, we wouldn't want to risk losing them."

"One final thing about these coins. All three have had a small hole drilled into them. My guess would be that they've been worn, probably around the neck on a chain or something. Certainly our Mr James next door had worn a chain. I found minor bruising to the back of his neck to substantiate this."

"Interestingly, Peter, we found a chain at the scene," Hart said as Stacey produced it from his pocket and laid it down onto the table. "It was close to where the body had been found. In fact, I trod on it."

Picking it up, Peter offered it up to one of the coins.

"I can't say for sure of course but it certainly looks promising, wouldn't you say? It's about the right thickness. The bruising on William James's neck would certainly have been caused by a chain similar to this." Peter lowered it slowly back onto the table in a neat little heap.

"There's also, Peter, the question of the Latin characters found scrawled on the floor," Hart scribbled the figures down and passed the slip of paper to Peter. "XXIV/XLI. "Obviously it means something to the killer?"

"Yes Hart, but what exactly? Unfortunately that part

of this puzzle has me beat." It was evident from his expression that Peter, too, was baffled by the significance of this marking.

"Peter, do you think it would be possible for you to speak with this Anton fellow and arrange for us to meet with him, preferably at the museum and obviously as a matter of urgency? There are several things that I'd like to learn more about and not just about these coins," Stacey asked.

"Of course," Peter replied.

"James will be thrilled to help, I'm sure."

"Great."

"Actually you've just reminded me of something. It's been bothering me all day," The urgent tone in Mitch's voice worried Hart for a moment as he wondered what was coming. "When the three of us were poking around William James's house earlier, I noticed an answerphone on the table in the hallway. I know it's a long shot but did anyone think to check it, you know, see if there was any messages left on it or not? Only, to be honest, I don't remember it being mentioned anywhere on the incident report."

"It wasn't in the report," Hart added.

"Jesus." Stacey ran his hand through his hair as this observation suddenly hit home.

"Mrs White stated in the report that she had been woken by the phone but that it had rung off once the answerphone had cut in." He added.

"It's essential that we retrieve its tape if there is one." Hart said urgently.

Stacey glanced down at his watch and was shocked to see that it was almost six.

"Peter will you ring me as soon as you have spoken

with the museum?"

"Yes, of course."

"Should we go back to the house now?" Mitch asked.

"No, it's important but it's getting late now I'm sure it can wait until the morning," Stacey said confidently.

"Look, I don't know what you both think but I suggest that we leave it at that for today and resume tomorrow." Hart stood and produced a pen from an inside pocket, "Peter, this is my new telephone number," he quickly scribbled down the number on a slip of paper and handed it to his friend, "give me a ring if you think of anything else that might be relevant."

"I agree, it's been a traumatic day all things considered," Stacey added turning to Peter. "How can I put this, Peter?" Stacey said holding his hand out. "It's been quite an experience."

Peter grasped Stacey's hand firmly and just smiled, "I'll be in touch as soon as I've spoken with James." Peter said grabbing Hart's hand.

Turning to Mitch, Peter took her hands in his and held them firmly. "My dear Mitch, it has been a real pleasure..." Then pulling her towards him he gave her an affectionate peck on the cheek.

"I'd like to say the same but ... no offence, you understand."

"None taken, my dear. Come, I'll show you out," Peter said holding open the door.

"I'll ring James now and arrange for you to meet with Anton as soon as possible." He said confidently then allowed the door to close.

Back in the car and with the heater up they turned out of the gates and were soon heading for Wolverton.

CHAPTER SIX

Over the loud hissing and rhythmic clatter of the two large printing presses – and now some 72,000 impressions later – Steve and Neil kicked a ball of screwed up paper, tightly wrapped with a dozen or so thick heavy duty rubber bands, between them.

Other than its visual appearance the less than obvious difference between this paper ball and the real thing would be its value. This hastily constructed item was probably worth somewhere between two to three thousand pounds sterling and was made up from a handful of running sheets collected straight from the delivery end of Neil's press.

Soon the metallic clatter gave way to a deep resonating thump from the first press, shortly followed by similar sounds from the second, signalling to both players the end of their match and the end, for today at least, of their print run.

With one final effort Neil kicked out, sending the paper ball spinning high up into the rafters where it stayed.

"You dick," screamed Steve, lobbing a twelve-inch plastic rule in Neil's direction.

"Leave it mate, we'll get it later," Neil said, as his friend attempted to dislodge it with a well-aimed pallet knife, "we'll use the forklift."

"It's on charge."

"Then we'll have to do it tomorrow won't we? Neil replied as sarcastically as he could.

Steve gave his friend the kind of look that didn't invite conversation.

"Come on mate lighten up, don't be such a tart, it can wait honest,"

"It'll be your bloody funeral if he finds out,"

"He won't see it, trust me I'm a doctor,"

All Steve could do, was shake his head in disbelief at his close friends complacency. Neil sensed his victory and grinned,

"I'll tell you what. You wash my press up for me, and I'll sort the stacks out and we can be on our way."

Without waiting for a reply Neil jumped onto a pallet truck and scooted his way down to the far end of the factory, weaving from left to right between pallets of paper and machinery.

Strapped tightly to each of these pallets and covered carefully with a thin plastic sheet to protect the contents from damp air was a little over 14,000 sheets of unprinted, untrimmed paper. Each pallet stood almost four feet in height and weighed in at just over the ton. Although undoubtedly valuable now, what was certain was that by the end of the week once printed each pallet would be worth significantly more.

Almost an hour later both stood in reception. Steve switched off the lights and waited while Neil entered the four-digit code that would re-arm the alarm system.

"See you tomorrow, gay boy," Steve hissed as he went out into the cool night air.

Neil thrust his middle finger into the air as a direct response to this accusation and locked the door.

"See you later, tosser," he shouted.

With both engines revving loudly and music turned up high they each exited the small car park at full speed, watched by an elderly man out walking his dog.

Tuesday was a better day. Although fresh, the sun shone warmly and looked as though it might be here to stay, at least for a while.

As arranged, Hart met up with Stacey at his office and made a good job of hiding his disappointment once he'd learnt that Mitch had taken the day off. Both agreed that the first job of the day regrettably was to go back to William James' house and if it existed, recover the answerphone tape. Looking back on it now neither of them could believe that such an important item could have gone unchecked. This tape, if there was such a tape, could prove invaluable in this inquiry and thank God that Mitch had been on the ball.

Stacey drove, which allowed Hart time to take in the journey while contemplating what lay ahead. The possibility that the answerphone may have recorded a message which could supply them with further leads was at the very least encouraging.

Some twenty minutes or so later Stacey was turning off the A5 and on to the gravel driveway. At the entrance a uniformed policeman complete with cape stood arrow straight and waved them on as he recognised Stacey.

"I'll tell you what, I'm beginning to hate coming back here," Stacey remarked as he brought the car to a halt directly in front of the garage door.

Stepping from the car, both stood square on in the bright sunlight looking up at William James' magnificent and rather imposing house. Although the weather was still brisk it was somehow comforting to feel the heat from the sun penetrating their clothing and warming aching backs.

Standing at the front door Hart watched as Stacey produced a slip of paper from his pocket, punched four numbers into the electronic keypad and waited for the door to unlock.

"May I?" Hart said sharply holding out his hand palm up.

Stacey frowned as he passed the slip of paper to Hart.

"What's this?" Hart now held the note between finger and thumb and waved it slowly in the air.

Stacey's face reddened slightly. "To be honest I couldn't remember the code number to get in, so I wrote it down," he laughed nervously.

"Not on this you didn't, Stacey. This is a piece of notepaper from my hotel room. I gave you this yesterday when we were in there with Mitch," Hart said anxiously.

Hart slowly unfolded the paper, watched closely by Stacey.

"You see, this is my handwriting, I wrote that number down," he said.

Snatching the paper from Hart, Stacey now realised the enormity of what Hart had just discovered. He felt numbed as he stared down at Hart's carefully written numbers.

"Christ, Hart, I didn't bloody realise."

"Too much of a coincidence, wouldn't you say? We had better find out from Mike if the London and Dunstable addresses had the same alarm systems fitted ... and if they had, who supplied them and when. I'll bet you a pound to a penny, Stacey, that the alarm codes turn out to be the same number as this one," he said confidently.

Folding the note Stacey slid it into his inside pocket then, wiping away the light condensation that covered the metal keypad, looked closely at the small logo etched into the surround.

"It's a Praco system."

"Well, I can't say that I've actually ever heard of that make before, Stacey, but I'll eat my bloody hat if the others don't turn out to be of the same make too." Hart watched as Stacey gave the door a shove and then on reflection added, "I'll wait in the car for you. Pointless us both going in," he said taking a step back.

"Okay, sir, I'll be as quick as I can," Stacey said and was swallowed instantly by the unwelcoming darkness of the hallway.

Hart checked his watch as he pulled the car door closed. Tucking his coat around him he rested his head on the side window and shivered. The heat from the sun warmed his face and became just too much to resist. His fatigue swept over him like an old cloak. Closing his eyes he let his head fall back onto the head rest.

Hart shivered as he came out of his nap and put a hand up to his mouth in a vain effort to stifle a yawn. Looking around him he was confused for a moment then remembered where he was. He rubbed the sleep from his eyes and turned to look out of the back window. He could just make out the blue cape on the huddled figure at the gate, turning to his left he noted that the front door to the house was still open.

Hart pulled back his sleeve and looked down bleary-eyed at his Timex, trying to focus on the small Roman numerals.

"Fuck."

He had been asleep for almost thirty minutes. Where

the hell was Stacey?

He yanked at the door handle and almost stumbled to the floor in his haste to get out of the car. Quickly regaining his step he sprinted towards the house.

"Stacey, Stacey!" he shouted as he approached the open door.

Hart waited for a few seconds, trying to get his head together, then called again. Still nothing. Something had to be wrong, he thought, Stacey had only gone in to get the tape. That was almost half an hour ago.

He made to approach the house then hesitated and with a furtive glance over his shoulder, ran towards the policeman at the front gate. "Quick, constable, get up here now," he said in a hushed tone.

The young PC faltered for a moment then slipped his cape off his shoulders and with one hand clutching at his helmet sprinted towards Hart.

"What's wrong?" he shouted through gasping breaths as he approached Hart.

"I fell asleep."

"What?"

"In the car, I fell asleep. Stacey went into the house to recover something. He's been gone half an hour, something's happened."

As they reached the front door Hart grabbed at the enthusiastic PC almost pulling him to the ground.

"Wait," Hart hissed stepping to one side of the door frame raising his finger to his lips. Hart listened to the silence. He could hear nothing. The policeman stood opposite eyes fixed firmly on Hart, waiting eagerly for a signal.

"Perhaps we should call for him?" the PC suggested.

Holding his hand up Hart shook his head and tried to

tune into the deafening silence ... then he heard it!

"There, did you here that?" Hart looked the policeman directly in the eyes and waited for some reaction. Suddenly a door slammed shut followed by the crashing of glass.

"Quick, around the back. The bastard's legging it."

Hart didn't wait for a reply, turning and running at full pelt along the front of the house and past the garage. Turning left at the corner he almost slipped on the gravel.

With the young policeman close behind, they sprinted across the lawn towards the back door.

"Mind out, there's glass everywhere," Hart shouted thrusting his hand into the air.

Then suddenly, somewhere in the distance, they could hear the unmistakable sound of an engine turning over, slowly at first then becoming quicker as the battery warmed to its task.

Hart spun around, cupping both hands around his eyes in an effort to shield them from the low sun.

"What's that?" He tried focussing in on a point at the far end of the garden from where the sound appeared to coming from.

"Quick, he'll get away." Hart yelled then took off across the wet lawn.

In the distance above the pounding of their feet on the sodden ground they could clearly hear as an engine fired up, it coughed at first then spluttered, cleared then the engine note rose almost to a scream followed quickly by the sickening sound of crunching metal as the driver tried to find and engage first gear.

Then suddenly all went silent.

"He's stalled it!" Hart shouted triumphantly.

Both kicked out trying to get a better grip on the wet grass as they sprinted towards the end of the garden. As they neared the fence an engine burst into life again. Hart gulped at the air with lungs fit to burst but pushed on, his legs had almost giving out.

Out the corner of his eye he caught a glimpse as the PC slowly passed him and took the lead.

Again the driver attempted to find a gear. They could hear as the engine note increased and as he let out the clutch the rear wheels spinning, tyres scrabbling as they tried to grip on loose gravel.

Hart watched as the Policeman vaulted the wooden fence then disappeared from view.

As he approached he could still here the car in the distance, its engine screaming as the driver made good his escape.

Climbing up onto the fence he sat astride, gripping the rough timber with his knees. From this position Hart could just make out the speeding car in the distance.

Both men gasping, watched as it headed for the horizon.

Only the occasional glint of light through the trees as the sun reflected on its windows gave away its position.

"Fuck it!" Hart rasped as he dropped down from the fence.

"Sorry, sir, I didn't even see what make it was other than it was white."

Hart was bent double, his hands clasping his knees as he tried to regain normal breathing. "I'm too bloody old for this shit," he gasped then straightened.

"No point getting the car I suppose?"

"He's long gone," Hart said shaking his head, his

voice raspy and dry as he tried to get air into his lungs. He reached for the top of the fence and with much effort hauled his exhausted frame up. He sat astride the panel then paused as he looked down at the obviously frustrated policeman.

"There'll be another time, make no mistake," Hart encouraged.

"We were so close though!"

Hart held out his hand and pulled the policeman up onto the fence, both pausing for a moment to look down the road where the speeding car had made its escape.

"Trust me, our time will come, but for the moment we had better make sure that Stacey has come to no harm." Trying to conceal his real concern for his colleague, Hart swung his leg over and dropped to the lawn below.

Eager to get back to the house they broke into a jog.

"What's your name, constable?" Hart asked, still trying to control his breathing.

"Paul, sir, Paul Edwards."

"Well, Paul Edwards, you did okay."

"Thank you, sir."

As they neared the house Hart could clearly make out a shape standing up at a window.

Once they had reached the back door both did what they could to clear the thick clinging mud from their shoes, then stepping carefully over the broken glass Hart tried the back door. It was locked.

"Try 2441, sir," a gruff voice suggested.

A startled Hart looked up. Stacey stood some six feet into the room, his face pale and drawn. His left hand held what looked like a tea towel to his head.

"Are you all right?" Hart asked relieved that his new friend appeared relatively unscathed.

"Yes, did he get away?" Stacey asked already knowing the answer.

"We almost had him, Stacey, so close, he stalled the car."

Hart punched 2441 on the keypad and waited for it to unlock, then pulling open the door stepped inside.

"I bet the bastard was after this." Stacey stepped back and waved the tape in the air.

"You've got it, that's great!" Hart exclaimed.

"He surprised me, gave me a bit of a crack on the head."

Stacey bent forward removing the towel from his head.

"No blood, you'll live," Hart said coldly.

"He must have been pretty desperate to chance climbing through that," Hart said pointing to the broken glass in the door.

"I'm not sure that he did, sir."

"What do you mean?"

"Well, for one thing there's no glass inside and if you look there's none on the doorstep, all the glass is out here." Stacey moved outside and pointed to the smashed window strewn over the lawn. "It's almost as though he broke the glass when the door was already open."

"You should have a crack on the head more often." Hart grinned.

"Why the hell would he bother doing that?" the PC asked from the doorway.

"So that we would think that it was just another chance burglary," Stacey said turning to the policeman.

"Exactly, so we would be most unlikely to change the code number to the alarm and then that way he is free to come back when things have quietened down," Hart explained.

"He must have heard us at the front door and then hidden somewhere," Stacey said stepping back into the house. "I stepped into the hallway, which I admit was quite dark, but eventually found the table just under the stairs. The answerphone was on top. I pressed the eject button on the tape player. It was then that I heard something. I was pretty sure that it came from the kitchen. Anyway, I knew that it couldn't have been you, sir, so just to be on the safe side I popped the tape on top of the door frame and went through into the living room."

"Quick thinking Bat Man, then what?" Hart asked keenly.

"That's it, unfortunately I don't remember anything else, well, not until I heard you shouting."

"Did you get a look at him?"

Stacey shook his head slowly.

"I'm sorry, Hart, no, not even a bloody glimpse."

"Never mind, Stacey, at least he didn't get to nail you to the floor," Hart replied, giving him a sharp slap on the upper arm.

"Paul, I think it would be a good idea to ring in, don't you?" Hart suggested, pointing to the telephone. "Could you also ask them to arrange for someone to come out and check for fingerprints? It's probably a waste of time but you never know, we might just get lucky? And while you're at it you had better get them to send someone to sort the door out."

"Sir."

"Come on, Stacey, we'd better get you looked at."

Hart closed and locked the damaged door and led Stacey back through the house, both waiting in the hallway for a moment until the PC had finished his call.

"Twenty minutes, sir," He said replacing the receiver back onto its rest.

"Good, you'd better stay here until they arrive. If they find anything, ring us, we should be back at the station by then," Hart replied stepping through the doorway. "I'm going to drop by the hospital first and get someone to have a quick look at Stacey, make sure there's no concussion."

"No, Sir, I'd rather not," Stacey bleated. "I'm okay, really, just a bit of a headache, that's all, nothing a couple of aspirin couldn't sort out."

Hart turned surprised that this large and very fit young man was so obviously rattled by the thought of going to hospital.

"I would sooner go back to the station, sir, honest. Anyway, I'm more than just a little bit keen to see if there's anything on this tape or not." Stacey patted his breast pocket.

"As you wish, Stacey, but any blurred vision and you had better let me know."

"Don't worry, if I feel the slightest unwell you'll be the first to know." Stacey turned and gave a wink to the PC before following Hart out into the driveway.

"If it's all the same to you, Sir, I think I'd prefer to wait here at the doorway rather than inside," the PC called after them.

"Whatever," Stacey replied without looking back. "You'd better drive, sir, if you don't mind," he added quickly.

Five minutes later and with Hart at the wheel the two were speeding along the A5 towards Stony Stratford.

"Are you hungry, Stacey?" Hart asked pointing to the large swinging sign ahead of them.

"To be honest, I could eat a horse, sir."

Hart slowed up and turned into the near full car park of the Sizzling Sausage. Although busy with lunchtime trade they managed to find a table over by the window. Stacey mumbled something about putting too much weight on lately, but still managed, Hart noted, a full English.

Having settled their hunger and the bill, they made their way across the packed car park towards the car. Soon Hart had rejoined the busying traffic on the A5 and keeping his speed up as they entered Old Stratford tried to make the traffic lights but was unlucky.

"I take it that you've got a tape player back at the station, Stacey?" he asked, keeping one eye on the lights.

"Yes, though I'm not exactly sure where it is."

As the traffic lights changed Hart engaged first and accelerated down the hill, keeping his speed constant they were soon entering Wolverton. Passing the school to his right he indicated then swung the wheel over and brought the car to an abrupt halt directly opposite the police stations main entrance.

Stacey drew several deep breaths as he stepped from the car, in an effort to clear his numbing head before going in. "I thought you had the day off," he said stepping through the doorway.

Hart's smile visibly broadened as he spotted Mitch sat behind the glass screen.

"It's a long story so I won't bore you. Let's just say it was a bit of a let-down," she replied, holding both hands in the air in mock surrender.

"Well, next time you have a day off and it looks as though it could be a disaster let me know and perhaps we could have some lunch together or something." Hart suddenly checked himself. He pulled an apologetic face and quickly backed off. "Sorry, I mean—"

"That'd be nice ... sir." She smiled.

Hart's smooth Irish ascent had won him another chance. "That's a date then," he said, punching the air as he walked away.

Stacey, Hart noted, looked oddly displeased, which surprised him. He gave a wink as he passed, which Stacey chose to ignore. Hart didn't let it bother him and headed for the men's room.

When Hart returned to Stacey's office he was on the telephone. He went over and sat with Mitch. He could just detect her perfume, his heart thumped so violently he was sure it could be seen through his shirt.

"What about tonight, are you doing anything this evening?" he asked, trying to sound confident fully aware that he was probably being a bit quick of the mark. "Perhaps we could go to the pictures and then onto a restaurant or something afterwards."

"Don't push your luck," she replied without looking up.

Hart looked shocked. He could feel heat bristle at his cheeks.

Mitch relaxed, although it seemed to Hart that she was enjoying this brief burst of power that held him entrapped.

"I can't tonight, that's all."

"I'm sorry, Mitch, I'm being pushy."

"Of course you are," she replied, trying unsuccessfully to hide the glint in her eye. "That's what

I like about you, isn't it?"

"You do?" Hart raised an eyebrow. Was she playing games? Getting her own back for his earlier faux pas? He guessed he would have deserved the rebuff but something about her sent him dizzy. Not just her looks, something else. He was beginning to get the real measure of her – confident, strong, intelligent. She was nobody's fool, and Hart liked it.

"It's my mum," said Mitch.

"Excuse me?"

"You see, I always go visit her on a Tuesday – she's in a hospice." She turned away for a moment.

"I'm sorry to hear that, Mitch, I didn't know. What's wrong with her?"

"Cancer ... she hasn't long now," she sighed.

Hart instinctively grasped her hand.

"If it's of any consolation I do know what it's like, it's not easy," he said thoughtfully.

Giving his hand a light squeeze she let go and turned to Stacey as he replaced the telephone rather heavily back onto its rest.

"Guess what? You won't have to eat that hat after all," Stacey mused.

Mitch turned to Stacey and frowned.

"That was Mike Sharp." Stacey now seemed hardly able to contain himself and had become noticeably fidgety. "The alarm system fitted to the London address was exactly the same make as that fitted to William James's house."

Hart couldn't help but smile at this news from Mike. This really was a step in the right direction.

"And it gets better," Stacey said his face now flushed with excitement.

"Let me guess, the code number's the same, correct?" Hart added confidently.

"Yes, just as you thought – 2441."

"What about the Dunstable address?"

"He's going to check that out and come back to us," Stacey said getting up from his desk.

This news from Mike Sharp was extremely encouraging and interestingly Stacey had learnt from a colleague that the inquiries being carried out from Bletchley were not going so well. In fact, rumour had it that the officers involved were soon to be put on other duties. Sitting back down Stacey turned to Mitch and gave his best helpless expression.

"Be a mate and pop next door and get Tom's tape player for me, would you?" he asked, retrieving the tape from his inside pocket. "I want to hear what's on this."

"No problem," Mitch said jumping to her feet.

He waited just long enough for her to close the door behind her then turned to Hart. "What's going on?" Stacey's expression had changed, his body language almost offensive. He sat with both hands clasped tightly in front of him like some headmaster.

"What?" Hart asked, surprised at Stacey's offensive manner.

"Don't act the innocent."

"I'm not. I have no idea what you're on about."

"I'm not stupid, Hart."

"Nothing's going on, as you so quaintly put it. All I've done is ask her for a date, that's all. What's your problem?" Hart couldn't for the life of him understand this aggressiveness from Stacey, then the penny dropped. "You're jealous," he mocked.

"I am not. I just don't want anything happening that

might interfere with this investigation."

"Bollocks, Stacey, admit it, you don't want her seeing me, that's the real reason isn't it?" Hart half smiled, knowing better than to let his Irish temper show.

"Listen, Hart, I don't expect you to understand this but I'm fond of her, very fond of her, but only as a friend, nothing else. I don't want to see her get hurt, especially at the moment with her mum so ill." Stacey's face had reddened.

"Listen, Stacey, I don't want to make a big thing of this." Hart did his level best to keep his voice down and his growing temper controlled. "But back off. It's got fuck all to do with you. Has it occurred to you that I, too, might be fond of her?" He scowled.

Suddenly the door opened.

"I can't find it, Stacey."

Mitch stood in the doorway and shrugged her shoulders. Stacey looked up and attempted a smile but it didn't really come off.

"What's happened?" she asked as she stepped into the room.

Both men looked at each other, neither wanting to be the first to answer her.

"Something's up, isn't it? You both look as if you've just swallowed a wasp."

"It's nothing, Mitch, honest," Stacey replied, looking sheepishly to Hart.

"Stacey here was giving me some ideas on where to take you on our date, that's all." Hart said cheekily.

"Well, I hope it's somewhere expensive." She chuckled.

"But of course, Mitch, nothing but the best." Stacey's expression was close to normal now.

"Good, I could do with some serious pampering, but until then perhaps someone would tell me where I can find this tape player. I've looked everywhere in Peter's office – nothing."

"I'm sorry, Mitch, I am an idiot," Stacey replied, tapping his forehead with the palm of his hand. "It's not in his office, I forgot. It's under the front desk. I spotted Rob with it the other day."

"Okay, I'll go and have a look there," she said, quickly disappearing again.

"Hart, I'm sorry for that outburst. I really don't know what came over me?"

"Forget it, Stacey, it's not a problem, trust me!" Hart's Irish blood had cooled.

"I found it," Mitch called excitedly as she burst through the doorway carrying the small tape player.

"Put it down here," Stacey said clearing space on his desk.

Pressing the play button produced the faint sound of music as the tape player kicked in. Mitch turned the volume up; it was the Rolling Stones.

"Here you go, Mitch." Stacey passed the tape over.

Quickly pressing the eject button she replaced the Rolling Stones with William James's tape. Closing the cover shut with a click she hit the play button again. All three listened patiently as they waited for something to happen.

"Try rewinding it, Mitch," Stacey suggested.

Mitch pressed rewind and the machine responded instantly. They waited as it noisily rewound the tape then clicked off.

Mitch pressed play again.

"William, its Lucy, can you hear me? If you're there

please pick up the telephone." There was a pause. "I waited for almost an hour ... please ring me."

Then silence. They listened to the faint hum from the tape player's motor followed by a loud click as Mitch pressed the stop button.

"Well, Lucy, I wonder who you are." Hart directed this question to the tape player.

"Do we have anything on his girlfriend yet, Mitch?" Stacey enquired.

"Not yet, I'm afraid. Hopefully we should have an answer in the morning. Do you think that she's involved in the killing, sir?"

"Who knows? But until we know otherwise we should treat everyone as a potential suspect."

"First thing in the morning I'll speak with Mrs White again. Perhaps she'll come up with something."

"Good idea, Mitch, and while you are at it, find out if Mr James had any other visitors, and if so, who and when."

Looking down at his Timex Hart was surprised to note that it was almost 4.30.

"I think I'll call it a day, that's if you both don't mind. Can't keep up the pace anymore," he mocked.

Stacey looked up at the large clock hung above the door. "I didn't realise the time myself."

Hart stood up and held out his hand. "See you tomorrow, Stacey."

Stacey glanced quickly at Mitch who was busy writing.

"I'm sorry about earlier," he whispered, giving Hart's hand a firm shake.

"As I said, forget it, it never happened. See you tomorrow, Mitch," Hart called as he walked to the door.

"Hold on, sir, I'll walk with you," she said lifting her coat from the back of the chair. "Is it okay if I finish now Stacey?" she added quickly.

"Yes, yes, that's it, bugger off and leave me," he joked.

"I can stay on if you like," she offered sheepishly.

Suddenly the telephone on Stacey's desk rang. "Go home, would you, I wont be much longer myself," he said picking up the handset.

Hart gave Stacey a wink before closing the door quietly behind him.

"What happened then? Did you both have a falling out?" Mitch shot a look at Hart that didn't invite anything other than a straight answer.

"Just a minor difference of opinion, that's all. It's okay now, so don't worry."

"What was it over?"

Hart put his hand on her shoulder in an effort to calm her obvious concern.

"Mitch, forget it! It was nothing really."

"You would tell me if it was something serious, wouldn't you?"

"Yes, now come on, let's get out of here. I need a smoke!"

It made a pleasant change to be outside in the fresh air far away from the pungent odours of a busy police station. They walked side by side across the car park towards Mitch's car.

"Well, quite an eventful day all things considered," she said fumbling in her handbag.

"You can say that again," he replied and sent a small stone into the hedge with a short sharp kick.

"Hart, over here. Good news." Stacey called out, "that was Mike on the telephone and guess what? The

Dunstable address had an identical alarm fitted and used the same entry code. I'll speak with you both tomorrow." Even at this distance the expression on Stacey's face spoke volumes as he closed the window.

"Now I don't know about you, Mitch, but I think that bit of news deserves a quick drink, don't you?"

"I really can't, Emit. I would love to, honest, but I always visit my mum Tuesday's. She would think something was wrong if I didn't show up."

His heart leapt with excitement to hear her call him by his first name. He knew this was bloody childish really but all the same it was a nice signal.

"Of course, I quite forgot," he replied sincerely. "I don't want you worrying your mum. What about tomorrow? We could perhaps have a meal?" He gave her his best smile.

"Yes, that would be nice." She took his hand and squeezed it gently, and for a split second he was hopelessly lost, and in more ways than one.

A door slammed abruptly. She smiled up at him.

"Until tomorrow then?" he said stepping back.

He stood alone for a moment as she drove off, then, realising that someone had come out of the building behind, he made his way towards his car.

As he drove through the town he tried to keep his mind focused on the case and the progress that they appeared to be making, but just occasionally her face would enter his head destroying any sensible thoughts.

His journey back was uneventful and worryingly unremembered, and soon he was turning off the main road and into the hotel car park. Almost forgetting to lock the car he sprinted across the car park and up the worn steps.

CHAPTER SEVEN

Just north of Stony Stratford and straddling the A5 is the small hamlet of Pottersbury. The picturesque stone-under-thatch buildings stood in stark contrast to the speeding traffic that had all but destroyed the once popular village. Number seven, The Green, could be found on the left along a narrow footpath that served as access to three other small cottages in the quaint little row.

Built by a wealthy landowner to house farm workers that cared for his land, it now provided dwellings for three families and one recluse known only as Marcus.

Mr and Mrs Abbot had lived at number eight for almost thirty years. Mr Abbot, now retired, had tried on several occasions to strike up a conversation with his new neighbour but this had always fallen on deaf ears. This rudeness was unacceptable for Mr Abbot. He had even spoken with the other neighbours, Mr and Mrs Jay who lived at number nine, and the Griffith family at the far end in number ten. Mr Griffith had suggested to Mr Abbot, in the nicest way possible, that he should let the man be and accept that, perhaps, he was just not like everyone else in the row, and intended to keep himself to himself. Mrs Jay on the other hand believed that the man was simply deaf. This complacent and negative attitude from Mr Abbot's supposed friends only added to his frustration. He had become obsessed by this quiet stranger that lived next door, and he often deliberately positioned himself in the garden so that he might intercept his neighbour on his return home.

This was such a day. Mrs Abbot had complained that the return spring fitted to the garden gate had jammed in the open position. Ordinarily this would not have been a problem. However, they had recently been visited by a large stray dog. Mrs Abbot hated dogs, big or small. This phobia had worsened one Tuesday afternoon when she had been bitten on the calf by a small yapping dog that she had tried to quieten with the help of her yard broom. Although the wound had not been deep, it had necessitated the use of Mrs Abbot's second phobia, an injection. It had taken much patience on behalf of the nurse to convince Mrs Abbot of the need for protection against infection.

Mr Abbot was only too pleased to see to the gate for his wife. He had been careful in positioning himself just so; that way he could be sure of spotting his prey as he came up the narrow pathway.

Unbeknown to Mr Abbot, the small but fit figure of Marcus watched quietly from the tiny leaded window that looked over the front garden from his single bedroom. A smile, which was almost undetectable at first, cracked the tanned, leathery face as it mused at the bobbing head of Mr Abbot attempting to repair the gate while keeping watch.

Muttering something to himself, Marcus let the net curtain fall back and went downstairs. The cottage was small but tidy with very few luxuries. The low beamed ceiling in the living room, together with the dark wood floor, could have made the room feel oppressive to some, but not to its inhabitant. He was used to it now. He sat alone with the curtains drawn and switched on one of the few modern devices permitted to him. Daytime television wasn't his favourite but it would do.

Outside, Mr Abbot was just about to give up; the gate repair was beyond him. It would require a new spring mechanism, he had decided. He closed the lid to the toolbox that his eldest son had bought him and stood up straight. He was about to walk off when he spotted a figure strutting up the path towards him. Mr Abbot's heart skipped a beat. He wasn't sure any more that this was such a good idea. The purposeful arrogance of the man's walk was a little disconcerting. Mr Abbot made one of those quick decisions that most of us are forced to make occasionally and decided better of it. He turned and made his way reluctantly down the footpath towards his house. Hesitating for a moment, he then turned around deciding that he would, after all, confront the man. Why ever not? This was silly he had done nothing wrong. All he intended to do was introduce himself.

As he turned he was amazed to see the figure climbing over the fence. This was drastic, Mr Abbot decided, surely he wasn't that hard to talk to? "Oh well, his loss," he whispered and continued towards the house.

Inside number seven, the lone figure of Marcus sat in the only comfortable armchair in the room, mesmerised by the images before him. Today's programme was a remake of an old film, the subject of which was hopelessly lost to its viewer. But he was enjoying it all the same.

While John Wayne convincingly wrestled his enemy to the floor and despatched him with a single blow, the newly painted latch on the cottage stable door was being raised with extreme care.

Suddenly a pick-axe handle arched through the air and was brought down heavily, sending John Wayne reeling. Marcus sat forward clasping his head with both hands in mock horror. The ceaseless gunfire that followed as they attempted to rescue Mr Wayne only served to mask the noise of groaning floorboards. As the intruder approached, he reached into a pocket and withdrew a small but heavy hammer. Now only a single step from the armchair, his narrow eyes firmly fixed on the back of the seated figure.

Outside Mr Abbot had reappeared carrying a large green plastic watering can, which he now poured slowly over dry plants. Although his hearing was not as it once was, he did pause for just one split second. Was that a scream? He cocked his head to one side as though directing his good ear towards his neighbour's house would allow him to hear better.

Inside number seven, John Wayne dived for cover behind a large wooden barrel just as a hail of bullets hit. The small figure dragged the face of the hammer slowly across the back of the chair, leaving a long crimson scar.

His unsuspecting victim lay unconscious, face down on the floor. Placing the hammer down on a small table, he stepped forward and pulled the plug from the wall. With the television now off he bent down and rolled the limp figure over on to its back. The face was almost unrecognisable, the gaping hole that was once a mouth now toothless and bloody. A small piece of severed tongue slid slowly down the cheek and fell to the floor with an audible slap. The eyes, although tightly closed, flickered as three large nails were dropped noisily onto the floor.

Outside Mr Abbot had finished the watering and had

just started back to the house when he heard the unmistakable sound of someone hammering from within number seven. He glanced down at his wristwatch and shook his head in a way that only grumpy old men seem able to do before continuing towards the house, his poor hearing missing the brief cries for help.

A few miles away the Blues Brothers had just finished "Gimme Some Lovin" and were now starting "Minnie the Moocher".

"For Christ sake, Steve, turn that fucking noise down, I cant here myself fart."

Steve shouted back something but it fell on deaf ears. The volume was reduced to something just above deafening.

They had both had yet another profitable day having produced between them somewhere in the region of £864,000.

With both presses running flat out and while under the watchful eye of Neil, Steve stood with arms folded in the far corner. The Heidelberg Platen 10x15 with its circular brass badge identifying its year of manufacture as 1950. This was Steve's baby, and the machine that he did his apprenticeship on. With its flailing mechanical arms hissing and rattling it was singly responsible for applying the thin foil strip to each and every note.

Proof of their hard work and acknowledged skill stood along the far wall: four wooden pallets. On each stood five layers of standard printer's cartons, each layer containing twelve cartons and each carton holding £12,000 sterling.

It was unlikely that anyone would be bothered

enough to count the contents that stood innocently against the wall. Only Neil and Steve knew there real worth, holding somewhere close to £720,000 per pallet, any one of which would be enough to set someone up for life.

Both had been tempted, in fact both had talked of nothing else over the past few days, but each secretly knew that they would probably never live long enough to reach the bottom of one carton let alone a pallet or two.

As the feeder boards of both presses ran dry the sheet detectors automatically cut in and shut down pumps and motors signalling the end to another day.

With skill learnt over many years as a minder, Neil darted from one press to the other pushing and pulling a confusing array of chrome leavers and knobs until both presses were turning their large impression cylinders over slowly. One by one each of the eight plates were cleaned and gummed before being removed and stored safely.

"I'll shrink wrap these four pallets, gay. You get on and wash up. I hope he's not bloody late tonight, I must be home by eight tonight or my life won't be worth living," Neil shouted.

Steve acknowledged this statement with a customary single finger thrust high into the air before turning up the tape player and singing along badly to Jailhouse Rock.

Forty-five minutes later with both presses now washed up and the Platen shut down and covered for the night the pair went through to reception.

They sat leaning back in high-backed leather chairs, with careless feet scuffing the highly polished desks.

To the casual observer everything looked as it should. Carefully placed plants, telephones, desk pads, staplers, even paper clips, but someone looking more closely may have noticed that the desks were empty of any paperwork, the telephones were unconnected, and the plants were maintenance-free plastic. Even the schedule board that hung so convincingly from the wall showing the work in hand was fake.

"He's fucking late, it's almost seven, I'll give him ten more and then I'm off."

"Stop whining, Neil, he'll be here," Steve replied confidently, "I'll go and put the kettle on."

"Sit down, gay, I'll do it," Neil said springing forward violently and sending the chair crashing against the wall. Passing Steve at speed he flicked something from the end of his finger.

"You dirty sod," spat Steve, attempting with little success to dodge the incoming object, while at the same time sending a stapler curving through the air, which landed heavily against the wall opposite leaving a large scar in the white painted plasterboard and narrowly missing its intended target, which was now out of sight and heading for the kitchen.

Steve sat shaking his head in disbelief at this childish antic from his close friend who never ceased to amaze him. Pulling open the desk draw he decided to amuse himself with linking paper clips. His attention to this meaningless task was interrupted briefly by the sound of a key as it was inserted into the door lock. He continued linking even as the door opened, shivering momentarily as the cold night air hit him.

"Good evening, Neil," a gasping voice whispered.

"It's Steve, actually," he replied without looking up,

still linking.

"So it is. Where is Neil?"

Steve looked up and grinned at the three figures standing huddled together in the small confines of the entrance.

"Come on in and shut the door, you're letting all the heat out," he said getting to his feet. He let the paper clips fall from his hand onto the desk. "Take a seat, I'll go and find him."

The largest of the trio stepped forward and sat down. Steve watched with interest as this fat, overfed man attempted to cross his legs. This task, which to most is taken for granted, was totally beyond him. Having given up he sat back in the chair and tried desperately to regain his breath.

Steve didn't like these men and certainly didn't trust them, a view shared by Neil. His heart skipped a beat as the taller of the three locked the door and stood squarely in front of it, arms folded. His body language left Steve in no doubt that for the moment at least neither Neil nor himself were leaving yet.

The third, a smaller but heavier built man, moved forward and stood to the side of the seated figure who, although still panting heavily, was now trying to stem the beads of sweat that rolled down from his forehead with a less than white handkerchief.

Steve moved around to the front of his desk and made his way down the narrow hallway, making sure that he held his breath as he passed. He found it difficult not to gag on the sickly sweet mixture of perfume and stale cigars. He met Neil halfway carrying two mugs of steaming tea.

"Fat man is here with his two buddies, Titus and

Cassius," he whispered with a flick of his head.

"And about bloody time. Here, hold these, the quicker they see what they want the quicker we'll be away."

Neil handed over the two hot mugs of tea briefly keeping hold of the handles.

"Shit, there hot," Steve complained putting them down onto the floor for a moment.

Neil laughed then whispered something that went unnoticed as he pushed roughly past.

"Hello, Guv," he said cheerily holding his hand out to the seated figure.

"The name is Galba not Guv, and you would be well advised to remember it," he hissed through stained teeth.

"Sorry, Galba," Neil replied nervously lowering his hand.

"Have you my samples?" The fat man asked rudely.

"Yes, of course. If you would care to follow me, they're through here?"

He waited as Galba slid his massive weight forward then with a hand on each knee rocked slowly back and forth until he had gained enough momentum to stand. Once upright he stood with hands on hips and gulped at the air; even this relatively easy movement had drained his lungs.

They waited patiently until he signalled that he was ready to walk then with Neil leading them they followed him down the hallway.

Neil smiled to himself at the thought of Galba forced to walk crablike behind, this the only way possible for him to pass along the narrow hall.

Galba appeared from the hallway still mopping his

brow followed closely by his two colleagues.

"Would you like some tea?" Neil asked giving them a pleasant but blatantly force smile.

"I want my samples. That is all," the fat man replied curtly.

Neil pulled back slightly to avoid the spray of spittle that came at him on the word samples.

"But of course." He turned wiping his face with the back of his hand, which luckily went unnoticed by Galba.

Once in the pressroom, the air that greeted them was a mixture of spirits, heady ink fumes and hot electric motors.

"The smell in here, it is so strong is it not?" Galba stated.

"I can't say that I can actually smell anything," Neil replied cautiously as he led them to one of the presses. Positioned to one side was a large light box on which was placed several untrimmed running sheets. Taking one from the top he passed it to Galba. "That's one of our make readies but its cock on," Neil exclaimed proudly.

Galba lifted the sheet close to his face as he scanned the image carefully. Then without speaking replaced it back on the light box, his large round face inches from it.

Neil glanced over at Steve who had positioned himself near the second press well out of range of Galba's foul odour.

Both Galba's colleagues moved closer. The taller of the two whom Neil knew only as Titus peered over Galba's shoulder and whispered something that Neil didn't quite catch.

Without taking his face away from the sheet Galba

held out his hand palm up. "An eye glass if you would." His fat fingers clawed at the air like an upturned crab.

Steve rummaged around in a tray at the side of his press then finding one passed it to him.

"Are they all as this?" he quizzed.

Neil turned to Steve. His face had paled slightly.

"What's wrong with it?" he asked.

"I won't ask you again." Galba straightened slowly and turned.

Neil coughed into a clenched fist in an effort not only to clear his drying throat but also to give him time to think.

"Well, I'm waiting."

"Yes, Galba." Neil held his breath. "All as that."

Galba stepped forward closing the distance between himself and Neil, his face expressionless. Neil froze, unsure what to say or what to do. He stood expecting Galba to explode though he didn't know why. Suddenly Galba raised both hands into the air exposing damp patches under his arms. Neil instinctively backed off.

"Excellent, my friends. Truly excellent," he shrieked exposing stained teeth. "Please, Titus," he said passing the eyeglass to his colleague. "You must see, tell me what you think!"

Titus moved forward and squinted into the little lens, moving his head back and forth in an effort to focus on the complex image.

"Well, Titus, they are good are they not?" Galba could hardly contain himself.

"Very," Titus said looking up.

"You two certainly know your stuff, and both worth every penny I must say," Galba added. "Hopefully you are left alone here?" This was more a statement than a question.

"No problem, we have the odd rep drop by but they're no hassle," Neil replied quickly.

"You are aware, I hope, that we would take an extremely dim view of any breech of security. This project is most important to us." The smile had gone from Galba's face now and his voice had dropped a couple of notes becoming deliberately more menacing.

Neil watched with anticipation as Galba produced a black leather cigar case from an inside pocket and slipped the top off.

"We are aware, believe me," Steve stuttered.

Removing a cigar from the case Galba replaced the lid and slid it back into his pocket. He pulled at a thick silver chain that was buried deep within the folds of flesh around his neck and produced a small pearl handled cigar cutter, and snipped the end off then rolled the large Havana slowly between his wetted lips before lighting it.

The thick smoke curled high up into the roof of the unit leaving Neil gasping for air.

"Believe me," Neil replied nervously. "We are very careful. Neither of us have any intention of spending time at one of Our Majesty's hotels."

"That is a comfort. It would distress me greatly to resort to any form of punishment," Galba warned as he puffed heavily at the cigar in an effort to keep it going.

Neil was no fool, but this man was worrying. In an effort to change the subject he pointed over to the far wall. "I think you'll be interested in this."

Neil led them over to the four pallets that stood against the wall then, producing a small pen knife from his pocket, slit through the shrink wrap to expose brown cardboard cartons. Lifting one out, he turned and placed it onto a nearby bench and slit through the brown vinyl wrapping tape. He pulled open the lid and tipped the carton forward, spilling its contents out onto the bench.

"Oh, how wonderful." Galba's fat stumpy fingers stroked the bundles of notes almost seductively. "Absolutely wonderful. I'm so impressed with you both, you have excelled." He drew heavily on his fat cigar, sending a cloud of dense, acrid smoke twisting through the air. "How much?" He mumbled clenching the cigar in his yellowed teeth.

"Twelve thousand pounds per box, that's seven hundred and twenty thousand pounds on each pallet," Neil replied stepping back in an effort to avoid the cigar smoke.

"Four pallets finished." Galba looked thoughtfully in the air. "That's just over two point eight million if I'm not mistaken," he said turning.

"About that," Neil replied confidently, then smiled.

"Delightful, simply delightful," said Galba slapping Neil heavily on the back. He removed the cigar from his mouth and sent it spinning through the air. It landed some fifteen feet away showing glowing ashes over exposed rags and paper.

Steve reacted quickly stamping out what he could before anything ignited.

"With respect Galba, you don't want to be doing that in here, not with all this paper around," he yelled, shaking his head angrily.

"My goodness, yes, your quiet right, Steve, don't want a fire just yet now, do we?"

Neil repacked the bundles neatly into the carton and taped the top shut then replaced it back on the pallet.

"Will you be finished by Friday as planned?"

Neil hesitated then turning answered the tall stocky figure that stood to his left. "Possibly sooner, I would say."

"Excellent," Galba interrupted. "We will arrange transport as originally planned for late Friday afternoon. It will attract less interest loading a lorry in the week."

"And most people around here on a Friday afternoon will be busy trying to finish up early so they can get off home," Neil added quickly.

"Good, we shall leave it at that then," Galba turned to his two colleagues, "We must go now my friends. I have much to do." he said smiling knowingly. As he reached the entrance to the inner hallway he hesitated as though lost in thought for a moment then added quietly, "Take great care of our goods, my friends," Then slid the door open.

"We will, Galba, make no mistake."

Turning his large body sideways he shuffled forward and out of sight. Neil waited for a second until Galba's men were in the hallway before following.

"What a fucking state, eh!" Steve whispered prompting a warning scowl from Neil.

As they reached the end of the hall Galba stood in reception with his shoulder against the wall gasping. Pulling the stained handkerchief from his pocket again he wiped his forehead.

"Well my friends," he panted. "My colleagues and I will be off now. Please if you will, lock the door behind us."

Every word spoken by this large man was an immense effort for him.

Both Neil and Steve watched with some amusement as Galba, now almost totally exhausted, was helped by his two men down the small flight of stairs towards his large car.

Neil closed and locked the door as Galba had requested.

"What a strange bunch of bastards," Steve hissed shaking his head.

"I'll tell you what son, I'm not too happy about any of this, especially the way he hinted about not having a fire just YET!" Neil deliberately emphasized the word yet, "What the fuck did he mean by that?" He added.

Steve sat on the corner of the desk and continued linking the paper clips that he'd started earlier. "What do you mean?"

"I think that they intend to load that money up on Friday," he said pointing into the print room, "and then torch this bloody place," Neil replied dropping into the nearest chair.

"But I thought that this was to be an ongoing project, that's what they said originally." Steve let the string of joined paperclips drop onto the desktop in a neat little pile.

"We're going to have to box clever here, mate, otherwise we're going to be out of work and out of pocket. I was more than banking on this to pay for my new house," Neil replied urgently. "We've got to try and stay one step ahead of them," he added.

"Perhaps we should have some away, careful like." Steve smiled waiting for Neil's reaction.

"They'd kill us if they found out."

"They would never know," he replied confidently.

"Let me sleep on it," Neil suggested glancing down at

his watch. "Christ, I've got to go, I promised her that I wouldn't be late. She'll bloody kill me! We'll talk tomorrow."

"Steve, if you're out tonight, keep schtum. Not a word, not to anybody. Do you understand?" He wagged his finger menacingly close up to Steve's face.

"You don't have to worry about me, mate, Isa know anuzzing," he answered tapping the side of his nose with his first finger.

"And don't forget to put the alarm on when you leave." Neil said pulling the top off a pen, "I'll stick the number on this so you don't forget." Then licking the back he slapped the yellow slip of paper less than gently onto Steve's forehead.

"See you tomorrow, gay."

CHAPTER EIGHT

The previous day's news from Mike confirming identical alarm systems fitted to all three addresses had certainly raised the morale amongst the team and, although he had been unable to confirm the existence of a wooden sword having been found in Dunstable or indeed any reference to the word Mithras, they were confident that having sent men back to the address it was now only a matter of time.

Hart declined with a polite smile the offer of more coffee from the young waitress and thanked her for breakfast. On the way out of the restaurant he bid good morning to an elderly couple sat by the window but didn't stop to talk. He had done so the morning before and had regretted it.

He replaced the newspaper back in the rack and checked the time. Reception looked like a war zone, a coach had just arrived and its passengers were all busy checking in. Luckily there were three girls on duty this morning and he soon stepped forward to be greeted by Sarah.

"Good morning, Mr Hart, how are you this morning?"

Sarah was aged about twenty-three, very slim and quite stunning, and a favourite of Hart's.

"Hi, Sarah." He said resisting the temptation to look down the front of her baggy white blouse.

"I wish that I was staying longer, I'm really getting quite used to all this pampering," Hart said holding his room key just above the desktop.

"Did you want to check out now then?" she asked holding her hand out palm up.

Hart let the key drop into her hand and risked a look.

"Not until later this afternoon if that's okay!" He beamed, sure that he'd just been caught out.

Sarah reddened slightly and straightened her top then hung the key on a small brass hook just under the room number on the wall.

"I'll get your bill together later then. Where're you off to now?" she asked pleasantly.

"It's not raining so I thought I'd pay a visit to my house and make sure the builder's finished and that my furniture has arrived safely."

"We'll see you later then Mr Hart." She said with a smile.

A grinning Hart side stepped a group of over fed Americans that stood in the doorway and pushed his way outside, he stood for a moment at the top of the steps, breathed in the fresh country air and resisted the strong urge to light up. As the clock struck in reception he checked his Timex, slipped the pack of Raffles back into his pocket and with a noticeable spring in his step descended in a manner more befitting a dancer auditioning for a lead role in a new dance show. The sun warmed his back which helped relieve the sort of ache that only hotel beds seem able to offer. Once in his car he waited as a large coach reversed up to the hotel then skirting around the front of it headed off down the drive, once out in the lane he was soon passing Bullington End and heading for Wolverton.

Although the thought of a relationship with Mitch was now playing a large part in Hart's waking day he was still eager to get to his new home and see what the finished job looked like. He had been remarkably lucky with his builder, John. John Young was a highly respected local builder with a well earned reputation. They had first met almost seven years ago, a friend of a friend. A softly spoken man with a gentle manner, John had been working for Hart for some time now and often through his now vast experience been able to advise Hart on how best to tackle this complicated refurbishment. The house was very old and over recent years had become derelict, but through a combination of skill, time and money it would soon be Hart's home.

Taking the sharp right Hart eased off of the accelerator as he entered the small hamlet of Haversham. Once at the bottom of the hill he was soon passing the old Wolverton Road and climbing the steep hill that swept sharp right passed the rail station. The traffic in the town was unusually heavy the cause for this became apparent as Hart got closer to the police station. A large articulated truck had shed part of its load onto the road effectively blocking off one side of the high street. Although the police were in attendance there didn't appear to be any casualties other than the embarrassed driver. As Hart was signalled through the narrow gap he had just enough time to catch a glimpse of Mitch's car parked as usual under the large old oak in the station's small car park. He was tempted for a split second to turn off but decided against it, instead carried on passed the school and down the hill.

With the town behind him the traffic thinned and he was able to pick up speed and soon was passing over the River Ouse. He tried to make the lights but wasn't quick enough and was forced to bring the car to a dramatic halt which appeared to amuse a group of builders stood in a driveway off to his right. Winding down the window Hart took a deep breath in an effort to calm his racing heart, brought on not by the sudden braking but the realisation of this developing relationship with Mitch.

A car horn from behind signalled that the lights were now green, Hart shoved the gear lever forwards and gunned the car. Now on the Deanshanger Road he brought his speed down and went back to his thoughts. He had to admit to himself that initially his first reaction had been one of self preservation and had questioned in his own mind his intentions. Once he had realised that the way he felt about her appeared mutual, instinct cut in, but should he back off?

Having travelled for about a mile the sight of the call box ahead was enough to call his bluff. He would ring her!

He slowed up and pulled onto the gravel lay-by and switched off the engine.

For several long and agonising minutes he sat trying to decide whether this was a good idea or not, then as a large truck thundered past rocking the car he grasped the door handle.

"Bugger it! In for penny, in for a pound," he said opening the door. He stood for a moment in the freshening air, lit a cigarette and leant against the side of the car watching the world drive by. Taking one final drag he flicked the half finished cigarette into the road and rubbed his hands together briskly in an attempt to get some heat back into them. Pulling open the door he stepped inside and waited for the self closing mechanism to finish squealing then lifted the handset and dialled directory enquiries and waited for the connection to be made.

"Directory Enquiries, which town please?"

"Wolverton Police Station."

"The number is 0908 555491."

"Thank you." Hart clicked the rest up and down several times and waited for the dialling tone again then dialling the number he pushed the money into the slot and waited.

"Wolverton Police Station."

He recognised the voice instantly. "Mitch, it's me."

"Emit," she said softly, "how are you?"

"I'm fine. Did you get to see Mrs White?" he asked trying to buy time.

"Yes, it was very useful, I think." There was a pause then she added. "I can't understand it, what's going on Emit? You're on my mind all of the time. I've only just met you and yet I feel as though I've known you all my life."

Hart couldn't help but grin. His heart pounded in his chest again as he tried to conceal his excitement.

"I know what you mean, I feel exactly the same. I just don't want to come across too pushy and risk ending something before it's begun."

"Don't be silly."

"Shall we meet up?"

"Tonight?" she replied quietly.

"Yes, tonight. I'm going to pick up my gear this afternoon and check out of the hotel."

"Are you moving into your new home today then?"

"Yes, I'm on my way over there now. The builder telephoned me this morning to say he was finished and that my furniture had arrived."

"Shall I pick you up? I'm off duty at two. You could show me around your new home then I'll run you back to the hotel," she suggested.

"Meet me at the hotel first then we'll go back to the house. Have you got a pen?"

Hart gave Mitch the hotel details just as the pips started he quickly pushed two coins into the slot.

"Mitch can you hear me?"

"Yes!"

"I'll see you just after two then? That'll give me a chance to sort John out." he suggested.

"Two it is then."

Hart replaced the handset and waited for any change to drop.

Back in the car with the engine running he picked out a gap some twenty cars back, waited for his moment then floored the pedal. The engine coughed, backfired and then in a cloud of gravel he shot out into the traffic.

Approximately two miles on from the telephone box and Hart was indicating right. He turned into the lane and moments later pulled up behind a white Ford pick-up. He sat for a moment looking ahead, then got out of the car as John appeared from around the side of the house carrying a kettle.

"Hello, Emit, how's life?" he called then, waving his arm in the air, added, "Come around this way, would you?"

Hart thrust his hands into his pockets and walked slowly up the path towards the house, it looked so tidy. At last it was finished and it was his. No more half filled skips and piles of sand and gravel. No trenches, scaffolding or tools. All the painting was finished, even the gate was on.

He pushed open the gate and went through into the garden. John stood at the back door grinning, one hand clutching the kettle, the other extended. They shook hands warmly.

"You have done the house proud, John," Hart said stepping through the doorway and into the kitchen.

"I was just about to put this on," John said. "Do you want one?"

"No, I'm fine, mate."

"Your stuff arrived this morning," he said filling the kettle, "Come on through." He led Hart into the dinning room. "I've put all the furniture where you wanted it, the bed's together, in fact it's made up, well after a fashion." He chuckled. "There's some wine in the fridge, my treat, and my misses got you some food in, nothing fancy mind but it'll get you by for a day or two."

"John, you've thought of everything."

"You sure you don't want a coffee?" he asked taking a mug from the pine dresser that stood against the wall.

"I'm sure."

John shrugged his shoulders then disappeared into the kitchen.

"I'd better show you where things are before I shoot off," he said stirring the drink briskly.

Hart spent the next three hours re-arranging the furniture with John. Although John had taken great care in following Harts original plan, now, with the furniture in place it just didn't feel right to him. John's other task was to explain to Hart where the water cut-off point was and how to use the heating system.

"I'll leave all the paperwork in this drawer," he said gathering a selection of sheets together. "I know it's a bit difficult to take in all at once," he said placing the documents into one of the empty drawers in the dresser.

Hart stared blankly for a moment at the drawer as

though he hadn't taken a word in, even his face had assumed a wooden appearance.

"Are you okay, Emit?" John placed his hand on Hart's shoulder.

"Yes, mate, sorry, I've just got a lot on my mind at the moment." Hart replied.

John gave Hart's shoulder a friendly slap before going into the kitchen. "You should learn to chill out Emit, life's too short," he said running a mug under the tap.

"I know, mate, and chilling out is exactly what I intend to do once I've moved in here," said Hart as he appeared in the doorway. "I just have one or two things to sort out beforehand."

Hart who was often quick to catch the moods of other people was always the last to realise his own. John put the mug down on the drainer.

"You should make sure you do. You're retired now so you have no excuses."

Hart pulled his sleeve back as he heard a clock chime from the living room.

"Christ, is that the time? I'm going to have to go, John," he said hurrying towards the back door. "I was supposed to be checked out of the bloody hotel twenty minutes ago."

"You'd better have these," John said taking a set of keys from the hook on the wall, "or you'll find it hard to get back in."

Hart stopped just long enough to take the key fob together with the half-dozen keys that were hung from it.

"It's the Yale," he shouted as Hart sprinted the last few yards to his car.

"See you later, John, and thanks."

Hart slammed the car door shut fumbling for a moment until he could get the key into the ignition. Unusually the car started first time. With one arm draped lazily over the back of the passenger seat he reversed out into the lane then selecting first sped off.

Thirty minutes later and he was bounding up the stone steps and into reception.

"I know, I know," he said panting, "I'm late."

Sarah did what Sarah always did when in the company of Hart, puffed her ample chest out and smiled.

"I'll be packed in no time, I promise."

Sarah didn't say a word, she didn't have too, the frown said it all. She removed the keys to room 212 from the wall behind her and put them down on the blotter. Hart took the lift as the doors were open but not before giving Sarah a cheeky wave as they closed. Room 212, which had been his home for a few days now, was at the end of the narrow corridor.

Gripping the polished brass knob Hart pulled the door towards him while turning the steel key in the lock then gave it a shove with his shoulder.

As it swung open Hart was totally unprepared for what greeted him. The room had been trashed. Whoever had got in had gone through all his belongings, systematically emptying all the contents of the drawers into the middle of the floor. His paperwork was strewn across the bed along with his clothing.

Flushed with anger, he stepped in and closed the door behind him. He stood quietly and looked around him, his chest tightened with frustration. They had been very thorough. If only he'd returned on time, he thought.

Taking great care not to move anything he made his way across the room, stepping over the mound of clothing and upturned drawers.

"The bastards," he whispered. The fury swept over him now like a hot towel, but it didn't last, it never did with Hart.

Fortunately there had been nothing of real value in the room so he was pleased that the thief or thieves would have gone away relatively empty handed.

He considered calling the police for a moment then decided against it. It was then that he spotted it. Lucky really – he could so easily have missed it. Just above his bedside lamp a calling card from the intruder. Hart picked his way carefully between discarded clothes and ripped paper then leant forward and inspected the object with rising interest.

His mouth dried. Even the hair on the back of his neck stood to attention as it suddenly dawned on him what might have happened had he returned on time or worse still, if he'd been asleep in the room.

Gouged with obvious deranged ferocity into the soft plaster wall the now familiar inscription   XXIV/XLI.

Hart allowed his finger to trace slowly over the strange markings. Just below and nailed to the wall hung a cheap wooden doll. He brushed the back of his hand curiously over it causing it to swing like the pendulum of an old clock.

A feeling of nausea swept over him as he looked at the grotesque shape hung limply from a rusted nail. Suddenly as though waking from a strange dream Hart straightened and lifted the telephone from its rest and waited for a moment.

"Would you give me an outside line please? Thank you." He said calmly then tucked the phone under his chin.

He looked down at his watch then dialled the number, it was just gone two so with a bit of luck Mitch might still be there. Hart recognised the deep gravely voice immediately.

"Hello, Rob it's Emit Hart. If Stacey's there could you put him on for me?" he asked keeping his eye on the doll as though waiting for it to somehow magically pull itself from the nail and attack him.

"Hello me duck, hold on won't you?" He sounded busy. Hart could here someone in the background shouting. Occasionally the odd swear word could be heard above the noise.

A few moments passed then the telephone clicked as Stacey was connected.

"Hello, sir," a voice answered cheerily.

Hart didn't answer immediately; he was now thinking of Mitch.

"Stacey, listen, this is important. I want you to get hold of a camera or at least someone you can trust with one, also a fingerprint kit. Mitch if she's around, and then meet me here at my hotel," he paused for a second, then added, "I think I've had a visit from our man."

"What man?" Stacey said dumbly, "what on earth are you talking about Hart?"

"The killer, Stacey, the killer, he's been and paid me a bloody visit. Just get up here now," he ordered.

It took Stacey less than twenty minutes to get the camera, fingerprint kit and, pleasingly, Mitch to the Hatton. Hart was still holding the telephone in his hand when he heard the car speed up to the front door and stop with wheels locked.

They both arrived looking flustered and worried. As Mitch came into the room she hesitated momentarily before closing the door behind them, Stacey had spotted the doll from the door.

"Fuck me, Hart, this isn't good!" he exclaimed.

"Stacey, sometimes your deductions are right on the button," Hart replied. Stacey turned and gave Hart a quick flash of his teeth before lifting a black hold-all onto the bed. He produced a small Pentax and matching flash unit which he hurriedly assembled. Once he was satisfied he pushed the test button on the flash then waited until it had recharged.

"Well, it appears to be working okay," he said raising the camera to his eye, then, clicked the shutter button several times making sure that each shot was taken from slightly different angles and distances.

"Are you okay?" Mitch asked turning to Hart.

"Yes! Just a bit of a shock really. Last thing I expected. Only came back to pick up my stuff and pay the bloody bill. If I'd been a bit earlier I might have missed all this," he said making light of the situation.

"If you had come back any earlier, you may have found out who this fellow was the hard way," Stacey interrupted giving the doll a sharp nudge.

Hart tried to smile but failed and sat heavily down on the corner of the bed. He watched as Mitch removed a fingerprint kit from the bag and unfastened the small clasps. Taking a roll of clear tape a large brush and a jar of white powder from the bag she started dusting the small doll and the wall around it.

"There may be fingerprints but probably not the ones we want," she said flicking the brush quickly from side to side over the surface. From the doll she worked her way down onto the bedside table. Satisfied that she had dusted everything intended she removed from a side pocket in the case a powerful magnifying glass and skimmed slowly over the surface of the fine powder looking for any signs of a print. After several agonising minutes she sighed, her frustration obvious.

"You know what I'm going to say, don't you?" she said turning to Hart and shrugging her narrow shoulders. "There's nothing, not even one, plenty of smudges but not one clear print."

"He wouldn't have been that stupid," Hart said irritably.

"It was worth a try," Stacey said in a firm voice. "Have you had a good look around? Found anything missing?"

"Not that I've noticed," said Hart gloomily.

"Well, if you do discover that they've had something, better let me know pronto so I can put the word about," Stacey said putting the camera back into the hold-all.

"I know this may not be the time to say but, in a perverse way he's warning us off and that, appeals to me." Stacey said zipping the case shut.

"I'm bloody glad you're happy about that." Hart said folding his arms, his tone leaving Stacey in little doubt that for the moment at least, that opinion was not shared by him.

"It means we're getting close to him, too close for comfort." Stacey wanted to explain in more detail but decided that this probably wasn't the time or place.

"Look, I'm about done here now," he said lifting the bag from the bed. "I want to get back and get these developed ASAP. Are you coming, Mitch?"

"I think I'll stay, help clear this mess up if that's okay with you." Mitch turned and waited to see if Hart agreed.

"Yes, that would be good if you don't mind. I could do with the company to be honest, Mitch."

"Oh! I nearly forgot," Stacey said turning, "wouldn't do to forget the bloody evidence now, would it?" he said pulling the doll, complete with nail, from the wall and slipping it into the side pocket of the hold-all. "I'll ask reception on the way out if they remember anyone asking after you or if there's been anybody walking about the hotel that shouldn't have been. In the meantime," he said pulling the door open, "Unless anything untoward happens I'll see you both in the morning bright and early."

Once Stacey had gone Hart sat with Mitch on the edge of the bed, he felt exhausted and new that it showed.

"Although I don't want to admit it I agree with Stacey, this visit is a real plus for us," he said coolly.

"A plus?" Mitch's raised voice was out of character, "I fail to see what's good about some lunatic paying you a visit." replied Mitch as she squeezed his arm.

Hart wanted to put his arm around her and hold her close but resisted.

"The thing is, this visit to my room proves that we must have discovered something, something so important to him that it's rattled him." Hart got up and walked over to the window. "He put himself at great risk coming here." He added picking up a drawer and placing it back into the dresser.

"I wonder what we've done to panic him," said Mitch trying to put aside her concern for Hart.

"God, if we only knew that!" Hart exclaimed.

"Emit, let's hurry up and go, this room makes me feel really uneasy," she said holding out her hand.

Hart grasped her hand and they stood for a few moments in the centre of the room. He looked into her eyes, wanting to pull her towards him and embrace her. He knew instinctively that she wanted this too, but not now, not here. She slipped her hand from his and gathered the papers that still lay strewn on the bed.

"Come on," she said dropping them into the case, "the sooner this is done the sooner we can go.

It had taken almost two hours to pack and more importantly try and leave the room in some kind of acceptable condition. There was little they could do about the damage to the wall, he would have to explain that later he decided. Picking up the receiver Hart rang down to reception.

"Hello, it's Hart, room 212. Could you make up my bill? I'm ready to check out now," he said then turned as Mitch went and stood over by the large window.

"Hello. Oh! Okay, put him on," he said with a frown. "Hi, James, no, I don't think we have met." Hart sat down on the corner of the bed. "Very good, yes, of course I understand, no, don't worry, I wont let on, I promise." He chuckled. "James, many thanks, that's really very helpful. Please thank her for me, would you? Yes, goodbye." Hart replaced the handset on the cradle and turned.

"What's happened?"

"James works in the kitchen here. Anyhow, he'd just been speaking to Julie one of the receptionists and she happened to mention to him that Stacey had been asking questions about my visitor."

Mitch moved away from the window and sat in the chair by the desk. "Go on."

"Well, it would appear that a man telephoned this morning asking for me, said he had some invoices for me that I needed to go through, evidently for work that he'd been doing on my house. Normally the receptionist wouldn't have disclosed the room number over the phone."

"Why did she then?" Mitch said angrily.

"She didn't. It was James. He was covering for the girl who was on duty while she went out the back for a smoke."

"Hart, how the hell does the killer know about your house?" Mitch's face had visibly paled.

"I really don't know but I think it's important that we don't jump to any unnecessary conclusions."

Hart didn't say so, but he was clearly worried now that the killer might become more adventurous and decide to make contact with Mitch.

"This seems to be going from bad to worse," she added coldly.

Deciding not to enter into a debate over this recent news, Hart gathered together his cases and bags and with Mitch's help loaded them onto the trolley that had been left outside his room.

Once in reception Hart settled his account, thanked everyone for looking after him then, with Mitch guiding the trolley at the front and Hart pushing from behind, they headed out into the car park.

CHAPTER NINE

Hart slid onto the cold driver's seat, instinctively arching his back in an effort to pull away from the skin-numbing vinyl. He leant across and released the lock on the passenger door for Mitch.

"God, it's cold in here," she groaned wrapping her arms tightly around her body.

"It'll be okay once the engine has warmed up," he replied rubbing his hands together vigorously and wincing at the pain in his stiffening fingers.

The condensation from their warm breath soon turning to ice as it made contact with the inside of the windscreen.

Hart fumbled for a moment with his keys eventually finding the ignition key.

"Come on, old girl, don't let me down now," he pleaded as the engine turned over slowly. Pausing for a moment he tried again. This time it coughed, fired then cut out.

"Perhaps we should get a taxi!" suggested Mitch tactfully.

Hart didn't answer. Instead he crossed his fingers, gritted his teeth and tried again. The battery was now struggling to cope then, unexpectedly, the engine burst into life.

Mitch clapped her hands together loudly in response to this welcomed sound.

Hart kept his foot planted flat on the gas pedal in an effort to keep the engine alive. Eventually it settled down and, clearing what he could of the ice from the inside of the windscreen with a gloved hand, engaged first gear and headed out into the countryside.

For several minutes they drove along in silence, not wanting to mist up the windscreen again.

"I'm really getting worried about the way this case seems to be turning out, Emit," said Mitch finally.

Hart slid the heater control to hot and switched on the fan.

"Just think what has happened so far – three people dead. Each of them had their Cricket Cartilage or whatever the hell it's called cut out."

"Cricoid Cartilage," Hart corrected.

"Oh, you know what I mean, don't interrupt. We have a collection of old coins that for some bizarre reason the killer inserts into his victim's throat. Then finally he nails them to the floor. And now to top it all you have a visit from this maniac who, just so that you're left in no doubt who it is that's ransacked your room, decides to leave a doll nailed to the bloody wall." Mitch's voice had risen and was now almost a scream.

"You forgot about the number," Hart said flippantly.

"What!" Mitch yelled grabbing at Hart's left arm, the action of which momentarily caused him to swerve towards the curb.

"Careful, Mitch, you'll have us off the bloody road." He said firmly. "Look, I know you're right and I am concerned, honest."

"Emit, he knows about the building work being done to your house, remember? He said to the receptionist that he had some invoices that he wanted to discuss with you, remember? Oh Great!" she cried as the penny dropped.

"What now?" he said turning to her.

"Bloody marvellous, don't you see what this means? He obviously knows where you live." Mitch sounded far from amused at this revelation.

Hart didn't want to admit it to her, but he knew that this was probably very likely. What concerned him more though was the distinct possibility that the killer might also know where Mitch lived.

They drove along in relative silence through Wolverton High Street, which was still surprisingly busy considering the truck had gone, and down the hill towards Stony Stratford.

"Why has this killer singled you out?" Mitch said turning to Hart.

"What do you mean?"

"He could have come after me or Stacey. Why you? I mean you're not even in the force anymore."

"Listen, don't go tempting fate. The last thing you bloody want is a visit from this idiot!" Hart replied angrily.

Mitch didn't reply and for the next five minutes they again travelled in silence. Hart slowed up as he approached the junction then stopped. He waited for the traffic lights ahead to change then turned left towards Buckingham.

"Look, Mitch, I know you're worried about me and I'm flattered." Hart didn't look but he could feel her staring at him. "No, I am, really, but you have to understand, helping both you and Stacey on this case has opened up old wounds." He risked a look at her then back at the road ahead. "I want this killer as much as you two, if not more." He pulled out and overtook a cyclist. "Some good might come of his visit to me, you know," Hart said hopefully.

"Good! What bloody good could possibly come of having some madman after you?" she replied still feeling frustrated by Hart's apparent lackadaisical attitude to the whole thing.

"Mitch, I'm big enough and ugly enough to look after myself, trust me!" he said looking down at his wristwatch.

"I wonder how many of his other victims thought the same way just before he killed them," she replied sarcastically.

"It's obvious that he thinks you know more than you do. You're a threat to him and next time it might not be the doll that he nails to the wall."

Hart changed down as he approached a slow-moving tractor in front of him, then once it was clear ahead he pulled out and accelerated passed.

"Mitch, please, don't let this get to you. I really will be careful and I want you to do the same."

"You don't have to warn me to be careful. I have absolutely no intention of running into this maniac," she replied earnestly.

"Good, I'm pleased to hear it. Anyway, with any luck my builder John may still be at the house. Perhaps he'll remember if anybody has been asking after me, and if so, he might even be able to give us a description of them."

Just before reaching Buckingham town centre Hart indicated right, slowed down then locked up almost missing the turn. Checking his rear view mirror and seeing it was clear behind him he swung the wheel over and turned into the lane soon bringing the car to a skidding halt in front of a freshly painted garage door.

"Emit, it's lovely," proclaimed Mitch, keen to change the subject.

She was right. Even though the light was failing he could appreciate what she meant. John had done a magnificent job renovating this old cottage. It had definitely been worth the wait.

"That's a nuisance. I was rather hoping he'd still be here," Hart said stepping from the car. "I'll catch up with him tomorrow and see if he knows anything. Come on, Mitch, I'll show you around the garden before it gets too dark."

They walked up the path together hand in hand Hart holding the gate open for Mitch as she passed under the brick archway that John had convinced Hart to have.

The garden mainly laid to lawn was of a manageable size, not too big. There were many trees; most were of apple, some of pear. Around its perimeter, a six foot high shiplap wooden fence kept prying eyes out.

At the very end of the garden John had constructed a small gazebo for relaxing in the afternoon sun, something that Hart had promised himself to take up now that he was retired.

"It's so peaceful," she said slipping her arm inside his. Hart turned to her, his heart thumped so heavily in his chest that he was sure she would hear it.

"You're cold, shall we go in?" he said rubbing his hand briskly up and down her arm in an effort to get her warm.

"Please," she replied with a smile then rested her head on his arm.

"I'll give you the grand tour if you like?"

"That would be nice."

Hart put his arm around her narrow shoulders and

hugged her, giving her a gentle kiss on the head. The pleasant sweetness of her hair sent his heart rate soaring.

"We'll have to go around to the front. I don't have a key to the back door yet." They stood for a moment huddled together at the door while Hart tried each key in turn. "That would round the day off nicely, wouldn't it? Not able to get into my new home." He chuckled, happily the next key fitted and Hart pushed the door wide.

Fortunately for them both John had put the heating on so the house was now quite warm; Hart closed the door behind them, and in the confines of the small hallway turned. He looked slightly uneasy.

Mitch smiled. His heart thumped in his chest again. It was now or never, he thought.

He leant forward, their lips not quite touching; he could feel the warmth of her sweet breath as he held his. He embraced her, gently pulling her to him; their lips met, and with eyes closed they were lost in each other's arms.

"Christ, I'm sorry, Mitch," he bleated and was now blushing deeply something Hart rarely did. Mitch put a finger to his lips.

"Don't be, I wanted you to kiss me," she whispered.

Sensing his embarrassment she slipped past him and pushed the inner door open, stepped into the living room and switched the light on.

"This room is wonderful, Emit. Who chose the paper?" She asked trying to conceal the excitement she felt at their first kiss.

"I would like to say that it was me but that would be lying. The credit for the decorating has to go to John's wife, Joan. She has a talent for it," he admitted.

Mitch moved towards the patio doors, pushing both glazed doors open, she stepped through into the newly finished conservatory.

"I do love the smell of new paint," she said turning to Hart who had followed close behind and now switched on the light that hung from the centre of the glazed roof.

"Sit down and make yourself at home, Mitch. I'm just going to stick the car in the garage then I'll get us a couple of glasses and a nice bottle of plonk."

Choosing the large comfortable sofa near the window she sat then, bringing her legs up under her, she settled, pushing her back into the soft velvet feather cushions.

Hart wasn't long and soon returned with two long-stemmed glasses, a bottle of Chablis and an opener. Sitting down in the chair opposite he pulled the foil wrapping from around the neck of the bottle.

Mitch patted the empty space beside her. "Come and sit with me, Emit. You can keep me warm."

"Sorry about the bits of cork."

"Oh! Don't worry," she said lifting her glass, "here's to your new home, Emit."

"And to us!" he added.

They sat for some time huddled together on the comfortable sofa just talking.

"You know, I don't even know where you live?" He said topping her glass up.

"I'm staying at my Mum's at the moment while she's away, it would worry her if the house was empty, this way it keeps things more normal if you know what I mean?"

Hart didn't really know what to say so he just squeezed her hand and held her closer. Sensing his awkwardness Mitch then added, "I'm going back to my place tonight to collect my mail and to make sure things are okay, you know? No burst water pipes or worse."

"So where is this place you call home?" He asked.

Mitch sat forward and drained her glass before answering. "Nothing very grand I'm afraid. I have a small," she paused for a moment, "a very small," she corrected, "one bedroom house in Newport Pagnell." She said holding up the empty glass. Hart took it from her and stood.

"Are you hungry, Mitch?"

"Yes, a little." She nodded.

"Great! I'll rustle something together. Do you like pasta?" he asked picking up his glass and the empty wine bottle from the coffee table.

"That sounds good."

"You stay put, Mitch, and relax. I'll go and fetch another bottle."

"If you insist." She giggled.

"I do."

After several agonising moments trying to find where John had stored his groceries Hart was now excitedly preparing their first meal together.

"I had better warn you, Mitch, I'm not the best when it comes to cooking," he called from the kitchen.

Once the pasta was boiling he went through into the dining room and started laying the table then, taking a second bottle of wine from the fridge and this time having better success removing the cork, he placed the bottle on the table along with his glass.

He returned to the kitchen to complete his pasta experience and carried the two china plates through to the table before fetching Mitch.

He now realised why she hadn't replied when he had called out to her earlier. With her head tilted to one side she had fallen asleep.

"Mitch," he whispered shaking her gently.

"Mitch," he said again, this time more loudly. She woke with a start. "Sorry, I didn't mean to make you jump. It's on the table."

She stood then rubbed her legs briskly trying to get some feeling back in them before following Hart into the dining room.

"Emit, this looks great. I'm so hungry," she said stifling a yawn.

Pulling back a chair he flung a napkin over one arm and, in his best French waiter's voice, said, "If madam would care to sit I shall pour zee wine."

She quickly cupped her hand over the glass. "Only a drop, Emit. Wine goes straight to my head."

They sat opposite each other and for the second time that evening touched glasses.

Newport Pagnell is midway between Olney and Wolverton and is a small town with a growing community. Its most recent development of housing is the Green Park estate built on reclaimed farm land and an ideal place to live especially if you work in Wolverton. Mitch's home lay back from the road and was one of seven terraced properties each separated by an alleyway. This alleyway served as access to the rear gardens and although not intended was perfect cover for those not wishing to be seen. Even Mitch's vigilant neighbours would have been hard pressed to spot this determined visitor as he hauled himself effortlessly over the solidly locked gate and dropped cat-like onto the concrete path below. Turning, the small but muscular figure slid both steel bolts back that held the gate fast allowing him a speedy exit, should one be needed. The window locks although well able to deter the opportunist were no match for this attacker as he slid the thin hardened steel blade into place. Once inside he pulled the heavy curtains across both downstairs windows then made himself comfortable in the soft leather chair positioned in the corner of the room, his powerful hands tightly clutching the smooth wooden handle of the hammer that lay in his lap.

CHAPTER TEN

Jilly's was a favourite watering hole for many early morning drivers. A converted Sprite Major caravan complete with its many plastic pennants still stuck firmly to the windows, informing anyone who could be bothered enough to read them of its various holiday destinations.

Now with serving hatch cut neatly into one side it served as a refreshment stop, meeting place and somewhere to lust after Jilly.

Tall, with shoulder length crow-black silky hair, dark smouldering eyes and a figure usually seen in Playboy magazines. She started the day off nicely for many drivers who cared to stop, and most did.

Today, although cold, it was at least still dry. Jilly entertained a small group of customers who stood huddled around the hatch, each enjoying the aroma of bacon and eggs sizzling in the hot pans.

With her back turned and busy cooking this gave ample opportunity for all gathered to ogle her pert denim-covered bottom.

Neil elbowed Steve violently in the ribs, "Wouldn't you just like to get your hands on that for ten minutes?" he whispered.

"I heard that. Do you mind?" Jilly said looking over her shoulder.

"Sorry, Jilly, just joking," Neil replied thrusting both hands into the air.

"Just dreaming, more like," Steve barked.

"You wouldn't have said that if Frank had been helping me today, now would you?" she scoffed.

Frank was Jilly's husband. Six foot six and built to break bones. He was often known to join in with the regulars when flirting with his wife. Most knew where to draw the line though, and those that didn't, rarely came back.

"Here you are, you dirty bugger," she hissed and thrust a bacon roll forwards, "Money first young man," and held her hand out for payment.

"See you tomorrow, Jilly," he said dropping the coins into her upturned palm. "Do you think we'll be finished tomorrow?" Steve asked closing the car door.

"No choice, mate, we have to," Neil answered. "They're sending a truck in the afternoon to pick it all up, remember?"

"Is fat bloke going to be there, do you think?"

"Galba, you mean? I would think so. I don't think he would want to risk us disappearing with a lorry load of his money, do you?" Neil scoffed.

"Are you still up for taking some of it, Neil?" Steve whispered as though someone might hear. "He wouldn't miss a few boxes now, would he?"

Neil reached for the radio and switched Noel Edmonds off. "I bloody hate that prat," he said, then wound down the window just far enough to allow him to squeeze the greasy paper napkin through the gap and let the wind dispose of it. "Come on, mate, we'd better get on. We can talk about this later."

Steve wiped the condensation from the inside of the windscreen, started the engine, then sending a cloud of debris into the air shot out of the lay-by and into the busy traffic.

Thursday morning Hart woke, slowly at first. Eyes still closed he lay motionless for a moment listening to the countryside come to life – birds chirping; somewhere far off in the distance he could hear a tractor; a dog barked.

He could smell perfume, warm breath on his cheek, then a gentle kiss as a soft hand stroked at his chest. Slowly he opened his eyes. Surely a dream, he thought, then turned his head to the side.

"Did you sleep well?" Mitch asked softly.

All he could do was nod as his mind rewound quickly. He couldn't recall anything, his mouth dried up and his head thumped. Too much wine, he thought.

She laid her head gently back on his chest. "You were very drunk last night, Emit. How do you feel?" she asked tugging playfully at the dark hair on his chest.

He tried in vain to remember more of last night, cursing himself for being so foolish. Why had he drunk so much? Bloody Irish pride, he thought.

"I don't remember coming to bed. We must have drunk more than I thought," he said wearily. "Did we?" he asked. His face reddened slightly.

She lifted her head and sat up slightly. He could feel her left breast just teasing his skin.

"No, Emit, nothing happened. You fell, asleep." She gave his chest a playful slap and laid her head back down.

"I'm sorry, Mitch," he replied sheepishly. Secretly, though, he was gutted.

They lay there in each other's arms for almost an hour until Mitch started to get restless.

"I'd better get up. Can I use your bathroom?" she

said, her fingertips tracing lightly across his chest.

"Of course, you don't need to ask. I'll get up and make us some breakfast."

She went to sit up then hesitated pulling the cover tightly around her. "Don't watch me," she pleaded, pushing his head to the side. "I know its silly but I'm easily embarrassed." She giggled.

Hart pretended to comply then relented, turning just as she disappeared into the bathroom.

"My dressing gown is on the back of the door, Mitch," he called out.

Hart sat up fluffed the pillow and lay back, content to stay there all day if he could. He hadn't felt this good for ages. This woman was really getting to him and the best bit was he liked it. All around the room lay the evidence of them being together, a couple.

He waited until he heard the shower go on then swung his legs out of the bed and went downstairs. Turning the thermostat up, he stood in his underpants and filled the kettle, then dropped four slices of bread into the chrome toaster and pushed the leaver down.

"Coffee and toast, is that okay?" he said pushing the door open with his foot,

"Sounds great,"

He placed the tray down onto the dresser keeping one eye on Mitch who stood by the window rubbing a towel briskly over her wet hair.

Hart sat, picked up a steaming mug of black coffee and finished it in one go, the hot liquid thankfully replacing the taste of stale wine that lingered in his mouth with something more palatable.

"It's a great view!" he said cheekily.

"It is, Emit, you can see for miles. However did you

find this place?"

"Luck really. I saw it advertised in an estate agent in Stony. It'd only come on the market that day. I arranged to view it straight away and put in an offer there and then. An hour later the agent rang to say my offer had been accepted. Doesn't happen like that too often, does it?"

Hart made to go over to her just as the telephone rang. He went to answer it then hesitated. "Shall I?"

"You'd better, Emit, it might be important."

"Hello, Emit Hart speaking."

"Hello, Hart, its Peter," the voice at the other end announced loudly.

"Peter, how are you?"

"Fine thanks, but it's bad news, I'm afraid. I spoke with Anton at the British Museum early this morning. Unfortunately today is his last day. He's taking his annual holiday, going back home for a bit of warmth he said, bit of a last minute thing evidently. Anyway, he's going to be away now for two weeks, perhaps longer, lucky bugger."

Hart sat down heavily on the corner of the bed, his mind trying to work out the implications that this might have. News of this nature wasn't what he wanted to hear and he wondered for a moment where home was for Anton.

"However, all's not lost I'm happy to say," Peter continued cheerily. "I remembered afterwards that some time back Anton had introduced me to a colleague of his, a David James. Anyway, to cut a long story short I rang back about an hour ago and was put straight through to him. Apparently he's now the head honcho there. I explained more or less everything that we know so far and he's agreed to meet with you," Peter exclaimed.

"Well done, Peter, that's great news," Hart replied excitedly. "When can we meet with him?" he declared.

"Is tomorrow good enough?"

"Brilliant, mate, I really appreciate it, I owe you one." Hart felt even better now.

"A pleasure, Hart. Let me know how you get on, wont you?" replied Peter earnestly.

Hart replaced the telephone.

"I assume by the expression on your face that it's good news?"

Dressed in a surprisingly revealing black lace bra and matching briefs she sat down on Hart's knee then, with one arm draped loosely around his neck, leant forward and scooped up a slice of slightly overdone toast.

"Come on then, what's happened?" she asked, wiggling her bottom playfully on his lap.

He could feel the warmth of her body against his and was immediately conscious of a stirring somewhere below his stomach. He shifted on the stool in the hope that she hadn't noticed.

"I think I had better get dressed, don't you?" she joked planting a kiss on his head.

"If you must," he replied dropping both hands to his lap in an effort at modesty.

"Was that Peter your doctor friend?"

"It was."

"What did he want?" she asked pulling on a pair of lightly creased black trousers.

"He's arranged for us to go tomorrow and meet with an expert in Roman history – a chap called David

James." He paused as she pulled a white roll neck over her head. "Hopefully he'll be able to shed some light on the evidence that we've got, and if we're really lucky he might even have an idea what that bloody number means."

Slipping on her shoes she went into the bathroom and switched the light on. "God I look dreadful without make up," she shrieked.

"Not from this angle, kid!"

"Hadn't you better get ready? You're going to make me late," she called out.

"I'm waiting for you to finish." He stood as she came out of the bathroom and kissed her lightly on the lips.

Second guessing him, she held him at arm's length.

"Emit, I have to go, really." Her tone was firmer this time, more insistent.

"I know, I'm sorry." With mouth turned down like a five year old that's been refused his favourite toy he allowed her past.

Having shaved in record time he had a quick shower, got dressed and went down stairs. Mitch had made more coffee and was now sitting in the conservatory.

Taking a mug off the hook Hart poured himself some coffee and went to join her.

"Emit, I've had a wonderful time, you know, I really don't want it to end. I wish we could stay here for the rest of today, or forever." She turned and gave his hand a squeeze as if sealing the deal.

"Why don't you come and stay for the weekend? We could go for a walk or something. There are some nice places to visit around here."

"That sounds wonderful, Emit, let me think on it, eh? I'll have to see how my mum is first?" she said finishing her coffee, "I hate saying this but, I really do have to go, I am sorry."

"It's not a problem, let me just grab my coat and we'll make a move," he said getting up from the sofa.

Hart closed the door behind them as Mitch pushed her arm through his and rested her head on his shoulder. The sun was warm on their backs as they made their way down the footpath that led to the garage. Lifting up the single wooden door Hart disappeared inside.

"Hold on, Mitch, I'll reverse the car out, it's a bit of a squeeze down that side," he shouted sliding into the driver's seat.

Fumbling for a moment in the near dark he eventually found the ignition, then turning the key ... nothing.

"Bollocks!" he cursed as he watched the dim red glow of the ignition light flicker then go out.

With a battery so flat you could have slid it under the garage door he got back out of the car and slammed the door in a way that for the moment at least made him feel slightly better.

"Left the bloody side lights on when I put the car away last night, I'm afraid. Battery's dead as a Dodo." He said holding his hand up to shield his eyes from the bright sunlight.

"We'd better ring in. Perhaps Stacey can send someone out to pick us up or something," she sighed now concerned that she was going to be even later.

"Under the circumstances that might prove a bit embarrassing, don't you think?" he responded quickly.

"Oh! I see what you mean." She sniggered. "Perhaps a taxi then?"

"Good idea." Hart pulled on the cord that hung down from the door, then stepped back quickly as it slammed shut.

They hurried back to the house. Fortunately for them both, and probably because it was a weekday, they didn't have to wait long. A loud blast on a car horn signalled the arrival of their lift.

"Look, Mitch, just for the moment I think it might be a good idea to keep last night, you know, you staying over, just between the two of us, no sense in rocking the boat if you know what I mean?" Hart had suddenly become noticeably fidgety.

"No! I'm not sure I do know what you mean?"

"I don't know exactly how to put this!" he replied.

Her grip suddenly tightened. "You're worrying me Emit, what's wrong?"

"No! No!" he quickly cut in. "It's nothing to worry about, well, it's just that..." He hesitated for a split second unsure that he should continue.

"That what?"

"I just don't think that we should make it too obvious, particularly to Stacey."

"Why ever not?" She replied angrily. "What the hell has it to do with him?"

"Because he likes you, Mitch, well more than that, I think he has a serious crush on you."

"Oh that." She giggled.

"You don't sound a bit surprised. Did you know then?" he asked, unsure whether or not he should feel relieved or just bloody angry.

"Yes, of course I knew, but he's harmless. I've known for some time actually."

"Are you offended?"

"No, don't be silly, not in the slightest, he's a lovely bloke, it's just a boyish crush that's all. Anyway, he's married."

Before Hart could respond the taxi turned into the police station's car park and pulled up directly adjacent to the main entrance.

Stepping out of the car Mitch waited as Hart paid the driver then together they went inside.

Big Rob was sat behind the re-enforced glass screen giving his biggest smile ever.

"Hello, me ducks, and what have you two been up to?" he asked looking over the top of his thick horn-rimmed glasses.

Mitch did her best at hiding her obvious embarrassment by simply laughing.

"Morning, Rob, is Stacey in?" Hart asked putting himself between Mitch and the glass screen.

"Yes, go on through, you know where he is," he replied still grinning, making sure he caught Mitch's eye as she passed.

Once in the corridor and out of view she turned. "It's as if he knows," she whispered.

"Don't be daft, Mitch, how the hell could he? You know him better than most. He gets a buzz out of putting you on the spot that's all."

This statement appeared to satisfy her, she shrugged her shoulders and opened Stacey's door.

"Morning you two," Stacey welcomed sliding a couple of chairs across the worn parquet flooring towards his desk.

"Here, sit down, I watched as you both arrived so I've organised some tea," he said sliding a manila file into his drawer.

"You appear to be in a better mood this morning, Stacey?"

"Definitely, at last I feel we're making some sort of headway with this bloody case."

There was a knock on the door as the tea arrived. Stacey paused just long enough for the WPC to leave then, sliding a mug towards Hart added, "the question now is, how long have we got before our killer strikes again, and when he does decide to strike who is it likely to be?" and gave Hart the kind of look that left Hart in no doubt whom Stacey thought it might be.

"I think it's pretty bloody obvious, don't you?" Mitch interrupted angrily, "why else would the killer have risked a visit to the hotel?"

Stacey raised his hand to quiet Mitch's sudden outburst. "I agree that on the face of it Hart might be on the list, so to speak, however I doubt it!" He leaned forwards and folded his arms. "It's more likely in my opinion that it was a warning, if he'd intended to harm him, well, I don't think he'd be sitting with us now." Stacey turned to Hart then added coldly. "We have a pretty good idea how this person thinks! If he'd wanted you Hart, I believe that he would have simply waited in your room until you had returned, just as he did with William James, and then bosh!" He slapped his hand violently on the desk. "Anyway, you're forgetting something, there's no motive." He put his hands together, as if in prayer, "why would he want to draw more attention to himself than he's already got? Killing a copper, even a retired one would only make everyone involved more bloody determined to catch him, and he would certainly know that for starters."

Mitch leant forward resting her weight on both arms

and stared at Stacey stony-faced. "The motive, Stacey..." She spoke each word slowly, her tone deliberately sarcastic. "The motive could be that he knew Hart had been involved in the original enquiries and he obviously knows that he is helping us now, and perhaps, just perhaps we are closer to him than you think." She slammed her mug down on the desk spilling most of the contents.

"Okay, Mitch, let's assume for the moment that you're right." Stacey said wagging his finger at her. "Let's say that he does think that Hart here knows something. Don't you see? This could help us we could use this to our advantage, use Hart as a decoy and flush the bugger out." He turned to Hart to gauge his reaction to this new idea.

"Hold up a minute." Hart said pushing back his chair. "I don't think I like the way this is going." He gave Stacey a sour look then went and stood by the window, "do you seriously think I'm mad enough to act as your bloody stooge?" He rested his forehead against the cool glass.

"You know how it works." Stacey responded quickly. "We would have you under surveillance all the time. He would never get to you." Stacey had become visibly excited at this new angle.

"Yes, Stacey, I know exactly how it works, thank you, and I also know that we have probably lost as many decoys in this type of scam as we have successfully protected." He said sitting back down. "No, I'm sorry, Stacey, I would like to help, I really would, but I don't think I'm designed to swallow old coins, do you?"

"I agree. You're expecting too much, Stacey," said Mitch grasping at Hart's hand.

"Okay, okay, I know it's a lot to ask, but would you at least sleep on it? This could be the break that we need, Hart," Stacey asked noting their tightly clasped hands.

"I'll think about it, but don't hold your breath."

Stacey was about to try a different approach when the telephone rang, he lifted the receiver reluctantly.

"Hello." He snapped. "You're bloody joking?" His expression had changed in the blink of an eye. Whoever it was on the other end now had Stacey's un-divided attention.

Seizing the moment Mitch leant forward and whispered, "Emit, I don't want you to let Stacey talk you into doing this. I know what male pride's like, it really isn't worth the risk."

Hart half turned and gave her a controlled smile his mind racing, she squeezed his hand tightly unsure whether this signal from him was in agreement with her request, or just in an effort to shut her up.

"Will you just hold on, Rob?" Stacey said clamping his hand over the mouthpiece, "you'll never guess who's on the other bloody line." He beamed. "Lucy Reed. She wants to report a missing person," he said quickly then, taking a deep breath, removed his hand. "Okay, Rob, put her through," and put a finger to his lips. "Good morning Miss Reed, I'm DI Stacey, how can I help?" Stacey's face remained expressionless as he listened. "Right, yes, okay, Miss Reed, please try to stay calm. Firstly may I have your home address? Good, telephone number? Great, and are you ringing from that number now?"

Stacey quickly scribbled down something on his blotter then, laying his pen down looked up, his face now beaming again.

"Miss Reed, I would like you to do something for me, would you? It's very important, good. I'll explain everything later. Firstly I want you to go and lock the front door. Yes, do that now, and then come back to the telephone." Stacey cupped his hand over the mouthpiece again.

"Mitch go fetch the car, bring it around the front would you? Okay, Miss Reed, I want you to stay exactly where you are and on no account do you open the door for anyone other than me, do you understand? Good, I'll come over to you now, is that clear? Good." Stacey slammed the receiver back onto its cradle.

"She's at William James's house." Stacey leapt from the chair. "I want you to join us if you would?"

"Of course," Hart replied following Stacey out of the office.

Five minutes later with blue lights flashing they were astride the white line and speeding north on the A5 towards Towcester.

"It would appear that Miss Reed decided to return to the house in an effort to confront William James and find out why he had dumped her."

"Does she know what's happened to him?" Hart asked.

"No, and until we get her back to the office I think we should try to keep it that way," and then as an afterthought added, "thank God I released the house yesterday and had it cleaned up."

Ten minutes later Mitch turned into the driveway and gunned the engine, the car responding instantly. At the end of the drive she swung the wheel over and stamped her foot down hard on the brake bringing it to a skidding halt directly in front of the garage door.

Stacey leapt out and with Hart close behind they sprinted up the path towards the front door, stopping so quickly they almost collided like two characters from a silent movie.

"Miss Reed," Stacey shouted. "Miss Reed, hello, it's DI Stacey, are you there?" He hammered his large fist against the wooden door.

They waited then tried again.

"Miss Reed, are you there?" Still nothing! "Shit!" Stacey cursed.

"Quick, Stacey, open the door!" Hart hissed as he dropped to one knee. "Lucy, open the door, it's the police," he shouted through the letterbox.

Stacey quickly tapped the four digits on the keypad and gave the door a hard shove then stepped inside. The hallway was in darkness and with no lights on in the living room it wasn't looking good.

"Hello, Miss Reed, its DI Stacey, where are you?" he repeated.

Mitch, with her heart in her mouth closed the door quietly behind her, even with care the click of the metal latch seemed mind numbingly loud. They inched along the hallway towards the living room in a tight little group half expecting anything to happen.

"Can you hear that?" Stacey whispered stopping mid stride cupping his hand around his ear.

"It's a radio," Mitch responded.

"I think it's coming from upstairs."

Avoiding the large coffee table in the centre of the room they moved cat like through the living room, the music growing ever louder. Once at the foot of the stairs Stacey called out again.

"Miss Reed, can you hear me?"

175

As though connected by some unseen force, just as he planted his foot on the first stair tread the music stopped and the house fell silent.

"Hello!" Stacey called out.

All three froze as they heard the heart stopping scream from somewhere upstairs.

Mitch responded by screaming in what was probably just a knee-jerk reaction but this was enough to cause Hart to falter.

Stacey meanwhile took off up the stairs, missing out every other step in an attempt to cover as much ground in as little time as was humanly possible. Realising that Mitch was okay Hart leapt forwards. Both men reached the bedroom door almost simultaneously, suddenly a small figure appeared hunched over in the doorway clutching both hands over the mouth.

"Shit, you made me jump," she spat, stamping her foot down angrily. "Why the hell didn't you call out?"

Lucy Reed, small, petite and very attractive, stood framed in the bedroom doorway; one hand now held to her chest, the other to her mouth.

"Miss Reed, I'm sorry to have startled you. I'm DI Stacey, this Emit Hart." He hesitated as Mitch reached them. "I did call out to you, several times," he assured then pointed to the radio sat on a small cabinet by the side of the bed. "You obviously couldn't hear us."

"Oh, I'm sorry, yes, I did have that on," she stammered apologetically.

Stepping back into the bedroom, Lucy went over to the bed and sat down heavily running both hands through her hair and sighed. "What's going on? Where is he?" She shook her head in despair. "I've rung William's work number several times. Nobody has seen or heard from him." She sat with her hands tightly clasped in her lap trying desperately to control herself. "I've rung here several times but still no reply. I would have left a message only he's removed the tape from the machine," she continued.

"No, that was us," interrupted Stacey.

She turned to Stacey. The puzzlement on her face spoke volumes.

"What's going on, have you arrested him?" She clamped her hand over her mouth again as it now started to dawn on her that something was wrong. "Oh my God, he's hurt, what's happened?" She ran her hand through her hair nervously. "Oh shit, he's dead isn't he? Tell me, I need to know." She was now sobbing uncontrollably, her eyes fixed on Stacey waiting anxiously for him to answer her. Mitch sat down at her side and put an arm around her shoulders in an effort to calm her.

"Please, tell me what's happened. Where is he? I want to see him. Was it an accident? He's an awful driver you know, I kept telling him to slow down in that bloody car of his." Her breathing became heavy as she wiped tears away on the back of her hand.

"Miss Reed, may I call you Lucy?" Stacey said trying to sound less official.

"Yes," she sobbed still trying desperately to gain control.

"You must trust us, Lucy. We're only here to help and we know you're worried, but, you could be in danger. Especially here."

Lucy looked up at Stacey with reddening eyes, she tried to say something but it just came out in a succession of sobbing gasps. Mitch squeezed her shoulder and whispered something that went unheard by Stacey.

"Let's go downstairs, Lucy, shall we?" Mitch repeated.

In the living room Lucy dropped heavily onto the couch, the soft cushions seemed to somehow swallow her petite frame whole. She laid her head to one side, eyes scrunched tightly closed. Hart who had gone through to the kitchen now returned with glass in hand.

"Would you like some water, Lucy?" Mitch asked as she sat down at her side.

"No, I'm fine," she replied keeping her eyes firmly shut then suddenly and without warning she sat up ram rod straight. "I'm sorry but I've got to get out of here."

A startled Mitch turned to Stacey waiting for him to say something.

"Look, if you don't mind I just want to go, and now!" she said looking directly at Stacey.

"Okay, Lucy, I think that's probably a good idea. We have a car outside. We'll go back to the police station."

"Am I under arrest?" she asked nervously.

"Of course not, Lucy, we just need to talk with you. It's just possible that you may have the answers to a few questions that we want to ask you," Mitch said resting her hand on Lucy's shoulder.

Hart didn't say anything, instead went over and held the door open. Lucy turned to Mitch and attempted a smile then stood. They followed Hart out of the living room and into the cold air all three watched in complete silence while Stacey closed the door and rearmed the alarm.

"Mitch, you sit in the back with her," Stacey said climbing into the driver's side. Once on the A5 and for the second time that day they sped down the centre of the road the wailing siren and blue flashing lights ensuring a clear route back to Wolverton.

Throughout the journey Lucy sat quietly with chin on chest fumbling nervously with the strap of her hand bag.

Stacey switched off the siren as he swung into the stations car park and brought the car to a halt directly opposite the main entrance.

"Come on Lucy," Mitch said, "Let's go in, shall we?"

Stepping from the car Lucy looked up at the blue sign hung above the door and hesitated, until now everything that had happened to her over the last hour could have been excused as some ghastly dream. Now though, well, this was as real as it was going to get.

Once inside Lucy had gone directly to the Ladies' room with Mitch. Hart took a fresh pack of cigarettes from an inside pocket and removed the wrapping.

"I'm just going out for a quick smoke," he said stepping through the doorway. He stood for a moment on the top step and pulled heavily on the cigarette, holding the smoke in his chest for a moment before letting it out slowly and watching as the wind swept it skywards.

"I've asked one of the lads to fetch her some tea," Stacey said as Hart appeared in the doorway of his office.

"I think she's probably going to need it don't you?"

"She looks pretty shaky. I hope she can hold it altogether." Stacey hesitated as Lucy appeared in the doorway with Mitch just behind her.

"Please, Lucy, come in and take a seat," Stacey said

pointing towards a chair.

Responding quickly Hart slid the chair across the floor towards Stacey's desk.

"How is she?" Stacey asked looking passed Lucy.

"Oh, as well as can be expected, sir, under the circumstances," Mitch replied.

"Please, Lucy, sit down if you would. I'll try to make this as painless as I can."

Mitch stood just behind her resting a hand on Lucy's slim shoulder.

"Lucy, this police officer is going to take some notes."

She turned slightly in the seat and nodded at the WPC who had sat to her left.

"Lucy, there's no easy way to do this so, I shall come straight to the point. We are a team that have been put together to investigate the death, or rather the murder, of your late boyfriend, William James."

The room fell silent. Only the traffic noise from outside could be heard. Someone in the room coughed.

"Did you understand what I just said, Lucy?" Stacey waited for some reaction from her.

She nodded without looking up from the floor still fumbling with the strap.

"I know this isn't easy for you but there are several questions that I need to ask you. Are you up to it?"

Stacey paused for a moment before continuing.

"Would you tell us how long you had, known Mr James?"

Everyone in the room watched with controlled silence as Lucy with head still hung low fumbled inside her handbag then snapping it shut violently turned to Stacey.

"We met about seven months ago," she replied softly.

"And where was that, Lucy?"

"Oh, it was a pub, The Crooked Billet." She coughed into her clenched fist trying to clear her throat, her tone was remarkably calm. "It's close to where we both work," she replied dabbing at her eyes with a paper tissue. "We met most lunchtimes, and occasionally after work too."

"Did you only meet there?"

"No, I see him most Thursdays too. I would catch the train after work and we would meet at the station."

"You mean Wolverton Rail Station, yes?" Stacey asked, already knowing.

"Yes," she replied vaguely.

"I'm puzzled, Lucy. Why if you both worked near to each other did you travel separately?"

"Oh, William worked very odd hours. Thursday always seemed to be the best day to meet. Apart from a Friday he always drove to work, you see. He never knew when he might leave so it was easier that way." She hesitated then turned to the WPC for a moment then back at Stacey. "Anyhow, we would spend the evening together then in the morning we would travel to work on the same train."

"That would be the Friday morning then?" Stacey asked leaning forward clasping and unclasping his hands in front of him.

"That's right."

"Are you okay to continue, Lucy?" Mitch asked over her shoulder.

She looked up nodded and attempted a smile. "Yes, I'm fine, thanks."

Lucy appeared to have got a second wind. Her face, Hart noted, had definitely got some colour back and although her breathing was still quite heavy she had at least stopped crying and appeared to have accepted what was going on now.

"Could you tell me what happened last Thursday then, Lucy?" Stacey asked.

"Yes, William telephoned me to say that he wanted to leave work early that day. He said that he would work through lunch instead of us meeting up." Lucy sat back in the chair, touching the sides with her hands and crossed her legs. "He said that he had to stop off in Watford to pick up something that he'd ordered from a shop there."

"Do you know what that might have been?"

Looking stony faced across the desk at Stacey her eyes filled and her breathing now gave way to greater sobs as she held the paper tissue to her lips.

"Yes, I know. A ring. We were to be engaged. He had planned it for weeks. He did try to keep it a secret from me but I found out. William wasn't very good at hiding things, I could always tell."

"Please go on, Lucy, you're really doing very well," Stacey encouraged.

Taking a deep breath then continued. "I arrived at Wolverton at about eight in the evening. The train was running late, it should have arrived at seven thirty. Anyway, I wasn't too bothered as William was normally late and I knew that he would wait for me. I waited for almost an hour and he still hadn't turned up." Lucy uncrossed her legs and sat forward, her hands now fiddling with the clasp on her bag. "The next train back was the nine thirty so I decided to catch it. Any trains after that and you risk getting in with a load of drunks, so I left."

"Why didn't you try to phone him?" Stacey questioned.

"I did, at Wolverton, well, eventually. Unfortunately all three telephones were out of order so I decided that I'd call him once I had arrived at Euston."

"And did you?"

"Yes, I used a payphone on the platform. I just left a message on his answerphone."

"Lucy, have you ever heard of something called 'The Cleaners'?" Stacey knew this was a long shot but one he felt worth taking.

"Oh, you mean that silly club in London!" she replied. A hint of a smile appeared and then was gone.

Stacey shot a look in Hart's direction, their eyes making contact for a brief second before he asked, "What do you know of them?"

"Not a lot really. William loved that sort of thing though – it was the intrigue, the mystique of it all." She chuckled. "It was like the one that he'd joined here, he loved it," she added simply.

Hart sat bolt upright at this last remark and for the first time during the interview cut in. "Lucy, what are you saying? He belonged to one here? What do you mean exactly?"

"He'd been a member of a club here, well, not far from here. As far as I know he joined it about two years ago." Lucy shifted in her seat and placed her bag onto the floor. "William would never speak to me of it. Whenever I mentioned it he would either change the subject or simply remind me that it wouldn't be a very secret society if all its members went around discussing it."

"How did you find out about it then?" Hart enquired, keen not to let go of the subject.

"Just by accident really. I'd used his car to go shopping one Friday morning," she said turning to Hart. "We'd decided to call in sick and spend the day together. Anyway, I was packing the shopping into the boot when I noticed this gold-coloured rope. I probably would have normally ignored it but it caught my attention because of a large ornate tassel, which was on the end. I thought at first that it was a tie back, you know, for a curtain. Anyway, I pulled at it but it wouldn't budge, so I lifted the panel up to free it."

"What panel?" Stacey interrupted. "Sorry, Lucy, what do you mean?" he added aware that his growing excitement was visible to all in the room.

"You know, where the spare wheel is kept? The rope was wrapped tightly around some red – well, crimson to be exact – material." Lucy stared at Stacey waiting for some kind of reaction from him.

"What did you think when you found this bundle?" Hart asked.

"I didn't really. There was someone waiting for my parking space so I put it back, shut the panel down and continued loading the shopping."

"Did you say anything to William?"

"Of course, I asked him about it as soon as I'd returned. He was annoyed at first, saying that I shouldn't have gone through his car like that. Once he'd calmed down though and realised that I'd come across it by accident, well, that was when he admitted to me that he belonged to this club. He said that they were just like the Masons and that it was no big deal."

"Did you believe him?" Hart asked.

"Yes, why ever not! There was no reason for him to lie," She replied with obvious distress.

"Lucy, do you know where this robe is now?" Stacey asked.

"I suppose it's still in the boot of William's car."

Stacey picked up the telephone on his desk and rattled the rest up and down several times then dialled zero, two.

"Hello, Rob, I need you to do something for me. Grab one of our lads and shoot up to Towcester to William James's house. The entry code for the front door is 2441. Go into the garage. I need you to get into the boot of his car – smash it open if you have to. Under the cover where the spare is kept you should find a bundle of red clothing." He shot a glance at Lucy who nodded in approval before continuing. "Bring it back here to me, would you? Great, thank you." Stacey replaced the telephone back onto the cradle.

"Why the interest in the robe?" Mitch puzzled.

"Well firstly whoever it was, that clouted me over the head might have been after the robe and not necessarily the tape as we first thought. Secondly the robe might tell us who or where it was made. If so, then we may be able to find out a little more of this so called club, its location and perhaps even a list of members. It's a long shot, I know, but still worth following up."

"Oh! I know where it is," Lucy interrupted. "Well, roughly where it is," she said looking at both Stacey then Hart.

"Hold on," Stacey said excitedly raising his hand. "Are you telling me that you actually know its location?" This was more of a statement from Stacey than a question.

"Well, sort of, I've not actually been up there but I know where it is," she replied, eager to help.

"Great, would you recognise it on a map, Lucy?"

"Of course." She sounded insulted by Stacey's question.

Mitch without being asked turned and hurried from the room leaving the door swinging in her wake.

She was back in moments. Stacey cleared off his desk and between them they laid out the large map.

"Right, Lucy, this is where you are now." Stacey drew a cross with his pen next to the word Wolverton. "And here is Towcester."

Lucy lifted her handbag from the floor and stood, leaning over the map she carefully traced a route with her slim finger, from Wolverton to Bradwell, then to Newport Pagnell. Both Stacey and Hart watched eagerly as she moved her finger along the road towards Olney.

"Here it is." She said tapping a finger on the map, "This road here. The first left is to Sherrington. The first right goes up to a farm. Next left is to Filgrave. Just passed this Filgrave turning and on the right, can you see? It's shown on this map as a path but it's not, it's actually a road, well, lane," she said confidently.

"Mitch, pop next door and see if we have an Ordinance Survey map of Olney, would you?" Stacey said without looking up.

Moments later she was back.

"Will this do?" she said unfolding the map.

Stacey laid the map on the desk and smoothed the creases out with his hand. "Great, it shows right up to the edge of Emberton village," with his mood now very upbeat he carefully plotted the route using a red marker pen.

"Lucy's right, look, it is a lane," Hart said excitedly.

"It runs for about a third of a mile up to these woods then skirts around to the right towards this old ruin."

"Oh! I don't think it's a ruin anymore." Lucy interrupted.

Stacey ringed the building several times with the marker.

"That's interesting." Hart tapped the map with his finger.

"What is it?" Mitch said moving closer to the table.

"According to the key it shows that it was once an old rectory."

"Mitch, get in touch with the Post Office. See what you can find out from them on a postal address if there is one. Then get someone to check out the electoral register, also the rating people, see if anybody owns the ruin." Stacey sat down heavily in his chair and allowed himself a celebrating smile. "I don't want anyone going up there either," he called out. "Not, that is, until we can find out more about it." Then turning to Hart he added, "If there is someone living up there no sense in warning them yet, is there!"

Hart's smile broadened as he watched Mitch disappear through the doorway.

CHAPTER ELEVEN

"Oh shit!" Neil exclaimed as they turned into the industrial estate. "Galba's already here."

Steve parked the car just a few feet from the gleaming dark blue Range Rover.

"They must be inside," Neil said hurrying from the car. He slammed the door heavily. Steve's curse went unheard.

Neil almost broke into a run, but not quite, pulling on the hand rail as he mounted the steps that led up to the main entrance. He signalled frantically for Steve to get a move on.

Neil spun around quickly as he heard the door behind him open. The small but powerful figure that stood framed in the doorway gestured irritably for them to enter.

Galba was sat behind the front desk attempting to snip off the end of a large Havana with his heavily engraved silver cutter.

Steve hesitated as he heard the door close and watched with growing concern as it was locked, noting the cynical grin that their new doorman gave.

"Good morning, my friends," Galba's voice welcomed. "You disappoint me." His tone had changed in an instant. Without looking up he busied himself sliding the cutter slowly over the tip of the large cigar. "I was expecting to find you both hard at it this fine morning."

The violent snip from the cutter left no one in any doubt as to the mood that this large man was in.

"Yes, Galba, I know, we're sorry we're late, we stopped off to get some breakfast on the way in, took longer than we thought though," Neil replied giving a nervous cough into his white knuckled fist.

"You're here now, that's the main thing, isn't it?" said Galba snapping his lighter shut. "We have dropped by to inform you both that there is to be a slight change of plan." The dense smoke spilled from his mouth with each word. He leant back, the chair complaining under his immense bulk, and pointed to the empty seats opposite. "Please sit, you're making my neck ache," he ordered rubbing the back of his wide neck with oversized hands. "My friends, why the long faces?" Galba's tone had changed again. He leant forward, his arms now supporting his great mass on the desktop. The chair became silent as his weight became less of a burden to it. Without waiting for a reply to his question he continued. "I'm afraid that it has become necessary for us to move the collection day of our consignment." He sucked noisily on the fat cigar like a baby with a dummy. "The truck will now arrive on Sunday, Sunday morning to be exact, so it's essential that you are both here to help with the loading." He paused allowing the thick acrid smoke to pour from his mouth like dry ice off a stage.

"That's impossible, I can't," Steve blurted.

Galba's face visibly reddened. His breathing became noticeably heavier as he tried to control his obvious anger, then suddenly, unable to stay calm any longer and watched by both his men, he leapt out of his chair like an athlete.

Both Neil and Steve were taken completely by surprise and cowed back as the large man launched himself at them, grabbing both around the neck and wrenching them up from their seats slamming them violently against the wall like two lifeless rag dolls.

This sudden outburst from Galba had him gulping for air but not once did he release his tightening grip.

"I'm afraid the matter is not open for debate!" he screamed, his face inches from them. "You will both be here and that is the end of it. Is that understood?" He stared at each in turn with eyes bulging before relaxing his grip on them. Galba shot a look at both his men standing against the far wall then smiled exposing stained teeth again.

"Good," he said stepping back from the two terrified men. "You should understand by now that I take no nonsense. You do as I say and question nothing. Is that understood?" Galba's voice had risen again along with his gasping as he straightened his clothing the best he could.

"We understand, Galba, it will never happen again, I swear," Neil reassured.

Galba stood as straight as he was physically able to, took several deep breaths until he had calmed then removed a dark mohair overcoat from the back of the chair and pulled it around his broad shoulders.

"I am pleased that you now understand," he said, turning to his men. He moved towards the door, his fat fingers closing tightly around the handle. "You have a few days left to complete our order. See to it that you do."

"You have no need to worry, Galba, it will be done, you have my word," Neil replied.

"I will have your life if it is not," he responded menacingly.

Neil attempted to smile but his drying mouth made it physically impossible.

"Well, my friends and I will bid you goodbye for now. Please don't let us hold you from your work, and ensure that you are both here Sunday," he warned putting more emphasis on the word both.

Galba stepped outside, followed closely by his two henchmen, and allowed the door to slam shut.

"Tosser!" Steve barked angrily.

Neil went over to the door and turned the catch. "What the fuck was that all about? Why the hell did you tell him that you couldn't work Sunday?"

"Because I didn't want to, that's why." Steve shouted back.

"Well, you're going to have to now otherwise, my old mate, he's going to throw another wobbly like that and next time he might not relax his grip so quickly."

"Did you feel that grip? Jesus, I was sure that he was going to kill us," Steve said pulling the blind down.

"I thought he was about to explode, didn't you? And his breath," Neil exclaimed.

"Fuck, what the hell had he been eating?" Steve said. His stomach turned at the very thought.

Neil slapped his friend on the back and gave him a less than gentle shove into the hallway. "Come on, you, we'd better get on. We've got a lot to do."

Friday morning and after a couple of mugs of tea and almost a whole packet of Digestives, Hart, Stacey and Mitch left the warmth of the office and headed for the rail station at the far end of the high street. Mitch dropped Stacey and Hart outside the white painted wood-clad building and drove off with a wave. Hart hesitated at the entrance for a second before joining Stacey inside the bustling ticket office.

"Hurry up, Hart," Stacey shouted waving a couple of tickets in the air. "The train's already in, platform two, come on."

Hart turned and sprinted after him, along the bridge and down the concrete steps. As they got to the platform the train was just on the move, slowly at first but gathering speed rapidly. Stacey grabbed at the nearest passing door yanked it open then with one long stride swung inside.

Above the sound of leather on concrete Hart could just make out someone behind him shouting at him to let this one go. He gave an extra bit and managed to grab hold of Stacey's outstretched hand and was pulled aboard. Having closed the door with some difficulty they made their way along the packed carriage to find some seats.

Unfortunately in their haste they had chosen an "all stations train" so the journey was longer than they would have liked. Almost one hour and twenty minutes later the train entered the labyrinth of murky tunnels that was the entrance to Euston station. Having already decided en route not to bother with the underground, they made their way across the vast brightly lit concourse and down the steps that led to the underground taxi rank and joined the end of a small but orderly queue.

Five minutes later and Stacey was pressing his face against the half open window.

"Can you take us to the British Museum, please?" he said shouting above the noise of the dimly lit taxi rank. This, together with the thick acrid exhaust fumes held captive within the poorly ventilated building, was already drying out the back of Stacey's throat.

Without replying the cabby nodded as he zeroed his meter and the slow clatter of the diesel engine rose as he waited for Hart to close the door.

"This is a much more civilised way of getting around London," Stacey said sitting back and crossing his legs.

Hart almost fell into the vinyl seat as the driver accelerated away. Lifting his briefcase up onto his lap he swallowed in an effort to get some moisture back into his mouth. "Anyway," Stacey added as they entered the exit tunnel, "I'll bung it on this month's expenses."

The taxi sped up the slope ignoring the speed ramps and out into the daylight, both passengers squinting against the blinding daylight.

"You know, I'm looking forward to meeting this bloke," Stacey said tugging the ring pull on a can of Pepsi.

London cab drivers aren't always the all knowing, inquisitive individuals that they're often made out to be, however, this one was the exception. They sat in relative silence as they listened to his ravings and obvious anger to the recent terrorist bombings that London had been receiving.

"We're almost there," Hart announced deliberately loudly pointing towards the large sign hung above the road pleased that his accent had now quietened the incensed driver.

Taking a left then a quick right the taxi came to a halt outside what appeared to be the main entrance. Hart pulled on the leather strap that released the door and stepped out of the cab. Now away from the warmth of the car he shivered as the cold air hit him, gripping the briefcase between his knees he pulled the collar of his coat up around his ears, hunching his shoulders in an effort to stay warm.

Stacey meanwhile was digging around in his pocket for some change while making small talk with the driver.

"Did you give him a tip?" Hart asked through tight lips.

"Yes, I told him to stop going on about the IRA."

Both made their way up the steep flight of concrete steps towards the large oak panelled doors and entered the great hall.

Although busy with tourists they soon spotted the reception desk at the far end. It was manned by three uniformed men. As they got closer they could see that two were on the telephone while the third appeared deep in conversation.

Joining the small queue it soon became evident to them both that the visitor speaking with the guard spoke poor English. With arms flailing through the air like a demented windmill the guard tried to explain to the confused man that he wasn't standing in the London Library. After a frustrating ten minutes the visitor, deciding that he was getting nowhere, stormed off. Both Hart and Stacey stepped forward.

"I hope one of you speaks bloody English," the voice said gruffly.

"Perfectly!" Hart answered quickly.

The guard raised an eyebrow in response to Harts accent then sighed. "Honestly, it's a wonder they ever get here," he added shaking his head. "Anyway, gentlemen, what can I do for you?"

His high-pitched voice didn't exactly go with his large

physique. Hart knew from experience that many of these museum guards were straight out of the armed forces, army usually, Hart visualised this one on a parade ground somewhere.

Stacey moved forward producing his ID from an inside pocket. "We're here to see Mr David James?" His voice tailed off almost as though it had been a question rather than a statement.

"Yes, sir, and you are?"

"Sorry, I'm DI Stacey and this is Inspector Hart."

"Is he expecting you, sir?" the guard asked glancing down at the ID.

"He is," Stacey replied quickly.

"Do you mind?" asked the guard pointing at the briefcase that stood on the floor.

Hart picked up the case and laid it carefully down on the desk and unfastened its buckles.

Pulling it towards him the guard opened the case and carefully inspected its contents. Occasionally he would remove a file or envelope holding each up to the light. His interest broadened as he lifted out the tightly bound bundle of crimson fabric.

"What's this?" He directed his question to a smiling Hart.

"That's one of the reasons we're here," he replied smoothly. "We're rather hoping that your Mr James will be able to tell us that."

Apparently satisfied with Hart's answer the guard replaced the bundle and refastened the leather straps. "Please take a seat," he said sliding the case forward. "I'll ring up and let him know you're here."

Hart smiled pleasantly as he took hold of the case and lifted it clear of the desk. He followed Stacey over to a row of wooden benches that were positioned against the far wall.

Hart sat and placed the case on his lap with both hands palm down on the top. Stacey deciding to stand contented himself to people watching, something he did often, "sort of came with the job," he would often say to his wife who thought it rude.

"Mr Stacey." It was almost a shouted whisper, something librarians seem able to do well. Stacey looked up as the guard waved them over.

"That's us," Stacey whispered slipping a leaflet on "What to do in London" into his inside pocket.

As they approached the desk they could see that the guard was holding something out in each hand.

"If you wouldn't mind putting these on, gentlemen," he said passing them both a visitor badge. "You can take the lift if you wish, it's the third floor." Then handing Stacey a slip of yellow card he added, "When you get up there turn to your left, keep on down the corridor marked staff only and present that to the guard at the end. He'll let you in."

"Thank you," Stacey said slipping the badge on.

Shortly both were standing by the lift watching its descent indicated on the dial above the door.

"Very hot on security, aren't they?" Stacey said as the lift doors slid open.

"It's as the cabby said, the IRA," Hart replied stepping into the lift. "Since they bombed the rail station up here a few months back all the public places have been put on alert." He pushed number three on the steel panel then watched as the doors closed. "They can't be too careful now, can they? Anyone with an Irish accent is bound to be treated with a certain amount of suspicion." He leant his back against the lift as it started its accent. Both men watched its progress displayed above the door as the arrow began to climb up the scale. As it approached level two both the arrow then the lift started to slow. The lift stopped with a firm jolt and the doors opened.

Hart straightened as a young woman dressed in a light blue two-piece suit entered the lift. Pressing number three she leant her shoulder against the padded side noticeably tightening her grip on the bundle of files under her arm. As the doors closed Hart could sense from her body language that she felt uncomfortable but was trying hard to hide it. Both men did their best not to stare at her but it was difficult.

Again the lift started to slow up signalling to the three of them its imminent arrival at level three. The doors opened, the girl was gone and only her perfume remained.

Stepping from the lift they did as instructed and followed the "staff only" signs. Occasionally they would hear the familiar clatter from a typewriter as they passed an office or a door slam somewhere far off, but mainly this large old building with its maze of intertwined corridors appeared empty of people.

"It can't be much further!" Stacey whispered.

Taking a left as the sign on the wall instructed this corridor led them onto a large landing with several doors and hallways leading off.

"This must be it," Stacey said pointing towards the guard that was sat at a small desk in the centre of the landing.

The uniformed figure stood as they approached, his arms down by his sides.

"Christ you wouldn't want to upset this one, would you?" Stacey said quietly.

As they got closer Hart realised what Stacey had meant. Apart from the sheer physical size of this man he was also armed. The holstered weapon strapped to his side was obviously evidence of how seriously people in London were taking the bomb risks.

"Can I help you?" he asked suspiciously, glancing down at Hart's briefcase.

"Yes, I'm Detective Inspector Stacey and this is Inspector Hart," Stacey replied passing the card to him. "We have an appointment to see Mr David James."

The guard scanned the card carefully before handing it back, then leant forward to read their visitor badges. Apparently satisfied that they were who they said they were he sat back down, lifted up the telephone and dialled two numbers.

Hart noted that this large man had not once taken his eyes from them.

"Hello, it's David." He paused. "I have with me two gentlemen from the police. They say they have an appointment with Mr James." His large hand grasped the telephone tightly his other hand was worryingly out of sight. "Okay, I'll send them through," he said replacing the telephone back onto its rest. "If you would like to follow me gentlemen I will show you to his office."

He stood up from the desk, dwarfing them both as he strode off.

Stacey was forced to quicken his step more than once in an effort to keep up with this large figure as he led them along one of the many corridors.

"He's through here," the guard said opening one of the doors to his left. "Sue, this is DI Stacey and

Inspector Hart," he said peering into the office. Then stepping to one side added, "Sue will look after you from here on."

As they entered both smiled at the figure sat behind the well organised oak desk, Sue, who had shared their lift earlier, stood and held out her hand to greet them.

"Hi, please come in and sit down," she said as Hart grasped her small but warm hand. "I'm David James' PA. He's on the telephone at the moment, I'm afraid, but he shouldn't be too long."

"Pleased to meet you, Sue," Hart said letting her hand slide from his.

"I'm DI Stacey," Stacey said holding out his hand. "And this is Inspector Hart," He added giving Hart a wry smile.

"Please take a seat. Would you like a coffee or something?" she asked politely. Her manor was polished and professional, not over friendly but undoubtedly efficient.

"No, we're fine thanks," Stacey replied sitting down next to Hart.

Sue's office was large, well laid out and as you would have expected on meeting her for the very first time, extremely tidy. The office must have been recently redecorated as the heady odour of new paint hung thickly in the air. On each of the pale cream walls were various framed drawings and prints depicting historical scenes; most appeared to be of ancient Rome. Several featured in intricate detail the impressive Colosseum including a cut away illustration showing the various floor levels within the building.

To the right of this drawing and cordoned off by a thick plaited rope strung from brass poles, stood a display containing two life-size figures. The nearest was dressed in full body armour with one hand clutching a spear, the other on the hilt of a short sword.

Hart, intrigued by the realism, stood.

"May I?" he asked.

"Please. Visitors are always impressed with Anton's display. He has incredible knowledge of that period, you know." The pride in her voice was obvious.

Hart squared up to the figure before him. The detailing was truly amazing, almost scary.

"You feel as though at any minute it could just step over that rope and walk off, don't you?" she laughed.

"I know what you mean," Hart replied. "Jesus he looks so life like. How accurate is it?"

"Well, according to Anton, very. The problem for Anton is that he has extremely strong views on the Roman period, he can be very insistent and that sort of behaviour hasn't always been met with open arms."

"What do you mean?" Stacey cut in.

"His opinions seem too knowledgeable for some people here to accept. Then there are the relics that he has unearthed. Most are in outstanding condition for their age. People don't like change, especially experts."

Hart stepped closer to the figure. Although smaller, he could visualise how effective he would have been in battle. Multiply this soldier by one thousand and you had a ruthlessly efficient fighting machine, almost unstoppable. Running his hand up the thin steel shaft of the spear Hart tried to imagine what it would have been like to come face to face with someone like this.

"It's a form of javelin. It's actually called a Pilum," Sue advised, "they were very clever, you know?" she continued. "Anton told me that it was designed like that so that when it was thrown and on the very rare occasion it missed its intended target it would often be bent on impact if it struck the ground or any hard object."

Hart frowned, as though missing the point.

"So it couldn't be thrown back, you see, very clever don't you think?" She smiled knowingly.

Hart returned her smile before turning back to the Roman soldier; the highly polished breast plate carefully sculptured to intimidate, the short crimson skirt protected by thick dried leather, powerful legs browned from years of exposure to the sun.

He turned to the second figure. Again like the first the detailing was impeccable and clearly both were a work of art.

"He's wearing the Toga Purpura. It indicates that he is an emperor, possibly Trajan according to Anton. The Toga Purpura, or Purple Toga, was only ever worn by an emperor," Sue said pushing her chair back. "It's all in here," she said passing Hart a small folded leaflet that she had taken from the plastic dispenser stood on her desk. "The colour of the toga indicated rank, you see. Purple for the emperor, a white toga with a broad band of purple would have been for senators, while people in public office would have had narrower bands. If I remember correctly they were called Toga Praetexta or something like that. Anyway, plain old white was for people like you and I, we were known as plebeians." She giggled.

Hart flicked through a few pages of the leaflet.

"I'll keep this if that's okay, it will give me something interesting to read on the journey back," he said slipping it into his side pocket.

Suddenly the door behind Stacey was flung open and David James' disembodied voice called out gruffly.

"Good afternoon, wonderful to meet you, please come in."

"I'm afraid that you'll have to excuse him today," Sue whispered. "I should have warned you earlier, he's had the raving hump all day ever since Anton announced to him this last-minute holiday that he has insisted on. He gave no warning, you see, and that's against the rules, just phoned in."

Hart smiled sympathetically as he followed Stacey into the office.

"Please take a seat. Would you like some tea or coffee?" the seated figure asked.

"That would be nice," Hart replied sliding his chair nearer to Stacey.

David James was forty-two, married and had three children. He had started working for the museum straight from having qualified at Cambridge University with top honours. Through dedication and pure hard work he had, to the surprise of many around him, been appointed the head of the museum after only two years.

Of medium build with close-cropped hair and horn-rimmed glasses David had a reputation amongst colleagues as someone who took great pride in his appearance, which pleased the Board.

He pushed the intercom button on his desk. "Sue, would you be good enough to bring us all some tea? Thank you."

"Mr James, this is Inspector Hart." Hart shook hands then sat. "And I'm DI Stacey."

"Nice to meet you both. Please, call me David."

"It's very good of you to agree to see us both so

promptly. I know that you're a very busy man," Stacey said sitting down.

"Please do forgive me. I'm not normally that rude," he replied gesturing towards the door. "I've just had a lot on my plate lately, what with the bomb risks and staffing, etc. Anyway don't mind me," he said with a wry smile. "I just hope that I can be of help to you?"

There was a single knock on the door followed by Sue carrying a tray.

"Would you like me to pour?" she said placing the tea down onto the desk.

"No, don't worry, Sue, we'll do it, thank you anyway." He turned his attention back to Stacey. "I understand from what Peter was telling me that you'd like an opinion on some evidence that you've come across, is that correct?"

"Yes, that's right." Stacey replied removing a small envelope from his inside pocket. "Firstly we would like you're opinion on these." He handed the envelope to David who promptly slit open the top using a silver paper knife and let the contents slide into his palm.

"These are Roman Denari," he announced. "Pure silver," he added looking directly at Stacey as if waiting for confirmation before swinging the large magnifying lens which was fixed to the corner of his desk over his palm. He switched it on and a light flickered momentarily from somewhere beneath the lens. "Yes," he said confidently, turning each coin over in his palm. "Definitely Denari, and all in pretty good condition, only a couple have been clipped."

"Can you tell us much about them?" Stacey said leaning forward.

"How much do you want to know?" he asked slipping

his glasses on.

"Everything. If you get too technical we'll stop you," replied Stacey.

Keeping hold of one coin David allowed the remainder to slide from his palm onto the desk, then gripping it between finger and thumb he held it under the bright light of the magnifier, this time though more closely, occasionally rubbing it against his sleeve.

"What we have here is a coin showing the bust of a man called Aelius Hadrianus, better known to most as Hadrian."

"As in the wall?" Stacey cut in.

"Exactly," David smiled. "Anyway, he was born in AD76, the son, or rather the adopted son, of the emperor Trajan. Hadrian became emperor of Rome himself around AD117." David peered over the top of his glasses then pushed them up his nose. "Unlike most emperors that ruled, he was considered a good leader by his people and died in AD138. Unfortunately this has been clipped rather heavily which would make the coin pretty worthless."

"What do you mean clipped David?"

"It was common practice back then to snip off small pieces around the edge of the coin to sell. The silver used to produce the coins, especially in the early days was very pure and therefore valuable. It goes without saying that it was also a pretty risky thing to do, if you were discovered it often meant the death penalty.

Placing the coin down onto the desk he picked up the second and again using the sleeve of his jacket gave the coin a clean before holding it under the bright lamp.

"Tiberius Claudius Nero. Tiberius to you and I. This is actually a much older coin. Born in 42BC he was the stepson of Emperor Augustus who had died in AD14 leaving Tiberius to rule, which he did successfully until his death in AD37. He was 78 – which was not a bad age to reach considering."

Picking up the third he paused while Hart made notes.

"Incidentally, just for the record, the crucifixion of Christ occurred during his reign as emperor. This third one though is very rare, very rare indeed," he announced holding it closer to the lens. "It has virtually no clipping at all and would be extremely valuable if like the others it hadn't got this damned hole drilled through it." He looked up. "May I ask how you've come by these? They're in remarkable condition."

Stacey turned to Hart for a moment. The subtle nod from Hart went un-noticed by David but signalled to Stacey that it was time to come clean. David sat motionless as he listened to Stacey's calm and methodical explanation of how and where the coins were found. This was a side to life that was far beyond David's comprehension and one that certainly held no appeal for him.

"Why is that particular coin so valuable?" Hart asked, certain that David needed a distraction.

David faltered for a moment then picked up the bright coin and held it under the lens again.

"It's very rare, in fact I've only ever seen one before and that was one that Anton owned. The bust shown is that of a rather unpleasant chap called Caraculla. He was given the title of Caesar at the same time as his younger brother Geta. They ruled Rome jointly. Unfortunately for poor Geta his brother refused to accept this arrangement and in February AD212

Caracalla murdered him, then just to make sure that none of Geta's acquaintances would ever become a problem to him in the future he put them to death too, all twenty thousand of them."

David sat quietly for a few moments to allow Hart time to make more notes in the black book that he had cradled in his lap.

"This Caracalla wasn't a very nice chap, by all accounts," Hart said looking up.

"There were very few emperors that ruled Rome that were, as you put it, nice," David replied. "Most murdered and got murdered, a very advanced civilisation for its time, and incidentally if you want my opinion all three of these coins have been worn on a chain around the neck at some stage hence the hole."

Hart lifted the briefcase up from the floor and sat it on his lap then slid the straps from their buckles.

"Would you mind taking a look at these photographs for us? I'm afraid they're not very pleasant."

Hart handed David several five-by-four black and white prints from a brown envelope.

"Good grief, I see what you mean."

"They were taken at the mortuary. You will see that I've marked in the top left hand corner on the reverse of each print who is who."

"As you can see, each of the victims had suffered a severe wound to the throat. We're told by Peter that, in his opinion, this was almost certainly done with a single slash rather than a hacking action."

For the moment Hart had decided not to mention to David their crucifixion or indeed any other injuries that they had received.

"What we'd like to know David is, that in your

opinion could the wounds have been inflicted with a knife or maybe a sword?"

"Definitely not a knife, no weight to it. My guess would be a sword, a sword could easily do this," he blurted unable to take his eyes from the photographs.

"I'm still of the opinion that a sword is the wrong weapon," Stacey said shaking his head. "After all it would be almost impossible to conceal, just too risky for the killer."

"If you would both give me a second I'll go and fetch something that I'm sure will change your opinion on that subject."

With a broadening grin David slid his chair back and left the room, shortly he returned carrying a highly polished wooden case, which he put down gently on the desk. He sat back down and slid his chair forward.

"This, gentlemen, is a Gladius."

He undid the two brass catches and lifted the lid back and slowly withdrew the weapon.

"It is widely thought that the Gladius was first developed and used by gladiators. Its potential as a military weapon soon became obvious and was quickly adopted by the Roman army."

David offered the short sword across the desk to Stacey. "Take care, it's extremely sharp," he advised.

"I don't know about sharp but its bloody heavy," Stacey said surprised by its weight, he turned it over in his hand. "How old is it?"

"Almost two thousand years," David answered proudly puffing out his chest.

"How the hell can it be in such good condition?" Stacey was baffled.

"Almost mint," David replied quickly. "It was found

by Anton while on a dig in Spain a year or so ago. Fortunately for us we believe that its former owner had been extremely careful in the way he had stored it. That combined with the warm climate of Spain has helped to keep it in such remarkable condition." David was almost ecstatic.

"Can you imagine how much damage you could cause with this, especially if it was in the right hands?" Stacey was thinking of the display in Sue's office as he passed the heavy weapon across to Hart.

Grasping the hilt, he noted immediately that it fit his hand perfectly and made several short slashing movements through the air with it.

"Its main function actually as a weapon was that of a stabbing sword. Being short it was easily carried and very effective in close combat."

David held out both hands signalling an end to Hart's role playing.

"You may recall from history lessons at school how the Roman army fought, often in rows and all the time surging forward, their large square shields held out, they were very effective and highly trained. Once they made contact at close quarters the longer more conventional swords used by most of their enemies became almost useless. The Gladius would be thrust out from behind the shield, stabbing and slashing as they advanced." David closed the lid down on the box and run his hand lovingly over the smooth grain.

"Would something like that be easy to get hold of?" Stacey asked.

"Good grief, no. Very, very rare. They do come up for auction occasionally but always command high values and never in this condition." He tapped the lid of the box confidently. "We have been very fortunate since Anton joined us. He has remarkable knowledge of the period and the most amazing contacts. Our stock of Roman antiquities has more than doubled since his appointment and almost everything in mint condition."

"Almost the perfect weapon, wouldn't you say?" Hart jibed, looking at Stacey for some reaction.

"Yes and easily capable of inflicting these injuries." David slid the photographs back across the desk towards Hart, "and as you have now seen, quite small enough to conceal." David sat back, his hands clasped tightly behind his head.

"So Hart, we may have our murder weapon. All we have to do now is find the bloody killer."

Hart leant forward and removed a second envelope from the case along with William James's crimson toga, which he placed on David's desk. Then, pushing a finger into the flap he slit open the envelope and withdrew three more five-by-fours which he laid face down on the desk.

"Would you take a look at these and let us know what you think?" he said pushing them forward.

David's face remained expressionless as he turned each of the prints over. What little colour he had regained over the last few minutes had now drained completely away as he stared at the shocking images before him.

"My God, how can anyone do this, what sort of killer are you dealing with here?" He said taking in a deep breath, "those poor bastards, can you imagine the suffering they would have gone through before they died?" he continued as his mind raced wildly.

"As you can see from the photographs, each victim

had been crucified. They had also had their wrists slashed." Hart paused for a moment, unsure if he should disclose what had up until now been a closely guarded secret.

"There is something else," Stacey said prompting Hart.

"The killer had removed the Adam's Apple from each of them," Hart added coldly.

The room fell silent as both detectives waited for some reaction. David let his head drop back on the chair. His breathing had become noticeably heavier as he stared up at the high ceiling. It was several agonising moments before he spoke but when he did he was back as the Historian.

"I must say that, historically speaking, this is incorrect." He stated tapping his well manicured finger on the nearest photograph.

"What do you mean?"

"Well," he said, "contrary to popular belief, the victim of a crucifixion was never nailed through the hands. They were almost always nailed through the wrist. A piece of wood, about two inches square and perhaps half-inch thick was used. They would pass the nail through this first and then drive the nail on through the wrist and into the timber. The wood block acted as a type of washer, you see, to stop the victim from pulling their wrist off the nail."

It was Stacey's turn to loose some blood, even Hart had noticed Stacey's lack of colour now.

"And the victim actually suffocated, you know," he added confidently.

"What do you mean? Surely they would bleed to death or something?" Hart was genuinely surprised at this revelation.

"You see, if you think about it, there you are on your back, arms outstretched. You have a nail through each wrist and your feet are nailed together. They now hoist you with the aid of ropes into an upright position; the base of the cross drops neatly into a hole, which is now filled. The ropes are removed and you are now some twelve feet up, maybe more. The pain is intolerable, firstly you try desperately to pull your arms off the nails that hold you, but you can't; it's those little wooden washers, you see. You now, in an effort to reduce the pain that you're experiencing in your wrists, transfer your body weight to your feet by standing. But remember, your feet, too, are nailed to the cross. You can only take this pain for so long then you go back to hanging by your wrists. The muscles across your chest begin to tighten you stand again to relieve the pain in your wrists and now also from the tightening chest muscles. This goes on hour after hour day after day perhaps. Eventually your chest muscles go into spasm, contracting and stopping the lungs from inflating. Together with the pain and the cold you have no chance; a very slow death."

Both detectives sat motionless as David's history lesson sunk home. Suddenly, without warning the telephone on David's desk clattered.

"Sorry about that." David chuckled. "Would you excuse me for a moment?" he said lifting the phone. "Oh yes ... thank you, thanks for reminding me ... I had forgotten." David replaced the receiver back onto its cradle.

"I'm sorry, gentlemen, I don't wish to appear rude but that was Sue, I had clean forgotten that I have an appointment with the curator from the science museum this afternoon."

"No, please, David, we quite understand we've taken up more than enough of your valuable time. But before we go, just quickly there are a couple of other things we'd like your thoughts on," Hart said placing his hands palm down on the desk.

"Fire away," David enthused.

"Well, firstly there's this." He said pushing the toga forwards. "That was found by the deceased girlfriend in the boot of his car. We're pretty confident that it was his."

"It's a toga," David said confidently unfolding the garment.

"Unfortunately there's no label inside it. We had hoped that it might give us a clue as to who manufactured it," Stacey said sadly.

David held it up to the light then swung the large lens around.

"Oh, I'm pretty sure that I can tell you who manufactured this," he said confidently pulling gently at the fabric and inspecting the weave.

Stacey turned to Hart. "Are they local?" he asked hopefully.

"Not unless you're able to go back in time. This is a remarkable find. If I'm right, and I think I am, this is almost certainly the real thing."

"But it's almost new," Hart said, baffled by David's statement.

"Like the sword this robe has been stored carefully under controlled conditions, otherwise it could never have lasted this long. Don't quote me on it, but I would say that this is probably getting on for some fifteen hundred years old or so." David fondled the material almost lovingly, occasionally holding it to his nose. "Do you mind if I keep it?" he asked. "I'll run some tests on it. That way I'll be able to date it exactly."

"Sure, I don't see why not, but whatever you do don't lose it," Stacey joked.

"Lastly there's this!" Hart said soberly. Removing a slip of paper from his case he handed it over. David's eyes visibly widened as he stared at the large characters that Hart had written down: XXIV/XLI

"All three of the victims had that scrawled above their heads," he said, hopeful that David's vast knowledge would supply an answer.

"What possible significance could that number have to the killer?" Stacey added.

"My God, this is truly unbelievable." David removed his spectacles and sat forward.

"VIRGINTI QUATTUOR, QUADRAGINTA UNUS." His Latin was near perfect. "It is a number," he said confidently. "2441 to be exact and given the circumstances it would be my considered opinion that its reference -." He stopped mid sentence and slipped his glasses back on. "You see, until Julius Caesar had come to power, Rome had been a republic. Power was the responsibility of the senate; the senate was a council made up of all the leading citizens who were either chosen by rank or birth. Unfortunately this delicate balance between the power of the people and the power of the senate led to some serious problems, then in 49BC Caesar became dictator; he became Rome's absolute ruler. As you may remember from your history lessons at school he was eventually assassinated by a couple of fellows called Brutus and Cassius in 44BC."

Hart marvelled at David's seemingly boundless knowledge.

"It's generally accepted by historians today that once he'd been assassinated his adoptive son Octavian had come to some arrangement with the senate, which gave him supreme power. He was then renamed Augustus and ruled the Roman Empire for almost forty-five years." David noted both Stacey and Hart's blank expressions. "I hope I'm not boring you both?"

"No, not at all, David, please continue."

"I'm sure that things will make more sense in a moment," he assured. "After Augustus there was a succession of different rulers. One in particular was a rather unpleasant chap called Caligula. He was a real head case and had a severe problem mentally. He was renowned for his orgies and love of the gladiatorial games. An example of this man's insanity was demonstrated when he appointed his closest friend, Incitatus as consul. This made Incitatus one of the most powerful rulers in the Roman Empire. The only problem with this appointment was that Incitatus was, in fact, his favourite horse.

"Emperors were always protected from the public by their own private army; these were known as Praetorian Guards. They were highly trusted and often highly paid. Caligula, who was disliked by his people and it has to be said by most of his army, was eventually assassinated by a group of his most trusted Praetorians, Casius Chaera and Cornelius Sabinus, both officers, together with their commander, a man named Arrecinus Clements and a palace official. They were all believed to have had connections with a secret society known as MITHRAS."

Hart turned to Stacey but remained silent.

"Within this society they had formed a small group that had plotted the murder."

Stacey appeared agitated, which David noticed.

"I'm sorry if you think I'm rambling on a bit but if you just bare with me for a moment," he said apologetically. "You see, what is most interesting is that Caligula was killed on the 24th of January 41 AD." David paused. "They slit his throat and in one final act of humiliation to him they stabbed him repeatedly in the genitals. It's well documented that after the assassination the group gained an almost cult like following and soon became known within the MITHRAS society as the VIRGINTI QUATTUOR, QUADRAGINTA UNUS, or put more simply twenty four forty one." David pushed his back into the chair and chewed on the end of his glasses.

For several minutes all three sat in silence. The only sound was from the clatter of Sue's typewriter outside.

"We know from the writers of that period that the society went to ground after the killing. We also know that they had been responsible for the murder and removal of many of the unwanted emperors and officials.

"Are you saying that this Mithras society or group could still be in existence today?" Stacey questioned.

"It certainly seems a possibility, don't you think? I mean look at the Masons, they're still around."

"What about the coins, where do they figure in all this?" Hart asked.

"Do you think they may have been worn by members of the Mithras?" Stacey added.

"That, I can't say." David shrugged. "There's certainly no record to my knowledge which suggests that, but that's not to say it wasn't done. It's possible, I suppose, that they wore them secretly, perhaps as a means of identifying each other."

David pushed his chair back away from his desk.

"Look gentlemen, I really don't want to appear rude," He said pulling his sleeve back. "But time is getting on and my colleague isn't best known for his patience, I'm afraid."

"Yes, I'm sorry we've taken up more than enough of your time, David." Hart said returning the photographs to their envelopes. "You've been of great help to us. Obviously it goes without saying that what we've discussed here today is highly confidential."

"Of course, yes, please don't worry, it will not go beyond this room, I promise." David removed his glasses and lay them down on the desk then, held out his hand. "I'll get back to you as soon as I have an answer on the toga."

"Great, if you would." Hart stood up and placed his chair against the wall.

"It's been good to meet you both. Makes me realise now how boring my line of work must seem, compared to yours I mean."

Hart smiled politely without actually answering him.

"I'm pleased that it was you that we got to see," Stacey said grasping David's outstretched hand. "Not that I've ever met your assistant Anton, I'm sure that he would have been more than capable," He added quickly.

"Yes, Anton. I'm not best pleased with him at the moment. Dropped me right in it to be honest, taking off on holiday like that. Anyway, that's for me to sort out."

"I guess so." Stacey smiled.

"We can see ourselves out, David, and we'll await

your call."

"Give me a couple of days, that's all."

Hart closed the door quietly behind him as they left.

"You'll need that yellow slip that you have," Susan reminded. "Otherwise you'll be questioned all the way to the main entrance," she added with a knowing smile.

Both men thanked her then left. They made their way out of the building without being stopped and were soon outside in the cold air. Happily they didn't have to wait long for a cab and twenty minutes later were standing on platform 5 at Euston station waiting for their ride back to Wolverton.

CHAPTER TWELVE

Mrs Patricia Spencer – Pat to her few friends – switched off the television and reflected on her favourite programme, Charlie's Angels. How she admired that female threesome. Tonight's story had been even better than last weeks she thought as she took a long swig from the pre-mixed gin and tonic, winced as it hit the spot and lit a king size cigarette.

Inhaling the smoke deep into her chest she held it there for as long as she possibly could before snorting it out through her nose in a series of controlled bursts. Taking a second shot of her G and T she replaced the lid and slipped the small aluminium flask back into her unconvincing copy of a Gucci handbag and set the alarm. The loud regular bleeping from the internal horn screwed high up on the hall wall allowed her just enough time to gather up her few possessions, pop an Extra Strong Mint into her mouth and exit before the alarm became active.

Just two short steps from the safety of the front door activated the security lamps. She was glad of their powerful light as she made her way carefully up the gravel path towards her silver Triumph.

Having fumbled for several frustrating moments in her handbag she eventually located her keys and, taking a long pull on the cigarette that hung from her bottom lip, she slipped the key into the lock and with a flick of her wrist unlocked the door. She paused for a moment to take one last look over her shoulder, then satisfied that all was well she removed the cigarette from her mouth, cursing loudly as the filter pulled skin from her lip.

Running her moist tongue across drying lips she flicked the glowing cigarette angrily into the cold night sky, only a thin trail of hot ash arching skywards giving any evidence of its direction.

Having slid into the driver's seat she tilted the interior mirror towards her, the dim yellow glow of the interior lamp giving just enough light for more rouge and a second coat of lipstick.

Satisfied with the result, she put the key into the ignition and closed the door. She checked that the gear selector was pushed firmly forward and turned the key while pumping at the accelerator. The car started on the third attempt. She pulled out from the "staff only" car space and headed towards the market town of Olney and her next job.

Married with three kids, life had been hard for her. She had done her best, particularly with the children, but now as teenagers they had become unruly and, although she refused to admit it publicly, a disappointment.

Her relationship with husband Richard was strange to say the least. Professor Richard Spencer had distanced himself from her years ago with endless hours spent tutoring medical students at the local university. She, left to her own devices, had discovered another world; an exciting world that frequently allowed her to indulge in casual affairs. Most ended quickly, her extravert behaviour more than many were prepared to put up with.

Her day job could be tedious and often entailed long

hours sitting alone behind a reception desk with only a book for company. Working for a Hotel group though could sometimes be fun and she certainly had met some strange people over the years.

Pat pushed the heater button on the dash and fumbled in the door pocket for a tape. Switching on the player she slid the tape in and turned the volume up, tapping happily on the fur-covered steering wheel to her favourite Rolling Stones number.

She detested spending time at home; it was boring. There was more to life than just cooking and cleaning. Mostly she would make excuses to Richard and visit neighbours or friends, often staying out until the early hours.

Now, though, things were different. That was all behind her. By chance, almost one year ago to the very day, she had met someone while working her shift. They had got on well together and he had arranged to meet with her in the bar that evening. But for whatever reason, whether it was guilt perhaps or simply cold feet, he had stood her up. Feeling dejected and alone she had started drinking, it wasn't long before she had been joined by a hotel guest who had mistaken her for an escort. With the alcohol now taking effect she was capable of anything. Accepting his generous proposition, she soon found herself back in his room and quickly discovered that this new career satisfied both her lust for sex and for money.

Now, and many clients later, she was an old hand at the game. She would mostly meet them once her shift had finished, although she had, on rare occasions been known to disappear for half an hour or so which often puzzled her colleagues. Working in the hotel made it easy, as a receptionist she could come and go whenever she pleased. She knew which rooms were occupied and which were not.

Tonight's client, though, was different. Pat smiled to herself. Her heart thumped heavily in her chest at the thought. She was so excited, so eager, almost wet.

She had been hired to entertain a small but very select group of young men. This appealed to her. Often her services were required to entertain men of her own age, which she openly enjoyed. Much older than that wasn't so pleasant but it went with the job. This, though, this was much better, with young inexperienced men. She liked them best, early twenties, so easy to dominate, and they were very often grateful of the experience.

This introduction, although unusual, had come from a trusted regular. The fee that he had offered her she certainly could not refuse. Yes, this was definitely going to be a night to remember.

CHAPTER THIRTEEN

Reginald Arthur Pinnock, a name he wouldn't have chosen himself, stood impatiently in the doorway to his office. Now almost forty-two, overweight and certainly unfit, watched the hunched figure before him with a hatred so strong he could almost taste it.

"For Christ's sake, Stan, please, get a move on!" He yelled looking down at his wristwatch for the fourth time in the past ten minutes.

Back home Reg had a wife and two kids, both of which had been a handful to bring up. His wife Julia, not unattractive, had lost interest in him some years ago so home life was sometimes difficult. He liked a drink, which had put a strain on their relationship. Although so far away from them now he didn't really miss them, which was just as well at the moment.

"We can't afford to be late again," Reg pleaded.

His so-called business partner peered over gold-framed glasses as he shuffled towards him, a grey sack slung over one shoulder, his oversized shoes dragging on the concrete floor. He let the sack drop heavily onto the weighing platform of the large grey painted industrial scales.

"Twenty Pounds," he grunted, then burped loudly from somewhere deep within his stomach.

Reg winced at the stench. Even at this distance he could smell the heady mixture of stale smoke and onion.

"They'll just have to bloody well wait, won't they!" He burped more loudly this time; almost a bark.

Reg disliked the rudeness of this man, his arrogance. In fact he hated him. He turned and walked back to his desk.

To this day he could never understand why they had let this person join him here. Sure, he worked hard, they both did, but he had never realised at the time how much he would get to him.

In the past and before Stan, Reg had enjoyed being out in this new and exciting world of business but not now. He sat watching through the doorway as Stan did the other thing that he hated: smoking – a popular habit here and one thankfully he hadn't given in to.

With each pull on the cigarette his face would contort, his lips drawn back tight over clenched and heavily stained teeth, then he would snort thick blue smoke down through his nose.

Reg closed his eyes in an effort to expel the scene from his mind, a sort of cleansing. When he opened them again Stan's stunted figure was standing in the doorway feeding on a stale cheese roll like a starved ape, most of which was dropping to the floor.

"Ready?" he grunted, spitting bread.

Reg closed his eyes again. This wasn't speech, he thought.

"Yes, I'm ready." He stood slowly, fighting back the almost overwhelming urge to put his hands around that leathery neck and squeeze very tightly.

"We'll be late if we don't get a move on," the hunched figure mumbled as he walked off.

Taking his jacket from the back of the chair, Reg switched the lights off and closed the door to his office. He waited patiently while Stan armed the alarm then opened the front door and stepped outside.

"You drive," Stan ordered rudely as he shuffled towards the light grey Jaguar parked twenty feet away. "I can't get on with this knacking car."

Reg followed some several steps behind, watching the hunched figure with distaste as he dragged his feet lazily across the concrete path.

"For fuck's sake, Reg, we're knacking late, get a move on," he grunted. "It's almost nine."

The powerful Jag started as always first time. Reg moved the shifter to drive and floored the accelerator. The car shot forward, and soon both men were heading along the Sherington road towards Olney, and as usual when they were together in total silence.

CHAPTER FOURTEEN

It was unusual, meetings normally took place on the last Friday of the month and had done for almost two years now. Today, though, was Saturday. The large four by four slowed then came to a halt in the centre of the road. Fat, stumpy fingers tapped impatiently on the smooth, highly polished walnut steering wheel waiting for a gap.

After several vehicles had passed the driver pulled the selector lever into drive and stabbed the accelerator down sending the heavy car surging forward, tyres scrabbling for grip as it rumbled over the cattle grid and on through the gateway watched by a pair of stone lions.

It resumed a more sedate pace, travelling along a single-track lane with heavily ploughed fields to each side. Halfway up the gentle climb towards the woods a lay-by allowed passage of oncoming traffic, but not this evening.

Skirting closely to the edge of the woods, the car swooped down past a large barn, the lane twisting left and right before climbing once again. With headlights switched to main beam the driver gunned the car forward sending wildlife for cover.

Now almost three quarters of a mile from the main road the car slowed. The driver quickly checked the rearview mirror before swinging left at the fork in the road.

Hidden amongst the trees a small wooden sign was picked out by the cars powerful headlights: MITHRAS

HOUSE.

"Solute Vila Bela," the driver whispered excitedly to himself as he brought the car almost to a halt opposite the sign. He could visualise the house now, especially the inside and what was planned for tonight. He smiled quietly to himself. He increased his speed slightly. In the distance he could just make out the familiar shape buried deep in the woods. His grin broadened as the headlights picked out the large whitewashed building ahead.

MITHRAS HOUSE hadn't always been considered beautiful. In fact, up until a few years ago, most locals did what they could to avoid it. To many, its ruins were a danger and a menace, to a few they were haunted and best left alone. The building – or what was left of it – was believed to be almost three hundred years old and had once been a rectory. Rumour had it that several people had perished in a mysterious fire which had engulfed it. Now, though, having been completely renovated to the highest of standards by a local builder it was, as stated on the deeds in bold type, the headquarters to a large private company. There had been no expense spared and no shortcuts taken to ensure that the completion was on time. Cost had never been an issue.

As he approached, Galba switched the headlights off, now relying on tiny sidelights and memory alone. Turning right then left he swung the car around and brought it to an abrupt halt, before reversing silently backwards. Only the faint hissing from its power steering pump could be heard within the Connelly and Wilton interior.

Its occupant, with unimaginable effort, pulled

himself out from the car and stood for several seconds to regain his breath then, opening the cavernous boot, took a large sports bag out before slamming it shut.

Galba's large frame rocked steadily from side to side like some monstrous pendulum as he made his way towards the house, his breathless panting sending vast clouds of vapour up into the cold night air. Six feet from the house a shaft of yellow light cut through the darkness as a door was opened.

"Good evening, Galba," a voice whispered respectfully.

Squeezing through the doorway and still panting loudly Galba could only manage a courteous nod to the crimson-robed figure. The door closed behind him, its large iron hinges creaking under the weight of solid oak.

A simple wooden bench placed against the wall groaned as it took the full weight of this large and overfed man. Head hung forward he tried to gain control of his breathing. He swallowed repeatedly to moisten his drying throat then looked up.

"Are we all here, Titus?" He sucked in more air.

"We wait for only four more, Galba." The reply was instant and humble.

"Who?" Galba barked looking down at his wristwatch. "It's almost nine," he added, his face reddening with anger.

"We are still waiting for Nero, Vespasian, Caraculla and, as always, Marcus."

The large man threw his head back and drew a long but measured breath before speaking. "Unfortunately for our colleague Caraculla, he will not be joining us this evening or sadly any other evening." Galba struggled to his feet, the collar of his shirt noticeably damp with perspiration. "And the whites?" he added pulling the collar away from the folds of flesh around his neck.

"All assembled, Galba, just as you requested."

"Good, would you please arrange for the others to be ready while I get changed? We can't afford to wait any longer – this is far too important," he ordered.

Titus, with noticeable relief, waited until Galba had gone through to his room and slammed the door shut before following. He had almost reached the far end when there was a succession of rapid knocks. Recognising it immediately as the entry signal Titus smiled and hurried back. The knocking was repeated, this time louder, more urgent.

"Okay, okay," he called out. "I can hear you, have patience."

Sliding back the heavy steel bolts he pulled hard on the large round handle.

"You're late," he growled as the door swung open. "Galba is already here and is extremely displeased." His jaw dropped as he added disappointedly. "Is Marcus not with you?"

"I'm afraid not." Vespasian replied quickly.

As they entered, the smaller of the two belched loudly, the stench of stale smoke and onion forcing Titus to step back and hold his breath. Like many, Titus also disliked this small arrogant man. He closed the door behind them and slid the bolts home.

"It's good to see you again, Vespasian, my old friend."

"And you, Titus." Reginald Pinnock gripped Titus's outstretched hand warmly.

They were old friends and had been for most of their lives. Both had been brought up as children in the same small town. They had schooled together and had shared many good times. Eventually Titus had gone into the army but not before seeing his youngest sister Julia marry his close friend Vespasian.

"Come, you must hurry, the other four are already waiting," he urged. "I feel sorry for Marcus, he will have much to explain." Titus led the two men quickly along the narrow hallway. "Here, on your right," he instructed opening the door. "I will come back for you shortly, don't be long," he pleaded placing his palms together as though in prayer.

Closing the door behind them Titus crossed the hallway and entered what was referred to by all as the Great Hall. Although too small to really have been considered a hall, this large room never failed to impress with its high, vaulted ceiling lit brightly by the yellow-white light from twenty large ornate oil bowls, their strong heavy vapour scenting the air. The floor was of the finest white Italian marble. In its very centre, carved skilfully into the hard surface, were the words Senatus Populus Que Romanus. (The Senate and the People of Rome.) The walls were decorated in richly painted and highly ornate frescos. Each scene depicted lavish wealth and most appeared to be of ancient Rome and its Colosseum.

Along three of the walls, the floor, which rose in a series of steps, gave a small if not hard seating area for the fifteen or so men that sat around the room. A few sat quietly on their own while others whispered in small groups. Most wore a simple white toga. A few, though, were dressed in dark crimson and all had sandals on their bare feet.

Titus clapped both hands together loudly as he entered and gently touched the tip of his finger to pursed lips. The hall quietened, almost as if one as each member focused on this small but intimidating figure. He was well respected amongst these men and he knew it. Once satisfied he turned and exited through a small doorway to his right.

The hall remained silent as they waited only the occasional nervous cough broke the uneasy silence, as everyone's attention was now fixed firmly on the doorway in the far corner. A few moments later Titus reappeared ahead of six men, each dressed in identical crimson togas. As the group entered Titus smiled to himself. He enjoyed these meetings, the role playing and the secrecy, and best of all he liked being amongst his own.

Stepping to one side he waited with chin on chest until all six had been seated, then left again, this time though through a large panel skilfully concealed in the far wall which slid silently open.

Someone sitting at the back tapped a leather sandal annoyingly on the hard floor. Occasionally someone would cough, the strong and pungent odour of hot scented oil drying throats. This together with the incredible heat given off by the numerous lamps placed around the room gave everyone a thirst that was longing to be quenched.

Immediately Titus entered everyone stood. Behind him the large and unmistakable figure of Galba shuffled forwards then, as the small pale figure appeared in the doorway, there were several gasps. No one had expected this. Why hadn't they been told? Many were left open mouthed as the small arrogant figure dressed in purple silk strutted past with head held high. For most this was the first time that they had actually seen him, rumours of his albinism now proved true. With heads bowed low they strained to take in every detail. Galba, with obvious difficulty, climbed unaided up onto the marble step his face reddened with effort. He allowed himself a faint smile almost undetectable to those around him as he waited for his emperor to be seated.

Then raising his arm in the air with his hand clutching a small gold staff he waited until everyone had sat. This was a proud moment for Galba and he intended to make the most of it.

"Good evening, gentlemen, and welcome to this hastily convened Forum. It's good of you all to join us, I know that many of you have travelled far to be here tonight." His smile broadened.

This rare attempt by Galba at humour was rewarded with much laughter and applause.

"We are truly honoured, nay, may I say privileged this evening with the presence of our beloved leader, Emperor Caligula, who has agreed to join us and I hope take part in our festivities later."

Almost instantly the hall erupted with nervous applause. Galba raised the short staff again, patting the air slowly with the palm of his hand.

"Please, please," he pleaded. "Before this evening begins I have news for you – extremely important news – and I must insist on your undivided attention." His large head moved slowly from left to right as he observed his concerned audience.

"We have been forced to call this unscheduled meeting of our senate for a number of important reasons. You will all by now, I know, be aware of the demise of our colleague Caraculla. He is the third member of Mithras to have been murdered." His voice tailed off as he paused for a moment to get his breath. "Caraculla had been a member for only a short time – two years, I believe. In that time he had proved himself worthy of living in the outside world and coped with it well. He will be missed by us all, I know. However, we are concerned now that all three of these killings are connected in some way with our project. If that is so, then none of us are safe – we are all at risk." He swept his arm in a great arc through the air.

This news from Galba was not welcomed by his audience and several in the room had stood in protest.

"Please sit back down, I have much to say. You will each get a chance to speak, I swear." Panting heavily now, he waited for a moment before continuing. "In view of this I urge you all to be on your guard. Trust no one unless you are absolutely sure. As you are aware, all three were slaughtered while in their homes, somewhere that you would so rightly expect to be safe." He hesitated, "I believe the risk to be so great to each and every one of us sat here that I have respectfully advised that our beloved emperor Caligula also come in." He paused then added triumphantly, "I am happy to report that he has agreed."

"Long live Caligula." a voice shouted anxiously. Sensing what might happen Galba quickly raised both hands high into the air in an effort to suppress any desire for further chanting.

"Please, please." He shouted, "As you well know, always it has been our custom to only ever allow twelve members within the inner sanctum at any one time, twelve that have been carefully chosen and trained to live beyond these walls. Those twelve have all earned the privilege and the honour to wear the crimson toga and to continue the important work of 2441." He wiped the perspiration from his brow on a fat hairless forearm. "Now with three of our inner sanctum members murdered their places must be filled."

Almost immediately this most obvious revelation caused much excitement. To be selected was a high honour, one that all members longed for but few ever achieved.

"But not yet," Galba announced boldly. "Not, that is, until we have found our Judas." His voice had risen in pitch matching this sudden mood swing that few in the room had seen before.

"Judas." Cassius erupted angrily, "What Judas?" he shrilled ignoring his colleagues' pleas to sit down. "What do you mean, Galba, our bloody Judas?" The last two words from him seemed to hang momentarily in the heavily scented air.

"We have it on excellent authority that once again the police are investigating us. They know of our society but as yet they don't know of our location. We must make sure that they never find out." Although still out of breath, Galba tried to speak more calmly, aware now of the rhythmic thumping going on somewhere deep within his chest and deliberately ignored Cassius' rantings. "Our colleague Caraculla was found in his home, murdered. Slain, we now know, by the very same hand that was responsible for the deaths of Hadrian and Tiberius." Galba turned to Caligula as though waiting for permission to continue. "We believe that the traitor is amongst us." Galba scrutinized closely the bemused expressions sat before him. "Not just amongst us." He added bitterly, "But almost certainly he is a member of the inner sanctum." He held his audience captive with this latest revelation. "How else would the killer know of our membership, or where to find our people? This traitor is sat amongst us as I speak, I guarantee it."

"Unless, Galba, one of the whites has dared to venture out," Caligula suggested, turning to the now passive audience.

"It is possible, my Caesar, of course, but I doubt it. Unlike you they are not gifted in living beyond these walls none are trained. They would be discovered immediately, I'm sure." He turned his attention to Titus and added, "We have debated this long and hard, I'm afraid that it has to be one of us nine sat here. Do you agree, Titus?"

"I do."

"But why, it just doesn't make any sense? What could anyone here achieve by killing our own people?" someone from the back shouted.

"Six million might be reason enough."

This seemingly absurd suggestion from Titus prompted an angry response from several members as they demanded an explanation from him.

"Are you so blind that you cannot see?" Titus stood up. "Six million split five ways or even ten is better than splitting it by twenty or more."

"No, no I don't believe that it is the money alone that is the motive," Galba interrupted confidently. "It is something else, don't you see? I believe the killer enjoys this. It is for this reason, and this reason alone that it makes him particularly dangerous."

"Whatever the motive and whatever his reasons one thing is for certain, we must all remain vigilant and be on our guard as Galba has said." Caligula stood, pulling his toga around him tightly before adding, "It's more than possible that someone amongst us is indeed the killer. Only a few of you know each other well, and well enough to feel safe, most of us have come from different backgrounds and different places. We cannot afford to lose any more of our number. Rest assured that we are doing our very best to expose him before he can strike again. My advice would be, for the moment at least. Trust no one not even your closest friend until he is discovered." Only the very observant sat within those stone walls that evening would have noticed Caligula's obvious amusement at this last statement from him.

"First, let us see an end to our project." Galba said, "We have but a few days left and all will be finished, then my killer friend, whoever you are, beware." he warned, "Until then, I really can't emphasise it enough, we must all be very careful, especially when home. As for the police finding us, I am not greatly concerned. As most will know we are fortunate that Cassius here is well placed to keep us informed of their progress. If our location was ever discovered I feel confident that we would have plenty of time to depart."

"Have we recovered Geta's toga?" Caligula asked firmly.

Galba's face reddened again as he turned to his emperor. "I am embarrassed, Caligula, we have not, not yet anyway, but we will." He swung around, hands resting on oversized hips.

"I will get it personally, Galba," Titus said quickly.

Galba gave a measured smile that spoke volumes with his displeasure. He struggled desperately to conceal the rage forging through him. To forget to recover something so important was inexcusable, and worse, to find this out now, in front of Caligula. He tried to calm himself by taking long deep breaths. A distraction was necessary.

"Gentlemen, please, may I again have your attention." he shouted, clapping sweating palms together loudly. "On a much happier note, as you all know, our newly formed business venture is doing rather well – very well, in fact."

The concern for the toga had now vanished from Galba's face and he smiled confidently. He enjoyed giving out news, especially good news.

"If all goes according to plan, and I have no reason to think otherwise, we shall collect tomorrow." It had become necessary now for Galba to raise his voice in an effort to be heard above the clapping and cheering. "I visited the factory personally on Thursday along with both Titus here and Cassius. Our two young men have excelled themselves. They really were a good choice and have worked hard. They have informed me that by the end of today they will have printed a little over six million as planned."

Galba drew a deep breath as someone from the back shouted rudely, "Why is the pick-up tomorrow?"

Then a second called out. This time, though, the tone was different. "Yes, why have we not picked up as planned? It was agreed that it would be collected Friday, the money should be here now, that's half the reason for being here tonight."

Galba raised the staff in an effort to gain control but was ignored.

"I thought you had called this meeting to show us our money!" a voice screamed.

"This all stinks. You'd better not try to fuck us all off,

Galba."

Suddenly the figure to the left of Galba jumped up. "Be silent, you fools."

Almost instantly the hall fell silent and those that stood dropped submissively to the cold marble.

"Do you think for one moment that this hasn't been well thought out?" The small figure scanned the hall with narrowed eyes, his face contorted with rage and an aggression that could almost be tasted. "We in the inner circle planned this project, we have cared for it, watched over it, we will run it as we see fit and not be ordered by plebeians such as you." He paused, almost taunting some reaction.

"Thank you." Galba nodded, pleased for the interruption. "Trajan here is right. We have spent almost one year putting this plan together. You whites must trust in our judgement, we would do nothing that might put us or the project at risk."

"Then explain to us, Galba if you would." A sarcastic voice asked.

Galba raised his hand into the air again. "It was decided not to pick up yesterday as planed for two very good reasons. Firstly, it was felt that the fewer people around the better. Very few people here work on a Sunday, you see. It would be safer, less chance of someone asking an awkward question. Secondly, and perhaps more importantly, we have to decide what we are to do with our two little workers."

"I thought that had been agreed. We were going to put an end to their ageing process," someone called out, prompting much amusement from other members.

"I admit that at one point we had more or less agreed to that form of action. However, we're not convinced now that we need to adopt such a severe plan. To kill them would put us all at risk. Believe me when I say that it's not the same as disposing of a few sluts. Both these men are traceable. They have backgrounds and families who almost certainly know where they've been working and for who. The authorities here are very good in what they do as we have found to our cost in the past."

"Then what do you suggest, Galba? Make them both members? Perhaps we should even give them a toga each and tell them who we really are," a voice shouted cynically.

Galba, with palms together begged his audience for order.

"We believe it would be more prudent to pay them off just as they expect," he said wiping sweat from his forehead again.

"Why don't we just stick to the original plan, it would be far simpler? They could go and keep the ladies company."

This last remark surprised Galba as it came from Cassius, one of the inner members and not normally known for sarcasm.

"I thought Cassius, that, we in the inner sanctum had all agreed." Galba shrugged his shoulders and gave a puzzled look to the colleagues sat around him.

"It would be tidier, that's all, they would never know and they would certainly never be found," Cassius cut in firmly.

"I have heard enough," a voice hissed.

Galba turned to face this new interruption and paled. "Caligula." Galba lowered his head submissively and sat.

Caligula stood, an expert in drama, knowing just how long to keep his audience waiting.

"I have sat here tonight and listened carefully to this debate. I have remained silent in the hope that you could agree between yourselves. It is evident that you will not, therefore it falls to me as your Caesar to decide," he paused, conscious that he had everybody's attention. "Mithras and more importantly 2441 and its existence is paramount, nothing can ever be allowed or tolerated that could put the society or its members at risk."

The wise and calming tone of Caligula's voice could never be underestimated. He had in the past been known to explode into violent fits of uncontrollable rage for little or no reason and on rare occasions even kill.

"We have more important matters to consider than the livelihood of these two workers and must put an end to this bickering. I have therefore reached a decision." Again he paused. "The two men will remain unharmed. We will pay them as arranged. We will keep them under our wing and tell them that there will be more work in the future if they want it, and that working alongside us will make them extremely wealthy. But we shall make it quite clear to them that we will not tolerate betrayal. There must be no doubt in their minds that careless talk will only result in violence and that we will always be able to get to them and their families." Caligula sat before adding, "After a period of twelve months has passed I'm confident that they will have forgotten about us and anyway, by then we shall have moved on."

Galba raised himself up from the cold marble and attempted a respectful bow. "Caligula, as ever your wisdom is a gift to us all."

Pleased with Caligula's intervention and with the matter now closed it was time for Galba to impart good news once again. His sweating and reddened face beamed broadly as he attempted to build on the already excitable atmosphere.

"I believe that it is almost time." He said gleefully, rubbing his palms together then locking fat stumpy fingers together in prayer.

His expectant audience responded wildly to this news with many stamping their leather clad feet on the hard floor.

"Until then, my friends, we should feast!" he shouted above the growing frenzy.

Although most were excited at the prospect of what was to follow, some, particularly the more recent members, had reservations. To the older, more experienced members it was the games held within these walls that were the unmistakable attraction of being a member of the Mithras society and with most, possibly the single biggest reason for attending.

The bustling group led by Caligula pushed and jostled its way noisily from the Great Hall and into the inner sanctum opposite.

The Sanctum was much larger and noticeably, more grand. Its walls were decorated with finely painted frescos, most depicting splendid orgies and mountainous feasts while a few portrayed in graphic detail Gladiatorial combat.

Like the Great Hall it, too, was lit by large oil lamps, the heat from them smothering everyone like a welcoming blanket. Although remote, mains power did exist to the property but was rarely used. The society preferred to live as they would have done in the past.

Oil lamps were the only means of light and these were favoured by most as they provided both atmosphere and warmth. Members who were allowed to live on the outside were envied, and this privilege when it became available was hotly contested. However, most that did would readily admit that they were more at home within, there was much safety to be enjoyed living amongst your own kind, well, at least until more recently.

The newer members were in awe of the Sanctum's lavishness. It didn't disappoint. Couches encircled the magnificent room – at least twenty of them – each positioned end to end and covered in the finest Italian silk, their detailing perfect in every way. To the side of each stood a small but plain wooden table displaying golden platters filled with exotic fruits that most had never seen before. Large silver flasks filled with sweet wine stood along one wall. On a small, low silk-covered table in the centre of the room was placed a selection of gold and silver goblets, each decorated with rare and precious stones.

Caligula led the surging group into the centre.

"Come," he welcomed with arms extended. "Take a flask and be seated."

The heady smell from the strong wine added to the already intense atmosphere; the anticipation of what was to follow was almost heart stopping.

Caligula, having selected a flask and goblet, went and sat at the far end flanked by both Galba and Titus. They watched with much amusement as the group pushed and shoved all eager to be seated as close to the centre of the room as possible.

As the evening progressed and with so much wine

consumed some gave in to its effects and lay prone on their couches in a state of drunken delirium; others talked excitedly of impending wealth. Tonight most had put aside concerns of danger and well being.

Outside in the warmth of her car Pat was nearing her destination. Her heartbeat quickened and her stomach flipped at the thought of what could happen this evening.

"Almost there," she whispered excitedly shrugging her shoulders as she passed the sign to Sherington, and ahead just as directed the turning on the right. Missing the first she turned into the lane and brought the car skidding to a halt directly opposite the gate, then switching off the headlights stepped from the car.

The silence was deafening. For a moment she was certain she could hear the blood as it was pumped around inside her head.

Leaning back into the car she checked the time, the small white numerals on the round face confirming that she was early – almost half an hour to kill.

She placed her handbag on the roof of the car and unfastened its catch. Although dark, she eventually found what she wanted and sighed as she unscrewed the cap from the small silver flask. Throwing her head back violently she gulped greedily at the cool liquid until it was all gone then, replacing the lid, dropped the empty flask back into the bag and snapped it shut.

There was a violent burst of light followed by the sweet smell of sulphur as Pat touched the lighted match to her cigarette. Drawing deeply on it she let the acrid smoke spill from her mouth before tossing the match to the ground.

She leant back on the car and marvelled at the clusters of bright stars, trying to remember their names. She wondered which one was the Plough. Slipping a mint through pursed lips she took another drag on the cigarette before walking to the front of the car. Staring blindly ahead she could just make out the woods in the distance silhouetted against the night sky. Her heart thumped excitedly in her chest again, her breathing laboured. Taking one last pull on the cigarette she sent it spinning through the air before walking back to the car. She took a deep breath as her stomach churned and held it for a moment in an effort to calm herself before getting back in.

Checking the time again she started the engine and waited for it to settle before engaging drive. She allowed the car to move slowly forward on tickover, needing only a small amount of throttle to pass over the rumbling cattle grid and between the two stone lions.

Judging by the noise the evening was progressing well. Only Titus was aware of the silver Triumph that had pulled up outside. Getting up from the comfortable couch he finished what little wine was left in the goblet before whispering something to Galba. The fat man waved his hand drunkenly in the air and nodded. Titus smiled as he walked towards the exit. It went largely unnoticed too, that Cassius had followed.

Out in the hallway both men exchanged jokes as they made their way to the main entrance, both for the moment glad to be away from their drunken colleagues.

Titus pressed his face against the warm timber and squinted through a tiny peephole drilled discreetly into the centre of the large door. He could see very little at first except smoke curling up into the night sky, then, a figure approached.

He chuckled quietly to himself as he watched the figure stumble then trip and fall to the ground. Lost from view for a few moments, Titus debated whether or not to open the door. Then suddenly the figure reappeared. As the woman got to her feet Titus was forced to clamp a hand over his mouth in an effort to suppress the laughter that he could feel welling up from somewhere low in his stomach. As she approached he could now see a cigarette in her mouth. It had been bent in the fall and the end was missing. She puffed vigorously several times in an attempt to reignite it then gave up and let it drop from her mouth to the ground. Brushing herself down with the palm of her hand she walked up to the door.

Titus instinctively pulled back as she spotted the peephole and put her eye up to it then realising that she could see nothing she stepped back. Titus watched as she adjusted her hair then fumbled around for several moments in what he assumed must be her handbag as it was out of sight.

"Cassius, come, my friend, you must see," Titus whispered, moving away from the door.

Cassius put his eye up to the peephole. "What is she doing?" he sniggered as she, with lipstick in one hand and a small vanity mirror in the other, attempted to freshen up in the dark.

"Here, let me see." Titus pushed Cassius roughly aside. "We will have fun with this one, I'm sure," he said looking at her slim form. Both men laughed loudly as the heavy doorknocker rattled on the polished wood.

Titus took a step back as he opened the door. Both men eyed her up and down as she stood framed in the doorway.

"Please, come in, it looks very cold out there," Titus said cynically, noting she wore no bra.

Pat stepped through the doorway and stumbled on the doorstep.

"Take care!" he said grabbing her arm. "We don't want you to come to any harm now, do we?"

He closed the door behind her and grinned broadly at Cassius.

"Please, let me take your coat. It's Pat, isn't it?" Titus could smell an odd mixture of alcohol, tobacco and mint on her breath as she turned her back to him and allowed her coat to slide off narrow shoulders.

"Yes, so kind." Her speech, although slightly slurred, was well educated, which surprised both men. "Where's this party then, boys?" She giggled looking both men up and down seductively. "I could murder a drink," she insisted, lunging playfully at Titus's crotch.

With catlike speed he pushed her groping hand aside.

"Oh, don't be so nervous, I won't eat you," she hooted. "Well, not yet."

Deciding to ignore her, he let her coat fall in a heap on the small bench.

"Please, would you hand my colleague your car keys and follow me? He will park your car for you."

Opening her bag she tossed the keys in the air playfully but Cassius's reactions, even though numbed with wine, were far quicker than Pat's and he scooped them out of the air before they could land back in her palm.

"Spoilsport," she hissed, deliberately snapping her

bag shut up close to his face.

"I should hurry if I were you," Cassius whispered sarcastically.

Turning, Pat ran off in pursuit of Titus who was now some twenty paces away. He could hear her behind him, her shoes clip-clopping on the wood floor as she tried to catch him up. At the far end of the hall he turned and waited. As she approached he noted that she was very slim, not unattractive, more flirty looking, her small bust pushed up by a tight-fitting low-cut top.

Holding open the door he signalled for her to enter then followed her into the darkened room.

He fumbled momentarily before locating the light switch. There was a faint hum as the single fluorescent tube lit. Closing the door he turned, Pat stood facing him some ten feet away, her head tilted to the side as she ran her fingers through her dark hair.

This room was not large, only fifteen feet by twelve, and probably the smallest in the building. Its walls were painted white and the floor was tiled, there were no pictures. And like most rooms in this building there were no windows. It was, however, one of the few rooms that made regular use of technology. It had electricity, not only for its lighting but to provide hot water.

Against two walls and separated by a low table were two white couches. Standing in the centre of the table was a flask and a large earthenware bowl, which contained various fruits.

"Please make yourself comfortable." Titus smiled warmly in an effort to reassure her. "There is a shower in there for you to freshen up, if you wish?" he said then walked over to a small cupboard that stood against the wall. Opening the single door he removed a small white bundle from a shelf. "When you are ready, please slip this on." He undid the gold braided cord that fastened it then held up the thin silk garment for her to see. "There are several sizes of sandal in the bottom of this cupboard. Please choose."

"What is this place, and why do you all dress so strangely?" She tried to smile naturally but her upper lip quivered nervously, which amused him.

"Please don't feel alarmed, we mean you no harm." He draped the silk gown lazily over the back of the couch. She sat and stroked her hand over the cool smooth material as Titus moved around to face her; he sat opposite and leant forward, elbows resting on his bare knees.

"We are a society, a type of club, if you like." He gazed up at the ceiling for a moment as though deep in thought. "A little bit like the Masons only far more exclusive."

Pat smiled politely but looked unconvinced at this answer.

"Where are you from?" she asked. "You have a strong accent but I can't quite place it."

"I am from a small province close to Rome."

"So you're Italian."

"Almost," he answered dryly.

"Are you all Italian then, you know, in this club?"

"Pat, please." Titus was becoming impatient. "There will be plenty of time to answer any questions that you might have but for the moment I need you to get ready, I really do. We don't have much time now, it's getting late and many of my colleagues will have to leave shortly."

"Of course, how rude of me, I'm so sorry. I get carried

away sometimes. I get a bit nervous, you see. I'm okay once I get started though," she said proudly.

"Pat, I have every confidence in you and I know that you will enjoy yourself this evening just as we shall."

She sighed and took a deep breath. "What would you like me to do?" she asked boldly.

"You're here this evening to simply entertain, flirt around a bit, that's all. Nothing too difficult, just relax and have some fun." He stood and moved over to a chest of drawers that stood by the door. "As you probably already know, Pat, you have come to us highly recommended, which is why we are willing to pay so much."

Unseen by Pat, Titus removed a large wad of newly printed ten pound notes from the drawer.

"Five hundred, that's what was agreed, was it not?" he asked snapping the elastic band that held the notes together.

Pat grinned exposing a near perfect set of teeth as she stared at the large wad of money. Almost snatching it from Titus's hand she fanned the bundle and held it to her nose, smelling the fresh ink.

"I won't bother counting it, I'm sure it's all here," she said slipping it quickly into the fake Gucci handbag. "I'm sure that I can trust you." She snapped the bag shut. "How many am I to entertain?" Pat asked with renewed interest, any nervousness that she might have felt now gone, with the cash safely in her possession it was time to enjoy.

"Nineteen," replied Titus with a broadening grin.

Her eyes widened at this news as she struggled to tame her imagination.

"As I said, Pat, just flirt amongst them, tease them a

bit." He smiled and gave her a wink before adding, "I'm sure you don't need me to be too blunt now, do you?"

"Sex – I hope you don't expect me to have sex with all nineteen," she interrupted excitedly.

"No, not at all, just show them some flesh ... but not too much," he added quickly. "There may be one or two that might get a bit carried away. If that does happen, simply move on to the next, they will soon get the idea." He stood and held out his hand Pat grasped his powerful hand and allowed him to pull her to her feet. She stepped forward as he embraced her. She was hesitant at first but soon gave way to his kiss. He held her to him in a vicelike grip, almost crushing the air from her lungs. She pushed her wet tongue out and ground her slim hips into his crotch, feeling him grow.

Titus resisted the strong temptation that swept over him to snap his teeth shut and remove her tongue.

Pulling away from him she held him at arm's length and gasped for breath.

"Perhaps later, when everyone has gone," she panted then ran her warm, moist tongue over his chin.

Titus smiled, regretting that for the moment at least he had missed his chance.

"There is just one other thing," he said as he turned his back to her and headed for the door. "Later in the evening most of the guests that are dressed in the white robes will leave. Not all though." He thought for a moment before continuing. "They are, how would you describe it, beginners, no, novices, new to our group, if you like. Anyway, some will be allowed to stay. When most have gone I will let you know but once they have you will be expected to step it up a bit."

"How do you mean, step it up a bit?" she asked

running both hands over her hips seductively.

"Perhaps be a bit more enthusiastic with your act, strip or something. I'm sure you'll know what to do when the time comes."

Pat moved across to the bathroom and switched the light on. "Strip off you say, oh, that's no problem," she said confidently then, pointing to the white robe draped over the couch, added, "Not, that is, that there's an awful lot to remove."

"You have an hour, Pat, that's all, then I shall come back for you."

"Is there anything to drink in here?" she asked poking her head around the bathroom door.

"Wine, it's in the flask on the table."

"Lovely," she called out then closed the door.

With the bathroom door firmly shut Pat was unable to hear the key turn as Titus locked her in the room; neither could she witness the revulsion shown on his face as he wiped his tongue slowly across the crimson silk of his robe.

Almost one hour had now passed since Titus had returned to the Sanctum and many of the figures strewn across couches were obviously unconscious. A few had disappointedly vomited into their wine flasks and were now being removed.

Caligula leant forward and whispered something to Titus. The few men that were still reasonably sober looked on with renewed interest. It was almost time. Some called excitedly to each other, their expectations of what was to follow heightened by the alcohol. The mood in the room was becoming intense.

Titus stood and smiled as he produced a small black

bag from within his robe. Untying the drawstring at the top he widened the neck of the bag, then moving from one member to the next collected a small silver coin that each wore around their neck, once satisfied that no-one had been missed he returned to his couch and sat. He gave the bag a shake then, watched anxiously by all he thrust his hand inside and withdrew the first of six coins which he placed onto the small table to his left. The whole room was silent, the anticipation obvious. Picking up the first he read aloud the inscription. The response was immediate, Severus Alexander normally a quiet man leapt to his feet punching the air with both hands. Suddenly Domitian on hearing his name called screamed and fell back onto his couch his legs kicking in the air like a demented child. Titus continued until the identity of all six members was revealed. They now stood in the centre of the room as a huddled group arms entwined watched by expressions of blank envy, as their colleagues did their best to remain unaffected by this show of childish behaviour. Titus clapped and raised both hands into the air in an effort to bring some order to the room.

"My friends please calm yourselves," he smiled then turning added. "I know how disappointed you others must feel, but please, your turn will come, that I promise, and when it does you, too, will know what it's like to be one of these six." He looked over at Caligula lying prone on the couch. "And now, my friends, for the highlight of this evening – our entertainment has arrived."

The room erupted, those that could still stand clapped and whistled, slowly the clapping became more rhythmic as the mob sensed the imminent arrival of their visitor.

"Quiet please, you know the rules, they will be obeyed."

"Bring the bitch in!" someone screamed.

The whistling now gave way to chanting, Titus raised an arm in the air realising that he needed to gain control quickly to avoid any problems. "When you are told, you leave, no arguments – is that understood?"

Force was rarely used on these occasions and as the room slowly quietened and the mood calmed he was confident that he would be obeyed. Watched by everyone Titus exited through the large door to the left, as he strode along the dimly lit corridor he couldn't help but grin to himself, he loved these meetings and was confident that tonight Pat would make it one of the best. Yes, this had all the hallmarks of a wonderful evening.

He unlocked Patricia Spencer's door and pushed it open. Pat was laid out across one of the sofas; she grinned up at him as he came into the room then attempted to sit up. Looking more than a little drunk now she drew heavily on what little remained of her cigarette and stubbed it into the clay dish that rested on the table.

"I had just about given up on you darling," she said trying to string the words together coherently.

Titus smiled and held out his hand. She had some difficulty standing at first but once upright she appeared relatively steady.

"We have been enjoying ourselves, haven't we?" he said turning the empty flask over.

"A girl has to get some fun when she's on her own, you know," she slurred.

Titus stepped back and looked her up and down.

"Do you approve?" she asked turning slowly around. "It has a wonderful feel to it, this silk, so soft on one's skin." She untied the gold plaited cord from around her waist then, opening the front of the robe, she revealed her nakedness.

"Very pleasant," he replied glaring lustfully at her small but firm breasts.

"Later, remember," she said covering herself with the silk robe. "And if you're a good boy I might just let you have some."

Titus bent forward and lifted the gold cord from the floor and held it out for her.

"Thank you," she said knotting the cord around her slender waist.

"It's time," he ordered coldly and held out his hand.

Bending at the knees she went for the cigarettes that lay on the table.

"You will have to leave those here, I'm afraid." He tried to sound pleasant but it didn't come off.

"What?" she snapped steadying herself on the arm of the couch.

"We don't allow smoking, I'm afraid."

"Oh! I see, never mind." She let the pack fall from her hand. "I'm going to have a ball tonight anyway, I just know it," she said cupping her hand under his crotch, "several in fact." She squeezed him gently, her eyes widening along with her imagination. Saliva formed in the corners of her mouth. She flicked her tongue from left to right like some lizard ready to pounce then slowly ran it over her painted lips and grinned.

Titus ignored the revulsion that he felt surging through his body and pointed to his front teeth.

"Lipstick," he whispered.

She frowned, still trying to steady herself.

"On your teeth, you have lipstick on you teeth." He hated that.

"Oh, I see." She took a tissue from her bag and rubbed vigorously at her tightly clenched teeth, then with lips drawn back said, "Better?"

Without replying Titus nodded his approval and made a mental observation that one of her teeth was gold and that he might just remove it later and keep it as a souvenir.

He held the door open for her. She took a deep breath, gave him a wink and left the room.

As they approached the Sanctum the sound of laughter grew louder. Pat's confident pace slowed as she heard the sound of slow rhythmic clapping, which increased in tempo until almost a frenzy.

"They know you approach."

Pat half turned, her emotions confused. "I will be all right, won't I?" Her face had paled slightly, which now exaggerated her bright red lipstick.

"I will take care of you personally, Pat, that I promise." He grasped the door knob.

Confident that he would, she smiled, took a deep breath, pulled the robe tightly around her and stepped into the room.

Her heart skipped to the sound of enthusiastic applause. She stood for a moment as though riveted to the floor as she observed the manic scenes before her. The opulence of the room, the heady mixture of alcohol and oil, and best of all, so many young men!

"Just remember, Pat enjoy yourself," Titus whispered up close to her ear and breathed in her heavy perfume.

"Oh, believe me, I shall." Her voice had deepened

with lustful desire as she stepped forward.

Instantly she was in her element and adopted her role with ease, strutting provocatively from left to right, skipping from person to person doing what she did best.

Titus stood for a moment watching her perform. She had been a good choice and would be enjoyed to the end.

Over the next few hours most behaved. Pat was spotted on several occasions with her robe pulled down around her waist as she thrust her small breasts into the ecstatic faces that she entertained. On only two occasions that evening had it been necessary for Titus, with Cassius's assistance, to intervene. The first had been with one of the youngest novices, who had tried to take Pat against her will on his sofa. He had got as far as stripping both her and himself before he was tackled and removed to an outer room to calm down. The second was an older member who, had he not been so drunk, would normally have known better. He was soon pulled away from her to his obvious distress and embarrassment.

During those hours Pat, who had continued to drink heavily, was oblivious that the numbers within the room had gradually diminished. Only the six that had been selected remained, together with Galba, Titus, Cassius and Caligula.

They watched keenly as Pat, with little inhibition and happily for all present with far more enthusiasm, played out the performance of her lifetime.

She was also unaware that the small table that had stood in the centre of the room had now been cleared and the white silk sheet that had covered it had been removed.

What stood there now was a polished wooden table,

which although long was also quite narrow and only knee high. At the base of each of its four legs a thick leather strap was secured by several large silver rivets. At one end of the table two holes were cut side by side, both almost large enough for a head to pass through, but not quite. Along from them at the very end of the table the timber rose up, perhaps two inches or so, and ran the full width of the table. In its centre a curved indentation scooped out from the wood gave it the appearance of a small medieval stock.

Below the table and almost out of sight hung a larger, thicker strap, which had been riveted through its centre to the underside of the table. Each end of the strap was fitted with a heavy brass buckle.

Pat, completely ignorant of the act that was now to take place, went along with all that was asked of her. The table had drawn her attention and, having danced around it several times, was now sat naked on it.

It took very little persuasion from Titus to convince her that she would do better to kneel and lay face down across it.

Soon, to Pat's squealing delight, she was fastened to the tabletop. Her legs were forced apart and a strap around each just above the knees secured her to the legs of the table. This action only served to heighten her excitement. Her arms were pulled forwards and down with each wrist now fastened firmly to the opposite legs of the table.

Lastly, the thick strap that hung below was pulled up and over the middle of her back. This was tightly buckled, forcing her small breasts to hang down limply through the two circular holes in the table.

This last fastening caused Pat some concern but,

despite her pleading, remained firmly in place.

Her mood had now changed from one of excitement to one of fear, which was now made worse as she realised after straining her head upwards that Titus had produced a video camera.

Adding to her distress was the knowledge that her lecherous audience had moved closer. While they watched they continued to binge greedily on both the sickly sweet wine and fruit. All ignored her tearful requests for freedom.

As Titus moved around her, filming, she hung her head down shamefully, trying desperately to keep her face from the camera. This didn't work and instead prompted one of the audience to lean forward and jerk her head violently upwards. All Pat could do was scrunch her eyes tightly closed as if it was all a bad dream.

She jerked violently as someone just out of her line of vision gave her a painful slap on her exposed rear while someone to her left squeezed one of her hanging breasts roughly.

Her fear and vulnerability were now so intense that she started to urinate. She realised through her dizzying haze of alcohol that these men meant her harm and there was little or nothing that she could do to stop it.

She shook violently as though fitting as she realised her ordeal was about to unfold. With Titus taking great care not to film any faces except for their bound victim, Pat was systematically raped by all but him and Caligula. Most of her tormentors were conventional, while others including Galba showed more unusual perversions.

At one point it was necessary to use the gold cord that had hung from around her waist to gag her screams. Finally exhausted, she lay like a discarded doll over the tabletop. Many, having satisfied their need for lust, had staggered exhausted from the room while others had slipped into a drunken coma. Galba had collapsed in a pale and sweating glutinous heap almost dead from exhaustion his chest slowly rising and falling as his abused body tried to recover.

Titus in one last cruel act stood in front of Pat and snatching a handful of matted hair wrenched her head from the table. Her eyes were tightly closed. He put his face up close to hers, so close that he could smell mint again then, whispered her name.

Her eyes opened slowly. He wanted to be sure that she knew that he was to be next. He let her head drop then, passing the camera to someone to his left, began to rape her. She tried to scream out but the gold cord was yanked back and she began to choke.

Pat then became aware for the first time that evening of voices chanting. She could feel the cord as it was undone from behind her head, snagging painfully at her hair. Relief now showed on her pallid face, though this was short-lived as she stared into the camera lens.

Every single moment, every violation felt by her recorded on thirty minutes of Betamax videotape.

As the cord was allowed to slip around her slim neck she gazed into the camera almost knowing what was to happen next.

Titus increased the pressure on the ligature as he thrust into her. Pat's eyes began to swell. Her breathing came in short laboured gasps. A long string of thick white foaming saliva hung from her bluing lips, which now swung pendulum-like from side to side.

The few members still present watched quietly. Some disguised their horror with nervous laughter but, although Galba was now propped up on one elbow breathing heavily, it was Caligula who was the most visibly excited as he unashamedly rocked backwards and forwards on the couch matching the grunting thrusts of Titus.

His sick grin widened, exposing stained and broken teeth. All the time his panting grew louder occasionally snorting down through his nose. His pink tongue darted over drying lips; his thrusting became more violent, more urgent as he pumped at his imaginary lover. Finally, in a breathless, excited scream he became still and watched with muted fascination as the life snorted from Pat's nose.

Her head became still, her lifeless form now slumped heavily over the table.

Caligula sighed and allowed his shoulders to relax as he wiped saliva from his mouth. Now aware of those around him he tried to control his breathing by taking deep nervous gasps.

Titus, now panting heavily, released his grip on the cord around her neck and allowed her head to fall forward. He straightened, pulling his toga around him before unfastening the heavy leather strap that had held Pat's body to the table. Releasing the bindings to her wrists and legs he stepped back.

The silence was broken by an audible click as the video camera was switched off.

Titus bent forward and slipped his right arm under Pat's waist and lifted her from the table then let her drop heavily to the floor, her head making a sickening crack as it made contact with the marble.

"Ouch!" a voice mocked.

Caligula, his face expressionless but still heavily flushed, rested his chin on his chest and whimpered quietly to himself as he rocked gently backwards and forwards. His blood red eyes stared blankly at the lifeless and naked form that lay on the floor. Soon this quiet whimpering grew louder until eventually it became a howl. He clapped his hands together, slowly at first then quickening as he was joined by the remainder of the sobering guests.

"Wonderful, Titus, simply wonderful, you have excelled," Caligula applauded almost crying with glee.

"The best one yet, I would say," Galba added excitedly.

"By far!" someone called.

"Thank you, I think I would have to agree," Titus replied dropping to one knee. "A small souvenir," he said thrusting a small bladed knife into Pat's stiffening jaw.

"Come sit with me, Titus," Caligula asked softly.

Titus stood looking down at the blooded gold trophy held in the palm of his hand. Caligula, turning to his few remaining guests, clapped his hands together.

"Please, if you would remove her. I wish you all to leave. Take her through with you and have her buried. Galba and you, Cassius, please remain, would you?" As Pat was lifted from the wet floor, Caligula added coldly, "So undignified, death, don't you think?" Pointing to the small pool of urine left on the floor. "Did she arrive by car?"

"Yes, Caligula, it will be disposed of," Cassius answered confidently.

"Good, and now before we have to depart I would like to drink a toast with you to celebrate this wonderful life. Soon we shall all be very wealthy."

"We have only you to thank, Caligula," Galba replied picking up a flask from the table and swirling the contents around.

"To our future, may it always be as entertaining," Cassius added raising his goblet.

"Yes, to our future."

CHAPTER FIFTEEN

"Yes!" Neil screamed and for the second time that morning sent the ball blasting passed Steve and crashing heavily against the metal shutter. "Two nil, tosspot."

Steve, with a lengthening stride, went across to the ball and sent it spinning across the floor with one violent kick. "Fuck you, Neil, you think you're so fucking brilliant, don't you?"

"Going to throw a little tantrum, are we?" Neil mocked, knowing Steve would rise to it.

"I'll get my own back on you one day, wanker," he threatened and thrust two fingers into the air.

Fortunately and before the situation could worsen someone outside hammered repeatedly on the shutter. Neil spun round and touched the tip of his finger to his lips. This was followed by the unmistakable heady stench of diesel; then a flat reverberating drone, which grew louder and louder until the metal shutter rattled noisily on its runners.

"They're here," said Neil glancing down at his wristwatch. "And dead on time."

Steve hurried over to the shutter, slipped the lock off and began to pull on the heavy chain.

"Steve."

"What?" he replied curtly as the shutter began to rise slowly from the floor.

"Remember, mate, keep schtum about our tip."

"Of course, what do you take me for?"

Dropping to one knee Neil counted several pairs of feet under the widening gap. "Great, there's a few of them," he said brushing the dust from his leg. "I thought we'd end up doing this alone."

"I'm not sure if that's a good thing or not!" Steve added dismally.

Before the shutter was more than just a couple of feet from the ground, two figures suddenly appeared from under it.

"Good morning, Neil," Titus beamed. His ill-fitting jacket looked oddly out of place stretched over his small but powerful frame. "Cal, if you would be so kind."

"Who's your friend?" Neil asked nervously as Cal complete with oversized sun glasses shoved Steve roughly aside.

"What's his fucking problem then?" Steve cursed letting go of the chain.

"Ah! That, my friend, is Cal. Not a particularly pleasant chap, is he?" Titus said slapping his small powerful hand on Neil's shoulder. "Best keep out of his way if I were you," he advised.

"We get the message, Titus."

"Good, I thought you might. Now, let's get on, shall we? We have much to do this morning."

There was an audible click as the shutter locked in the open position. Steve put his hand up trying to shield his eyes from the bright sunlight.

"And who's this lot?" he asked squinting at the group of silhouettes stood against the morning sky.

"They are just colleagues of mine, or rather business partners, I should say. They have come here to see what you have both been doing for them." Titus gave a worrying smile again.

Neil stepped back quickly as the truck revved sending a swirling mass of dense black smoke into the factory as its driver tried to engage reverse. After several agonising attempts the truck suddenly lurched backwards then stalled.

"Try again, friend," Titus shouted impatiently shaking his head.

The driver restarted the engine and revved it loudly, sending burnt diesel into the air.

"Honest, Neil, what a bunch of tossers," Steve whispered out the corner of his mouth as they watched the driver attempt to reverse into the unit. Eventually on his third attempt he managed it.

"Get that door down!" Titus ordered.

With his men now assembled inside, the shutter was released and allowed to come down.

"Please, if you would like to join us," he urged stripping his jacket off.

"I don't think I like the idea of being shut off from the outside world with this lot, the sooner this is done and we're paid, Neil, the better."

"Not that we need the money now though, eh, mate?" Neil threw Steve a look and chuckled to himself.

"Good morning all," a confident voice shouted.

Half turning they could just make out Galba's unmistakable shape standing in the doorway, his immense size almost eclipsing the sun. "What a wonderful day, don't you think?" he applauded and put his arm around Neil's shoulder as he stepped inside.

Neil could smell that odd mixture of cigars and perfume again and swallowed discreetly.

"Shall we get on? I want to get loaded and off as quickly as possible," he said giving Neil a worrying squeeze. "Perhaps, Neil, you would be kind enough to use that?" he asked pointing his fat stubby finger towards a forklift that stood in the far corner. "As you have witnessed for yourself, most of my friends here make poor drivers at the best of times, and we wouldn't want any accidents now, would we?" He sniggered then gave Neil a sharp but friendly slap on the back. "And you, Steve, my friend, I suggest the pallet truck – load all but one, would you?"

"As you wish, Guv!"

Galba gave Steve the sort of glare that had he seen it, it would have had him running for cover.

"That young man needs to learn some respect, I think," he hissed.

"He's still young, Galba, he means nothing by it, honest," Neil replied pulling himself up onto the forklift.

Galba stepped back surprisingly quickly for a man of his size as Neil accelerated forward and scooped up the first pallet. This he positioned carefully onto the tailgate of the truck. Four of Galba's men leapt up onto the back and tried in vain to pull the pallet backwards.

"Leave it!" Neil shouted. "I'll push it further on with the next pallet if you wait."

Spinning the battery powered forklift around he dropped the forks and waited as Steve, using a small yellow pump truck, brought up the next pallet.

"I told you they were all tossers, didn't I?" he said as Neil lifted the pallet off the ground.

"Steve, do yourself a big favour mate and, keep your opinions to yourself. I think Galba may have it in for you," he said just loud enough for him to hear over the constant hum from the forklifts motor.

Turning around again, he lifted the second pallet

high into the air. Then creeping forwards slowly he lowered the forks until the pallet was just inches above the tailboard. As the two pallets made contact he increased his speed, the powerful electric motor surging the heavy forklift forwards and pushing the first pallet further into the truck. Once he was satisfied he lowered the forks and reversed back out to fetch the next. This process was repeated until all but one was loaded.

"Steve, bring that last one over here, would you?" Galba said, waving his arm in the air.

Steve pushed the trucks forks under the wooden pallet and pumped at the handle until it was lifted clear of the ground, then with some effort hauled it towards Galba.

Pulling at the release handle the pump truck gave an audible hiss as its hydraulics lowered the weight to the floor.

Galba stood over the pallet tapping the top of it with one hand while with the other he fumbled for something in his pocket. He produced a small knife and quickly cut away the shrink-wrap and lifted a carton from the pallet. The effortless way in which, Galba had picked up the carton surprised both Neil and Steve but it confirmed to them both exactly what Neil had suspected right from their first meeting. Although this man was obviously obese he was also incredibly strong. Resting it on the top of the pallet he sliced through the tape that held the box closed.

"I'm intrigued my two friends, what do you intend to do with your earnings?" Galba asked as Neil got down from the forklift. Neil watched eagerly as Galba removed a neatly banded wad of freshly printed notes from the carton and fanned them up close to his nose before offering them over.

"Spend it, Galba, what else?" Neil grinned while making a grab for the money.

He was far too slow, his hand slicing through the air as Galba pulled his hand back and out of range with lightning reflexes.

"Not so fast, young man," he said. His eyes narrowed as he noted Neil's expression.

Fearing the worst Neil stepped back then spun around as he heard footsteps closing in from behind him. Snatching at Steve's arm to warn him, they closed ranks. Just two short paces from them stood the stocky figure of Titus flanked by two others, one of which was Cal. Up until now Neil hadn't really taken too much notice of him but now wished he had. Although slightly smaller than Titus he had an arrogance that you could almost taste. Even under the glare of artificial lights Neil could tell that he was much paler than the others and there was something else. There was something about him that he couldn't quite put his finger on. Then it hit him, it was the eyes. With sun glasses tucked down the neck of his sweater Neil could now see what was so different with him. He was an albino. Neil had never come across an albino before and tried hard not to stare but the colour of the eyes intrigued him, this though, was short lived as he suddenly realised that it was almost like looking into the soulless eyes of the devil himself, and what was now worryingly apparent, the others (Galba included) were also frightened of him.

Then the penny dropped. Galba wasn't the leader. It was this small figure that stood before him.

"I don't like this," The panic in Steve's voice was obvious.

"Gentlemen, gentlemen, there is no need to be worried. We mean you no harm."

They could now see that Galba had sat down and was waving his hands through the air like some vast windmill. "You have done a wonderful job for us, we are all very wealthy, you included. I only wish that we used paper money back home. It would make things much easier for us."

Several of the men standing in the back of the darkened truck laughed.

"No good trying to leg it, I suppose?" Neil said under his breath, even his normally confident tone had gone.

"We wouldn't stand a chance, mate!"

"Leg it! What does that mean?" Galba questioned struggling to his feet. "What does leg it mean please?" he repeated.

"Run, to bloody run," Steve shrilled.

Realising that panic was starting to set in Galba attempted to defuse the situation by smiling broadly.

"Come, come, run, there is no need for you to run, please listen to me, we need you, we need you both don't you see?"

Steve met Neil's bemused expression halfway, "For what?" Steve's voice had deepened now. "Why would you need us now? We've done what you wanted us to do."

"We wish to keep you. We have more work to be done. Not from here of course, too risky, but somewhere close." Galba gestured for them to step forward. Both appeared reluctant at first. "We intend to pay you in full as arranged, nothing has changed, believe me!"

"We thought that you might back out on the deal." Neil appeared relieved.

"So you are going to pay us then? All of it?" Steve

questioned.

"Yes, all of it, but not all at once," Galba answered softly, his head crooked to one side.

"What the fuck do you mean, not all at once? Finance was never an option!"

Galba moved forward closing the gap between them, his large figure swaying from side to side.

"If we pay you all that you're owed two things will happen: the first will be that the police will wonder how two young men such as yourselves have come into so much money so quickly."

"How will they know?" Steve interrupted.

"Because you will both go from Fords to Ferraris that is how."

"What's the second thing?" It was Neil this time.

"Loyalty my friends, loyalty. By releasing the money to you gradually this will ensure that you remain loyal to us. You will think twice about who you speak with and what you say. We have the interests of your families at heart, believe me. We would not like to see them suffer in any way..." Galba's voice tailed off menacingly.

"That's blackmail."

"No, it's common sense."

"What if we refuse?" This statement from Neil was risky and he knew it.

Galba turned his stony glare into a faint and sinister grin. "If you were to refuse, then not only you but also your loved ones might suffer." Galba paused to allow this to sink in then added, "My colleagues behind you would make certain of it, trust me."

Neil froze as a strong hand gripped his right arm tightly, the tips of the fingers probing muscle.

"Okay, if we agree, how much, how much do we get and when do we get it?" Steve interrupted cautiously, his mouth dry.

"We let you have one box each now, that's twelve thousand. Then one box per month until we set up the new operation." Galba turned to Titus who then relaxed his grip on Neil's arm.

"Which will be when?" Neil said turning to Titus.

"Three months," Titus replied coldly.

"Then what?"

"You get the balance. By then you will both have had the taste of it as we have, and then like us you will want more. After all, you can never have too much money, now can you? Please, there is no room for debate here, trust me." Without turning around Galba pointed a single finger towards the group of figures standing in the back of the truck. "There are, I might add, some of my colleagues here that feel that they have a much better solution to this small and very minor problem."

"Which is what?" Neil's face paled already aware of what the answer would be.

"I'm sure that you would prefer me not to go into too much detail." Galba didn't wait for any response and instead lifted a second box from the pallet and placed it together with the first on a nearby bench.

Almost immediately, as though given a signal, two figures jumped down from the back of the truck and came over. Using the pallet truck they hauled the last pallet towards the lorry.

"Perhaps you will do the honours again Neil?" Galba asked stepping forward, his arm extended. This was not the first time that Neil had been forced to hold his breath when the large man got too close.

Neil reached up for the roll hoop of the forklift and pulled himself up onto the vinyl seat. Turning the key to the on position the whine from the motor was strangely comforting amongst this oddball collection of men. Once he had loaded the last pallet of cartons onto the truck he manoeuvred the truck towards a small pallet that stood in the far corner.

"What is it?" Galba asked curiously.

"It's our make readies. We've collected up all the waste sheets as you instructed."

"Oh! I see. Splendid," Galba acknowledged, his smile growing.

"All the films and plates along with the blocks are in the pack to the left," Neil said lowering the pallet onto the tailgate, "the only thing left for us to do now is to get rid of the personal stuff like mugs, radio, etc." he said switching the forklift off, "we're doing that tomorrow."

"I want it all out by tonight," Galba ordered flatly.

"Why tonight?" Steve frowned.

"No arguments, I want absolutely no trace of you or us ever having been in this building."

"But we have almost four months to run on the lease still! Why the bloody hurry?"

"Let me please explain. Firstly, it was planned that we would vacate before the lease expired. We deliberately paid the rent up in full. That way no one will suspect anything until the next rental period falls due."

Both had known Galba long enough now to recognise when not to ask questions; this was now one of those occasions.

"You both appear to have a problem hearing what I'm saying to you." Galba waited for some reaction from them both then, with his patience now at an end, he screamed, "I want it cleared out tonight, do you not understand English?"

"We understand, tonight it is." Neil replied humbly.

"Good. Titus please close up, its time." In an instant Galba's mood was back to normal again. The heavy doors on the back of the truck were slammed shut and locked. There was a sudden rattling of chain as the shutter was hauled up. Titus struck the metal tail gate several times with his clenched fist then stepped back as the driver started the engine.

All five watched as the truck moved forward then stalled. For what seemed like ages they listened as the driver tried to restart. It coughed a large dense cloud of black choking diesel from the exhaust pipe then fired. The driver revved the engine loudly then, again having some difficulty finding the correct gear, it suddenly lurched forwards.

They followed the truck outside and although the sun was bright in the sky it was surprisingly chilly. Both Neil and Steve exchanged furtive glances as they each listened to the grating of gears as the driver pulled out onto the main road and accelerated up the hill.

"Don't you have trucks like that back home?" Steve asked trying to conceal his obvious amusement.

"Not exactly," Galba replied softly. "That's rather a new model to us."

Steve watched Galba walk back to the shutter and not for the first time since meeting him, wished the fat man dead.

"Come on, mate, it's getting cold, let's get back in before they shut us out," Neil said slapping his hand on his friends back. They were greeted by a smug looking

Galba who was standing in the centre of the factory, belly pushed forward with hands on hips flanked by his two colleagues.

"I want you both, to remain here and clean up, make sure that there is nothing that can associate you or us to this place. We will return later to make sure that you have done as asked. Then and only then shall you be paid," he instructed.

"What?" Neil exclaimed angrily. "Why can't we have it now?"

"We will let you each have a box later," replied Galba pointing towards the two boxes that stood on the bench. "For now, though, they come with us, and please, we will be very thorough in checking that you have cleaned well. Make sure that it's done properly. Both Titus and Cal will meet you here later tonight."

They watched passively as the small figure of Cal with sun glasses still tucked down his neck stepped forward and picked up both boxes, Neil was suddenly aware of a muted gasp to his left and guessed that Steve had just noticed the eyes, and prayed that he'd keep his mouth shut, at least until they were alone.

"We must depart," Galba said signalling to Titus. "I will leave you both to lock up behind us please."

Staying a few steps behind, Neil followed them along the narrow corridor and out into the reception.

"Come," Galba said impatiently, his fat arm arching through the air. Cal suddenly appeared in the doorway of the small office. "We must leave."

The rush of cold air from outside as the door was opened was not the only thing that day to send a shiver through Neil.

"Until later, my friends." Galba said not waiting for a

reply.

Neil made the door in two long strides and turned the catch to the locked position before dropping heavily into a nearby chair, the relief on his face was obvious.

"Want a coffee?" Steves disembodied voice called out.

"I want something stronger than a bloody coffee mate," replied Neil lifting a slat in the blind just in time to see Galba's Range Rover pull out from the car park.

"Have they gone?"

"Yes, thank God. I wonder what old red eye wanted in here?" he said stepping into the small office and switching the light on.

"You noticed them as well!"

"You would be hard pushed not to."

"He's a fucking Albino, must be." Steve spat.

"Whatever he is I don't like him," Neil said forcing the door to the cupboard open, then turning to his friend beamed, "they're something else this lot!" he said holding up the carton.

"Our money!" Steve's head appeared to sink into his shoulders as he rubbed his palms together excitedly.

Neil tore open the lid, "This doesn't really change anything, mate, we still have to do as they want and clear up." He said pulling out a wad of notes.

"I know, but it makes it a whole lot easier to do when you know they intend to pay up."

He let the bundle of notes drop into Steve's upturned hand. "What should we do with the money that we've nicked, leave it hidden or take it with us now?" he asked fanning the notes out and waving them in the air.

"Leave it hidden just in case we get stopped on the way home. We've still got the duplicate set of keys that we had made so we can come back whenever we want to."

"What do we do if Galba or one of the others finds out that we've taken some of their money?" Steve's heart skipped a beat as this new thought struck him.

"They wont, don't worry, it's only a few boxes. Anyway, they've got more than enough," Neil reassured.

This answer appeared to satisfy Steve as he handed back the bundle of notes. "Here, you'd better put this back. No sense in rocking the boat now," he said giving the wad an affectionate kiss.

Neil put the money back and slid the carton back onto the shelf, making sure that it was positioned more or less as he'd found it.

"Do you want that coffee now?"

"Yeah, go on then, you've twisted my arm," Neil replied, closing the cupboard door.

After almost five hours they were nearly done. They had been thorough, very thorough. Everything they had used was packed: this included mugs, kettle, spoons, jars, even toilet tissue. They had been very careful since their arrival some three weeks earlier. Even when the presses had been installed they had been careful and worn gloves. Thin surgical gloves were common practice in the trade; printing ink was extremely difficult to remove from skin!

With all but one of the large brown cartons safely stowed in the boot of their cars it was time for a break. In reception the storage heaters had almost claimed back the heat that had been lost earlier.

"Well, we're almost done, mate," Neil said sighing, pleased that things appeared to be almost back to normal. "Just a quick wipe around with the bog paper," he said sitting on the edge of the desk.

"I'm bloody hungry,"

"So am I." Neil turned to the large chrome clock that was hung on the wall. "Christ, it's almost seven, I didn't realise the bloody time."

"What time did Galba say he would be back?" Steve asked checking his watch.

"He didn't."

"Great, so we could be here half the bloody night?"

"Could be."

"Neil, I'll do a deal with you," said Steve with fingers crossed.

"Go on," replied Neil suspiciously.

"Well, I'm supposed to be meeting this bird at the Coach Makers in Newport tonight. I need to get to a phone and rearrange it."

"And?"

"I've been trying to shag her for months. Neil, be a mate. You know these don't bloody work," Steve pleaded then, picking up the telephone on the desk, lobbed it angrily to the floor.

"What's the deal?" Neil asked spinning around in the chair, his legs tucked up tight under his chin.

"What?" Steve's face broke into a broadening smile as he realised that tonight might still be on.

"The deal, you said you'd do a deal."

"Food, I'll get us some fish and chips, bring it back with me, I don't need long, honest."

"It's Sunday, they're shut Sundays," Neil reminded him.

"Okay, a fucking Wimpy."

"With chips and a Coke?"

"Yes, with chips and Coke. Now can I go?" Steve begged.

Neil stopped the chair abruptly and jumped up then, looking down at Steve's puppy-sized eyes, smiled. "Go on then, piss off gay boy."

"Great, I won't be long, promise." Steve leapt out of the chair, any sign of exhaustion now gone.

"And don't you dare forget the food or I'll take it out of your fucking arse," Neil threatened as Steve slammed the door behind him.

Turning the catch on the door he waited just long enough to hear Steve's car start before picking up a roll of toilet paper then went back out into the brightly lit factory.

That was the last thing that he could remember, hearing Steve's car start.

He woke slowly, his eyes heavy, his brain confused. Lifting his chin from his chest he struggled to focus. Looking down at the floor he now realised why his knees ached. He struggled awkwardly to his feet, the pain sending tears streaming down both cheeks. Eventually with much effort he was upright. His head thumped, his neck ached. He tried to tune into something familiar, a sound perhaps, but nothing. He sniffed the air then let his head fall forward, his chin resting on his chest again.

Ink – he could definitely smell ink. He tried to smile but stopped as the pain from his neck stabbed into the base of his skull. He shook his numbed head from side to side, slowly at first then more rigorously in a feeble attempt to bring some sense to his brain. He concentrated on the far wall until it came into focus then realised that he was still at work.

Panic now set in. His stomach churned and he

swallowed bile. Turning his head to the left he could see that he was tied firmly to the chrome handle of one of the machines. He tugged at the yards of sticky brown packing tape that held him. His right hand, he could now see, was tied in a similar fashion to a large wire cage. He cursed aloud as he struggled to get free, yanking and pulling, the vinyl packing tape tearing at the hair on his exposed arms and wrists.

"Steve, you bastard, untie me or else!" he screamed, anger coursing through his pain-racked body.

His voice echoed around the workshop, tailing off somewhere high up in the rafters. He listened carefully and could hear a familiar sound. At first he couldn't quite place it. Then he realised; it was the forklift, the soft whine from its electric motor getting louder as it approached him from behind.

"Steve, I'm warning you, if you don't untie me I'll punch you senseless." Neil strained his head around ignoring the pain in his head and neck. He could just make out in the corner of his misting eye the yellow shape as it approached. He turned his head forwards in an attempt to relieve aching muscles. His face was drawn and white; something was terribly wrong. Steve would never do this, he hadn't the bottle. Again he yanked violently on the tape, but it just wouldn't break. Not even his sixteen-stone weight could match its strength. He jerked his body violently from left to right with mounting frustration hoping something would give.

Fear now took over and he started to cry. He craned his head around again. He could still make out the yellow shape of the forklift but something was different. Beyond the pulsating noise of blood rushing through narrow blood vessels in his head he could see that it had now stopped some ten feet away.

"Please, who the fuck are you, what do you want?" he sobbed, his saliva thick with fear.

The silence was crushing. In the distance he could just make out the familiar sound of traffic; the outside world suddenly became oddly comforting.

"Don't you know me, Neil?" a voice asked softly. It was low almost calming and came from somewhere to his left.

Neil turned his head to the side, his breathing nervous and heavy. His whole body began to shake uncontrollably. A damp patch swelled from around his crotch and became warm as the hot liquid ran down his leg. A puddle appeared on the grey painted concrete floor. He looked down at his feet and felt ashamed.

"How mortal we are," the voice mocked softly.

"Why have you tied me? I've done nothing to you." Neil waited for a reply that never came. The silence hurt and again he struggled to free himself. He pulled harder at the wire cage but still it wouldn't budge. He tried to gain some control of his shaking body by taking several deep breaths. As he calmed he became aware of someone breathing from behind him. He craned his head around and this time he could just make out a figure as it darted away to his right and out of sight.

"Look, let me go, I won't say anything to anybody, honest. If you think I've said anything to anyone about the money your mistaken."

"What money is that, Neil?"

Neil froze as the familiar whine from the forklift's motor cut the silence. He tried to look over his shoulder. He knew deep down who this was but wanted to see, to be certain, the pain from his neck causing him to hold his breath, but still he couldn't see. Just above the low hum he could hear the squeaking of soft rubber on smooth concrete as it approached. It was getting close, too close. Neil called to its driver but his anguish fell on deaf ears. He could hear the whine and the clatter of chains as the forks were raised, then waited for the truck to make contact with him. Eyes firmly shut and head hung low he tensed his body, waiting for the impact.

Some seconds passed before Neil became aware that the whine from the forklift had ceased. He raised his head slowly, listening.

"I know you're still there, I can hear you breathing, please, let me go," he begged.

"It was a mistake for you both to think that we would not find out." The voice seemed to smother Neil like an old cloak.

"You can have it back, all of it."

"Too late for that, Neil, I'm afraid, far too late now." The tone had changed to almost a hiss now.

"It's here, it's in this building, honest, let me go and I'll get it for you."

"I think not, we have all the money we need now – thank you anyway," the voice whispered.

"What have you done with Steve?" Neil questioned.

"Nothing, Neil, I promise, well, not yet."

"He'll be here soon. You'd better let me go. I know who you are! Cal."

"Neil."

"What?" Again Neil yanked violently at his bonds.

"I suggest you get ready to take a deep breath."

The contact was slow at first, almost a gentle shove,

just to the left of his spine and six inches above the small of his back.

Neil didn't resist; instead he allowed his body to bend outward from the pressure behind. His stomach pushed forward until he could go no further. The brown packing tape stretched slightly but still held him fast. Then he gasped, his face white with shock. He retched from deep within his stomach then vomited, the truck all the time forcing him forward and outward. He spat then tried to speak but couldn't. The resistance finally gave way and his body slid backwards to an almost upright position. He tensed then swallowed; sweat ran down and wetted the floor.

He coughed, at first lightly then with more effort, sending a fine mist of red into the air. Blood oozed from his nose and ears.

He felt pain in his stomach, then gasped as he looked down and watched his shirt-front move outward to a growing crimson point.

He screamed as the thin silver spike burst through his belly button and then his sodden shirt. His whole body danced and jigged as the steel rod grated against his spine; blood fell in torrents making slapping sounds as it hit the cold floor. His last moments came as the whine from the truck's forks were raised, jolting Neil and lifting him up from the wet floor. With the tape now cut away the forklift raised him fully into the air. He hung almost fifteen feet above the ground, a heavy, lifeless doll.

CHAPTER SIXTEEN

Steve closed the door to reception quietly and slipped the lock on, he was late and certain that Neil would be pissed off. His only chance would be to get on his good side rapidly. He had to pull a prank; Neil appreciated a good laugh.

He placed the now cold burger and chips down onto the desktop, with lightning reflexes he quickly snatched the can of coke before it could roll off onto the floor and give the game away.

Crouching low so that he wouldn't be spotted passing the window, he tiptoed quietly along the darkened hallway and out into the print room stopping momentarily to allow his eyes time to grow accustomed to the dark.

"Why the fuck has he turned the lights off?" he said under his breath.

Convinced that Neil lay in wait for him somewhere, he proceeded cautiously. He pushed open the swing door that led into the plate room and had a quick look around to satisfy himself that all was clear. Then moving forward, his back pressed firmly against the wall, he inched his way towards the presses. He could just make out their shape to the left.

It was then that he spotted something. Despite the poor lighting he immediately recognised the shape of the forklift stood in the centre of the pressroom, and worryingly he could also just make out what looked like the silhouette of a figure.

"The bastard," he whispered with a grin, his eyes now almost accustomed to the dark. "If you think that you're going to jump down and shit me up you've got another thing coming mate."

Knowing what Neil was capable of Steve was determined to get the upper hand quickly. Dropping to the floor, his eyes fixed on the figure ahead, he shuffled on hands and knees across the floor, mostly sticking close to the benches which offered the best cover.

"I'm going to give you such a shock, you nonce," he whispered trying his best to suppress the excitement coursing through his body.

He was now some thirty feet from the forklift when he realised that there was light coming from under the toilet door. He halted for a moment unsure if this would give the game away. Then, deciding that it was safe, he continued, swearing as he crawled into a wet patch which was sticky and oddly warm.

"What the fuck's this?" he cursed jumping to his feet. He searched for something to wipe his hands on but finding nothing suitable decided to put an end to this ridiculous game.

"Okay, div, game's up!" he called out, switching the lights on.

In the eerie flickering blue white light Steve could now clearly make out the limp figure hanging from the forklift. It was as though he was watching a silent movie, only this wasn't Charlie Chaplin, each flicker of light revealed more of the horrific scene.

In an act of shear panic he brought his hand to his mouth, and tasted blood. Staring blankly at his reddened palms he instinctively rubbed them vigorously on his clothing.

As the lights grew brighter he stood as if riveted to the floor, his whole body numb with shock as he looked up at his friend hanging lifeless in the air with eyes wide and staring blankly ahead. His tongue hung gruesomely from his bloodied mouth.

The deathly silence was now broken by the sudden rhythmic pit-patter of blood as it dripped down from Neil's dark-stained trainers and slapped onto the cold concrete floor.

Then as his mind registered the familiar sound of the toilet being flushed, Steve quickly realised that whoever had taken his friend's life was about to make himself known.

He was too late. The door swung open and slammed heavily against the wall making him jump.

As if frozen in the smallest moment in time both men stared at each other as though acting out a gun fight scene from an old Western, neither of them making a move.

Suddenly the small muscular figure sprinted from the doorway. Steve turned, his feet scrabbling for grip on the wet floor. He leapt over the pallet to his side and headed flat out for the hallway.

He felt so scared he just wanted to scream out, but he resisted. Instead he concentrated on getting to that front door. Once there he would be out in the open and safe.

Behind him he heard the killer curse as he ran into something; Steve took this opportunity to look back. The figure had fallen. He couldn't see what had tripped him but now watched as he struggled to his feet and sprinted towards him.

Turning to his left Steve disappeared into the

darkened hallway, stopping briefly to yank the sliding door shut that separated the offices from the production area. As he reached the front door he heard the crash from behind as the sliding door was wrenched from its tracks, followed by breaking glass. He didn't risk looking back. Instead, gasping for air, he fumbled with the door lock.

"Fuck, open, will you!" he screamed, his skin wet with fear.

Eventually it burst open. He gulped at the cold night air, slammed the door shut and sprinted up the pathway, his speed renewed as he heard the killer crash through the door. He could hear footsteps ringing out on the paving, getting closer, and further quickening Steve's pace. He knew that he mustn't stop running; if he did he would die.

His legs ached and his lungs were fit to burst. He sucked in the night air. He was running now on will power alone.

Having turned left and right he slowed to a jog and risked a look back over his shoulder. He smiled nervously and listened; the only sound was that of his lungs wheezing. He stopped and looked back along the path, his body bent over, with hands on knees he peered into the darkness.

"Fuck!" he screamed as a figure darted across the path some three hundred yards up on the left.

Steve turned and sprinted all in one swift movement. The stinging blow to his forehead was instant and final; he dropped heavily to the floor.

CHAPTER SEVENTEEN

Hart was woken suddenly by a loud ringing. At first he was confused. His mind struggled to make sense of the sound. Perhaps this was part of his dream he thought. He opened one eye. It was light. Closing his eyes tightly he tried to ignore the sound in the hope that it would go away, then unexpectedly he was nudged rudely back to reality with a sharp jab of a single finger.

"Shouldn't you answer that?" a sleepy voice whispered.

Hart half turned and rubbed the sleep from his tired eyes.

"It might be urgent," Mitch suggested quietly.

He lifted himself onto one arm then leaning across picked up the telephone.

"Hello." His voice dry and husky, he coughed into a clenched fist in an effort to clear his throat. "Stacey, how are you?" he said trying to sound more awake than he actually felt. "...Yes ... I think I know it. It's just off the A5, isn't it?"

Mitch fluffed up a pillow then stuffed it between Hart's back and the headboard as he sat up.

"Good grief," he exclaimed planting a kiss lightly on Mitch's forehead. "Who found him?"

Mitch sat up and pulled the white cotton sheet around her.

"Okay, give me half an hour," he said as Mitch shook her head. "Better make that an hour, Stacey." He corrected quickly.

Mitch smiled, slid out of the bed and went through to the bathroom.

"Sorry, Stacey, I missed that, what did you say?" he asked, distracted for a moment by her nakedness. "Jesus, that's not the sort of thing that you expect to find when you're out walking your dog, now, is it? ... I will, I'll pick her up on the way in, don't worry." Hart replaced the telephone, swung his legs out of the bed and pulled on a pair of boxers. He ran his hand over his head and stood looking out at the garden.

"What did Stacey want?"

Hart turned just as Mitch appeared in the doorway of the bathroom rubbing at her hair with a towel.

"Apparently some old boy who was out walking his dog on an industrial estate this morning discovered a break in." He sat down on the edge of the bed watching Mitch comb out her drying hair in front of the dresser. "Anyway, his curiosity got the better of him and he decided to take a look inside."

"And?"

"The poor old sod had a bit of a shock unfortunately. Evidently he'd had a good look around before discovering someone impaled on the arm of a forklift."

"A forklift?" Mitch said turning.

"That's what he said."

"Dead?"

"As dead as it gets." Hart replied coldly.

"Male or female?"

"That I don't know, Mitch, I didn't think to ask. Anyway, we'll know soon enough. Stacey wants me to pick you up and meet him there." He grinned.

CHAPTER EIGHTEEN

Stacey stood motionless in the half-light of the factory trying to familiarised himself with his new surroundings. He sniffed at the air and made a mental note of the strong odour. He'd smelt it before but for the moment couldn't place it. Listening at the silence he turned and stared upwards.

Above him and almost fifteen feet in the air, the reason for his visit. The grotesque shape hung like fresh meat, a steel spike jutting out from the stomach.

He took great care not to disturb anything as he walked around to the side of the yellow forklift and fought back the urge to vomit. Blood still lay in vast pools on the floor and was now drying at the edges. He could smell the strong but unmistakable smell of faeces.

Dragging a wooden workbench up close he climbed up. From this elevated position he could now see the extent of the victim's injuries. The steel spike was in fact jammed into a slot at the back of one of the two forks where they met with the lifting mechanism. From here he observed that the steel rod ran along the top of one fork and protruded beyond it by some twenty inches. The rod was held tightly in place by yards of what appeared to be brown vinyl packing tape wrapped around it and the actual forklifts arm.

Impaled on the spike the body hung limp and marble white. The head oddly erect on slumped shoulders. The same tape that fastened the spike to the fork was wound around both wrists.

"Excuse me, sir."

Although whispered the voice startled Stacey.

"What?" he replied irritably glancing down at the uniformed figure stood by the bench.

"Sorry, sir," the PC stuttered nervously, making sure the forklift was out of his line of sight. "The old boy that found him, he's next door in reception. He said that you'd asked him to come back."

"I had," he said straightening his tie. "Tell him I'll be out shortly."

Using his right hand to steady himself he reached up. What had attracted his attention was the thin red line that ran across the victim's throat. As he touched the body the head turned, Stacey froze then reeled back as the head rolled from the slumped shoulders and fell with a gut retching crack as bone met concrete. Stacey went to say fuck but it came out of his throat in a mixture of gas and bile, half turning his head he spat the vile concoction out. He forced himself to look back at the headless corpse and then down on the floor. The head had rolled so that it was only partially visible beneath the bench opposite. He could see one eye looking up at him. At that precise moment it would have been so easy for him to have left via the metal shutter and got a job stacking shelves.

Stacey jumped down from the bench, landing more heavily than he would have liked. Looking around him he soon found what he hoped he would find. The brown warehouse coat hanging from a nail on the wall wasn't ideal but it would do for now. With the head covered he went back to reception.

"Any sign of Mitch yet?" he asked.

"Not yet, I'm afraid." The uniformed officer replied

shrugging his shoulders.

"While I think of it," he said smiling at the figure sat opposite. "Would you get on to Traffic? Give them the registration details of the two cars parked outside, find out who owns them. You'll have to use your radio. Apparently the phones here aren't connected."

"Sir!"

"Also, see what you can do to improve on the lighting back there. It's probably a fuse or something," Stacey said, then turned to the seated figure again.

"Mr Adams." Stacey held out his hand. "No, please don't get up, I won't keep you long. I know you've already given a statement to us but the reason I've asked you back..." Stacey moved over to the window and raised the blind. "The two cars outside, have you seen them here before?" he asked keeping his back to the old man.

"Oh yes, they're always here, well, when the presses are going. Noisy bloody things."

Stacey turned around and gave a reassuring smile to the frail figure.

"You see, I walk my dog past these units twice a day, once in the morning and then again in the evening, that's the way I stay so fit ... I'm sixty-two, you know." Mr Adams stood in an effort to qualify his last statement then sat back down.

"Mr Adams, can you tell me how long they've been parking outside here? Roughly will do? One week, a month?" Stacey had now sat down opposite.

"Well, let me see," Mr Adams said looking skywards. "I would have to say at least a couple of weeks, perhaps a little longer. Two young chaps! Always speeding off and making rude signs at each other." His expression changed for a moment as the penny dropped, "My goodness, do you think that's one of them?" He gestured.

"We don't know at this stage, Mr Adams, but it might be." Stacey looked up as Hart appeared in the doorway. He stepped inside followed by Mitch.

"Good morning, sir, it's a bit early for this isn't it?" She said cheekily lifting a cold burger from the desk.

"Morning. Not guilty, I'm afraid," Stacey replied quickly. "This is Mr Adams. He's the gentleman that found the body this morning."

Mitch smiled and sat down opposite crossing her legs. "Good morning, Mr Adams, it's nice to meet you," she greeted holding her hand out.

Mr Adams coloured up slightly and gave a nervous cough as he grasped her small hand.

"Hart, you had better come and have a look at this," Stacey said getting up and moving towards the hallway. "Perhaps, Mitch, you could stay here with Mr Adams for a moment?" he suggested firmly.

"Of course, sir, it would be a pleasure," Mitch said smiling at Mr Adams who coughed again.

"Excuse me, sir." The young constable appeared in the doorway and handed Stacey a slip of paper. "Traffic has confirmed the registration numbers on both cars. They're local, a Neil Becker and a Steve Ackerman."

Stacey scanned the note quickly before handing it back.

"Great, get some help. I want you to check out both addresses, see who's who. If you get a result I want you to bring them in. Arrest them if you have to." He glanced over his shoulder. "It's a bit early in the morning for this I'm afraid."

At the far end of the hallway Stacey could see that it

was now much brighter in the factory than earlier.

"Good, someone's managed to get the other lights to work." He stepped into the brightly lit work shop. "You can see by the amount of damage Hart that whoever was responsible for this killing was obviously very keen to get away." He stopped and lifted the shattered door from the floor with much of the glass falling out of the frame and smashing onto the hard floor. "The odd thing is Hart, that the door in the main entrance definitely appears to have been kicked outwards, which suggests to me that the killer might have been caught out by someone and whoever that someone was chased him off."

"Or maybe the killer was doing the chasing," Hart suggested tactfully.

"The other printer you mean?"

"It's possible."

Stacey shrugged his shoulders and let the door drop back onto the floor. "Come on, you'd better take a look at him."

With Hart following close behind Stacey led the way through to the machine room.

"Jesus!" Hart exclaimed running his hand over his head.

"Well, I did warn you," Stacey said walking around to the side of the forklift, taking care not to step into the drying puddle of blood.

Hart had spent most of his working life with CID and during that time had seen the result of many brutal murders but, the sight of a headless corpse or disembodied head still rated very highly on Hart's what not to see again list.

"Where's the head?"

Stacey pointed down to the brown coat just visible under the bench.

"Whoever did this new exactly what would happen once someone moved the body."

"Was that someone you by any chance?" asked Hart already knowing the answer.

"It was," Stacey answered coldly. "I know it's a bit early to say for certain but it looks to me as though he was fastened between the press and the cage over there using the packing tape." Stacey went over and tugged at a length of brown vinyl tape that hung from the wire cage. "I reckon the forklift was driven into him impaling him on the spike then, he was simply lifted up into the air."

"Any idea who he might be?" Hart said struggling to get up onto the bench.

"Not yet but I'll bet you a pound to a penny it turns out to be one of the lads that worked here."

Hart pulled roughly at the brown tape that hung from the wrist, causing the arm to shake violently. "No rigor mortis yet so he hasn't been dead for long."

Stacey walked towards the metal shutter and stood in the centre of the factory turning around slowly. "You know this doesn't feel right, there's something missing," his voice echoed.

"Yes, I know what you mean. There's no work for a start!" Hart called back.

"Sorry?"

"There's no printing in here. You'd expect to see at least some work in progress, on a pallet or in the back of one of the presses or something." Hart jumped down and lifted the lid from one of the many bins. "I admit that I've not had much to do with printers in the past but they've always struck me as places of organised chaos. There's nothing here, no paper, no waste, look, even the bins are empty, nothing." Hart let the lid slam shut.

"They must have been printing something. Mr Adams reckons that the pair were always here and had been for a couple of weeks or more," Stacey said striding off. "I'm going to let Mr Adams go home, and get some help to search this place from top to bottom."

"Stacey, see what you can find to cover this up. I really don't fancy staying in here with him looking like that."

Fifteen minutes later and Stacey had returned with several uniformed policemen and a large white sheet.

"I've asked Mitch to drive Mr Adams home, and told her to go back to the station afterwards. No need for her to see this shit," Stacey said climbing up onto the bench.

He carefully unfolded the sheet and with Hart's help they managed to position it over the corpse. As they lowered the fabric and it made contact growing patches of crimson appeared. Jumping down Stacey stood to the front of the forklift.

"Well, not ideal but I'm afraid it will have to do for now," he said turning to Hart.

"When will they come to remove him?" Hart asked.

"Not until the doctor has been out to confirm time of death." Stacey approached the group of policemen huddled together against the far wall. "Okay, you rabble, I know none of this is nice but we've got a job to do so split yourselves up. I want you to go over this place with a fine tooth comb. If you find something, shout out." Stacey watched as his men formed an orderly line and started working their way slowly forwards.

After almost an hour it became quickly obvious that Hart had discovered something. Stacey watched as he dragged a workbench noisily across the concrete floor and positioned it carefully beneath one of the large red beams that supported the steel roof.

"Stacey, get over here, I think I've found something," he said placing a chair on top of the bench. Stacey grasped the legs of the chair to help steady it as Hart climbed up.

"What is it?" From this position Stacey could now see what had attracted Hart's attention.

"I'm hoping that it's what I think it is," he answered, balancing precariously on the fragile chair.

"Here, try this." Someone produced a broom and handed it up to him.

"That's it, it's almost free," Stacey encouraged as Hart prodded with the handle.

The paper ball dropped to the floor several paces from Stacey and rolled lazily towards him. Hart climbed off the chair and stood looking down from the bench top. Both men recognised the bundle immediately. Someone whistled as Stacey picked up the ball and removed the elastic bands that helped hold its shape and pulled a sheet away.

"Jesus!" he exclaimed straightening out the crumpled paper.

"Well, Stacey, there's your answer, now you know what they've been doing in here."

"I can't wait to hear them explain this one away," Stacey said holding the sheet out.

Hart jumped down from the bench and stood the broom against the wall then turning to Stacey added soberly. "I think you can drop the, them bit, don't you?"

CHAPTER NINETEEN

Mitch settled back in Stacey's high-backed chair, glad of its comfort, and sipped at her steaming mug of hot tomato soup. Her mind recounted the previous evening spent with Hart. She smiled to herself at the thought of their lovemaking. It had been good, very good, and more importantly for her he had been tender and considerate. On a recent visit to her mother and in a rare moment of weakness she had admitted that although they had not known each other long she was falling in love with this softly spoken Irishman. Her mum had tried to warn her of the dangers involved in whirlwind romances but in the same breath had admitted that she had only known Mitch's father for a few days before realising that he was the one for her. They were married just three weeks later and spent their honeymoon in Southend. One week later he was in Normandy fighting the Germans.

This private reflection was suddenly interrupted by a gentle but insistent tapping on the window pane. She grinned at Hart's distorted face pushed up hard against the cold glass.

"I don't know what's got into him today!" Stacey said striding into the office. "If I didn't know any better I'd say he's taken something or was bloody drunk." He let the Marks and Spencer bag that he had been carrying under his arm drop onto the desktop. "It's okay, Mitch, stay where you are," he added as she went to stand.

"Do either of you want a coffee or something?" asked Hart as he popped his head around the door.

Both declined and Hart shrugged as he stepped into the office. He closed the door behind him, deciding that it was too much bother to make one just for himself. Instead he settled for a seat.

"You look about as bad as I feel," Hart mocked.

Stacey dropped into the less than comfortable chair by the door and swung his feet up with some effort onto the small desk, let his head fall back then sighed as the phone rang.

"Hello," Mitch offered cheerily. "Yes, he's here, I'll get him ... put him through though, would you?" She cupped her hand over the mouth piece. "It's for you Stacey. It's a David."

Stacey sat up and gave a puzzled frown as he put the phone to his ear. "Hello, DI Stacey speaking ... David, I'm sorry, I was miles away. How are you? Good, glad to hear it ... yes, we're both fine, bit knackered. So, David, I hope its good news..." Stacey said tucking the handset under his chin

"Who's David?" Mitch whispered.

"He's the museum curator that we met. We left the toga with him. He was going to run some tests on it and try and date it or something."

"Date it – why?"

"Well, apparently he seems to think that it may be the real thing," Hart answered raising his eyebrows in an effort to add some weight to the statement.

"Jesus, you're joking!" Stacey stammered loudly. "Who the bloody hell would be bothered enough to go to all that trouble?" he added excitedly. "No, David." Stacey said, suddenly jumping to his feet. "No don't do that. I'll arrange for someone to come up and collect it from you." he threw a look at Hart. "As you can imagine

David that toga is extremely important to us, I don't want to take the chance that it might get lost or, more importantly, stolen. If it does belong to this group, and I believe it does, then they might just attempt to recover it."

Taking an educated guess at what had been suggested Hart nodded his head in agreement.

"David, listen, thanks for your help with all this, it's been invaluable it really has. We will probably be in touch with you again, Good, that's nice to know." He paused then added, "And you, David, you will, soon ... and again many thanks, goodbye." Stacey replaced the receiver back onto the rest.

"Okay Stacey, we're all ears. What did he have to say then?" Hart slid his chair closer to the desk.

"The toga's real. He reckons it dates back to around 209AD." Stacey wrote the date down on the blotter then circled it several times with his pen. "Someone has taken great care in storing it, almost certainly under carefully controlled conditions otherwise as he said it could never have survived. To quote David, it's almost new."

"Why would anybody be bothered?"

"Its value, perhaps it's worth loads," Mitch cut in enthusiastically.

"That's the point, it's not. Well, not financially, or so he believes." Stacey went over to the window, "Its true value is its rarity. But the question is what else might this group or society have in its possession? As David just said, historically speaking, this could be immense," he said excitedly.

"That's obviously why David's so keen to help. He's realised the possibilities himself. We owe this society a visit, I think." Hart narrowed his eyes mockingly as he turned to Mitch.

"Be serious," she said tossing a crumpled sheet of paper at him, which he promptly headed neatly into the corner of the room.

"That reminds me," Stacey said taking hold of the Marks & Spencer bag. "Changing the subject for a moment, Mitch, take a look at this."

With the neck pulled wide open he tipped the bag up and shook it, "That's what they were up to, forging tenners," said Stacey, letting the bundle of notes roll lazily across the desk.

Mitch leant forward and picked up the paper ball inspecting it with growing interest.

"Clever boys," she said holding it up, "how many have they printed?"

"That we don't know."

Mitch peeled a sheet away, and smoothed the creases out on the desk top with the palm of her hand.

"Twelve images on one sheet. You wouldn't need to print many of these to make yourself pretty wealthy." She whistled.

Stacey looked up as someone knocked loudly on the door. "It's open," he shouted.

"Sorry to interrupt you, sir, but I thought you'd like to know, we have one of the car owners outside." The uniformed officer leant his shoulder against the door frame waiting for some reaction.

Stacey turned to Hart grinning broadly. Things were looking up.

"It gets better," the officer added with a smile, "he's admitted that he was one of the printers."

"Excellent, I think it's time that we found out what's

been going on don't you?" Stacey said rubbing his palms together briskly, "Better bring him in."

"Sir, just one thing"

Stacey turned to the young officer who now stood ramrod straight in the doorway.

"He's in a bit of a state. We found him hiding in his garage, well, in the roof of it to be more exact. The odd thing is, sir, he was actually pleased to see us. He kept mumbling about how they had tried to kill him."

"Who was going to kill him, who are they?"

"I don't know, sir, but he mentioned the name Cal several times, and someone has certainly had a pop at him, he's got a pretty bad bruise on his forehead."

"Go get the young man." Stacey said firmly sitting down behind his desk.

"Perhaps Stacey we now have our killer," Hart suggested calmly, "Greed can be a funny thing."

"That would be just too much to ask," Stacey replied as the door swung open.

"This is Mr Ackerman, sir, Steve Ackerman."

Hart got up and slid a chair forward.

"Please sit Mr Ackerman. I'm afraid there are a number of things that we'd like to talk to you about. You will, of course, be required to make an official statement later so please be patient with us."

"Am I under arrest?" the exhausted figure asked sitting down heavily.

"No, you're as we like to say – helping us with our enquiries at the moment."

It was obvious from his appearance that he was a physical wreck. He had a massive bruised swelling just above his left eye, his face was pale and his clothing dirty and torn. He sat motionless staring blankly at the floor, his breathing nervous and heavy.

"Mr Ackerman, we need to know what's been going on. Firstly, what can you tell us about the body in the factory? Was that you're doing?"

Steve lifted his head slowly, looking directly at Stacey. His eyes filled as he fought to hold back tears. "No, sir, Neil was my mate, my best mate."

"I want to know exactly what you've been up too. I also want to know who it is you've been working for. And more importantly, I want to know everything that has happened that has led to this young man's violent death, do I make myself clear, Mr Ackerman?" Stacey's voice had risen in both pitch and volume.

"I'll tell you all I know," he stammered, trying to gain some control.

"Fetch Mr Ackerman some tea, Mitch," Stacey said looking directly at him. "Okay let's start with your employer, or did you both do this off your own backs?"

"No, no, we were employed," he jabbered nervously.

"By who?"

"Galba, his name's Galba."

"Surname?"

"He didn't have one, well, not one that we were ever given."

"Okay, so how did this Galba employ you, when did you first meet him?"

"I can't answer that, I don't know. Neil met him first. I was only introduced to them once I had started work. They never interviewed me, only Neil."

"Them, you said them. Who are them exactly?"

"There were three of them, well, apart from when they turned up with the truck. Galba, he was the boss, there was one that I heard called Cal, the third they called Titus. I think they were sort of bodyguards or something."

Mitch returned with a large mug of steaming tea, which she handed to Steve. He looked up at her and attempted a smile.

"So, there were three of them, you say. Did they work with you?"

"No, it was only the two of us." Steve raised the mug to his lips and sipped carefully at the hot liquid. "They would only come in occasionally, about once a week, usually at the end of the week." He lifted the mug to his lips again before continuing. "They would come to check on what we'd done, you know, make sure that we'd been working and not pissing around."

"You mentioned a truck," Hart interrupted.

Steve flexed his neck in an attempt to relieve the pain that his tightening muscles were inflicting on his exhausted frame.

"How often did this truck visit?"

"Only once, that was when they came to pick up the printing." Steve's face had reddened slightly, which hadn't gone unnoticed.

"How many came with the truck?" Stacey asked quickly.

"I don't know exactly, seven, maybe ten, I couldn't say for sure. I didn't really take that much notice to be honest."

"What was it that you were printing for them?" Stacey asked, lifting the Marks & Spencer bag onto the desk again.

"Leaflets," he stammered nervously, his face now completely flushed.

"Steve – you don't mind if I call you Steve, do you?"

Hart said softly. "Let's get things straight, shall we, Steve? Save all of us wasting our time. If you're not responsible for your friend's death, and I don't think that you are, it's vital that you don't conceal anything that may hamper our investigation. We know exactly what the two of you were up to trust me."

Stacey pulled the paper ball from the bag and tossed it directly onto Steve's lap.

"How much of this did the pair of you actually produce for them and, more importantly, where is it now?" asked Stacey his tone now much firmer.

"I told him, I bloody said that we should've got this down," Steve hissed.

"How much, Steve?" Stacey repeated.

"A shit load, that's why they needed the bloody truck!"

"Where is it now, do you know?"

"We were never told where they came from, or where the money was going. They were very careful like that."

Stacey turned to Hart and shrugged his shoulders. Steve put the mug down onto the desk and rolled the ball slowly between his hands for a few moments.

"There is something," he said taking a deep breath. "Neil followed Galba one night, from the factory, I mean."

"Go on!" Stacey insisted.

"Neil said that he was careful to keep his distance to make sure that Galba wouldn't spot him. Anyway, according to him he had turned off the main road between Newport and Olney just before you get to Emberton, I don't know exactly where though."

The room fell silent as this last statement sunk home. Hart could now hardly contain himself.

"It has to be the same place, it's too much of a coincidence, don't you think?"

"I agree." Stacey leapt from the chair. Both men huddled around the small desk against the far wall. On it a map held down by four half empty mugs that now grew penicillin.

"How far is it, do you think?" Hart asked studying the map closely.

"Not far, maybe seven miles at most," Stacey replied tracing the route with his finger.

"Let's take a drive out there," Hart suggested tapping his finger heavily on the map. "You never know, Stacey, we might just strike lucky."

Both men, their expressions almost identical, each trying to conceal the excitement that welled up from somewhere deep down in their stomachs. Stacey turned just as Mitch leapt out of her chair.

"Don't worry, I'm on my way," she shouted leaving the office door swinging behind her.

"I'm sorry to say Steve that you're going to have to stay with us for a little bit longer." Stacey stood arms folded looking down at the pitiful figure sat in the centre of the room. "The constable here will take you back through to the interview room where you will be cautioned. You will be required to give a full statement so you will need to appoint a solicitor, do you understand?"

Steve looked up as he felt a hand grip his upper arm then stood. "For what it's worth, I hope you get the bastards," he hissed.

"We will, Steve, I can promise you that," Stacey replied confidently.

Outside the air was crisp but refreshing and a

welcome change to the stale air of the station.

"You really should knock that on the head, you know," Stacey said nodding at the packet that Hart was about to unwrap. Ignoring the advice he lit the extra strong Raffle, then drew hard on it sending a great cloud of dense smoke swirling upwards.

"So what's the plan? Do you intend to go knocking on their door?" Hart asked, keen to change the subject.

"Good Lord, no, too bloody dangerous. Who knows who or what we're dealing with here? No, I thought a discreet look around, that's all, nothing too adventurous."

"Here she is," Hart interrupted as Mitch appeared from around the corner and accelerated towards them. Inside the car Stacey fiddled with the heater control trying to get some warmth from the still cold engine.

Soon they were driving through the town centre and heading towards Bradville.

"I got the distinct impression that young Steve was pleased when you told him you'd be keeping him in, didn't you?" Hart grinned.

"The thing is, if you were in his position and you'd seen your mate strung up like a piece of dead meat and you knew for certain that that very same someone was after doing the same thing to you, wouldn't you be bloody glad to be out of the way for a while?" Stacey said over his shoulder.

"Put like that, then my answer would have to be a definite yes."

The car picked up speed as they headed out into the countryside, soon passing the gravel pits to their left and on up the long but gentle hill towards Newport Pagnell.

Newport town was small but well kept and famous for two things, Mustard and expensive hand built cars. Aston Martin who, were by far the biggest employer in the town employed a large part of the town's population. Passing the church on the right the road swept left and down over the river. Once over the stone bridge Mitch turned the car right and followed the road towards Olney. The traffic was light so they made good progress.

"Slow up, Mitch, we're coming up to the Sherrington turn." Stacey said leaning his weight on the dash board.

Mitch eased her foot off the accelerator.

"There you can just make out the gateway to your right, just past the next turning."

"Shall I stop?"

Hart half turned looking out of the rear window. "Pull over for a moment, Mitch, there's no-one behind."

They sat at the curb side, the engine still running.

"That has to be it wouldn't you agree?" Stacey said turning to Hart.

"Without, a doubt"

"It's pretty concealed. You'd be hard pushed to see that, especially at speed," Mitch suggested.

"That could be handy," Stacey said pointing to the bus stop two hundred yards further up on the left.

"When we get back, Mitch, get on to the bus company, tell them that we want to paint their bus stop for them."

This suggestion from Stacey caused much amusement.

"I'm serious. We can get a couple of our lads up here for a few days and see if there's anything going on."

"Come on, let's see what's up there," said Hart motioning towards the lane.

Mitch gunned the car forwards and stopped directly opposite the turning.

"Wait for this group of cars to pass then turn as though you're turning around. The blue Range Rover, behind the leading car, its indicating left," Hart said resting elbows on the front seats.

They watched as the lead car passed and the four by four slowed up.

"Shit, he's just flashed me!" Mitch exclaimed.

"Turn then, you'll have to go."

Mitch raised her hand to acknowledge the driver and turned into the lane and came to a halt.

"He's stopped just behind us. He's staring directly at me. I can see him in my mirror."

"Move forward a bit and stick your indicator on. Perhaps he'll get the idea and move around you."

"I'll have to go after this truck, there's no other traffic." There was panic in her voice.

Hart chanced a look out of the rear window then regretted it as he made eye contact with the driver. "He's a big sod," he said, smiling politely at the large figure sat behind the wheel.

"Go, Mitch, it's clear." Stacey ordered.

Mitch pulled out onto the main road but not before taking a second but longer look in her rear view mirror.

"There was someone sitting in the back. I just caught a glimpse of him as we pulled away."

"What are they doing now?" Stacey had wound down the window and was trying to find the image of the large car in the passenger mirror.

"No good, they're gone," Mitch said glancing in her rear view mirror again.

"I don't think they were suspicious. We looked too

natural. Anyway, if you drive around in one of those I'm sure you get used to being stared at," Hart said.

Some twenty-five minutes later they were back at the police station.

"Mitch, give the bus people a call, would you? Then come back here," Stacey said, he waited until Hart had entered the office then allowed the door to close behind them.

"Have you a plan then, Stacey?" Hart asked sitting down in the nearest chair.

"I think so," he replied perching himself on the edge of the desk. "Assuming that the bus company doesn't have a problem with us painting their shelter, we put two men out there starting tomorrow to keep an eye on the lane. Once we have a reasonable idea as to who or what we're dealing with we can gear up accordingly. I don't want to go in like a bull in a china shop, just in case."

"How long do we watch the place before going in?" Hart said curiously.

"One, maybe two days at most, I don't think we can give them any longer than that. Beyond that and we risk them covering up or at worst doing a disappearing act on us."

Mitch appeared in the doorway running her hand through her hair. "No problem with the bus company. Teak."

"Sorry?"

"Teak, it has to be painted teak." She giggled. "I'm serious, they're quite happy about it provided we paint it teak. Something to do with planning evidently."

"Who do we send?" Stacey asked already knowing the answer.

"Don't look at me Stacey, I'm not painting it. Besides, it would look odd, a female painter."

"Don't worry, I'm only winding you up. Big Rob and Trevor, they both get on well," Stacey said looking over at the large clock hung above the door. "Almost five-thirty," he said turning to Hart. "I'll get them up there early in the morning. Do we have any ladders?"

"Step ladders," Mitch offered. "They're out the back."

"Even better, what about brushes, overalls and the like?"

"I can get them from the hardware shop in the high street first thing," Mitch suggested.

"Excellent, you'd better see if they have some teak paint as well. I'd better go and break the news to Rob before he slopes off home."

"Don't forget Trevor, he was talking to someone at the desk when I came through, and I know his shift is almost finished," Mitch called out as Stacey left the office.

Mitch turned to Hart and took hold of his hand. "Well, things look as if they could be coming to an end," she said giving his hand a gentle but firm squeeze. "What will you do when this is all over Emit?"

"Hopefully Mitch, very little. I'm retired, remember? Other than seeing a lot more of you if you'll let me," he replied softly.

She leant forward and kissed him lightly on the lips. "I'll let you, you soft old Irishman."

"Less of the bloody old you," He quipped.

Suddenly the door swung open, "Hart, everything's in place," Stacey said as he entered the room.

"Rob will be dropped off around 5a.m. Trevor's coming here first to pick up their gear."

"How will we keep in touch with them?" Hart asked.

"Radio, both will be equipped with long range two-way radio. They're new, scrounged them from Bletchley, I don't want them using normal Police channels just in case. " he said excitedly.

"Do you think two days will be long enough to see what's going on?" Mitch asked.

"It's got to be!" Stacey replied quickly. "I'm convinced any longer than that and we risk losing them."

"I have to say I agree, and I think it's best to assume that they know we're on to them, and that it will only be a matter of time before they try to make their escape," Hart added.

"So when do you plan to go in?" Mitch asked getting up and closing the door.

"Wednesday, I've arranged for three vans to be here by four. I've planned two strike teams, each with ten men." Stacey crossed his arms and leant forward. "I'll lead one along with you Mitch. I was rather hoping that you would take the other along with big Rob." Stacey asked turning to Hart.

Hart's expression was obvious, Stacey needing no answer from Hart.

"Good, I thought you would be up for it." Stacey smiled. "I've planned for a briefing here tomorrow with both teams, probably late afternoon." Stacey stood up, his excitement mounting. "If there are any changes to that I'll let you both know."

Although Stacey remained, both Mitch and Hart decided to call it a day. Outside Hart suggested that they both call into the nearest pub and have something to eat. Although not late the sky had darkened and it looked soon to rain. Mitch decided to leave her car and go with Hart, which didn't go unnoticed by Stacey when he made his way across the car park to his own car some thirty minutes later.

CHAPTER TWENTY

Tuesday morning and the weather was definitely not for painting, especially outside and particularly not remote bus shelters. The rain came across from the exposed field opposite almost horizontally and hit the sides of the wooden shelter like two-inch nails.

Crouched low and out of sight from passing traffic big Rob kept a vigilant watch on the lane opposite. His companion was wrapped tightly in two very thick blankets, huddled in one corner with only his head and a mug of steaming coffee grasped between frozen hands visible.

"We must be bloody mad!" a muffled voice complained.

Outside and leant perilously against the wall was one brand new stainless steel ladder, complete with price tag, together with several tins of unopened teak paint. Apparently the stations only set of step ladders had been stolen the previous week. Some fifty yards up from the shelter a portable triangular sign weighted down by two small but heavy sandbags warned oncoming traffic of the work in progress.

"Want some coffee, Rob?"

"No thanks, me-duck," he replied holding his hand up in an effort to protect his tiring eyes from the merciless rain.

With each taking it in turns to keep watch, the hours dragged by, and both by mid-afternoon were bored and struggling to stay focused. The intense cold despite the warm blankets and an endless supply of hot coffee from two large Thermos flasks had now reduced the pair to near exhaustion.

"Hold up, I think we've got a result," Rob stammered, relieved that at last something appeared to be happening.

Trevor let the blankets fall from huddled shoulders and shuffled on all fours across the hard and unforgiving floor.

"It's about bloody time!" he hissed through chattering teeth and pressed his face against the damp wood, the cold air blasting his unprotected eye through the newly drilled hole.

A truck had stopped and now waited for the road ahead to clear before turning into the lane. Someone ahead slowed up and flashed their headlights. The truck lurched forward and swung into the lane, then in a cloud of dense black smoke accelerated slowly up the hill and out of sight. Rob quickly slid the single buckle off his waterproof holdall and flipped back the cover. The shortwave radio inside lit up instantly as he clicked the small button several times on the hand-held microphone.

"Rob to control, Rob to control, are you receiving me?" He waited a few seconds before repeating his call sign. "Rob to control."

"Come in, Rob." The reply was instant but the signal weak. "I can only just about hear you though."

He instantly recognised the voice and, with cheeks reddened from the cold, smiled. "If it isn't me old mate." He beamed.

"Hello, you old softy," the voice answered.

"Hello, Mitch, is that nice Mr Stacey with you?"

"No, but someone's gone to fetch him. Have you finished that painting yet?"

"Almost," he replied holding the mouthpiece closer.

"Rob!" Trevor shouted above the howling wind, his face still pressed against the peephole. "Someone else is about to turn into the lane."

Risking a quick peek over the top of the shelter, Rob could now see that not one but two cars had stopped and were waiting to turn.

"Hello Rob, are you there?" Stacey's voice said excitedly.

Rob lifted the receiver to his mouth again and pressed the send button. "Stacey, something's going on. A truck went up the lane not long ago and now we've just had two cars go up."

"Okay, stay put for the moment, Rob, but let me know if anybody else shows up."

Stacey clicked the receive button, and listened to the wind howling above Rob's straining voice as he signed off. He put the handset down and swung around in the swivel chair. Both Hart and Mitch were sat opposite their anxious expressions only too obvious.

"It's started. We don't go tomorrow, we're going in tonight," he said brazenly. "Mitch, get in touch with the rest of the assault group. I want them here for a briefing by five this afternoon."

Stacey walked over and opened the window. He stood quietly for a moment inhaling the cold but cleansing air deeply then turned back and added, "Mitch, you'd better arrange for someone to go fetch Rob. I want him in on the briefing."

"What about Trevor?" Hart asked, concerned that both men now would be suffering from the cold.

"No, I want him to stay on," he answered quickly. "We'll pick him up on the way in. Anyway, he's probably better equipped to handle a bit of hardship than Rob."

CHAPTER TWENTY-ONE

"Would you like some help with that?" Hart's smooth Irish accent was unmistakable.

Mitch lifted the chair from the stack and turned, the beginning of a smile formed at the corners of her mouth. "That would be nice," she replied placing the chair down onto the floor.

"How many more do you need?" he asked lifting a stack of four up.

Placing both hands in the small of her back she straightened, attempting to ease the ache that was now developing, then counted the rows of seats that she had just laid out. "Six more should do it, I would say."

The briefing room was almost thirty by forty and positioned at the very rear of the police station. Normally it was used for less dramatic purposes such as storing the forces fete equipment and its many orange traffic bollards. This afternoon, though, was different the room had been cleared, with the tombola relegated to the bike shed outside, it now contained several rows of neatly arranged blue plastic chairs ready for Stacey's briefing.

"Okay, you rabble, in you go, grab a seat," a voice ordered.

Hart sat with Mitch as the group spilled into the room and took their seats.

"Gentlemen, and believe me, I use that term very loosely," Stacey joked as he entered the room. He dropped a manila file onto the desktop and perched himself on the corner, keeping one foot on the floor. He looked around the room, occasionally nodding as his gaze met with a familiar face.

"By now you probably all know what this is about. For those of you here that don't, I'll give you a quick summary. Acting on information received, we believe that a group, number unknown, have been operating from a remote building on the edge of the woods just outside Emberton. We have it on good authority that they are some kind of cult or society. Exactly how long they've been up there we're unsure of at the moment. We also believe that they have been responsible for organising a counterfeiting scam close to Stony Stratford. This operation has for some time now been producing very convincing copies of U.K. ten pound notes."

He paused for a moment pleased at least that most assembled were busy taking notes.

"Also so that you're all aware of the fact, we have been assisted on this case by Inspector Hart who is ex-Scotland Yard. Unofficially I might add, so that bit of information goes no further than these four walls." Stacey signalled to Hart to stand, which he did, albeit reluctantly.

"We also strongly believe that someone within this organisation is responsible for the murder of one of the employees that worked for them. We have the other safely tucked away." Stacey looked around the room and was happy to note that he still had everyone's undivided attention.

"What's the plan then, sir?" someone called out from the back of the room.

"I've arranged for three Transit vans to pick us up

together with our gear from here tonight at ten on the dot. I want to hit them for ten-thirty or as near as damn it."

"Do we know how many will be up there tonight then, sir?"

"None I'm afraid. I've had two men keeping watch on the place all day. They've reported seeing cars arriving but there's no way of knowing for certain. All we can do at this stage is offer a rough estimate, which I believe will be around twenty or so."

Suddenly the door swung open. Stacey turned as the oversize figure of Rob appeared in the doorway.

"Have I missed much, me-duck?" he asked closing the door behind him heavily.

"Not really, well, nothing that you don't already know," Stacey said, pleased that his large colleague had made it. "Go find yourself a seat and take a rest while you can." Turning to the room he added. "Most of you know Rob here. He was one of the two unfortunate buggers that I've had watching the place."

Someone produced a chair and put it down at the front. Rob slumped down, stretched his legs out and yawned.

"It's bloody cold up there I can tell you," he said blowing into cupped hands then rubbing them together vigorously.

"How's Trevor doing?"

"Complaining as usual, but he'll survive. You know he loves it really." Rob shrugged his shoulders then, added, "He said he'd go walkabout once it had got a bit darker and take a look up the lane. Have a nose around."

"Jesus, let's hope he doesn't blow it for us," Hart

interrupted.

"Don't worry, sir, not much chance of that happening," Rob insisted. "He said he'd go across the field, not up the lane. Anyway, sir, he's more than used to this sort of thing – it's in his blood."

"Ex-Para," Stacey said turning to Hart. "To be honest with you, we're bloody lucky to have him on board."

"He's taken the radio with him, said he'd be in touch," Rob added.

"Okay then, unless anybody has anything else to ask I suggest that we take a break, get something to eat. It's likely to be a long cold night. I've arranged for cook to stay on and put together some grub in the canteen." Stacey slid off the desk rather awkwardly, surprised that he's legs had gone numb.

"Just one thing sir. Is there any chance that this lot might be armed?" a young voice called out.

A silence swept over the room as suddenly as a wave over sand. Stacey scanned the group for a moment but it was Hart that answered.

"We really don't know is the honest answer but we doubt it."

"I've requested for some armed support just to be on the safe side but as yet I've heard nothing." Stacey added doubtfully.

"Don't forget lads," Rob stood. "We'll have the element of surprise on our side, they won't know what's bloody hit em!" then punched his fist into his open palm.

"Right you lot, if that's it let's knock this on the head. Get yourselves down to the canteen and get some food inside you."

"What the fuck are we going to do if this lot is armed?" Hart said lazily.

Above the irritating noise of, chair legs being dragged across worn parquet flooring Stacey's look of concern was obvious. With no answer to give Hart he just shrugged his shoulders then followed his men to the canteen.

CHAPTER TWENTY-TWO

Stacey pulled the elasticated cuff of his bomber jacket back. "Ten-thirty," he said to no one in particular. Someone in the room coughed. "We'll give them five more minutes then we'll have to go in cars." This time he was looking at Hart.

Stacey turned as his team of twenty filed into the room, each dressed in dark blue, almost black bomber jackets and matching trousers. Footwear was standard issue: Doc Martens complete with steel toe caps and padded ankle protection. Each man was equipped with cuffs, twelve-inch rubber truncheon and shortwave radio.

No one spoke, the tension tight. Someone at the back quietly whistled an unrecognisable tune. Most were eager for the off while others appeared more mindful at what they might face.

"They're here!" called Mitch as she appeared in the doorway, both hands grasping the frame tightly.

"Good, about bloody time. Get them to drive around the back, we'll load up from there," Stacey ordered. "Okay, you rabble, listen up!" he shouted bringing both hands together in a loud clap. "Load up the gear in the last van then, divide yourselves up between the other two: my lot in the first van with Mitch; Hart's team in the second with Big Rob." Stacey turned to the figure that had been standing quietly by the door. "David, if you wouldn't mind, I'd like you to stay with Hart."

David stepped forward, his face now lit by the lamp

overhead.

"Don't worry, David. Rob here will look after you," Stacey seemed fixed on something over David's shoulder.

David spun round. Under different circumstances it would have been funny as Rob had positioned himself without David's knowledge directly behind him. As he turned, his face now had the full and unrestricted view of Rob's breast pocket. Startled he stepped back.

Hart fought back the urge to laugh but instead settled for an introduction. "Rob, this is David James, we have him on loan from the London Museum, I would like you to look after him if you would. David, this is Rob."

David winced as they shook hands but tried not to let it show.

"One last thing!" The room quietened as Stacey's voice bellowed out. "You all know what to do, no heroics, I want us all back with or without the target. Remember, we don't really know what we're dealing with here, and although I'm not expecting any problems there's always the chance that one of you might come up against a 'have-a-go-Joe'."

Although this last remark caused a few sniggers it was evident from Stacey's expression that he was serious.

"Okay, that'll do, let's get going."

Mitch who had already begun to organise her team appeared to be quite calm, in fact keen to get going, this concerned Hart. He moved forward to grasp her arm

"You take it steady, Mitch. Promise me you won't do anything stupid," he whispered.

"Or you," she replied pulling on her glove then

patting him gently on the cheek.

"It's time," a voice called out.

"Okay, you lot, let's get going!" she shouted, pausing momentarily before disappearing through the doorway and out to the waiting vans.

Hart watched as she left. He took a deep breath and held it for a moment in an effort to control the thumping in his chest.

Stacey stepped forward. "Grab those, will you?" he ordered, "better let Big Rob take charge of that." pointing to the large sledgehammer that was leant against the wall, then with outstretched arms herded his team through the doorway and into the cold night air.

"Onwards and upwards," someone mocked.

"Good luck, sir," a voice shouted.

Stacey raised his hand in the air and then was gone.

With all three vans loaded the procession left, followed closely by two Panda cars. Each car contained five uniformed men whose job it would be to seal off the entrance to the lane and ensure that the entry teams could work without interruption.

Once out of the gate the convoy turned right keeping to the speed limit through the high street.

Stacey's team remained relatively quiet during the journey. Occasionally Stacey would lean forward and check the wing mirror to make sure that they were still together. Soon they were indicating right as they passed over the Great River Ouse just outside Newport Pagnell.

Again Stacey leant forward.

"It's alright, sir, I'm keeping an eye on them," the driver reassured.

"I don't want us to get split up that's all."

"What's the time, sir?" a nervous voice asked.

Stacey pulled his sleeve back and shone the small pencil torch at his watch. "Almost eleven."

Once they had reached the top of the hill they turned left and followed the sign for Olney. Although they had left later than planned they had made good progress, turning in the seat Stacey aimed the beam of his torch at the row of figures huddled in the back.

"Switch it off, sir, would you? We can't see a bloody thing back ere," for a split second the unmistakable accent of sergeant Jones reminded Stacey of the film Zulu where a Welsh regiment were preparing to defend a small farm house at a place called Rorks Drift. He prayed that tonight's little foray wasn't going to be a remake.

"Sorry, lads," he said switching the torch off. "I just wanted to make sure that you were still here, it's been that bloody quiet back there."

He'd half expected some response from someone but surprisingly there was none.

"We're coming up to the Sherington turn now, sir." The driver said tugging at Stacey's sleeve.

"Better slow up. See the second left?" Stacey pointed, just visible in the van's headlights they could make out the reflective signpost on the left. "Can you see the lane to the right?" he asked turning to the driver.

"Yes, I see it." The driver flicked the indicator switch and slowed.

"Okay, lads, we've arrived," Stacey called out.

Even above the rattle of the diesel engine Stacey could hear a few sighs and the odd nervous cough. In the back, expressionless faces were lit intermittently by the orange-red glow from the indicator light as the driver turned into the lane.

"Switch the headlights off and go between the two statues," Stacey ordered. "Pull up over there on the left," he said glancing at the wing mirror again.

The driver followed Stacey's instructions and parked up on the left, bringing the van to a halt rather abruptly.

"Steady on, driver!" someone shouted as they braced themselves in the back.

"Sorry lads."

Stacey opened the door then quickly slammed it shut; he fumbled for a moment trying to switch the interior light off then in a moment of frustration removed the lens and pulled the bulb out. He stepped down from the van and watched as Hart's group swung into the lane, the driver immediately turning the headlights off.

With the vans now parked one behind the other Stacey sprinted towards the entrance closing the heavy gate behind the last car.

"Block the gate with the cars." He yelled.

Once both cars were in position and satisfied that no one could get out he walked quickly over to Hart's van.

"Make sure the interior light doesn't come on when you open the door, no sense in giving our position away just yet."

Hart stood alone in the dark glad to be out of the van, he took several deep breaths and prayed that the feeling of nausea would pass and hoped that it was travel sickness and not last minute nerves.

"The barn is up this lane about three quarters of a mile on the left," Stacey said to a startled Hart.

"Eleven-ten, we didn't make bad time." Hart said

looking at the luminous hands of his Timex.

"I still haven't been able to make contact with Trevor," Mitch said climbing out of the van.

"Try out here, it might be the steel sides of the van blocking the signal," Stacey suggested.

Hart, still not feeling a hundred percent, went and stood with Mitch as she tried to make contact again.

"Hello, Trevor." She paused. "Come in, it's me, Mitch, can you hear me?" She released the send button and waited – still nothing. "I don't like this, what the hell was he thinking of going up there on his own?"

"Still no luck?" Stacey asked suddenly appearing from nowhere.

"Nothing Stacey, it's as dead as a Doe-Doe."

"Okay, Mitch, forget it. We'll just have to hope that Trevor sees us coming." Stacey turned to Hart then added, "Well, I suppose we might as well get the show on the road."

Climbing into the van Stacey closed the door quietly, "Okay, lads, its time, and remember? No lights."

The van started at the second attempt. Stacey waited for a few moments then gave the signal to move off. The small convoy travelled slowly along the narrow lane. Even with a clear sky this would have been a difficult enough task without lights but tonight with the sky now clouding over, it was almost impossible and very risky.

They had been on the move for only a few minutes when the driver started to slow down.

"What's up?"

"Someone's just run across the lane, up there to the left, see? They've crouched down in the ditch."

"Keep going, it must be Trevor," Stacey ordered gripping the door handle firmly.

As they approached, the figure stood and hurried towards them. Stacey flung open the door just as the figure leapt forward.

"You had us worried!" He said looking at a muddied face, only the white of the eyes showing in the dark.

"Mitch has been trying to get you on the radio, what's happened" he continued.

"Lost it, sir, dropped it while climbing a bloody fence, had a quick look around for it but just too bloody dark," Trevor replied closing the door.

Stacey produced a flask of coffee from beside his seat and poured the contents into a mug. Trevor took hold and cupped his hands around it for some warmth.

"There's definitely something going on up here tonight. Lots of cars have been arriving," he said before gulping down the coffee. "I hid in the trees about thirty yards from the building. All the windows have been blacked out so not much to see. Sometime ago now this woman showed up and went inside." He paused to pour some more coffee from the flask. "Moments later this figure appeared and drove off in her car. He went towards some barns which are at the very back. Anyway, I decided to try and get a bit closer, when he returned he was on foot, I couldn't see him clearly but as he went inside I got a brief glimpse of him. Stacey he looked like a bloody film extra for Sparticus." Trevor half laughed then drained the last dregs of coffee and handed the mug back. "You don't seem surprised, sir." He frowned.

"I'm not." Stacey dropped the mug over the flask and gave it a twist. "How much further is it?" he said, keen to change the subject.

"That's it ahead," Trevor replied pointing up the lane,

"just beyond the trees."

Changing places with Trevor he wound the window down. A blast of cold air hit him full in the face as he stuck his head out of the window trying to make out the building ahead. His heart, for the first time that evening, thumped heavily in his chest as the reality of what was about to occur struck home.

"Right, lads, we're almost there," he said winding the window back up. "Remember, no noise."

The van continued at a snails pace along the lane, the driver hunched over the steering wheel taking care not to let the wheels run onto the soft verge where they risked getting bogged down, the valve gear of the diesel engine sounding louder than usual.

"Take a left here, just by the sign," Trevor instructed.

The gravel driveway crunched noisily beneath the tyres of the heavy van as they turned off the lane.

"Follow the drive around."

Stacey checked the wing mirror just as Hart's van turned off the lane behind them.

"Don't go all the way around, this is the only way in or out."

"Pull up here," Stacey ordered. "Turn it across the drive, that'll put paid to anybody trying to have it away." He added as an after thought.

The driver did as instructed and swung the van into the curb. As the second van pulled up alongside Stacey gave the order.

"Time to go Mitch," he said giving her a nudge, "out lads, and keep it quiet."

Outside the van the silence was almost deafening, Stacey watched as the third van turned off the lane and positioned itself across the driveway. Satisfied that no car could get passed he gave a short sharp whistle.

"Okay, people, gather around, you each know what you're doing," Stacey whispered. "Remember, no heroics. My lot follow Mitch, go!" Stacey turned to Hart. "Good luck, see you inside."

"And you." Hart turned to the assembled group of men behind him. "Okay lads, this way." Then keeping low sprinted off towards the building.

As planned, Hart, together with David James, stood to one side as Rob and two very fit, very large policemen struck the heavy door precisely on time – 11.30 to be exact.

The first few blows had little effect.

"That's it, again," Hart encouraged.

They could now clearly hear the commotion that Stacey's team were creating around the opposite side of the building.

The fourth blow was more damaging with the wood coming away from around the steel lock.

"One more should do it, Rob!" Hart yelled.

Pulling back the sledgehammer over his right shoulder he hissed loudly, then with tremendous power brought the hammer swinging in a large arc and crashing down onto the lock. This combination of sheer physical size and hardened steel was no match for a wooden door.

"In, in, now, let's do it!" Hart screamed as he kicked at the door and sent it swinging open.

Rob then Hart followed closely by the rest of the squad, stumbled and pushed their way over the debris that had once been a very expensive door.

The first confrontation to take place that evening was as two short but stocky figures both dressed in white togas appeared ahead of them to block the hallway.

"Quick, let's have 'em, lads."

With that Rob charged off down the narrow hallway followed by the rest of the team. The effect of this charging group caused both figures to hesitate momentarily. As they got closer Hart noticed in the dim light that the one to the right had stepped forward and pulled something from the wall.

"Fuck!" Rob screamed and dropped to one knee.

Hart, in a heart beat instinctively turned and pressed himself against the wall, still squinting in the half-light to see what was going on.

There was a glint of steel in the candlelight followed by a faint hiss. Whatever the object was, it had narrowly missed both Rob and Hart, but had struck one of their group behind with a sickening thud.

With Rob now back on his feet, he continued his relentless charge towards the two figures. Hart took a fleeting glance back at his colleagues before sprinting off after him. He was horrified to see that one of their number, he didn't know who, lay prone on the floor. Two of his men had stripped off their shirts and were now frantically trying to stem the flow of blood that pumped from the victim's chest. A third, whom Hart recognised as David James, was attempting to steady the end of a lance that had speared the policeman through the chest.

"Shit!" Rob called as he reached the end of the corridor. "Get the sledgehammer, quick." He hammered his large fist in frustration on the door as it was slammed shut and locked.

Hart heard the anger in Rob's voice and ran for all he was worth back down the hallway. Luckily Terry

Springer had also heard Rob shout and was now running towards Hart clutching the hammer. Hart sidestepped him to allow him past then, turning on the spot, sprinted after him.

"There's a lot of commotion going on behind this door, can you hear?" Rob shouted, snatching the heavy hammer from his colleague's grasp and bringing it down on the door without hesitating. The first blow did little other than to punch a hole through the timber.

"On the handle Rob, hit the bloody handle," Terry panicked.

The second impact wrenched the handle off but the door remained firmly shut.

"Out of the way, Rob." Hart pushed Rob's large frame to one side and peered through the gaping hole in the door. "Stacey must be trying to get in through the door opposite!" he said stepping to one side to allow Rob a quick look.

"I think your right," he replied, his face pressed up close to the hole. "They're in a complete panic," he said stepping back. "Stacking everything they can lay their hands on against the door."

With renewed energy Rob attacked the door, bringing the hammer down on it again and again.

"That's it, its going." Rob let the hammer drop to the ground then, pressing his back to the wall opposite, kicked out ferociously with his oversized boot at the loosening door. Terry now joined Rob in butting against it with their shoulders.

Suddenly the door gave way causing both Rob and Terry to stumble through.

Hart pulled Rob to his feet and watched in horror as the same two toga-clad figures that they'd encountered earlier, having pushed their colleagues through yet another doorway, had drawn their short stabbing swords.

"Watch out, lads, they're armed," Hart shrilled yanking Terry to his feet.

Both figures approached slowly, kicking away upturned furniture that lay strewn across the marble floor.

Rob stepped back into the hallway then, without taking his eyes of the approaching figures, reached down and scooped up the sledgehammer from the floor. Terry stepped slowly back through the doorway and drew his short truncheon.

"Not good odds, I would have to say. Let's see if we can draw them out into the hall," Hart shouted.

The three stepped back carefully as the two figures came through the doorway.

"For God's sake, don't trip on anything," Hart said backing up a hand on each of his colleagues' shoulders in an effort to maintain the same pace of retreat.

They had almost reached the others when, without warning, the two armed men charged them. The first sweeping slash of the short sword hissed above Rob's ducking head and buried itself deep in the plaster wall. Rob straightened and just in the nick of time side-stepped a vicious stabbing thrust from the second attacker. This allowed Rob just enough room and time to send a powerful left hook crashing into the attacker's jaw, which sent him swiftly down, his head making a sickening crack as it hit the ground followed by the clatter of steel as his sword spun across the marble floor.

There was a flash of bright steel, followed by a heart-stopping hiss as the blade sliced through the air. Hart's call to Terry was just too late.

It all seemed to happen so very slowly. Hart watched in horror as the blade travelled in a wide arc and came down onto Terry's left shoulder just where it met his neck, slashing flesh and snapping bone. Terry made no sound. He just dropped to one knee before toppling sideways, blood pumping in great spurts into the air. The attacker had no option other than to release his grip on the sword, as it was jammed between muscle and bone.

Hart and Rob both froze as they watched Terry die in front of them.

They were suddenly aware of voices shouting from somewhere behind them and looked up just in time to see the fleeing attacker disappear through a doorway.

Hart watched as Rob retrieved the dropped sword and took off down the hall in pursuit but he was too late. Rob rattled violently at the handle and hammered the hilt of the sword against the door.

"No good, sir," he screamed. "The bastard's locked it."

Hart ran forward and punched at the door in frustration. "Bollocks!" he screamed.

"I'm sorry, Hart, we've lost that young lad."

Hart spun round. "What?" he snapped.

David James had suddenly appeared and was now pointing down the hallway. "The young chap back there, I think his name was Paul." He paused for a moment before continuing. "The spear caused massive blood loss, there wasn't anything that we could do for him, I'm sorry." David appeared agitated. "There's something else, Hart," he continued. "It's all very strange, I just don't understand…" David stopped mid-sentence.

"Sir!" Rob shouted grabbing Hart's arm.

Hart turned around just as Rob pointed to the brass door handle. All three watched in horror as the handle moved slowly downwards. Rob increased his grip on the short sword and took a step back, readying himself for a second attack.

The door inched open slowly, very slowly. No one spoke. The only sound was as each man tried to control their breathing, trying to stay calm, and focused. Rob drew back the short stabbing blade ready to strike at anybody who tried to come at them through the door.

"Hart!" a voice called out. "Hart, is that you?"

"Stacey!" Hart shouted back. The tone in his voice showed his relief.

The door was pulled wide and Rob relaxed his grip on the sword as Stacey appeared framed in the doorway.

"Christ, am I glad to see you?" Hart grinned.

"Have you taken any casualties?" Stacey asked, his blooded face showing evidence of a struggle.

"Unfortunately, yes, two and both dead, I'm afraid," Hart replied looking past Stacey.

"Fuck," Stacey hissed. "Who?"

Hart's relief on seeing Mitch was obvious, "Paul Edwards and Terry Springer." He said sadly. "The other one is one of theirs."

"Who the bloody hell are they?" Rob cut in, his face drawn back in anger. "They look too bloody comfortable with these," he suggested thrusting the short sword into the air.

"God knows," Stacey cursed.

"Hart." The quiet voice went almost unnoticed at first. "Hart!" This time it was louder, more urgent. It was David. "Would you come here?" David stood some twenty feet away next to the fallen attacker.

"What is it?" Hart asked as he strode towards him.

"It's this," he said pointing to the body on the floor. "I've been trying to tell you. This is Anton, my assistant. You know the one that went on leave."

Hart crouched down and put his fingers on the neck as Stacey turned the lifeless body over.

"He's dead, I checked, must have fractured his skull on the floor. Why would he be dressed like that?" David asked. "And why would he try to kill us?"

"David, right now I don't know." Hart stood up. "In fact, I know less than you do," he said turning to Stacey. "What the fuck is going on, Stacey?" His Irish accent had thickened.

Before he could answer Rob appeared at the far end of the hallway. "Hart, Stacey, come here, you'd better take a look at this," he shouted excitedly.

Rob stood to one side to allow them into the room. "There's twenty-two of the bastards here somewhere," he hissed as he followed them in. "It looks like they've been having themselves an orgy or something."

Stacey stood with hands on hips and sighed, there were twenty-two white couches positioned around him. He suddenly felt sick.

A bewildered Hart came over and sat down heavily. The exhaustion showed on his reddened face. He picked up a large bunch of red grapes from a small table at the side and pulled one from its stalk, its sweetness instantly refreshing his drying mouth.

"It's straight out of Ben Hur," someone shouted boldly.

"I'm Sparticus," a voice mocked.

"No, I'm Sparticus!" a second shouted above the

rising nervous laughter.

"Listen up, you rabble, this isn't funny." Stacey scowled.

The room fell silent and many had sat in an effort to make the most of a few minutes of respite.

"Stacey, take a look at this. What do you make of it?"

Hart was now standing to one side of a small wooden table, which was positioned in the very centre of the large room. He lifted up the thick leather strap that lay across the middle.

"If I didn't know any better, Stacey, I'd say this was for torturing someone." He said letting the strap fall from his hand.

"For torturing a woman, you mean?" Mitch hesitated as she realised what she was saying. "The two holes." She gestured. Her face had visibly drained. "They've used it, or at least it was their intention, to strap someone down, a girl, and God knows what…" She was unable to finish the sentence as her mind raced at the thought of all the possibilities.

Hart stood, his hand extended. She clutched at it as if she feared it might disappear. He put his strong arm around her shoulders and led her away.

"Okay, you lot, the break's over." Stacey watched as his men struggled to their feet, knowing exactly how they felt. "My team split up into two groups. Robin, you take your lot outside, see what you can find, particularly over where the outbuildings are. Derek, I want you to take your group around the back of the building, stick close. We'll see if we can flush them out." Pausing for a moment then added, "And all of you be careful, I don't want any more casualties, is that understood?" He waited for a moment to allow this last remark to sink home. "Right, what are you waiting for? Get on with it!" Stacey turned to Mitch. "Take Rob and his team, Mitch. I want you to search all the rooms that are open from top to bottom. And be thorough, I don't want anything left to chance. Any that you find that are locked leave a man on. Hart, you and David come with us."

In the hallway Stacey stood for a moment over the covered body of his new recruit Paul Edwards and wondered how he would break the news to this young boy's mother, then, it suddenly dawned on him that Paul may be one of many tonight. Spurred on by this last thought and determined not to loose anyone else his pace quickened as he headed towards the locked door at the far end of the hall. He tried the handle just in case, then, pressed his ear against the warm timber.

"Shhh!" he said holding up his hand.

"Anything?" Hart moved closer.

Suddenly Stacey dropped to one knee and put his eye up to the keyhole.

"What do you make of this?" he whispered moving to one side.

Hart squatted down, cursing the stiffness in his knees, and peered through the small hole.

"It's a flash, a camera or something. I can't see anybody in there though, it's too bloody dark, just the odd flash of light." Hart took a second look before standing up.

Grasping the smooth wooden handle tightly Stacey stepped back.

"Move over, let's have a go with this." He said and with that brought the hammer crashing down on the lock and sent the handle spinning across the floor.

Now more experienced at breaking things, it wasn't

long before the door was swinging freely.

"Okay, slowly does it," Stacey whispered as he stepped into the darkened room.

They had entered what appeared to be a changing room. In the half-light they could just make out a row of benches that stood against the far wall with clothing and holdalls hung from the hooks above and shoes arranged in neat rows below.

Keeping their backs to the wall they continued further into the room slowly inching their way towards a door which was some fifteen feet away and slightly ajar. Suddenly and without warning there was a blinding flash of blue white light which forced them to shield their eyes.

"Jesus," Hart exclaimed, "Whatever, or whoever is causing that, I bloody hope he's got sun glasses on." Hart's flippant attempt at humour went ignored by his two colleagues.

As they got closer Stacey gave Hart a sharp nudge in the ribs and pointed to a sign fixed to the door.

"Aqua," David whispered, "water, it could be a well or something."

Stacey gave a nod and edged forwards until he was close enough to push the door open using his right foot. The door swung in noisily on dry hinges, and in the deathly silence of the room the sound was mind numbing.

"If they didn't know we were coming they bloody do now." Hart jibed.

They stood huddled together, each trying to listen out for something beyond their own breathing.

Suddenly the room was lit with a flash of burning white light followed by a mild but noticeable concussion and a low rumble somewhere distant.

"It's almost like being on the edge of a small explosion," Hart suggested as the bright light faded.

Stacey risked a quick look through the doorway. With eyes now more accustomed to the dark he could just make out a shape in the centre of the room.

"The room appears to be empty apart from what I think might be the well." He said then to Harts horror he was gone.

"Stacey, you fucking idiot!" he shouted, the hairs on the back of his neck suddenly standing to attention.

Moments later Stacey stuck his head around the door frame.

"Well, don't just stand there, what are you waiting for?"

Hart groped in the dark for David's sleeve.

"It's now or never, mate, stick close," he whispered then, with catlike speed, leapt through the doorway. Bent forward at the waist he shuffled quickly towards Stacey's form huddled against a low wall. He dropped heavily to the floor then watched as David sprinted towards them.

Suddenly and without warning all three were lit as a beam of intense light shot upwards. Hart cupped his hands over his eyes and kept them tightly shut. Stacey gasped as a blast of lung-burning hot air hit them. All three kept their faces covered as the strange wind buffeted and swirled around the room. Slowly, very slowly it subsided, the room cooled and again they were in the dark. Hart removed his hands from his face and squinted through half-shut eyes. He tried to control his breathlessness.

"I feel as though I've just run a marathon in the sun,"

he said.

"Are you all right, David?" Stacey asked looking past Hart.

David was hunched forward in a tight ball, his head between his knees. Slowly he allowed his back to make contact with the wall and straightened his head.

"Is it safe to look?" His voice was muffled by his hands.

"It's okay for the moment."

"What the hell was that? It felt as though someone had opened the door to a furnace!" David tried to focus on Hart's face.

"I really don't know, but I wouldn't want to catch that full on," Hart stammered.

"Listen up!" Stacey grabbed Hart's arm. "Can you here that?"

Slowly, very slowly, and muffled at first but growing ever clearer, they could hear voices.

"They're hiding in the bloody well, listen, you can hear them." David had straightened and was sat on his heels, his head cocked to one side close to the rim of the well.

Hart watched in horror as Stacey stood and looked over the top. "The bastards are going to get away," he cursed then spun round as he heard footsteps approaching from behind.

Several figures appeared in the doorway, Stacey's heart stopped.

"Quick, someone, I need a torch," He ordered.

"What the fuck was that?" Hart exclaimed as he peered down into the darkness.

No one answered; everyone seemed to be waiting for something to happen.

The room fell silent as the three men stood with white-knuckled hands gripping the top of the well.

"Listen, can you here that?" Hart said as Stacey encircled the well.

"Will you not follow?" The words taunted, the voice was eerily calm almost soothing and came from somewhere deep within the well.

Stacey's glare across the well was met with Hart's. No one spoke, the silence almost hurt. They could clearly hear someone below, the breathing deep, laboured, almost wheezing.

"Who are you?" The echo from Stacey's voice seemed to lack commitment.

"Come, you are all welcome." It mocked.

Stacey's grip tightened on the rim of the well, "Why don't you all come back up here and see us nice policemen."

His request was met with silence. "There's nowhere for you to go down there," he said reaching for the torch that someone had just held out. He fumbled for several agonising moments trying to find the switch. "I'm only going to get one shot at this, Hart," he whispered. "So for Christ's sake, keep your eyes open." With that he stabbed his finger on the button while leaning out dangerously over the edge, his feet scrabbling for grip on the smooth surface of the floor. The white pencil beam cut through the darkness like an arrow from a bow. Stacey had been deadly accurate. The light hit the shape below square in the face. For a split second all three were speechless. The figure screamed and threw an arm up to shield his fiery eyes then, cursing, ducked low and disappeared from view.

"Where the fuck did he go?" Before Hart could finish

Stacey had swung one leg over the wall. "Stacey, I hope you're not thinking of going down there!" he exclaimed.

Stacey aimed the torch then rattled the frail ladder that was bolted to the well wall. "We have to. How else will we know where they've gone?" Stacey said as several swinging beams of light approached. "Grab a torch, the pair of you." He pointed towards the door as more of his men arrived.

"Sir, we've discovered the cars," someone shouted.

Stacey responded to the voice by directing the beam of his torch in its general direction and watched as Robin tried to shield his face from the blinding light.

"What? What bloody car?" Stacey's face held a completely bewildered expression.

"The missing cars, sir." Realising that he wasn't making any sense, then added, "There are seven of them, you know, the girls that have gone missing." He waited for the penny to drop. "They're hidden under dustsheets in the large barn behind a stack of rotting hay bails – seven in all. We've checked with Traffic, they've confirmed the registration numbers on five of them. The missing women are here somewhere," he said triumphantly.

"Good work, Robin, good work." Stacey looked down into the darkened well. "Hart, I know I'm asking a lot, but will you follow me? You too, David?"

"Stacey, you can't expect David to go down."

David held up his hand. "It's okay honest, I wouldn't miss this for the world."

Stacey smiled then, gripping the wall tightly, swung out over the edge and lowered himself slowly until his feet made contact with the rungs below. Holding the badly rusted ladder firmly, he started his descent.

"Stacey, try not to stand in the centre of the rungs in case they give way," Hart shouted then grabbed David's arm. "Quick, David, you next, down you go or we'll lose him."

David did as instructed and clambered over the low wall. He looked down and hesitated for a moment. Then after a deep nervous breath he made sure that he had a firm grip and started his descent.

Hart watched David's progress, steadying the beam from his torch with both hands.

"Someone go and find some rope," he said turning to the group of men that had now gathered around the top of the well. "See if you can find some lights too, we might need them."

"I'm at the bottom," Stacey's disembodied words echoed up.

"David is on the way down. Can you see him yet?" Hart asked watching the beam from Stacey's torch inch its way slowly up the ladder.

"Yes, I see him!"

Hart could just make out David's form clinging to the side of the well.

"Not far now, David," Stacey encouraged. "Hart, when you come down I would suggest that you hold the sides of the ladder rather than the rungs, several of them are almost rusted through."

"I'm on my way." Hart swung his legs over and made contact with the ladder. He tucked the torch into his jacket and lowered his body slowly until he was happy that he was directly over the ladder, then started down.

"Hold up, Sir!"

Hart looked up as Robin's face appeared over the top.

"Lights and rope are on their way."

"Excellent, as soon as they're here get them lowered down. We're going to need all the light we can get down there."

Hart began to sweat as he made his climb down. Occasionally the ladder would flex and move away from the wall where the securing bolts had rusted through and snapped off. Stopping for a moment he looked up at the passive faces above then peered down past his elbow.

"You're almost down. David, just another twenty feet or so," Stacey called out.

"Are you okay, David?" Hart asked.

"Yes, no problem, I'm just hoping that you don't stand on my hands or something," he replied nervously.

"Just shout if I do." Hart laughed.

Stacey moved forward as David reached the foot of the ladder and steadied him. "Only one step to go," he said looking up at Hart who was now only ten feet away.

"They must have gone through there," David said excitedly as he played the beam of his torch on the far wall.

Hart jumped the last few steps onto the clay floor then pulled the torch from his jacket.

The three of them stood in the cool damp air, their torches clearly picking out the narrow opening in the wall opposite.

"I don't think we should go any further, do you?" stammered David nervously.

"We've got no option," Stacey answered noting that their breathing had become more laboured.

"We must be at least sixty feet down," Hart said swinging the beam of his torch skywards.

Stacey aimed the beam of light into the suffocating

blackness of the narrow cleft. "Not exactly inviting, is it?" he said turning his body side-on and sliding with some difficulty into the narrow space.

Hart waited until Stacey was several paces in before expelling the air from his lungs. With his chest size reduced and now satisfied that he would get through he pushed his body into the tight gap.

"Wait for me, you two!" David shouted, then, reluctantly followed.

The narrow cleft was cut from the dark stone and made smooth over the years by the flow of water that had once poured through to supply the well. For several yards its width remained constant, then slowly it widened until they were able to turn and walk more normally. They made slow progress, stopping occasionally to listen, the dazzling light from their torches cast ominous shadows across the walls. Suddenly Stacey halted abruptly.

"What is it?" Hart whispered, his heart pounding in his chest.

Stacey inched forward cautiously as the tunnel opened up. He aimed the beam of his torch slowly around the walls and up onto the high ceiling.

"We're in a chamber."

With the combined light from three torches they could now see that the narrow tunnel had led them into a large cave. Like the tunnel the walls were smooth granite and devoid of any foot or hand holds.

"I don't think there's been any water down here for years." Hart observed running his hand across the smooth stone.

"Christ! I hadn't even thought of that." Stacey stammered.

The chamber was slightly longer than it was wide Hart guessed about sixty feet by thirty and probably too perfect to have been natural.

"Why would anyone want to dig this out?" Stacey asked.

"God knows?" Hart said making his way to the far end of the chamber. Both Stacey and David watched from the relative safety of the tunnel entrance as Hart's torch scanned from left to right across the vertical wall and then stopped.

"The plot thickens"

"What have you found?"

"It's another ladder I'm afraid," tucking the torch under his arm Hart grasped the rusting metal and shook it violently watching it flex and bend.

"Here, let me I'm the lightest," David said tucking the torch into his waist band.

"What's it like?" Stacey whispered.

"The ladder's stronger than it appears it will easily take your weight," David's voice answered from somewhere high above.

Doing exactly as David, Stacey switched off his torch and stuffed it into the waist band of his trousers then placing his foot on the first rusting rung testing it to make sure it would hold his weight.

"I'll wait until you've reached the top before following," Hart suggested, "I doubt it could take our combined weight."

Hart watched as Stacey climbed until he was almost out of range of the powerful torch. He could just make out what appeared to be a shaft that Stacey was climbing up into.

"I'm almost there," Stacey called down. Hart watched

as Stacey reached the top of the ladder then swung his body over the top and was gone.

"Okay Hart up you come." Stacey said as he reappeared.

Hart switched off the torch and slipped it into his side pocket then grasping the sides of the ladder started to climb feeling for each rung one at a time in the smothering darkness. As he got level with the roof of the chamber he paused and looked up. With the light from Stacey's torch above he could clearly see that the ladder continued up inside what he guessed was probably another disused well shaft.

"Steady on Hart, just a few more feet," Stacey's hand reached out to guide him. Hart lifted his leg over the top rung and he dropped to the floor, "Guess what?" Stacey beamed, "another bloody chamber."

"Complete with a choice of exits," David added sarcastically and shone the torch to reveal the entrance to three narrow shafts that were cut into the rock face. The first appeared unfinished and only went for some ten feet or so. The second was higher up and lacked any means to climb up to it.

The third was the largest and Stacey now stood in its entrance aiming the weakening beam from his torch inside, "David perhaps you should wait here?" He said rattling the torch against the palm of his hand.

"Not on your life." He responded quickly just as Stacey's torch light flickered and then went out. "Shit, that's all we need."

"Perhaps we should turn back Stacey," Hart leaned against the wall.

"Sounds good to me." Said Stacey, relieved that someone else had suggested it. "We'd never find our way out of here without torches." He added.

The words were barely out of his mouth when suddenly from somewhere deep within the tunnel there was a tremendous rumble which reverberated around the small chamber. The ground shuddered violently. David lost balance and fell heavily to the floor. Both Hart and Stacey were saved from falling by clutching tightly to the wall of the tunnel. There followed a rush of hot stale air which roared out of the narrow opening.

"Quick, both of you close your eyes, now!" Hart screamed just as the intense light hit him.

CHAPTER TWENTY-THREE

"Where are they?" Mitch shouted as she burst into the room. The group gathered around the top of the well turned as though one. She stopped abruptly sensing something was wrong, "Jesus, please don't tell me they've gone down there." Mitch clasped her hands tightly behind her head and stared up at the ceiling in total disbelief.

"I'm afraid so, three of them," someone answered grimly.

"Who went?" she snapped.

"Stacey, Hart and the other chap, I think his name's David."

She grasped the cool stone work with both hands and looked down into the dark shaft. "Hart, Hart, can you hear me?"

"We could hear them talking to each other for a while," a voice said calmly. "And see the light from their torches, then, suddenly it all went quiet."

"I'll go down, Mitch," Rob offered stripping off his jacket. He swung his leg over and sat astride the wall.

"You'd better take this," someone said holding out a flashlight.

Rob switched the lamp on and aimed its powerful beam down into the dark. "Christ, it must be deep," he said hesitantly. "I can't even see the end of the bloody ladder."

"I'm coming with you," Mitch ordered looking him directly in the face. "No arguments, Rob, trust me, it's not open for discussion."

Rob, who knew better than to argue with her when she was this insistent, lowered his large frame over the edge and onto the ladder below.

"Mind the first step," he said with a faint smile. Rob looked into Mitch's eyes and saw genuine concern.

"It's the last step that worries me most," she said patting his hand.

He gripped the ladder tightly, climbed down several rungs. "Be careful Mitch, the rungs are metal and very slippery."

Someone switched on a torch and passed it to her.

"Thanks," she said firmly then waited until Rob had gone far enough down to allow her to get onto the ladder.

Stuffing the torch into the waist band of her black jeans she took a breath sat on the wall and swung her legs over the side. Someone to her right took hold of her arm to steady her.

"Thank you," she said trying to find a rung with her foot. Mitch descended slowly, one rung at a time, testing each before giving it her full weight. With each step she could feel the whole ladder flex under her weight.

"Are you okay, Mitch?" Rob called up.

"No problem. Have you reached the bottom yet?"

Gripping the cold ladder tightly she risked a look down. She could see Rob's flashlight some twenty feet below her.

"Almost!" he replied aiming the beam of the torch onto the ground below. "I'm down," he shouted as he swung the beam in an arc and then aimed it back up the shaft, its powerful light picking out Mitch's slim figure clinging to the side of the well. "That's it, you're nearly down," he encouraged as she felt with her foot for the next rung.

"Can you hear them, Rob?" she asked stepping down onto the cool damp earth. She turned to face her friend in the deafening silence. Even in the near dark the expression on his face spoke volumes.

"No, but I think I know where they might have gone," he said as the beam from his powerful torch speared the darkness to reveal a gap in the wall.

Mitch cupped her hands around her mouth and leant into the opening. "Hart, can you hear me?"

Rob shone the beam of light into the tunnel and waited for some response.

"It's no good, we'll have to go through," whispered Mitch, tightening her grip on her torch then, without warning squeezed into the narrow passageway and was gone.

"Mitch, hold on." Rob attempted to follow but his size made it impossible for him to pass through the narrow gap. "Mitch wait, I can't get through!" he shouted. "Mitch, can you hear me, are you okay?"

"Yes, don't worry, it widens once you get inside," she answered.

Rob kept the beam of light aimed into the tunnel. He could just make out her shape some twenty feet or so inside.

"Rob, it opens up into a much larger cave!" She was shouting now. "They're not here, it's empty." The desperation in her voice echoed eerily along the narrow passageway.

Rob turned and directed the beam of light slowly around the walls of the well in the hope that he might discover another way in. He steadied the beam just to the right of the opening and watched as the wall appeared to move forward. "Are you doing that Mitch?" He stepped closer trying to get fingertips into the widening gap.

"Yes, it's another opening, I could see your torch light through a gap, suddenly the whole panel swung out and Mitch appeared in the small opening, her face lit by Rob's flashlight.

"It's a large cave and there's a ladder against the far wall. I've had a close look at it. It's very old but I'm sure that it'll take my weight."

Rob sensed what was coming.

"No, Mitch. Definitely not. Let me get some men down here first."

"There's no time, I'll go ahead you wait here for me. The moment I'm unable to hear you I'll turn back, I promise."

Before he could answer she was gone. He followed her through the opening his torch lighting up the large chamber. He reached the foot of the ladder just as Mitch got almost level with the roof of the cave.

"Mitch!" he called up, "this isn't a good idea."

She hesitated for a moment, "Rob, I have to, they may need our help."

He watched as she scrambled over the top of the ladder and was gone, Rob could see the distant glow from her torch reflecting on the roof and walls of the chamber above, and hear her voice calling out but only just.

"Any sign of them?"

"No nothing." She shouted.

"Mitch, I think you should come back I can barely hear you."

He waited for a reply.

"Mitch, can you hear me?"

Rob strained at the sickening silence waiting for some response.

"Mitch, for Christ's sake, answer me!"

This was not good. He ran back to the foot of the well. "Someone get the fuck down here now!" he shouted then watched as a figure high up responded. "And get some lights down here," he ordered then ran back into the chamber. His face beamed as Mitch appeared at the top of the ladder. "Thank God," he sighed, "I was getting ready to come and find you."

"There are three tunnels up here that lead off from the chamber but they go nowhere," she said climbing onto the ladder, "one is only a few feet long, the second is just too high in the wall for anyone to climb up to. The third looked hopeful but it just narrows down to almost nothing, even a small dog would have trouble." As she stepped off the ladder and turned Rob could clearly see in the torchlight her eyes fill then slowly a tear rolled lazily down her ashen cheek.

"Rob." She gripped his arm tightly. "What's happened? It's just an empty cave, there's no possible exit. We're all this way underground. Where have they gone?"

Rob placed his hands on her slim shoulders and pulled her towards him. He embraced her as a comforting friend, a friend that could offer her no answers.

CHAPTER TWENTY-FOUR

Emit Hart remained motionless. His head pounded, his pulse raced. It felt as though he could hear the blood as it rushed around inside his head.

One thing was for certain, he knew that he was down. He could feel the warmth and texture of soil against the side of his face.

It was hot, very hot. The perspiration from his skin had made him wet under his arms, something he hated. Beads of sweat rolled down his face causing his skin to itch. He wanted desperately to wipe them away but couldn't. With his left arm trapped and numb under his heavy weight he tried in vain to move his right ... nothing.

He could feel the sun's rays burning his exposed face and arm.

Slowly his mind traced back what had happened. He could vaguely remember the chase with Stacey and David. Somewhere in the depths of his confused mind he recalled a room, they had broken into a room. A well, he could remember that too, and bright light, very bright light. Loud voices, people were shouting, screaming.

His thoughts were abruptly halted by the sound of voices, distant but definitely getting closer, and louder.

He winced then expelled air as his exhausted body absorbed a sudden and vicious blow to the small of his back.

The voices – he could make no sense of the language

– it was something that he'd never heard before.

He turned his head slightly, squinting in the bright light, the voice gibberish, angry and shouting. This was swiftly followed by a second stinging blow.

Hart lifted himself up onto one elbow and tried to focus. He could just make out a shape standing over him. The sun was behind the figure, making it impossible for him to recognise.

"Hart, Hart."

The voice was familiar but for the moment he couldn't place it.

"Hart, it's James, David James, can you hear me? Nod if you can."

There was a pause then again the voice repeated but more slowly.

"Hart, it's David, please nod if you can hear me."

Hart ran his tongue slowly over cracked and drying lips then, with enormous effort, nodded.

"Good, Hart, whatever you do, do not, I repeat do not get up. Do you understand?"

Again Hart nodded. He tried to speak but there was no sound. He coughed and tried to swallow in an attempt to moisten his drying throat.

Again the figure that stood over him spoke.

"I'm sorry, but I don't understand you," Hart croaked.

The voice spoke again, more loudly this time, almost shouting.

As his eyes grew more accustomed to the bright light Hart could now make out other figures; he could hear the clatter of metal, the creaking of dry leather.

He tensed as strong hands gripped his arms tightly, bruising his burning flesh, then suddenly lifted him bodily from the ground.

"Hart, for fuck's sake, don't move, don't do anything." It was Stacey's voice this time.

Hart did as he was told, his eyes fixed blankly on the figure that stood in front of him and listened bemused at the strange dialect.

Although the sun still blinded him he could now just make out a face. It was tanned and leathery from years of exposure to the sun, the features rugged as if carved from stone, the cool blue eyes cruel and unforgiving.

"Stacey, who are they? What do they want with us? And where the fuck, are we?"

The response to Hart's question was instant and painful. He would have dropped to the ground had it not been for the two men that held his arms in a vicelike grip.

He buckled as the blow struck. Just to the left of dead centre and under the ribs, it left him gasping for air.

"It's a form of Latin. I think he's saying that his name is Titus." It was David's voice. "They're soldiers, Hart, fucking Roman soldiers, and they're not amused." David sounded frightened and confused, "I don't know what's happened, but I think somehow we have travelled back in time."

Hart turned his head painfully in the direction of David's voice and fought the urge to throw up. Instead he stood with mouth wide, numbed by this revelation. Not more than two, maybe three paces from him he could clearly make out several figures holding his two friends hostage, their armour and weapons glinting and rattling in the bright sunlight. His attention was drawn to a banner that flapped lazily in the warm air. Just below a fox's skull and carved into yellow metal Hart could make out the inscription: "XXIV/XLI". His stomach churned.

Beyond this group and slightly to their left he could see a whitewashed building and several small trees. He turned his dizzying head slowly. To their right a neat row of wooden markers had been driven into the cracked and dry soil. He counted eight and each placed approximately four feet apart.

The enormity of what he could see hit him like an express train.

Carved roughly in the dry timber of the nearest were three large letters: "PAT."

He felt a tear roll lazily down his dry cheek as he went from one marker to the next. On each a girl's name, his head fell forwards as he read the final inscription.

He had found her at last.

EPILOGUE

"Just here will do fine."

The black cab slowed up and came to a halt against the kerb. The slim suited figure in the back slid forward on smooth vinyl, lifted the brown leather briefcase from the floor and, pulling on the chrome door handle, stepped out onto the pavement.

"That'll be four quid, love," the oversized cabby said yawning like a great basking shark hunting for food.

"Keep the change."

He touched his forehead with his finger and said something mid yawn that went unheard. Aware that her good looks often turned heads she did what came naturally to her and, keeping eyes fixed firmly on the floor to avoid an unwanted meeting of eyes, she set off towards the far end of the street. The morning sun was a welcome change to the weather of late. Although still early some shops were open but doing little business. With the odd mixture of office furniture shops, tobacconists, galleries and small eateries, you either love it, or loath it but, whatever your feelings, London is, if nothing else interesting. Even at this time of the morning the seemingly endless stream of people all eager to make it to work on time. The suffocating stench of exhaust fumes spewed from stationery traffic all waiting for traffic lights to change further down the street.

Having reached her destination she hesitated for a moment her hand clasping the cool brass hand rail, a sudden gust of wind snatched at her clothing whipping up small dust swirls along the curb. The building was a typical central London office block with wide stone steps leading up to an imposing entrance which in some select parts of London would have once concealed a huge family home now split into almost affordable flats. Tightening her grip on the handle of her case she stepped lightly up the few steps and pushed the door open.

"Good morning, Ma'am," a voice welcomed.

She turned and smiled at the saluting figure stood against the wall.

"Morning," she answered cheerily still unable to come to terms with her new role.

Her high-heeled shoes rang out noisily on the polished marble floor as she hurried towards the open lift. Pushing number three on the brass panel she watched as the stainless steel doors glided silently together. Both hands gripped the smooth handle of her briefcase as she tapped it lightly against her knees. As the lift slowed she breathed in and held her breath for a moment. She listened to her heart pound and reflected on the recent news. It had been a long time coming. She had shown patience, a quality which had proved invaluable in the past and one she was known for. She watched as the LED display lit green. A bell rang from somewhere above her head as the doors slid open. Stepping from the lift, she turned right and followed the corridor for several yards before stopping. She grasped the cold brass door knob and hesitated for a moment, looking up at the name plate screwed to the door. Even now she found it hard to believe.

She was greeted by Ruth's warm smile as she entered

the office.

"Good morning, Ma'am."

"Morning, Ruth, any calls?"

"Only one, Ma'am, reception rang to say that your new assistant has just arrived. They're keeping him in the waiting room downstairs until you call for him."

"Excellent," she beamed, almost unable to control her excitement. She could imagine what was going through her close friend's mind. Even with her colleague's help it had been difficult to keep from him, but the secrecy appeared to have paid off. She pushed open the half-glazed door and switched on the light.

"Would you like some coffee, Ma'am?" Ruth asked.

"No thanks, Ruth, I had a cup on the train coming up this morning."

Her office was the largest in the building with windows running along the length of one wall. Placing the briefcase down by the side of her desk she stood by the window, pulled the net curtain to one side and marvelled at the view below. From the street the building looked no different from any other in central London. This, though, was unusual in that it had its own private garden. The lawn was well kept, mowed with tramline-like patterns normally reserved for stately homes and football pitches. The whole garden was screened deliberately and effectively with tall, thick conifers, which not only kept prying eyes out but helped conceal the twelve-foot high brick wall.

She let the net fall back and sat down in the heavily studded brown leather chair. Lifting the briefcase from the floor, she slipped the two brass buckles off and removed a grey file. As she placed it down on the desktop she stared at the blood-red heading, still dumbfounded at what it contained.

HIGHLY CONFIDENTIAL.

Almost a year had passed and a lot had happened since. She paused for a moment as the thought of her mum came to her, she missed her greatly.

"Should I ring down and ask them to send him up, Ma'am?" Ruth's rotund figure stood framed in the doorway.

"Yes, I suppose you had better."

Ruth closed the door quietly behind her.

Slipping off the transparent sleeve from the file she leaned back in the chair and re-read the list of names that made up the privileged few who were allowed access to its contents. Feeling slightly confused over the whole thing and with emotions now put fully to the test, she turned the page and read on.

Outside, the large figure stood shaking his head from side to side as he read the name plate fixed to the office door.

DI Michele Glinn, Special Operations.

He could hardly contain himself as he opened the door. Ruth looked up from her desk as the figure put a finger to his pursed lips. Ruth gestured towards the closed door at the end of the room keen to play a part in this long overdue meeting.

"Hello, me duck."

Mitch looked up and just grinned.

"So this is where you've been hiding, is it?"

Big Rob stepped into the room and closed the door behind him just as Mitch launched herself at her friend. They stood for a few moments embracing each other just as long-lost friends do.

"I'm sorry about the cloak and dagger stuff, Rob, but

as you will see shortly it was necessary," Mitch reassured. "Anyway, please, come in and sit down, I have lots to tell you." she said dropping into her seat. Rob pulled a chair forward and sat opposite her.

"I was sure that after that fiasco you had just taken some quality time. It wasn't until a few months later that I was told you wouldn't be coming back. Now I know why," he stated, sweeping his large hand in an arc through the air.

Mitch chose not to comment but smiled instead.

"They were never found, you know," Rob added bitterly.

Mitch struggled with her emotions for a moment as she remembered the good times spent with Emit. It was simply just not fair, they had had such little time together, she thought angrily.

"There wasn't one stone left unturned. The whole building was taken apart. I was so sure that they were trapped in one of those shafts somewhere, we dug for days, nothing, absolutely nothing."

"I'm convinced Rob, that one day they will be found."

"Lets hope you're right." He answered doubtfully. "At least the case is still open, that's something."

"Yes, it most certainly is," she said pushing the grey file forwards, "They're back, Rob ... MITHRAS, I mean."

It is generally accepted that the Vatican holds secretly within the depths of its catacombs evidence of the world's past and, more worryingly, our future.

It is also widely believed that other than the Pope

this information is only known to a select few. All are sworn to secrecy whether they are of the cloth or scientists that have worked for the church.

Deep below the Vatican's public areas are the vast passageways and rooms used to store evidence and information. The whole area survives in a constantly monitored and controlled environment, its temperature set at an optimum level.

Along its passageways and inside its many rooms are rows and rows of hard wood shelving, the timber specifically chosen for its durability and strength.

Placed carefully on each shelf are identical containers. All are sealed. Many are sealed with the Pope's personal seal, indicating his knowledge of its contents.

As you pass along the ranks of containers it becomes obvious that all are numbered. This numbering system allows each container to have its contents meticulously logged.

One such container is number "due mila quattro cento e quarant-uno"; its English translation would be number "two thousand, four hundred and forty one". Beneath this, written in blue marker pen and highlighted by brackets, is the Latin number XXIV/XLI.

Within this container and carefully stored in hermetically sealed plastic bags are held contents that have baffled the most experienced and knowledgeable scientists of the twentieth century. These contents have been the subject of much argument and debate.

Fortunately over the years there have been great advances made in science, in particular the method of dating people and objects, DNA. This now allows us much information, more knowledge and greater success in solving crime. It allows the scientist to provide more detail.

Container XXIV/XLI holds the evidence of past lives: 202AD to be exact.

Each of the eight clear plastic bags contains the remains of a human, all of which are female. Extensive DNA testing has revealed that these women ranged in ages between twenty-two and forty-seven. How they died will never be known.

Below these eight bags and out of sight are two green opaque bags, each carefully positioned between protective foam strips. Their contents have been of particular interest.

The first is a bracelet, its value and beauty now destroyed by hundreds of years of moisture entombing it from view within thick, impenetrable layers of rust.

This once treasured piece of jewellery has, under careful cleaning, revealed a face; not a human face but a flat circular surface. On closer examination this face has revealed several Roman characters: to the top and in almost perfect condition XII; to its right IV; and below VI.

Just above dead centre is something truly baffling. Although parts of the characters have worn away it is still possible with the naked eye to just make out a word: "T I VI L X."

Written clearly in blue ink the attached label describes this item as a "Time piece". Manufactured in 1972 by TIMEX.

The slip of fabric contained in the second bag, although not much larger than a postage stamp, has also revealed under high magnification something equally startling. Something totally impossible but its existence is indisputable.

It shows that although it's a copy its origin was that of Rome. The manufacturer's name can clearly be read, woven into the fabric – GUCCI.

What they are is undisputed. The fact that they exist to this day is certain. How or why they exist no one knows. What is puzzling is that both items date back to a period when they clearly didn't exist.